DEATH AT THE SIGN OF THE ROOK

DEATH AT THE SIGN OF THE ROOK

A Jackson Brodie Book

Kate Atkinson

DOUBLEDAY   New York

2024

Copyright © 2024 by Kate Costello Limited

All rights reserved. Published in the United States by Doubleday, a division of Penguin Random House LLC, New York.

www.doubleday.com

DOUBLEDAY and the portrayal of an anchor with a dolphin are registered trademarks of Penguin Random House LLC.

Jacket images: (rook) by Andrew Howe / Getty Images; (Warwick castle) by RomanYa / Shutterstock; (frame) Tony Cordoza / Alamy
Jacket design by Emily Mahon
Book design by Cassandra J. Pappas

Library of Congress Cataloging-in-Publication Data
Names: Atkinson, Kate, author.
Title: Death at the sign of the rook : a novel / Kate Atkinson.
Description: First edition. | New York : Doubleday, 2024. |
Series: The Jackson Brodie series ; 6
Identifiers: LCCN 2023058793 | ISBN 9780385547994 (hardcover) |
ISBN 9780385548007 (ebook)
Subjects: LCSH: Art thefts—Investigation—Fiction. |
LCGFT: Detective and mystery fiction. | Novels.
Classification: LCC PR6051.T56 D43 2024 |
DDC 823/.914—dc23/eng/20240108
LC record available at https://lccn.loc.gov/2023058793

MANUFACTURED IN THE UNITED STATES OF AMERICA
1st Printing
First Edition

For Russell Equi

"The guilty always masquerade as the innocent but it is rarely the other way round."

—Nancy Styles, *The Secret of the Clock Cabinet*

DEATH AT THE SIGN OF THE ROOK

We Invite You To

Enjoy all the excitement of a Murder Mystery Weekend
in the charmingly atmospheric surroundings of Rook Hall,
a country house hotel located within Burton Makepeace House,
one of England's premier stately homes.

Enjoy a sumptuous four-course dinner in the splendour
of our magnificent Stubbs Room in the company of the owners
of the house, the Marquess and Marchioness of Milton,
and afterwards partake of coffee and liqueurs
in the comfort of the Library, designed by Robert Adam,
all the while being entertained with clues galore
to a fascinating "Whodunit?."

£1,250 per person exclusive of VAT, based on two people
sharing. Included in the price are all meals, including a lavish
breakfast buffet, served "Downton"-style in our charming
Morning Room. £300 deposit (non-refundable) per person.
Book early, places limited.
All enquiries to reception@burtonmakepeace.co.uk.

Red Herrings

As requested, they had all assembled in the Library before dinner. There were not enough seats for everyone, and someone wondered jokingly if they were going to play musical chairs.

"Do you think we will?" Major Liversedge asked, perking up a little at the idea. The Major and Sir Lancelot Hardwick had done the gentlemanly thing and elected to stand.

"What on earth is this about, do you suppose?" the Reverend Smallbones asked. "I hope there's going to be a good dinner to make up for all the waiting," he added querulously.

"And where are those drinks?" Guy Burroughs wondered out loud.

"Dreadful man," Countess Voranskaya murmured, unable to conceal her dislike of the brash American film star.

"Yes, where *is* Addison with the sherry?" Sir Lancelot said. He rang the bell again. Catching sight of the expression of distaste on the face of the fastidious little Swiss detective, René Armand, he laughed and said, "Don't worry, Monsieur. I have some excellent cognac."

"I fear we must make the best of things," the Reverend Smallbones said. "This snowstorm means that we're all going to be stuck here together for quite some time."

"Trapped!" Countess Voranskaya declared in gloomy Slavic tones.

The company fell into a rather awkward silence. There was an audible sigh of relief when Addison entered and said to Sir Lancelot, "You rang, sir?"

"Yes, Addison. We would—"

"I'm sorry to be so dim," Lady Milton whispered, "but I'm rather confused. Who is Addison?"

"He's the butler," Reggie whispered back.

"It's confusing. There are so very *many* of them."

"I know, Lady M, but I expect they're going to get picked off one by one. That's what usually happens."

"Is it?"

"Dear God Almighty," Jackson Brodie muttered. "If this goes on much longer I'll kill them all myself."

"It hasn't even begun properly yet," Reggie said.

The Mysterious Affair at the Willows

In fact, it had begun over a week ago when Jackson acquired a new client. Two new clients actually, although they came as a pair—twins, in fact—Ian and Hazel, the pensionable-aged progeny of the recently deceased Dorothy Padgett. Jackson had not warmed to Hazel when she contacted him on the phone, but she wanted to meet in Ilkley, the "scene of the crime" as she referred to it, and Ilkley boasted a Bettys Café Tea Rooms that Jackson had never visited. It wasn't the siren call of a toasted teacake that drew him so much as the promise of order, of sanctuary even. "A clean, well-lighted place," his ex, Julia, said when he had tried to explain the attraction. "That's Hemingway, and don't pretend you know that, because you don't." He didn't, but he was fairly sure you would never find Hemingway in Bettys, chomping on an iced fancy. Hemingway's loss.

＞

"And this is where the painting hung? In your mother's bedroom?" Jackson had asked, contemplating the ghostly outline, as if whatever had been on the wall had been vaporized. He was reminded of Hiroshima. He was in a dark mood, feeling the weight of history on his back. His teenage son, Nathan, clearly wasn't going to take up the burden.

"Yes," Hazel Sanderson, née Padgett, said. She had been a geography teacher before retiring. When Jackson was at school, "Geography" had consisted of tracing maps and colouring them in and getting a whack on the back of your hand with a wooden ruler if you made a mistake. Perhaps it had advanced since then. Perhaps not.

"It was a portrait," Ian said. "Small—about ten-by-ten without the frame. Approximately," he added, in case he sounded as though he had measured it. (He had, Jackson thought.) Ian was retired from "insurance" and had the dull, faded patina of someone who had spent their life indoors. "You could add on another two inches for the frame," he went on. "It was fancy—gold."

"Not real gold," Hazel intervened hastily. "Obviously."

"The whole thing's missing," Ian continued. "Not cut from the frame the way that thieves usually do." (He'd been on the internet, Jackson thought.) "It was very . . ." Ian searched for a word. "Portable," he concluded.

Portable? Jackson didn't think he'd ever heard that word used for a work of art. Made sense though if you were going to steal one.

"Dated from the Renaissance," Hazel said.

"Renaissance?" Jackson hadn't expected that either. Surely "Renaissance" equated to "worth a shedload of money." But what did he know? He would have been hard put to tell a Rembrandt from a Renoir. In the house Jackson grew up in, a Woolworths print of Tretchikoff's *Chinese Girl* was considered high art.

"Fifteenth, perhaps sixteenth century," Hazel elucidated, giving him a long look as if she was already doubting his capabilities. He supposed she was the sort of woman who thought he was an idiot from the get-go, although he seemed to meet no other kind these days. Hazel had a defensive stance, her folded arms resting on the rotund barrel of her middle. Visceral fat, Jackson thought darkly. He'd been learning, thanks to his daughter Marlee, the Ghost of the Future.

"It was the portrait of a woman," Hazel continued. "Of course, we've no idea who she is or who the artist was." The two Padgetts stared at the space on the wall as if they could magic the anonymous subject back to life.

"Valuable?" Jackson asked.

"Oh, we have no idea," Hazel said airily. "Probably not very. Its value was sentimental rather than monetary." Hazel didn't give the impression of being someone who had much time for sentiment.

"It was never valued or put on the insurance," Ian added, tag-teaming with his sister. "Nothing like that."

No insurance? To Jackson, the Willows seemed like a house that put its faith in insurance. Ian certainly did, it had been his job for, what—forty years? "Forty-five," Ian said. "Man and boy." Jackson's soul shrank at the thought of nearly half a century of indentured labour.

"The painting had no *provenance*, as they say," Hazel said, approaching the word carefully, as if it might be dangerous in some way. The word meant something to her, Jackson thought. "Dad bought it cheap at an auction after the war, in a house clearance."

"Nobody wanted old stuff in those days, did they?" Ian said.

Jackson had the distinct feeling that the two of them were reading from a script. One they'd agreed on beforehand. They were leaden actors, Ian particularly.

"Its origins are lost in the mists of time, I'm afraid," Hazel said. "It's been hanging in Mum's bedroom for as long as we can remember. Hasn't it, Ian?"

Ian responded eagerly to his sister's prompt. "Yes, yes," he said, nodding in strenuous agreement. He was going to hurt his neck if he wasn't careful, Jackson thought. "Mum said she liked to see it when she woke up," he said. "And when she fell asleep as well, I suppose. She loved that painting."

The spectral remainder—a square of wallpaper framed by a faint nebula of dust—was on the wall opposite the small double bed that their mother had died in. Deathbed, Jackson thought. No more waking up for Dorothy Padgett. Ever. She must have slept with the door shut. That was the only way she would have been able to see the painting.

He contemplated the frilled and flowery duvet cover with its matching pillowcases. A crocheted bed-jacket lay across the counterpane, and he had an urge to touch it to see if it was still warm.

Most poignant of all somehow was the pair of spectacles that were neatly folded on the bedside table and would never be needed again. They had the thick bottle-bottom lenses of the semi-blind. It would have taken some effort for Dorothy Padgett to see that painting when she woke in the morning.

Dorothy Padgett, ninety-six-year-old widow of this parish, had died in her sleep of a worn-out heart just a couple of days ago and now the vultures were picking at the remains. Jackson didn't want to die in his sleep, didn't want the Grim Reaper sneaking slyly up on him, he wanted to face him with his eyes wide open. Not that he was ready to die yet. He still had work to do—see his daughter happy, keep his granddaughter safe, persuade his son to get off his arse and put his phone away.

In the brief time since their mother had travelled on to whatever lay beyond, Hazel and Ian had gone around her house in Ilkley sticking coloured dots on her goods and chattels—red dots for Hazel, blue for Ian. Jackson wondered what colour would have gone on the missing painting, as the two of them seemed to be making an equal claim on it. Red and blue made purple. The imperial colour. He'd been reading Robert Harris.

This speedy pair had already been to the solicitors. "We knew what was in the will, of course," Hazel said. "We just wanted to check everything was in order. Just have to wait for the probate now."

"No surprises!" Ian had laughed as if they had perhaps been worried that their mother might have set an ambush in her final testament—her worldly goods to go to a cat shelter, or perhaps worse, her carer, Melanie Hope. But no, "Everything to be divided equally between the two of us," Hazel said. "Split right down the middle," Ian chimed in helpfully and received an icy stare from his sister for his trouble. There seemed to be a lot going on between the lines of their shared script.

Dorothy Padgett's home was an old-fashioned, chintzy kind of house in a quietly expensive street. From the upper storey you could see countryside and beyond that Ilkley Moor, of "Baht 'At" fame. "On Ilkley Moor Baht 'At" was a song they used to sing at Jackson's school, millennia ago. A hatless man catches his death of cold up on the moor, the worms eat him, the ducks eat the worms and then *we shall have etten thee.* The circle of life, long before *The Lion King.*

A house like the Willows wouldn't stay on the market long. It was worth way over a million (Jackson had become a connoisseur of property websites) although, apart from the view, there was nothing about it that he found attractive. Stone-built between the wars, four bedrooms, detached, with an enormous garden. No one built houses with enormous gardens any more. Jackson had become quite the connoisseur because he had been house-hunting lately. Most of his work these days was in this part of the world, his love life (such as it was, and love didn't have much to do with it) was also here and it seemed as good a time in his life as any to put down roots again. He was a grandfather now, after all, the head of a dynasty. (*Get over yourself*, his father would have said.) He congratulated himself for being so sensible and mature.

He had spent a good several weeks being sensible and mature and then he bought a Land Rover Defender instead. It was a rugged, blokey kind of vehicle. Brand-new, the model that had the top-of-the-range specs, 518bhp supercharged V-8 engine, plus every whistle and bell available to man. Cost an arm and a leg. No regrets. You could live in a Defender if you had to, but you couldn't drive a house. The whole macho construct only slightly spoiled by his granddaughter's baby seat in the back.

It wasn't so long since he had spent a month in his daughter's cramped, expensive London flat looking after that granddaughter. Marlee's childcare arrangements had fallen through just as she was due to return to work and he had been called up for service. It had been a baptism of fire for all three of them.

His granddaughter was called Niamh, after Jackson's murdered sister. Jackson wasn't sure it was a good idea to be named for the tragic dead, but Marlee had insisted that her baby be called after the aunt she had never known.

Shattered, knee-deep in nappies and various kinds of bodily fluids, Jackson realized how little he had contributed when his own children were babies. In Marlee's case hardly anything, in Nathan's case nothing at all (not my fault, he thought). A woman's world. "Well, you're an honorary woman now," Marlee laughed.

"Have been for a long time," he said.

"Not really," Marlee said.

~

"Shall we go into the living room?" Hazel ushered him out of the bedroom and downstairs into a room with large French windows and a view of the patio and the garden beyond. A well-worn, high-backed armchair looked out on to the leafless trees. The Willows did indeed have a couple of big weeping trees in the back garden, their branches winter-bare. "I remember Dad planting them when we moved here," she said. "They won't last much longer, willows aren't long-lived. Not like oaks, or pines."

"Beeches," Ian said, nodding his head sagely. "Sycamores." Were they going to name all the trees? Jackson wondered.

It was a big house for one small, very old lady (the bed-jacket was tiny, like a large doll's), but of course it had been the family home, "where we grew up," Ian said. "Me and Hazel. We moved here from Leeds in the Fifties."

School portraits had been dutifully hung on the walls, a variety of toothy children in uniform, shined and polished specially for their official photo. "Mrs. Padgett's grandchildren?" Jackson asked.

"She had great-grandchildren as well," Hazel said. "Ian and I both have two children and each of them has two children." It sounded more like a mathematical puzzle than a family tree.

There were more photographs on display on the sideboard. The sideboard was one of those sleek teak ones that had signalled the introduction of Scandinavian style into the grim post-war décor of Britain. It was probably some kind of modern antique now, if that wasn't a contradiction in terms. There was a matching shelved display unit and a table and six chairs in the dining room. The Padgetts must have considered themselves quite avant-garde back in the day. Jackson knew from his own forays into house-hunting that dining rooms were out of fashion now. There had been no such room in his own childhood home. They had eaten in the kitchen, digging into each other with their sharp elbows, around a little Formica-topped table. And then, one by one, his family members had disappeared, lost to murder, suicide, cancer, a trifecta of bereavement, transforming that small table into a wasteland.

There was only one photograph of the Padgetts *en famille*— a framed yellowing colour print from the Sixties, the two parents and teenaged Ian and Hazel. Dorothy had a sheepish sort of smile on her face, as if she was doing her best for the photographer to make up for the rest of her petulant family, who all looked as if someone had just said something extraordinarily aggravating to them. "Mum and Dad tried for a baby for years," Hazel said. "They'd been married for nearly ten years when they finally managed to adopt."

"Us," Ian added helpfully. "Adopt us." Hazel rolled her eyes at him. They were like a comedy double-act, but without the laughs unfortunately. Hazel, eager to exert her seniority, had been at pains to tell Jackson that she was older than her brother, born "a full half-hour" before him.

She picked up a silver-framed wedding photograph and handed it to Jackson, saying, "Mum and Dad on their wedding day." Dorothy was grinning for the camera, revealing crooked pre-war teeth. The young bride gave the impression that she would like to kick up her heels and dance, while the man at her side looked ready to settle down for life with a half-pint of Tetley's by his elbow.

"She was just eighteen. Thirteen years younger than Dad," Ian said.

"Eighteen," Jackson murmured. He supposed eighteen was older in the past. His son, Nathan, would be eighteen this year. The idea of him being mature enough to marry was ludicrous.

"The reception was a pork-pie tea in the village hall," Hazel said, as if she regretted the loss of such frugality. Perhaps she was right. Better than the entire wedding party decamping to the Caribbean for a week and having to pay for it themselves. Different times, different ways. Jackson was pretty sure there was Latin for that.

"And this?" he said, picking up another photograph. Padgett senior, in a wartime dispatch rider's uniform, standing proudly next to a motorbike.

"El Alamein," Ian said.

Harold Padgett was tanned, with pale circles around his eyes from wearing goggles. A filthy-looking khaki uniform—wrinkled shorts and shirt, dusty boots. Jackson imagined that personal hygiene was low on the list of priorities of the men fighting in the North African campaign.

"The bike's a Royal Enfield," Ian said. "And his gun's a Smith and Wesson .38/200."

Jackson had to suppress his cynicism (an art in which he was well practised). The nearest Ian Padgett had ever come to a gun was probably clay-pigeon shooting on a corporate jolly, and even Harold, as a dispatch rider, might have gone all through the war without ever shooting his sidearm.

"He was in the Signals," Ian said. "Attached to a lot of different regiments. Dunkirk, North Africa, Sicily, Italy, Germany. Ended up attached to the 11th Hussars, rode into Berlin with them. I'm a bit of a history buff, Mr. Brodie." He was in the grip of nostalgia now and battled gamely on. "Dad always loved motorbikes—rode one for years after the war. A Vincent Black Lightning, bought right off the production line in 1948. Before that he had an old BSA and a sidecar, took Mum all over England before we came along."

"Well, not 'all over England,' just the north," Hazel amended in her peculiar pernickety fashion. "He was a patriotic Yorkshireman. He'd never even been to London, said he had everything he needed right here."

As a "car fetishist" (his daughter's description), Jackson was largely indifferent to motorbikes, but he knew a brand-new Vincent Black Lightning wouldn't have come cheap after the war. Harold Padgett had not only afforded the Vincent but had the wherewithal to start his butchering empire. Where did the money come from? As if he'd heard this unspoken question, Ian said, "I think Dad was a bit of a wheeler-dealer in those early days."

Hazel looked daggers at him and said, "You make him sound like a criminal, Ian. He just liked a bargain, that's all. He was a pillar of the community."

"Master of his lodge," Ian said.

"Ah," Jackson said. He had an innate distrust of secret societies. Maybe because no one had ever invited him to join one.

"Stalwart of the local Conservative Club, too," Ian laughed. "Nothing Dad liked more than a couple of pints of bitter and a game of snooker with his pals. Fellow shopkeepers, mostly. They're a breed apart. Class of their own."

It was quite a CV they were building for their father. Were they polishing his bourgeois credentials to provide a cover for a "wheeler-dealer?" Or had they spent their childhood being endlessly lectured about their father's many attributes? Perhaps they'd had them beaten into them. He didn't know about Hazel, but even at seventy Ian had the twitchy air of a survivor. Jackson had seen it enough times to recognize it.

"Golf, of course," Hazel said, as if that went without saying. "He was captain of his local club for a while."

"Yeah, Dad certainly had a full and interesting life," Ian said. Jackson might have taken issue with that statement. Golf, Freemasonry and snooker may have some weird shibboleths but "interesting" wasn't necessarily the word he would have applied to them— "mind-bendingly dull" seemed a more suitable description. But what did he know? Harold had ridden his way, heroically or otherwise, across continents for an entire war. Jackson himself, several lifetimes ago or so it now seemed, had been in Northern Ireland, Bosnia, the Gulf. It had been many things, but not dull.

"And your mother?" Jackson asked. The woman who had just died, did she get a look-in? Did her children boost their mother's reputation with the same enthusiasm they applied to their father's, or was she just an adjunct to Harold's life with its male pastimes? Rewarded for wifely loyalty with the occasional dinner-dance at the golf club? Or perhaps he was being sexist, and the good wife Dorothy also knocked the occasional birdie out of the park or whatever it was that golfers did.

Ian laughed. "Not Mum," he said. "She liked ballroom dancing, but Dad had two left feet, so she had to go with a friend. A woman," he added.

"But not like *that*," Hazel said pointedly.

"And she liked her book club and evening classes, didn't she?" Ian said to his sister. "She did everything over the years—cake-decorating, flower-arranging, computing for beginners, not that she ever had a computer."

"Italian conversation," Hazel added, "although she never went to Italy."

"I don't think she had a conversation in Italian beyond 'Spaghetti Bolognese, per favore,'" Ian laughed again. He had an odd laugh, a kind of whinny that would get on your nerves after a while. It certainly seemed to get on Hazel's. "Not that she really went to Italian restaurants when Dad was alive. Mum even did a *cordon bleu* cookery course, but Dad had no truck with foreign food. One of those traditional meat-and-two-veg men. He knew what he liked," Ian said.

"And liked what he knew," Hazel added.

God Almighty, Jackson thought. Neither of them could open their mouths without a cliché falling out.

"Mum left school at fourteen," Ian said. "So she was always wanting to educate herself. And it got her out of the house, I suppose. Out of the shop, too. Dad was a bit of a bully," he added softly.

Ah, there it was, Jackson thought. Ian and Hazel went quiet for a moment, lost in a collective memory, and Jackson caught a glimpse of something long buried. Hero worship of Harold was a perverse kind of smokescreen.

"And she scribbled away all the time, didn't she?" Ian said, visibly pulling himself together.

"Ian," Hazel said sharply.

Her brother didn't catch the warning note in her voice. "Always writing little stories and—" He stopped short, and the rest of the sentence fell off a cliff. He shot a worried glance at his sister. Seemed like he was going off-script, improvising. "Mum was a wonderful woman," he said, changing tack and grabbing the nearest sentence and hanging on for dear life.

Hazel rushed to the rescue with a lifeline and said, "She was no Jane Austen. She liked to write romantic stories, you know, set in medieval castles or hospitals or remote Scottish islands." She gave a little shudder, at the idea of romance presumably.

"Shipboard romances," Ian said, "although she'd never been on a ship."

"She used to send them off to *The People's Friend*," Hazel said, "but of course no one would ever publish them. And really," she added stiffly, "she was quite fulfilled by being a wife and mother."

"Sometimes she lent a hand with the pies in the shop," Ian said. "She made a good steak pie. I miss those pies." (More than he missed his mother?)

She made a good steak pie. Not much of an epitaph, was it?

The tour of the sideboard ended at a china figurine of a woman in a long blue evening-gown. She was mid-twirl as if she were waltzing at a ball and could have stepped straight out of the Disney version of *Cinderella*. The little aesthetic value the figurine might have claimed was further marred by the red dot stuck on her face, nearly obliterating it. "I bought Mum that for her sixtieth," Hazel said, pleased with herself. For Jackson's own sixtieth, Marlee had recruited a babysitter for Niamh and taken him to Le Manoir aux Quat'Saisons for a slap-up lunch. Better than a china figurine any day.

"It's not like Mum and Dad were collectors or anything," Hazel said, interrupting Jackson's thoughts. They had drifted back to the Defender, as they often did. It loved rough terrain. He had a hard time finding enough challenges for its brawn, even with the moors on his doorstep.

"They came from very modest backgrounds," Ian chipped in. "Dad was a self-made man and very proud of that. Padgett's—the butchers—started after he came back from the war. He'd trained as a butcher before he was called up. Padgett's grew into a small chain across the north. Pontefract, Barnsley, Keighley . . ."

"Doncaster," Hazel supplied.

"Castleford," Jackson said, surprised to find himself adding to this litany. He remembered Padgett's—the sawdust on the floor, the aroma of the slaughterhouse, the same scent he would detect when he attended his first bloody murder—it all came flooding back. When his father was flush from the betting shop he used to send his son to Padgett's to pick up pork chops or a steak pie. Jackson could still summon up the smell of that steak pie warming in the oven after he brought it home. Enough for the two of them after everyone else was dead. And he could still see the rhythmic movement of the enormous slicing machine in Padgett's as it delicately shaved bacon, hypnotizing the young, permanently hungry Jackson. He would gladly have eaten it raw. Nowadays he was more circumspect. He wondered if he had also eaten one of the pies made by Dorothy Padgett's now dead hand. Six degrees of separation. Less, actually.

The Padgett siblings were sitting on the big old-fashioned sofa—linen covers with a faded pattern of roses—with a lot of distance between them, as if they were trying not to look like conspirators. They had spent the last hour telling Jackson a lot of things that had nothing to do with why they had called him in. He still wasn't entirely sure why they *had* called him.

"And so . . . the painting?" he prompted. "Can you give me a more detailed description of it?"

"I can do better than that," Ian said, taking a large envelope from a drawer in the teak sideboard. He plucked out a photograph and handed it to Jackson. "We found it yesterday amongst Mum's things. It's a photo of the painting, it gives you a pretty good idea of what it looked like."

A portrait of a portrait, the kind you might take for insurance, despite Ian's denials. The photograph was almost the same size as the painting must have been, the frame relegated to the margins. It looked professional. "We don't know when it was taken," Hazel said. "Mum never said anything about it."

Against a dark-blue background with a darker pattern of leaves just visible sat a young woman, her red-gold hair covered by an almost translucent veil. There was a coral necklace around her pale throat and her ringless hands, folded neatly in front of her, held a little spray of pink flowers. She looked as though she might know something that you didn't.

Jackson tried to remember any Renaissance portraits of women he had seen in galleries over the years but could only recall sharp features and pale, high foreheads. They never looked like real women. The one in this portrait did. She looked as though she could have hoiked up her skirts and clambered out of that "fancy gold" frame and had a chat with you. Perhaps even shared a drink. Maybe even told you what the secret was that she was keeping.

And she was beautiful, the kind of beauty that made you wonder if she wasn't painted from life at all but represented an ideal, conjured out of the imagination of the artist. All this aside, the most noticeable thing about her was the fact that there was a small furry animal on her lap. The little pink flowers looked in danger of being eaten by it at any moment. It was hard to say exactly what breed of small furry animal it was as its proportions looked all off. The artist has been good at women, not so good at small furry animals. The creature's beady little eyes stared at Jackson and Ian said, "A stoat, I think. Or ermine, perhaps."

"Same thing," Hazel said. "Ermine is when a stoat is in its winter coat." She frowned at the unintentional rhyme.

For some reason, Jackson thought of his mother. She had a "summer coat" and a "winter coat," the wearing of which was strictly demarcated by the calendar rather than the weather. The summer coat was a shapeless gabardine and the winter one was tweed, secondhand, sent from a relative "back home." Donegal tweed, she always said, and Jackson wondered if that was where her people were from in Ireland and why he had never bothered to find out. "How can you not know?" Marlee puzzled. The ghosts of the past meant more to her than they did to him. Perhaps because she was so far removed from the potato-grubbing poverty of it. Most of their ancestors had fled from the Famine, that much he knew because the folk memory of it had been in his mother's bones. He supposed he should find out more, for the new Niamh. Hire a genealogist. Who did he think he was?

Ireland was the place his mother called home, not the house she kept with her husband and children. Jackson had thought a lot about his mother recently. He didn't know why. He found it almost impossible to believe that she had been just over forty when she died, she had seemed so old.

"Mr. Brodie?"

"Yes, sorry. Might it be a ferret?" Jackson hazarded. Jackson's brother had kept ferrets, he poached with them. It was a northern thing. His father got rid of them after his brother killed himself, but Jackson never asked what he'd done with them. The memory of Padgett's seemed to have opened a porthole into the past. He slammed it shut. Don't let the ghosts in.

"A weasel," Hazel said definitively. "Mum called it a weasel."

Who had taken this photograph? Jackson wondered.

"No idea," Ian said. "As I said, we've only just found it."

"Can I borrow it?" Jackson asked.

"Bring it back, though," Hazel said sternly. Or receive a whack with the ruler, he presumed.

When he turned the photograph over, Jackson saw that someone had written—in the kind of handwriting that wasn't taught in schools any more—*September 1945. Ottershall.*

"Yes!" Hazel said. "In fact, we found this with the photograph as well." With a conjurer's triumphant flourish she produced a piece of paper and handed it to him. The paper was old, flimsy with age, and seemed to be a small poster from an auction house in Newcastle, announcing that on 20 September 1945 at 10:00 a.m. there was to be an auction "of the entire contents of Ottershall House."

"Evidence," Ian said with a self-conscious laugh.

"That's where Dad must have bought it," Hazel said, in case Jackson was too thick to make the connection.

Jackson didn't know why he felt so suspicious of the pair. He just did. Sometimes your gut feeling was all you had.

"Do you recognize the handwriting?" he asked.

They answered at the same time. "No," Hazel said. "Mum's," Ian said. They stared silently at each other for quite a while until Hazel said, "It could be Mum's, but it's quite generic handwriting for that age group, isn't it?"

"And your dad was back from the war by September?"

"He had an early discharge on medical grounds," Ian said.

"What medical grounds?"

"Can we just get back to the theft?" Hazel interrupted.

"Of course, sorry," Jackson said amiably. "Why don't you tell me exactly what happened on the day that the painting disappeared?"

"The day it was *stolen*, you mean," Hazel said mulishly.

"Tell me about Melanie Hope. She was your mother's live-in carer—did she come from an agency?"

"Well, we *thought* she had," Hazel said. "Mum's regular carer had left. Mum didn't need nursing as such, she was fairly mobile until the final few weeks. Mel just appeared one day. We thought, you know . . . Social Services, we thought Mum must have contacted them herself."

Mel cleaned, cooked, shopped. Like a daughter might have done, Jackson thought. Or a son, he amended hastily as the women at his back raised a collective eyebrow. "She didn't want to go into a nursing home," Hazel said. Or perhaps it was Hazel and Ian who didn't want to drain the inheritance pot with the astronomical fees nursing homes charged. Jackson knew about nursing homes because he'd had a recent case where a family, suspecting maltreatment, had asked him to investigate how an elderly relative was being looked after in her care home. Badly, they found out, thanks to a granny cam he'd installed in a clock in her room. So, it seemed that Dorothy Padgett might have been lucky to have Melanie Hope, and the theft of an old painting was perhaps a small price to pay.

There were no granny cams in the Willows, no CCTV cameras, no door-entry system, nothing at all to monitor Melanie Hope, or anyone else, inside or out. This was an expensive area and Dorothy Padgett was old and vulnerable—what kind of relatives didn't make sure an eye was being kept on her, even if it was only the lens of a camera?

"Talk me through what happened that day."

It seemed that Melanie Hope had brought Dorothy Padgett an early-morning cup of tea "as usual" but hadn't been able to wake her up. She phoned Dorothy's GP and then phoned Hazel. "Mum had died in her sleep," Hazel said.

"Obviously, we came as quickly as we could," Ian said, taking over the narrative from his sister. "Hazel lives in Halifax, I live in Otley, it's only fifteen minutes on the A65, although there'd been an accident that morning so I took Moor Road, which I can normally do in just over twenty minutes, maybe a bit more, but—"

Jackson's ex-father-in-law had been an Ian—slide shows of his holiday in Sitges, including the airport, the train journey and every drink and meal consumed. Shame for him that he died before Instagram. Ian was still going. ". . . West Lane, which is actually a shorter route but takes longer." Someone make him stop, Jackson thought.

"Ian," Hazel said in her schoolteacher voice, "enough." She picked up the baton. "The doctor had already been and gone by then. It's always a shock, isn't it? Even when you're expecting it."

"She looked so peaceful," Ian said. "That was a comfort to us." And that was also exactly the kind of platitude that people came out with at times like this, wasn't it? Jackson thought. He had seen a lot of dead people and he wouldn't call them peaceful. He would call them dead.

"And Melanie Hope was still in the house when you arrived?"

"Yes. She was very helpful," Hazel said. "She'd brushed Mum's hair, tidied her room, made tea for everyone—the undertakers had arrived by then—but then she had to leave because she received a phone call. It seems her sister wasn't well and she had to go and pick up her nephew from school."

"Did you hear her take the phone call?"

"She went into the hallway to take it. I didn't hear the conversation. I'm not an eavesdropper, Mr. Brodie," she said. She sounded offended. Jackson would have bet his bottom dollar that she would eavesdrop at any opportunity.

"And do you know her sister's name?"

They both looked blank. "Didn't even know Mel had a sister until then, I'm afraid," Ian said. "She never talked about her family. We weren't *intimate*." He looked shocked at the word that had just fallen from his mouth. So did Hazel.

"He means we had a professional relationship with Mel," she said quickly. "Not personal."

"Of course," Jackson mollified.

"And so she left, and you haven't seen her since?"

"She said she'd come back the next day—yesterday—and help with the funeral arrangements and get the house ready for selling, but . . ." Their mother's corpse was hardly cold and they were wanting to plant the For Sale sign in the garden?

"And when did you notice the painting was missing?"

"Later that day. We phoned Mel straight away to ask her if she knew what had happened to it, but she didn't answer her phone. Hasn't answered since."

"Did anyone see her leave?"

"Not really," Hazel said, "not with everything going on. You know," she said, "she always carried a big bag, a shoulder bag. I remember once saying to her, 'Goodness, Mel, what do you keep in there?'" Hazel had become almost as wooden a performer as Ian. "She could just have unhooked the painting off the wall and slipped it in that bag. To look at her, you'd think butter wouldn't melt in her mouth," she said bitterly. "But it was all an act."

"We found an address for her in Mum's address book," Ian said. "In Leeds. We haven't gone there, we thought maybe you could." Why? Jackson wondered. Were they scared of Melanie Hope? She didn't sound threatening, not according to Ian's generic description anyway—somewhere in her thirties, slim, regular features, fairish hair ("Mousy," Hazel amended), green eyes. ("No, brown.")

"Pretty?" Jackson asked, not so much interested in the answer as the question's effect, on Ian in particular.

He flinched, ever so slightly. "I suppose so," he said. That meant yes, Jackson thought.

Hazel shrugged indifferently, as if she'd never considered the question. She had, Jackson thought. Hazel had never been pretty. "She was what I suppose you'd call petite," she said. "Five foot two or three." Hazel was a big, raw-boned woman. Most women would look petite standing next to her.

And so to the big question—"Why didn't you call the police?" The two of them glanced at each other before Ian Padgett answered. "Mel was good to Mum, we don't really want to get her into trouble. If we could just sort it out amicably. No need to involve the long arm of the law. We just want to find her and get back what she stole from us."

"And get the keys to the house off her while you're about it, she never handed them back," Hazel said.

"She might have sold the painting on already," Ian said. "Fenced," he added with the same peculiar delicacy that his sister had approached the word "provenance." These people watched far too many cop shows on television, Jackson thought.

"But I thought you said the painting wasn't valuable," Jackson puzzled.

"I think," Hazel huffed, "that what I *said* was that we had no *idea* if it was valuable. We'd really like the painting back. It's not the monetary worth, just—"

"Sentimental value," Jackson said. "Yeah, you said that."

———

Melanie Hope had lived at the Willows for four months. What kind of person was prepared to give up months of their life to insinuate themselves into a household? Talk about playing a long game. Had she embedded herself there, waiting for her chance to take something that she knew was of more than "sentimental value"? Or was it simply an opportunistic act? After weeks of menial duties on low pay, did she seize the chance to better her circumstances?

Jackson had scrutinized the room that Melanie Hope had slept in. He couldn't have been more thorough if he had used a magnifying glass. The bedroom was next to Dorothy Padgett's and was a reasonable size with an en-suite, the floral peach décor of which screamed "Eighties." The bed had been stripped and, according to Hazel, the bedclothes washed and dried in the tumble dryer, neatly folded and put back in the airing cupboard. It was the kind of house that had an airing cupboard. There were a couple of items of clothing left behind in the chest of drawers—cheap, practical workout stuff that you would wear if you were on domestic duty every day, plus a tabard-type garment in brown with a yellow trim that would render any woman invisible. No ornaments, nothing personal, although a detective novel had been abandoned on the bedside table—*Hark! Hark! The Dogs Do Bark* by Nancy Styles. The name rang a bell—old-fashioned, so-called "cosy" crime. Jackson didn't read crime novels, he'd seen too much of the real stuff and it wasn't the least bit cosy.

Also in the room that Melanie Hope slept in was—clue alert!— a glossy, expensive hardback, titled *Renaissance Portraiture*. Perhaps Melanie had bought the book on Dorothy Padgett's behalf from the Grove Bookshop and they had spent some companionable time together looking it over, trying to identify the artist or the subject of *Woman with a Weasel*.

He could never know what occurred between Dorothy Padgett and Melanie Hope in those last few days, but the scenario at the Willows that Jackson preferred over all the others was the one where Melanie Hope had simply taken the painting because she wanted a memento of an old lady she had grown fond of. And perhaps she thought it would be morally right to keep the painting out of the grasping, greedy hands of Ian and Hazel. Or—and this was an even better scenario—it had been a keepsake, given in gratitude by the dying Dorothy Padgett to someone who had cared for her. (*Take it, dear, I insist—you've been so kind to me.*)

Melanie had still been here, hadn't she, when the Padgett siblings arrived? She'd made cups of tea, phoned the undertaker, been respectful in the face of death, yet at some point she must have brazenly taken the picture from the wall and walked out of the house with it. In her "big bag." (But who, he wondered, had made that fateful phone call that had spirited her away? A co-conspirator?)

"Anything interesting?" Hazel asked when Jackson had finished searching Melanie's room. She had been on his tail the whole time.

"Not really," Jackson said.

"So what about fingerprints?" she asked as he leafed through Melanie Hope's bedside reading. "Or a photo ID line-up?"

"Need the real police for that, I'm afraid," Jackson said, the word "real" sticking in his craw. The twins seemed disappointed that he hadn't put on a deerstalker hat, produced a pipe and pronounced some convoluted and unlikely explanation for what had happened at the Willows.

"Mind if I take a quick look at the garden before I go?"

"There's nothing to see out there," Hazel said.

"No stone unturned," Jackson said pleasantly. It was strange the way that Hazel and Ian gave off the aura of perpetrators, not victims.

Hazel was right, there was nothing to see out in the garden. The whole place was in hibernation, waiting to spring back to life in a few months. Dorothy wouldn't be here to appreciate it. No springing back to life for Dorothy Padgett.

The end of the garden was less manicured, there was a compost heap and a garden incinerator. For leaves, Jackson supposed. He looked inside. Something had been reduced to ash in there. What had been burned? And by whom? He poked around with a twig that he found lying on the lawn. There were a few scraps of paper on which some handwriting was visible. *Sir Edmund removed his armoured gauntlets and pulled Marjorie to his breast and said, "You little fool."* And *Where is my theatre nurse? I cannot operate without her.* And so on. Dorothy's romantic stories, presumably. Who had burned them? Melanie Hope? And why?

A big fat clue would have been nice. A bit of charred paper saying, *And the murderer is . . .* But Dorothy Padgett wasn't murdered. Why was he thinking that?

❧

Did he want this job? Not really, but he was intrigued by Melanie Hope, and if she had not stolen the painting—and there was no actual evidence that she had—then perhaps he could do a good deed and clear her name, innocent until proven guilty and all that. And he had to admit that he was drawn to the enigmatic, nameless woman in the portrait, gazing at him through the glass of time. She seemed as if she was part of the weight of history, too. Even the weasel added a couple of pounds to the total, he supposed, although he had no clear idea of the weight of a weasel.

"Well, better get going," Jackson said to Hazel and Ian. "Questions to ask, crimes to solve."

Ian escorted him to the front door, almost pushing him along the hall in his eagerness to be rid of him. Jackson slowed his pace on purpose. "Just one more thing," he said. It was one of those doorstep questions, the hook thrown nonchalantly over the departing shoulder. Jackson could see Hazel in the living room, busily adding more red dots to her swag.

"So, Ian," he said, adopting the kind of matey tone that he thought Ian would respond to. "Those stories your mum scribbled—do you still have any of them?"

Ian's eyes moved rapidly from side to side (fascinating to observe) as he tried to remember his lines. He was more easily flustered than his abrasive sister. No helpful prompt was forthcoming from the living room. "Um," he said eventually, "no idea."

"That's a shame, I'm sure they would have been interesting."

He clocked Hazel staring fixedly at him. Jackson could have sworn that Ian cringed when he spotted the expression on his sister's face. "So, what's your next move?" he asked Jackson, keen to change the subject.

No idea, Jackson thought. He resorted to TV police-drama-speak. "I expect I'll be pursuing several lines of inquiry."

Ancien Régime

It was over two years now since Lady Milton had been betrayed. She had recounted the events of that day so often, both to herself and the police, that they remained unusually clear in her mind. Lady Milton's memory was hazy on many subjects but not this one.

The day had started at a morning-coffee fundraiser for the local hospice—she was a stalwart of this kind of event, happy to be the "honoured guest" when they could never (ever) secure their first choice of Princess Anne.

This was followed in the afternoon by a Women's Institute meeting, where one of the members, Marian Forster, who had recently returned from "a trip of a lifetime" to Japan, gave a talk on Ikebana. Lady Milton thought Ikebana was some form of martial art and was disappointed to find it was just flower-arranging by another name. Surely anyone could stick a flower in a vase? The flowers in Burton Makepeace were from their own garden and were arranged by the housekeeper, Sophie. "I honestly don't know what I would do without you, Sophie," Lady Milton said. "You are the most thrillingly organized person I have ever met."

"I live to serve," Sophie laughed.

They had been taking tea together in Burton Makepeace's increasingly dilapidated conservatory. The morning's activities had left Lady Milton exhausted. The plants in the conservatory, sensing encroaching ruin, had abandoned it some time ago, leaving behind an earthy aroma that was not entirely unattractive. Lady Milton imagined that when she was mouldering in her coffin she would experience much the same scents.

"It must have been lovely once," Sophie said, casting an eye around the dusty glass panes and rusting ironwork.

"Everything was lovely once," Lady Milton said.

"Perhaps not everything," Sophie murmured.

"There were birds in here, too," Lady Milton added, after a lengthy contemplation of the tea-tray. "A cockatoo—quite mad. And a parrot—an African grey."

"Did it talk?"

"It refused. It was quite resolute."

Tea-time was Lady Milton's favourite time of day. By four o'clock all the difficult bits of the day were over and she could slide gracefully towards dinner and an early bed. Johnny—Lord Milton—had no interest in afternoon tea. Never had. They ate breakfast together and sometimes briefly came together for luncheon, but then rarely saw each other again before dinner. Absence was the foundation of a good marriage in Lady Milton's opinion. At night they each kept to their own bedroom. Johnny had never been terrifically interested in *that* side of marriage. The only thing he really enjoyed was shooting something. Once she'd secured the future of the estate with Piers, he rarely bothered her.

It was a surprise to her that they'd managed a third child— Cosmo. (The second had proved to be a girl, so was not much use to them as a "spare.") Not that any of them could be classed as children any more, of course. Piers and Arabella were well into middle age and Cosmo must be in his forties now. Lady Milton tended to lose count once they were over thirty. Even before that, to tell the truth.

Outside, the November sky was a sickly yellow-grey and everything seemed horribly barren. A few last leaves floated down past the window. Lady Milton—Honoria to a select few—disliked this time of year. It seemed so pointless.

"Shall I be mother?" Sophie asked.

"Oh, please do. It's always such a relief when someone says that."

Sophie poured the tea, a lovely pale Formosa Jade Oolong that she had tracked down recently. The two of them shared something of a passion for delicate China teas. It was surprising how many things they were in agreement over, given their different ages and positions in life. Sophie didn't seem like a member of staff, she seemed more like . . . Lady Milton hesitated even to think the word, but it was true—a daughter. She was certainly a good deal more pleasant to be around than Lady Milton's actual daughter, Arabella.

Lady Milton wasn't particularly fond of any of her children, preferring her dogs, two black Labradors, Tommy and Tuppence— a brother and a sister—reasonable creatures compared to her own children. "Sense and Sensibility," Sophie called them. ("It's a Jane Austen novel," she added cautiously, unsure of the shallows she was swimming in. Lady Milton wasn't much of a reader. "We had to read *Emma* at school," Lady Milton said. "It was torture.")

If she was forced to pick one of her offspring to keep, she supposed it would be Cosmo. At least he had a sense of humour, although rarely in the best taste. Was he Johnny's? She could never be sure. There had been a delirious summer when she had been quite, quite in love (first and only time, thank God) with the man—Pip—who had come to revalue the paintings. "Art lover," he would murmur, running his hands down her naked back. That was when they were preparing to open the house to the public for the first time. All those people coming to gawp at their things. Such shocking intimacy.

Pip turned out to be a bounder, of course. Wife and child in Montreal. Cosmo certainly had a look of him.

It was always the beginning of the end when you had to open a house. Burton Makepeace had survived the aftermath of the First World War when all the staff were either dead or had decamped to work in "jobs" rather than staying in service. And the house had come through the Second World War almost unscathed, only suffering a little damage to the East Wing when a Junkers had skimmed the roof before crashing in a fireball that destroyed all the glass-houses, not to mention one of their elderly gardeners, too deaf to hear his approaching nemesis. Not that Lady Milton herself was at Burton Makepeace then, of course, she had been a child during the war, evacuated to her father's country estate in Leicestershire where she ran wild with her older sisters. Not as much fun as it sounded— her sisters had been savages. Still were, although two of them were dead now. They all seemed very much alive to Lady Milton.

Johnny had been forced to capitulate to commercialism after his father's death. "The Old Marquess" as he was known. The death duties had been crippling—more than one Rembrandt, a Titian and a da Vinci sketch amongst (many) others all had to be fed into the open maw of the taxman and even then it wasn't enough. "Three days a week, six months a year, ten 'til four, main house only," he had conceded, and now look at them. Open all year round, gift shop, a huge café, a play area where children screamed so raucously that you could hear them from the house. Tuesday closing had been conceded because, according to something mysterious called a "focus group," it was found to be the least popular day for visiting. You would think it would be Monday but, no, apparently not. Fridays were Lady Milton's own least favourite day because that was when Arabella regularly spoiled the morning with a phone call.

Nowadays, Piers, the "heir apparent" as he grandiosely styled himself, was in charge of "the business." He was talking about adding a farm shop, petting zoo and an adventure playground, whatever that was. ("Zip line," he said mysteriously.) It wasn't a business, it was a home. It was *history*. Not Lady Milton's, of course, she had been the fifth daughter of a duke, very low down in the pecking order when it came to inheriting, and had jumped at the chance of getting a grand house of her own when Johnny Milton proposed. And she had known, even then, that when you married the man you married the house as well. Sometimes, indeed, that was the better part of the bargain. And Burton Makepeace had been a rather grand house.

She had been presented at court in one of the last years for debutantes. All those dances, all those frocks—Hartnell, Worth, Balmain. Her mother took her to Paris for fittings. Dancing the night away. The foxtrot—that had been the young Honoria's favourite dance. Johnny had two left feet, sometimes it seemed like three. The ballroom in Burton Makepeace housed the café now. A whale of a chandelier still hung there because there was no one left who knew how to get it down.

She had been introduced to Johnny Milton at a luncheon party— the debutante season was just a series of matchmaking events. Apparently Johnny was "VSIT," an older girl whispered in her ear. "Very safe in taxis." A queer thing to say. Honoria had no idea what it meant but it had seemed like a good thing at the time. Not that she had ever felt unsafe in a taxi because she had never been in one, as her family had their own chauffeur. She was only seventeen.

The Miltons had made their money from sheep and wool centuries ago. Later they had caught on to the idea of industry and built mills for the wool, and then not long after that they discovered the bonus of a massive coal seam that ran beneath the hooves of all those sheep. Their country seat—Burton Makepeace House— was miles away from the soot and smoke and the taint of trade and industry, "in the middle of nowhere," according to Arabella. It wasn't really in the middle of nowhere, it just felt like it. "Withering Heights," Cosmo called it.

Burton Makepeace could lay claim to being one of the greatest houses in the north, second only to Chatsworth. They had had their own railway line to take produce up to the London house. They had the second-highest jet of water in the world in their Nesfield fountain, the third-longest driveway in Britain. Vanbrugh designed the house and Capability Brown landscaped the grounds.

It was so big that it was said no one had successfully counted all the rooms. There was an old rumour that a manservant had accepted the challenge and set off, never to be seen again. And endless stories about ghosts and secret passages and women bricked up in walls or accidentally locked in marriage chests. ("Very *Northanger Abbey*," Sophie said. It was another Jane Austen novel, apparently.)

The Miltons had looked after their tenants, their land, their sheep, their miners. They had cared and nurtured, they *were* England, its heart and soul. Now everything was crumbling around their ears and they could barely afford to heat the breakfast room. And no one, but no one, had any sympathy for them.

Visitors came, but not enough of them, according to Piers. They were too far off the beaten track, apparently. Yet the Brontës up the road were off the beaten track and they managed to pull in the crowds, "and they're *dead*, for God's sake," he said. "And look at all the spin-offs, the merchandise—Brontë biscuits, liqueurs, cakes."

"We're not a grocer's shop," Lady Milton said.

"Well, we might make some money if we were. We're going down, Ma. We have to face facts." ("Burden Makepeace," he called the house.) He had already sold the dairy cottage a few years ago and was now planning to rent out the old workers' cottages on the estate as "holiday homes" and even sell off a few more of them. With *land*! You never sold land! Land was sacred! Everyone knew that. The dairy cottage, the forester's cottage, the shepherd's cottage—all going up for grabs. "It makes sense, Ma. No one's living in them. We haven't had a dairyman since the war."

She had been walking the dogs past Home Farm the other day and there was a sign on the gate—"Farmhouse for sale—offers invited." If she'd had any money of her own, she would have bought it herself. "And yet it's a strange idea, don't you think?" Sophie said. "That anyone can *own* land. Surely the land belongs to everyone. *When Adam delved and Eve span, who was then the gentleman?*"

"Are we talking novels again?" Lady Milton asked warily.

"The Peasants' Revolt," Sophie said, which rather put an end to the conversation.

Someone had been making enquiries about a "long let" for the Dower House. But that's mine, Lady Milton thought. The Dower House was where she was going to live when Johnny "kicked the bucket" (Cosmo's term) and Piers took over the title. She was looking forward to the Dower House, it had a sweet little morning room and a sheltered garden. And no one else living there, just herself and the dogs. It was to be her reward for putting up with the family all these years.

Most outrageous of all—Piers had already begun work on turn-ing the East Wing of the house into a hotel. A hotel! "A country house hotel," he said. "Offer people 'the Downton experience.' You know—shooting parties, dinner in evening dress, watching the hunt set off."

Rousing himself from the torpor he had begun to sink into, Johnny had said "Over my dead body" when Piers had first mooted the idea. "Not long, then," Lady Milton heard Cosmo mutter.

The East Wing—referred to as "the Rookery" due to the number of birds that flocked around it and possibly lived in it—was hope-lessly neglected. No one had lived there for decades, not since the Junkers; it would cost a fortune to turn it into anything, let alone a hotel.

The main house and part of the West Wing were given over to the visitors and so the family huddled cheek by jowl in what remained. Not Arabella, thank goodness. She was married (a miracle that anyone would take her on) and lived in Northamp-tonshire, where she was the Master of her local hunt. Arabella had grown quite stout lately. She had an enormous appetite and could eat the best of them under the table. Lady Milton felt sorry for her horse. And Cosmo, of course, spent a lot of his time debauching around London, creating one scandal after another. Not in Belgravia, their London house—that was rented out to a Qatari sheikh. Paid the rent in cash. "What's not to like?" Piers said.

They had sold off nearly all their Old Masters to pay the bills. The Raphael, the most valuable of them all, had gone, of course. The "Burton Makepeace Raphael"—a Madonna and child—was famous. It had been in the family for over two hundred years, bought with some of the compensation the Miltons received after the Abolition of Slavery Act when they had to give up their planta-tion in the Caribbean (and you definitely didn't talk about *that*).

Lady Milton had never particularly liked the Raphael. The Madonna had a simpering expression on her face as if she thought herself a better mother than other women. The Raphael was one of the first things Sophie had asked about when she arrived. She was very knowledgeable about art. (Sometimes Lady Milton wondered if you couldn't be *too* educated.) Unfortunately, Cosmo had sold the painting on the sly to someone who came on a pheasant shoot. A Russian, an oiligarch. ("Oligarch," Piers corrected her.) You heard about them all the time now, and not in a good way.

Cosmo had needed the money to pay off his debts to "some guys" who would kill him otherwise. "Let them," Johnny said.

They were all sworn to secrecy about the missing Raphael, something to do with tax liability. Whenever anyone asked about it, they said it was being restored. "You must promise you won't tell," Lady Milton said to Sophie.

Of course, they still had the big Turner, *Sunset over Fountains Abbey*, a view of the long vista from up at Anne Boleyn's seat. It had hung in the Red Room ever since one of Johnny's more avant-garde ancestors had bought it straight from the artist's studio. Not an Old Master but nonetheless "worth a bundle," according to Piers. Lady Milton presumed it would be the next thing to go. No art lover, she was nonetheless rather fond of the Turner. It represented something she couldn't quite put her finger on. Beauty, perhaps.

~

Piers was married to Trudi. Austrian. *"L'Autrichienne,"* Cosmo called her. Trudi's father was a minor Hapsburg with an unpronounceable title. The first wife, Ariadne, the daughter of a newspaper tycoon, had to be placed in a terrifyingly expensive "rehabilitation" unit. It was a mental asylum by any other name, but you weren't supposed to call them that any more. Best simply to keep one's thoughts to oneself. (Difficult.) The tycoon paid for his daughter's care because Piers refused, although he had to fob the tycoon off with the last of the Canalettos. Ariadne was no longer incarcerated but they weren't sure where she was. South Africa, possibly, Piers thought. There had been two children from the marriage—girls. The tycoon had insisted on taking them. They would be grown-up now, but they never heard from them, not even a Christmas card.

With Trudi, Piers had produced three more children. They were poppets really, all girls again—Miltons seemed to be lacking in whatever it was that made boys. Trudi's succession of nannies all spoke German because she wanted the children to be fluent in the mother tongue. Silly when they still had Nanny, who might be ancient but was perfectly competent (and certainly didn't speak German). She had looked after all three of Lady Milton's children. "The anti-Christ," Cosmo called her. The thought of Nanny always made Lady Milton feel slightly alarmed. She roamed free on the attic floors but sometimes she appeared downstairs—suddenly—like a character in a horror story. ("Or *Jane Eyre*," Sophie said.) Lady Milton's own nanny had been a sweetheart; she still missed her.

"Has Nanny had her tea?" she asked Sophie.

"I took it up myself. She was watching *Countdown*. It makes her unaccountably annoyed."

"It does, doesn't it?" Lady Milton mused. "I wonder why."

"Her hearing-aid battery needed changing again," Sophie said. "I don't know what she does to them."

"She *listens* more than most people, I expect," Lady Milton said, unable to prevent a slight shudder. "I always feel she's skulking somewhere, ready to pounce."

"She does loom rather."

Cook had made a plate of featherweight sponge drops. "Heavenly," Sophie said.

"Cook *is* wonderful," Lady Milton agreed. "Been with us for years, don't know what we'll do when she goes."

"She's going?"

"Not voluntarily. She'll drop in harness. Good old Cook."

"Have another sponge drop," Sophie said, urging the plate on her.

"I shouldn't," Lady Milton said glumly. "But I shall."

The thing that Lady Milton liked about Sophie (one of the many things) was that she could take tea with one and behave almost as an equal and yet still know her place. She wasn't a girl (woman really, but anyone younger than herself was a girl to Lady Milton) who kow-towed. She knew her place, but she didn't *crawl*, not like the last housekeeper, Mrs. Howitt, who more or less curtsied every time she caught sight of one.

And before that, of course, the "Awful Woman," as they called her. Johnny said he thought she might be a man. There used to be a time when you would keep a housekeeper for life. Those times were long gone, never to return. The Awful Woman had had no idea what was required to run a house like this. Whereas Sophie was so very much more than a housekeeper, forever going beyond the call of duty.

"She's more like a companion," Arabella complained sullenly. (Would that be so very bad? Lady Milton wondered.) "You should watch it, you don't want to let her get too close." There was something irredeemably coarse about Arabella, not just her size and her awful dress sense, nor even her gruff manner. It was an abrasiveness, a certainty about her own opinions that was unsettling. She would be a good person to send into battle, like a tank.

Arabella had produced twin girls, Flora and Faye. (More girls! No one *wanted* girls.) They were buxom teenagers with appalling manners, glued to their phones as though they were life-support machines. They would have to be surgically removed from them. "Flora and Fauna," Lady Milton often found herself accidentally calling them. One heard a lot about anorexia in young girls, but really it wouldn't do the twins any harm. Something else one couldn't say.

"Sophie's pretty fit though," Cosmo said, "beneath all that Elizabeth Fry clothing." Lady Milton was surprised that Cosmo had even heard of Elizabeth Fry. He had always seemed so resistant to education, despite Eton and a third in History from Cambridge.

"She *is* very fit," Lady Milton agreed. "She runs around the place all day long. I don't know where she gets the energy." That was another good thing about Sophie. She didn't set her cap at Cosmo, because he *was* a considerable catch. If Piers didn't produce a son then Cosmo would inherit the estate as the title didn't allow for a female heir. And they were overrun with girls! "Primogeniture," Sophie said. "Just like *Pride and Prejudice*." She seemed to have a way of relating everything to nineteenth-century novels. And, yes, Lady Milton had heard of *Pride and Prejudice*. She was not a complete philistine. Never read it, mind you.

All the branches on Johnny's once grand and flourishing family tree had withered and died. If Piers or Cosmo didn't produce a son there was simply no one left to entail the estate on except for a five-times-removed cousin who was a sheep farmer in Australia and who sent them a Christmas card every year "From your cousin, Brett." What an ignoble end, after all these years of hanging on to the estate like grim death. Trudi had "done her best," according to Piers (not good enough!), but now all their hopes lay with Cosmo.

"Perhaps we could steal a baby from somewhere," Sophie suggested. They both laughed at the idea. Sophie had a charming laugh, light and sparkling, like silver bells. Arabella neighed like a plough horse. When Lady Milton had first married into the Miltons they still had a couple of Clydesdales working the Home Farm, left over from the war. Big brutes. Lovely though. She used to walk down to their field every morning and give them an apple each. It was an escape really, getting away from the *ancien régime* of Johnny's father, the Old Marquess. Breakfast with him had been a terrifying start to the day.

Cosmo was a liability. There had been the dreadful affair with him and Johnny's last secretary (he had a young man now, thank goodness), not to mention—and Lady Milton never did—that girl who used to come up from the village to help out with the polishing.

Sophie, on the other hand, was professional, she didn't romanticize about a future with Cosmo. It wouldn't do anyway. It was imperative for their finances that Cosmo married money, however distasteful the source. Of course, he would want to keep it all to himself, but that was absolutely not going to happen. His girlfriend at the time was Thursday, the daughter of an American billionaire investment banker. It was just like the old days. Honoria's own grandmother had been the daughter of a Chicago industrialist— steel and railways. Sophie had shown her Thursday's Instagram account. "She's a real jet-setter, isn't she?" Sophie said as they looked at one photograph after another of a scantily clad Thursday drinking champagne and frolicking on yachts and in hot tubs. Just thinking about Thursday's name made Lady Milton feel tired, but they needed her, or someone like her, if they were to survive.

"Better than Monday," Sophie said. "That would be a rather depressing name to have. More tea? I've put hot water in the pot, it's not stewed or anything." She was a delightfully old-fashioned girl. Cosmo was right, she did seem rather Quakerly. She dressed in shades of grey and lilac, white blouses, modest hemlines and soft cardigans. Never in trousers. She wore old-fashioned wire-rimmed spectacles that gave her a studious air (all that Jane Austen). Mind you, anyone could look clever if they put on a pair of spectacles. Even Cosmo.

Lady Milton had tried Sophie's spectacles on once after she had found them lying on a table in the conservatory when she couldn't find her own. She had been trying to decipher a note that Piers had left for her. He tended to use the written word to communicate, even though he was usually only a couple of rooms away at most. He resented the fact that she refused to get a mobile phone. "I could text you," he told her. "It would be easier." But she preferred to be tethered to an old-fashioned telephone that you could just walk away from. She was such a Luddite, Piers said. It didn't sound like a compliment. Why would you want to be available to everybody all the time? And anyway, they were in some kind of "black hole" as far as mobile phones were concerned, apparently, something that drove Flora and Fauna hysterical when they visited because they couldn't "get a signal" and they had to go out into the deer park to "catch" one, frightening the deer in the process. If they did that in rutting season, they might find themselves on the wrong end of an antler. A cheering thought.

Sophie's spectacles had been no use to Lady Milton, they seemed to be a very weak prescription. In fact she wasn't at all sure that it wasn't just plain glass in the frames.

"Oh, there they are," Sophie had said when she had appeared suddenly in the conservatory, making Lady Milton jump. "I wondered where I'd left them."

Sophie's lovely fair hair was always neatly pinned in a French pleat. She was so clean it couldn't help but lift your spirits. She made Lady Milton think of a dove. A Quaker dove. So calm, so obliging. Not that doves were particularly obliging. Did Sophie go to church? "When I can," she said. "My father's a vicar, actually."

"Really?" Lady Milton felt quite thrilled by this information although she wasn't sure why. It just seemed so *right*. She imagined an ancient grey church, a village green, a fête in the summer with a splendid WI tent. England as it should be. You only found those places on television now, of course, and generally people were being murdered wholesale in them. Johnny used to throw a fête for the whole village, but really all they did was drink and do filthy things in the woods.

There was a lovely little Norman church—St. Martin's—across the deer park, but the congregation was almost non-existent and the vicar had to parse himself out between several different parishes. That was probably what had killed the old incumbent. His replacement was a bit of an oddball, "the trendy vicar," Piers called him. Lady Milton was not much of a churchgoer. She attended the occasional service, of course, more for form's sake than anything— Easter Sunday, the candlelit Christmas Watchnight service. She was an Anglican obviously, but God seemed a remote possibility at best.

If Sophie were to marry Cosmo, she would be a real daughter. It was a ridiculous thought, but strangely attractive when put into the context of a girl called Thursday.

"Oh, she's all right," Sophie chided gently. "She does have very nice manners. And she's good with horses."

"I suppose that counts for something," Lady Milton said grudgingly.

"The Burkett-Pitts are coming for lunch on Friday," Sophie said, taking out the little notebook she always carried with her. "I wondered whether or not you wanted to serve alcohol?"

"Why wouldn't I?"

"Well, I believe Sir William's a recovering alcoholic."

Lady Milton waved an indifferent hand. "No reason the rest of us should suffer. The pair of them are hard enough work as it is, I doubt whether I could manage without a couple of stiff gins."

"Right you are." Sophie wrote something in her little book. She was forever making lists and then ticking things off on them. Lady Milton found it very reassuring. It held out the possibility that one day everything would be finished.

She could hear Nanny clumping about somewhere upstairs like a troll. She felt suddenly terribly weary.

"Don't worry," Sophie said, getting up. "I'll see to her."

They ate a scratchy kind of supper, as they often did nowadays. Omelettes followed by baked apples and a bottle of Chablis. Lady Milton was separated from Johnny by the polished wasteland of a Chippendale table that Piers wanted to sell. ("Why not just sell me?" Johnny grumbled, but really, who would want him?) Lady Milton felt envious of Sophie, who ate in the warm, fuggy kitchen with Cook.

She remembered a time when dinner had been a proper five-course affair every night, when everyone dressed and the candles were always lit. Flowers on the table, the women in glittering jewels. Now they ate make-do, midweek food beneath harsh electric lighting. She hadn't even changed, was still in her old dog-walking tweed skirt and pearls.

"Good day?" Johnny asked.

"So-so," Lady Milton replied. She wished Andrew, the footman, wouldn't smirk so much at Johnny. What was the matter with the man? He had to double up as a valet as well, they ran the place on a skeleton staff these days. They weren't really footmen any more. They didn't even wear a proper uniform. When Lady Milton was a girl they still wore powdered wigs, white stockings, gold braid. Andrew wore a white jacket and looked as if he worked in a barber's shop.

Their butler—Chalmers—had retired. He had been very old and had just sort of faded away, so they hardly missed him when he went. He had been thoughtful like that. They still hadn't found a replacement for him.

After supper Johnny disappeared to his study, Andrew on his

heels with the whisky decanter. Still smirking. What did they *do* in there? "Chess," Johnny said. That seemed highly unlikely to Lady Milton. She had never seen a chessboard in there.

Sometimes after dinner Lady Milton played cards with Sophie. Sophie had taught her Cribbage. They played for matchsticks—they were both surprisingly competitive—and Sophie laughed and said one day she would cash in her matchsticks and Lady Milton would have to pay up. Sophie said Cribbage was the kind of thing old men used to play in pubs. "Well, I wouldn't know," Lady Milton said. Sometimes she wished she did know. Not particularly about old men in pubs, but just how life was for other people.

And, of course, they always had a jigsaw to fall back on. "Fascinating Norway" (more enjoyable than it sounded), a fiendish 3,000-piece, was on the go at the moment, laid out in what they referred to as the Stubbs Room, even though all the Stubbs had long since been sold to pay for repairs to the roof. Even that hadn't been enough.

This evening there was no sign of Sophie and anyway Lady Milton felt far too tired for the exigencies of cards or Norway, fascinating or otherwise, so she elected to watch television. There was an old set on its last legs in the Blue Room. One could hardly justify the expense of a new one when there were so few programmes that one enjoyed—*Grantchester, Midsomer Murders, The Chase.* Sophie always watched that with her. She was very good at general knowledge.

"You should apply to be on," Lady Milton said. "You would be sure to win."

"Oh, I don't know," Sophie said. "There's always something they catch you out on and I'm not what you would call a team player."

Lady Milton had never been a fan of *Downton Abbey.* It was such a painful reminder of one's family's glory days. And hopelessly inaccurate, of course. One would never have been so *involved* with the servants' lives. "The Downton experience" for paying guests. What nonsense. "But it wouldn't be real, Ma," Piers said. "It would be pretend. Like theatre."

She settled on a nature programme. A pack of hyenas was

stalking a gazelle. Lady Milton supposed it would end badly for the gazelle, although she missed the dénouement—she must have dozed off because there was a light tapping on the door that woke her with a start. There was something bizarre and raucous on the television now and some of the people seemed to be naked. Lady Milton reached hastily for the remote control.

"Still up, Lady Milton?" Sophie said. "Can I make you a cup of something? Cocoa? Horlicks? Cook's gone to bed."

"Thank you very much, dear, but I'm fine." Lady Milton heaved herself off the sofa. "I'm going to bed myself now."

"It's supposed to be cold tomorrow," Sophie said. "You must make sure you wrap up warmly." She held the door open for her and said, "Goodnight, Lady Milton." And then the girl did the oddest thing, she suddenly stepped forward and gave Lady Milton an affectionate kiss on the cheek. For one mad moment Lady Milton found herself wanting to pull the girl close and give her a responding hug. Reason prevailed and instead she managed a faint, "Goodnight, Sophie." Whatever next?

❧

The following day had been a Tuesday and the house was therefore closed to visitors. There was no sign of Sophie. Cook said she hadn't been down for breakfast, so Lady Milton went upstairs and knocked tentatively on her bedroom door. No answer. More tentative knocking on Lady Milton's part. She was not one to enter a room boldly. When younger, she had once walked in on her mother doing something unspeakable with one of the grooms. Even now she blanched at the memory. Eventually, when it seemed that Sophie must be either absent or dead, she entered her room. And if not dead, then perhaps she would find Sophie in bed, unwell. She imagined bringing her up a tea-tray or a bowl of broth prepared by Cook. How kind she would be to the girl, she thought.

No invalid in sight. No Sophie. The room was empty. The dogs followed her in, noses down, tails up, and did a quick efficient tour of the room as if they were searching for Sophie. The bed was neatly made but the drawers and cupboards were empty. Lady Milton felt like a terrific snoop but there was something fascinating about being in Sophie's room. Sophie's perfume—something faint and flowery—still lingered on the air. Lily of the valley possibly. A book sat on her bedside table. *The Secret of the Clock Cabinet* by Nancy Styles. What was a "clock cabinet"? Lady Milton wondered. Was it the same as a clock case? A page was folded down at the corner. Lady Milton opened the book. A passage was underlined. "The guilty always masquerade as the innocent but it is rarely the other way round." Too much like a riddle, Lady Milton thought, closing the book.

It was icy cold in here and the room itself was spartan. It felt rather like the cell of a nun. Lady Milton resolved to find some prettier furniture for the girl, there was some nice Hepplewhite in the neglected East Wing that might still be serviceable if the woodworm hadn't got to it.

She stood gazing out of the window for some time. She wasn't thinking about anything in particular, people spent too much time thinking, in Lady Milton's opinion. The dogs grew bored and flopped down on the floor, where they immediately fell asleep.

It was only later, when Lady Milton was pacing round the house, the dogs pattering at her heels, fretting about the whereabouts of a still-absent Sophie, that she noticed that although the Turner was hanging in its usual place, it was now merely an empty frame, enclosing not the fiery backdrop of a sunset beyond the ruins of Fountains but the red damask silk that covered the wall behind. At first, she thought that Cosmo must have sold it to another oiligarch, but he became quite testy when she accused him. It was only two large gins and several uncomfortable hours spent with the police later that Lady Milton was prepared to face the truth. Sophie was nothing more than a lying thief. A viper in their nest.

"Treacherous little trollop," Piers said, stomping around the drawing room. "Flogging's too good for her." And Trudi, who was in a funny mood, said, "Yet it's good enough for you, *mein Lieber,* isn't it?" Lady Milton had no idea what she meant.

"And you didn't see Sophie Greenway at all after she said goodnight to you?"

"No," Lady Milton said. "Why would I?"

The house had been crawling with police of one kind or another. Lady Milton had already been interviewed once (grilled, more like). They had all had their fingerprints taken, "for the purpose of elimination," the police said, but it made Lady Milton feel like a common criminal.

A Scottish child masquerading as a detective had been sent to interrogate her for the umpteenth time. Lady Milton knew that the police were young these days (everyone was young) but this girl was surely an imposter. "We said goodnight and then I retired to my room and so did she, I believe. I've told the other officers all this."

"I know, I'm sorry. It's just that sometimes a memory comes back when you go over it again." She was "not that long out of uniform," the girl said when pressed, and Lady Milton supposed she meant school uniform. "And the house is closed to visitors on a Tuesday, so I suppose it would have taken longer to discover the theft. She obviously planned it."

"There was no sign that she was a criminal," Lady Milton said. "She was here for nearly six months, for heaven's sake. And she had such good references. I spoke to Lady Boroughmuir on the telephone myself. She said the girl was an excellent housekeeper—and she was."

"I'm afraid we believe the woman you spoke to was Sophie impersonating Lady Boroughmuir."

"Goodness," Lady Milton said faintly. She was rather impressed by such depths of duplicity.

The girl gave her a card. "In case you remember anything else. DC Reggie Chase," she added. Lady Milton already had several cards from the various police officers. Like calling cards in the old days.

"Reggie?" Lady Milton queried. "Isn't that a man's name?" She had known a Reginald once, before she married Johnny. Handsome devil. Killed by a kick to the head from his own hunter.

"It's Regina, really," the girl said. "As in 'queen.'"

"How nice," Lady Milton murmured. She had met the Queen, of course, years ago. The real one. She had been surprisingly short, even then. One mourned her loss and moved on, but it would never be the same. "The past is a foreign country," Sophie had said to her once. From a novel, of course.

Perhaps Sophie read too much fiction, perhaps that was where it all went wrong for her. But she was right, wasn't she? You went to bed one night, in a happy daze because you had waltzed all night with eligible young men, and you woke up the next day and found yourself living on a bleak planet inhabited by alien creatures.

From an upstairs window Lady Milton had watched the police cars leaving. They had arrived several hours earlier with their blue lights blazing, sirens wailing—the hunt in full halloo—but now they were traipsing back down the drive, tails between their legs, with no quarry on show. Lady Milton wasn't sure which loss was the worse—the Turner or Sophie. Or whatever her real name was. It seemed unlikely that her father really was a vicar.

～

And not a trace of the perfidious girl had been found since. The housekeeping, such as it was, was done by the hotel staff, because, yes, Piers had got his way and the rooks had been evicted from the East Wing and it was now a hotel. "Rook Hall." Ridiculous. The hotel staff were rather resentful because they didn't get paid any extra to look after the main house.

Nothing had really been done properly since Sophie's sudden departure. No one ticked off items on lists. No one wanted to drink delicate China tea with Lady Milton or kill an evening by doing a jigsaw with her. "Fascinating Norway" had been tipped back into its box, its fjords unfinished and long forgotten. The Turner's empty frame had been left on the wall of the Red Room and every time

Lady Milton walked past the blank space she was unpleasantly reminded of the theft and all that had occurred since. Everything was in decline, almost as though the Turner had left a curse in its wake. It was not just Sophie who had gone, of course. Johnny was absent now, as were Trudi and the poppets.

Lady Milton thought of the French Revolution. Some of her own ancestors had been French, so it was personal. She thought of their heads being sliced from their bodies. Perhaps that was a better way to go than the painfully slow decline with its inevitable end. The Miltons would disappear into history.

"Lady Milton?" the butler said, interrupting what had become a distressing series of thoughts. Oh, God, the vicar, the last person she felt like talking to. Reverend Simon Cate was not really what Lady Milton looked for in a vicar (dogma, certitude, a lusty hymnal voice). He had rather wild hair and some odd ideas that hardly seemed to be part of the Protestant creed. "Mysticism," for example. And he talked about "Zen" and "Sufi," which were the kind of names Cosmo's latest girlfriend would choose for her children. She was a yoga teacher and an "influencer," whatever that was. Thursday, the American heiress, was long gone, having finally realized that what she had taken for charming British eccentricity in Cosmo was nothing more than straightforward idiocy. "Hugh Grant has a lot to answer for," Arabella said.

Lady Milton wondered whether Reverend Cate was due to retire soon. She wished that he would just get on with it and go. He seemed to approach everything as if it were a philosophical dilemma, and he was always irritating Lady Milton by saying, "Call me Simon, please." She would not. Why on earth would one want to be on first-name terms with one's vicar?

The deer park belonged to Burton Makepeace, but they allowed the locals to walk in it and sometimes, if Lady Milton ventured there, she encountered the vicar ambling around as if he had no employment. Once she had come across him attempting to put his arms around the trunk of one of the old oaks. He couldn't even get them halfway round, the tree had been there longer than the

Miltons. He was resting his head against the bark and when he saw her he made no attempt to move, just smiled at her and said, "I'm listening to her heartbeat."

"He's a nice man," Sophie had said to her on one occasion when Lady Milton had been grumbling about some of his strange quirks. He had, for example, held a service to which people were invited to bring their pets. An enormous number of people turned up, people who had never previously seen the inside of St. Martin's, or indeed any church. Not to mention all the cats, dogs, hamsters, guinea pigs, rabbits, two chickens, a donkey, a budgie (in a cage), two ponies and a snake. The place had been, literally, like a zoo. And afterwards, Marian Forster, the Ikebana woman, said it was "like cleaning the Augean stables." Lady Milton merely nodded politely. She had no idea what or where the Augean stables were. Lady Milton had made a point of not taking her own dogs. It might have given them ideas.

Sophie and the Reverend Cate had seemed to get on very well ("Platonic," Sophie reassured her). Lady Milton often spied them in the park together, chatting and laughing. She had to admit to feeling a little pang of envy at how easy-going they seemed in each other's company.

"Reverend Cate," she said now, with little enthusiasm. "How unexpected of you to drop in." He came regularly, begging bowl in hand. Usually he was looking for a contribution towards the church-roof fund, confirmed this morning by some primitive sign language when he steepled his hands together. (Had he lost his voice or simply gone mad?) Church roofs seemed very needy to Lady Milton. Or perhaps it was the belfry, because then he mimed ringing a bell. Lady Milton wasn't intending to donate anything, but she was sympathetic to his cause.

"I expect you would like some tea, Reverend Cate?"

The vicar nodded his head but still didn't speak. What on earth was wrong with the man?

"Or coffee, perhaps?" she offered. He nodded again. Did he want *both*?

He shook his head vigorously and mimed drinking from a cup and saucer, little finger aloft. Then he used his index fingers to form the letter T, smiling and nodding at her all the while.

"Tea it is, then," she said, resigning herself to his tomfoolery. "Shall we go into the conservatory?"

She reached out a hand for the bell-pull to call for the tea-tray, but it seemed unlikely that anyone would answer.

Return from Damascus

Simon Cate was meandering across the deer park on the way back from Burton Makepeace. He had drunk too much of the rather bitter tea that was served these days at the house. "The hotel," Lady Milton said, by way of explanation. "Bought wholesale. Tea bags," she added with a shudder of horror. He had hoped for a biscuit, but none had been forthcoming.

He was looking for flint arrowheads (he had, let's face it, the soul of a detectorist). The place was littered with them. He wondered what other treasure might be buried beneath the green acres of the deer park. Had there been a Neolithic settlement here once, long before the Miltons claimed this land for their own? Land ownership was a tricky issue, wasn't it? Technically speaking, the Earth belonged to God. The Church certainly owned enough of it.

When he was young, Simon had liked to think of himself as a bit of an anarchist, although really he had simply been spouting other people's beliefs. He would have done away with both Church and monarchy in those days—"bastions of the establishment"—but now, despite their gaping flaws, he felt rather fond of both. That was what age did to you—you ran the gamut from spouting gobbets of *Das Kapital* in your green youth to embracing Thatcherism by the end (he wasn't there yet, thank goodness). It was depressing. He supposed that anarchy, like sex, was best left to the young, as they were blissfully blind to the consequences of both.

It had been over a week now since Simon had been struck with the proverbial bolt from the blue. The day had seemed like any other day. He had begun it by drinking his morning coffee in his usual place, sitting in the front pew of the church. He had started to bring a Thermos flask from the vicarage. It was so cold in the church that his breath formed icy clouds in front of his face. Nonetheless he preferred the church to the feeling of being stranded in the big, inhospitable vicarage, also freezing cold. The original vicarage had burned down sometime during the nineteenth century and the one that replaced it was both ugly and impractical and hardly seemed to have been modernized at all in the intervening years.

St. Martin's had been Simon's church for over five years now. He looked after another two smaller parishes, rotating his Sunday services between them, but St. Martin's was the one he roosted in on a daily basis. The church had been here for as long as the village had. It had a very pretty graveyard where the residents of the village had been buried for centuries, since before the Black Death probably. Apparently there was a plague pit somewhere nearby that the diseased corpses had all been tipped into. He often wondered where it was. The recent dead were tragic, the ancient dead were a mere curiosity.

He poured another cup of coffee into the flask's little stainless-steel cup and raised a silent toast to the plague dead. They had never even tasted coffee. Or tea, for that matter. Or potatoes. Chocolate. He had to stop himself, the list of deprivations in the Middle Ages was a long one. He would have said a prayer for them, but the words stubbornly refused to form.

Simon didn't believe in God. Not at all. And when he had finally given word to this apostasy some years ago now, no cock had crowed. The sky hadn't fallen in, the devil hadn't come calling for his soul. Not that he'd expected him (or her) to, although it was easier to believe in the devil than it was in God. The devil was everywhere, whereas God was, clearly, nowhere to be found.

The church was on the edge of the deer park and Simon liked to walk there in the early morning before anyone else was up. He loved to see the mist rising off the grass and the trees emerging into view. The deer congregated near the church at night and were usually still there in the morning, wandering around in the graveyard. He thought of them as part of his flock, although obviously they were, technically speaking, a herd. There were many more of them than the human worshippers in St. Martin's, indeed in all of his parishes put together. The most congregants he ever managed was for his annual service on St. Francis's Day, when he held a service to bless people's pets. It was always lovely. He wished the pets would just come on their own every Sunday.

Sometimes Simon opened wide the great wooden double doors of the church in the hope that the deer might wander inside. They never did. Deer were essentially stupid, worse than sheep, the same blankness behind the eyes, but there was something wonderfully medieval about catching sight of them—something holy, too, that never failed to lift his spirits. They had been here for a very long time. Like most of the rest of the natural world, they must have munched their way disinterestedly through the Black Death. They had been indifferent to the recent pandemic, as they would be to the next one. Simon's lived faith was the imminence of the Apocalypse, a secular rather than a biblical one. He worried for the animals.

The deer were a "managed" herd, which meant they were culled regularly, something that felt decidedly unholy. Surely if they were left to get on with it themselves they would eventually self-regulate their numbers? They were shot by a marksman in the winter and then carted off to be butchered and sold as venison from the freezer in Burton Makepeace's new farm shop, recently opened in one of the old gate lodges.

Of course, Simon still didn't understand country ways. He had been brought up in an outer suburb of London and had spent most of his working life in the capital, in what were always termed "vibrant" multicultural parishes, to a soundtrack of sirens and traffic and late-night drunks. Every morning he had cleared the neglected churchyard of needles and used condoms that looked like empty sausage skins. Coming late to sex in the era of the Pill and early to celibacy (in the era of despair, he might have said), he had never used a condom, something that struck him as odd, but then the list of things he had never done was depressingly long.

He had been a vocal believer in Inter-Faith and had probably spent more time in the neighbourhood mosques and temples, and even occasionally a Kingdom Hall, than he had in his own dour, falling-to-pieces church in London. The closest he came to ecumenicalism now was the old Methodist chapel that had been converted into a house by a sybaritic couple from Leeds who were retired secondary-school teachers and who, in summer, sat in deckchairs in front of the chapel and raised their glasses of rosé to him when he passed. "Sun's over the yardarm, Vicar!" they called out gleefully. "Come and join us!" More like a challenge than an invitation. He felt like saying, "Come and join *me*!" They had never set foot in his church. Even Cosmo Milton was harried by his mother into making an appearance at the Christmas Watchnight service, but the rosé drinkers, like most people, gave religion a wide berth. Simon didn't blame them.

His rural parishes were very small and very white, and when the last of their worshippers died he supposed there would be no more church attendees. He felt as if he were overseeing the final death throes of Christianity. Someone had to, it may as well be him.

In Burton Makepeace, the soundtrack was birdsong and tractor engines, and the graveyard litter was mostly composed of leaves and the feathered remains of the wood pigeons that had been savaged to death in the night—by foxes, he presumed, but he always felt unsure about what predators might be prowling in the woods beyond the deer park. He wouldn't have been surprised to find himself face to face one morning with a wolf or a bear, but usually it was just stray cats. He put out a saucer of cat food for the hedgehogs every evening. More often than not, the cats got to it first. Fair enough.

He had been a vegetarian for many years now, but had begun to view this as a rather pathetic halfway house. If he really cared for animals, surely he would be a vegan? It had struck home for him last summer when he had blessed Fran Jennings' beehives. All that industry in the slavish service of humans! Bees were so smart you would think they would have rebelled by now.

Burton Makepeace was apparently the last step on the road to his retirement, but really Simon knew what had happened. He had been culled.

~

He sighed, finished his coffee and absent-mindedly left his flask on the altar, where it sat like an oblation, mystifying Marian Forster (a stalwart of the herd) when she came later to replace the wilting chrysanthemums.

He pulled himself together, both inside and out, and set off on his round of visits. Really being a vicar was more the job of a social worker or a GP, a visiting service for the elderly. The only people he ever saw who were under sixty (apart from himself, of course) were either tourists or young couples who wanted him to perform their weddings for them, even though they had never set foot inside a church before. Fine by him.

It wasn't that Simon had lost his Christian faith, it was just that he was no longer sure he had ever found it in the first place. It had been surprisingly easy to get by all these years, to say you felt you had a "calling" or even murmur mysteriously about "a Damascene conversion" without having to go into specifics—the burning bush, the holes made by the crucifix nails and so on. Once you had that collar round your neck, people rarely questioned you any more about your "faith." He had been placing the word in inverted commas for some time now, in his head anyway, although he'd noticed a few funny looks recently from his sparse congregants so perhaps he had been voicing his doubts out loud. He could never be sure, he spoke so much to himself. He was his own confessor.

It was perhaps not exactly that there had *not* been a moment—oh, God, he thought, listen to yourself, man, the equivocation and procrastination built into a simple sentence. He had developed a habit over the years of what he thought of as "vicar-speak," filling in the spaces where the spirit should be with extenuated grammar and endless conditionals and negatives—a misdirection away from the emptiness at the heart of his words.

What he *meant* to say (he was speaking to himself, so it hardly mattered really), what he meant to say was that there *had* been a moment. And it had been numinous and wonderful and transcendent and all those other words for the metaphysical, but that is what it was—a moment. As if he had been given a precious diamond and had held it for only a second before accidentally dropping it into the ocean and having to feel the agony of watching it fall, glinting, through the water, less bright with every passing moment, knowing it could never be retrieved from the depths. (Was he just remembering a scene in *Titanic*?)

"Perhaps you should have been a writer, darling," his wife, Rosalind, used to say, not without bitterness. "You like words so very much." She left, she said, because she couldn't bear to listen to him talking all the time. ("Nattering"—a word he associated, unfairly, he knew, with the elderly women in his flock.) He hadn't realized. He had tried to be quiet and discovered, not for the first time, how difficult he found it.

It didn't make any difference, because his wife was always going to leave. Both him and his "religion" (her inverted commas this time, not his). It was fifteen years now since Rosalind had renounced both him and Anglicanism as if they were the same thing and had fallen into the welcoming yet restrained embrace of the Society of Friends. One afternoon, when he was stuck in the middle of the harrowing tedium of sermon-writing, she had appeared in the doorway of his study and placidly announced that she was leaving him. "It's you, not me," she said.

A few years later, unlikely as it had seemed at the time (even more unlikely now), she was killed in a terrorist attack when she was on holiday abroad with her new partner, a man she had met at her Meeting. For some reason the bomb was not one of those "incidents" (a mild word for the depravity) that were seared into the public memory, like Bali or Lockerbie. If people were reminded of it now they usually said, "God, I'd forgotten all about that." Or they didn't remember it at all.

The new partner, whose name was Neil (lean, balding, keen cyclist), had found it necessary for some reason to visit Simon in order to recount the details. "Will you join me in silence?" Neil asked when he had finished his narrative with its inevitable and strangely banal dénouement ("and that was the moment when I knew that she had gone"). It was the Quaker way, of course, and they had sat together for what seemed like an eternity, Neil in intense worshipful silence and Simon staring at his feet while trying to get the occasional surreptitious glimpse at his watch, a skill at which vicars were particularly adept. He wanted to say, "It's been three years since I saw her, I can barely remember what she looked like, why are we doing this?" but obviously he didn't. He felt guilty because what he was remembering about Rosalind in the void of silence were all the things that had annoyed him. Irritation had not been entirely one-way.

Neil cleared his throat and Simon hoped it was a signal that the silence was ending, but it seemed it was a mere punctuation mark. He wondered if Rosalind had begun to grow bored of the absence of sound.

⌁

Simon's transitory moment of revelation had occurred in the Nineties, a decade that otherwise, like many, he struggled to remember. At university he had been desperate to be considered interesting and when religion reared its ugly head (he was studying Philosophy and Ethics) Simon used to tell people that he was brought up as a "strict atheist," because it made his background sound less mundane, more rigorously intellectual, more eccentric even, than it had been. In reality, the *Reader's Digest* that plopped through the letterbox every month was about as highbrow as it got during his solitary childhood in a 1930s semi in Bromley.

And "strict" implied commitment to an ideal, something his parents lacked. There was neither belief nor absence of belief in Bromley, just inertia. His parents were as apathetic towards politics as they were towards religion, he had never known them even to vote in elections. "People died for your vote!" the teenage Simon berated them. Had they? He wasn't sure. He was studying the 1832 Reform Act for O-Levels, but he didn't think anyone had actually sacrificed themselves to get rid of rotten boroughs. Still, it was the principle.

"We had the war, that was excitement enough," his mother said, although both Simon's parents had been young during the war in a Shire town that had been quietly left alone by the Luftwaffe, so they had no claim on the passion of conflict, in Simon's opinion. He would have given anything to have been in a war, even though he was nominally—and rather aggressively—a pacifist.

The teenage years had been unfortunate ones for Simon, living in a permanent paroxysm of indignation, fervid with hormones (or "feelings" as his mother called them) and stippled with such bad acne that he could have passed for a smallpox victim.

In Bromley he felt the world passing him by and he bitterly regretted being too young to experience the meaty stuff of recent history—the Vietnam War, Kennedy's assassination, the Bay of Pigs, the Civil Rights Movement, Haight-Ashbury and Bob Dylan. ("But that's all American," his mother puzzled.) The Sixties with their new, more vital rules of engagement had been denied him in his teenage years. All he had were Northern Ireland and industrial unrest, both of which seemed boring and neither of which he ever really understood. All he really remembered enjoying from this period was listening to *The Hitchhiker's Guide to the Galaxy* on the radio in his room and taking his first girlfriend to see *Grease* and holding one of her hands while she ate all the popcorn with the other.

Later he could laugh about his younger self. (Later still, he would weep for him.) He grew into adulthood, went to a concrete and steel university from which he graduated with a 2:2, by which time he had sloughed off his adolescent angst and resentment, along with his acne, and become almost handsome, with a "leonine" head of unruly hair (as described by one of his girlfriends) and an articulate, charming manner that he slipped on every morning along with his Hugo Boss suit, worn casually tie-less, before leaving his flat in

Camden and making his way to Television Centre in Shepherd's Bush, where he was part of the production team on an exhausting, purposefully chaotic Saturday-night entertainment programme.

He had plenty of female admirers, he took bottles of "good" red to dinner parties in Hampstead where people listened to his opinions and valued his arguments. After dessert—a lemon tart or a big bowl of strawberries—they would bring out cocaine and old-fashioned pot and roll joints and be remarkably pleased with themselves because they were part of the *Zeitgeist*. Simon was beginning to be "known," his star was in the ascendant. He was looking to make the transition into documentaries. Bromley had been left far behind.

And then he had his "moment," unlooked-for in every way. He had travelled north, for an old schoolfriend's wedding in York. He arrived the day before, rather than getting the early train the next morning. He was prone to laziness, and they were in the middle of a heatwave which had made not just him but the whole country lethargic.

It was an old city, ripe—even overripe—with history, and he had gone into one of its abundance of medieval churches, mostly to get out of the unwanted midday heat but also from a sense of architectural curiosity. There was not much in the way of medieval churches in Bromley, indeed precious few in London itself, thanks to the Great Fire, whereas in York you could barely go a hundred yards without coming across ancient stone and stained glass, not to mention the Minster, the great mother house, which dominated the city.

The fourteenth-century church he had ducked into was empty (he was yet to discover that churches were always empty) and Simon sat in one of the worn oak pews in the cool shade of plaster and pillar and wondered how much against church etiquette it would be to pop the top on the can of Fanta he had just bought, which was sweating, inviting with cold, in his hand. Very, he supposed, and he reluctantly put the can down on the stone slabs at his feet next to a kneeler—he thought that was what they were called—embroidered in blue and gold with a Celtic cross. He sat back up and lifted his gaze to the hammer-beam roof and its central gold bosses, too far away for him to discern any detail. If he could have seen them, he would have discovered that they were faces, modelled long ago on the medieval peasants of the town, gurning down at him for the fool he was.

But then—the moment. A kind of *whoosh*, more of a falling than a rising. A sense of great, overwhelming imminence and convergence. An unseen hand clutched his heart as his insides were hollowed out and filled with a flux of something that for ever after would be impossible to describe (although that didn't stop him from trying). And anyway, it was sensation not reason, perception not thought. (*Feelings*, his mother would probably have said.)

Without having to be told, he understood what it was—it was the Holy Ghost. What else could it be? He was transfigured. He had been touched by the hand of God.

For a time afterwards he liked to imagine it as a beam of light—the finger of God, finding him in the dark, the same finger that had reached out and created Adam on the ceiling of the Sistine Chapel. He had recently spent a few days in Rome with an American girl called Vanessa—on a gap year, quite a bit younger than he was—and had trudged dutifully behind her round the boiling-hot Vatican Museum when he would rather have been lounging in a pavement café beneath the shade of a parasol, drinking iced coffee or a deliciously cold vodka martini. You couldn't even see the ceiling of the Sistine Chapel properly. There were people there with binoculars, like bird-watchers. Instead, he studied Michelangelo's *chef-d'oeuvre* secondhand in the guidebook later. "Study" perhaps too strong a word for lying on the hotel bed, leafing carelessly through the pages while he waited for Vanessa to come out of the shower.

He had not felt the presence of holiness in the Vatican, not like he had in the little church in York. Although later, much later, he wondered if it was because he had looked down at the kneeler and then up at the roof bosses and had cricked a nerve in his neck or kinked a blood vessel and experienced ischaemia, perhaps. A physiological rather than a spiritual event.

He had left the church in a state verging on hypoxia and found a bench in the Minster Gardens where he finally drank the Fanta and lit a much-needed cigarette, which felt like a sacrilegious act to commit in the looming presence of the great cathedral.

At that moment—it seemed portentous at the time but was surely just a coincidence—the Minster bells began to toll. It was a simple round that was the precursor to a plain hunt peal. Of course, he didn't know that then. Years later he was press-ganged into service by one of his London church's band of bell-ringers and grew to love the plain bobs and the quarter peals and the desire for a once-in-a-lifetime go at an "extent." But he could never hear a plain hunt without thinking of that moment in the Minster Gardens. He loved the sound of church bells, it was something he would never tire of, long after religion itself had wearied of him.

Sadly, St. Martin's had a solitary bell, and it was Simon who tolled it and he didn't need to ask for whom it tolled, it tolled for him.

The Minster bells came to the end of their peal and Simon suddenly realized that he was getting burned in the sun and got up and tamped out the half-smoked cigarette underfoot and then seconds later went back and picked it up and put it in a waste bin, something he wouldn't previously have bothered doing. There was a whole new moral code to holiness.

On his return to London, in the first flush of evangelical fervour, Simon tried to describe his conversion to the liberal, artsy circle he inhabited. "The cloud of unknowing—apophatic rather than cataphatic," he said. (Ironically, the first thing he had done was to read around the topic as if he were still at school.)

Naturally, his new-found spiritual zeal was acutely embarrassing to everyone. He might as well have been David Icke turning up at those Hampstead dinner tables, and the invitations dried up pretty quickly. The prospect of working on documentaries also receded into the mists. Religion indicated bias, like being a Tory or admiring Wagner's music, no matter how left-wing or open to ideas he remained. You would think he had joined a cult rather than the Church of England. ("Isn't it the same thing?" one of his colleagues mused.) Vanessa, his gap-year girlfriend, didn't last a week with this new apostolic Simon. "You were fun," she said, packing her bag and heading for the airport, "and now you're not."

The very word "Christianity" was avoided by the people he knew. The word sat uncomfortably on his own tongue too, with its whiff of Cliff Richard and the Inquisition (different ends of the spectrum, it was true), but he supposed he would have to get used to it. Doctrine was doctrine.

Of course, these days he was a libertarian where canonical law was concerned and for a long time had been playing fast and loose with the tenets of faith. No one noticed, no one seemed to care. His flock treated him like a slightly wayward, rather bohemian nephew, even though they were not much older than he was himself. He had even kept St. Martin's open during Covid, appalled at the cowardly diktat to close his church and deny solace to those in need. During the Black Death priests had continued to minister to their flocks, dropping like flies as they did so. Sacrifice—wasn't that what religion was about? He had rather hoped that the police would come along and arrest him and he could make a stand, although apart from when the Turner was stolen he couldn't recall ever seeing a policeman in the village. He had spent his youth wanting to be lauded for rebellion—perhaps finally in his later years he could achieve his ends. A martyr, even.

It was the principle of the thing. Principle or not, no one came to his illegally open church, although Marian Forster surprised him by donning a mask, a visor and industrial-strength rubber gloves and braving the law to use the opportunity to polish all the brass.

━━━━━

The inevitable result of loosening the tethers of the creed was to find he no longer felt tied to it at all. He still believed in a spiritual dimension to the world—the deer, the trees, et cetera. He could spend hours just contemplating a leaf or a snail. All things bright and beautiful, and so on. He could understand the "from design" argument, he just couldn't pay lip service to it any more.

"I'm sure you're not the only cleric who finds himself an atheist," his bishop said gloomily when Simon went to him for pastoral advice. "Best just to carry on as if you still believed. I don't think it makes much difference, to be honest." At first, after "the moment," he had presumed that he must have been called to the pious existence of a monk, his days to be dedicated to contemplation and prayer, and so he applied to the Anglican monastery that was attached to the College of the Resurrection in Mirfield. He had not been so overwhelmed by transformation as to become a Catholic. ("Thank God," his mother said, the most heartfelt he had ever heard her.)

The monastery had existed side by side with a theological college and it wasn't long before Simon was being gently nudged, and then eventually rudely shunted, over to the college side. ("You're not made for silence," his advisor told him.) Before he really had time to consider what this would mean, he found himself on the path to ordination, a path that would end, inevitably, with him becoming a Church of England vicar. By then, the precious diamond of revelation—that spark of divinity—was already little more than a twinkle in the depths, but to renege on his conversion would have been to invite ridicule. There was no going back, the only way was forward, a good soldier marching onward in the ranks of the Army of Christ. Not that he thought of it in militaristic terms, but let's face it, he had joined the Ministry because he couldn't think what else to do. He put on the cassock in much the same way he had once put on his Hugo Boss suit. It was a costume, a disguise, covering the invisible man inside it.

If only he had taken a later train to York that day. He didn't even get to the wedding of his friend (to whom, in all honesty, he was not that close). Too discombobulated by the Holy Ghost, Simon had sent his excuses and caught the evening train back to King's Cross.

Smoking was abnegated within weeks and the vodka martinis and bottles of good red were largely gone from his life, too. Nowadays he drank a modest half-pint of real ale in the Milton Arms, on his own or with one or two of his male parishioners, or, if necessary, the occasional dainty sherry with one of his elderly female congregants, who plied him with enough homemade cake and shortbread to sink the Isle of Wight. Lately though, when giving communion, he had begun to think about wine again, not the blood of Christ but a full-bodied Barolo or a Malbec. Perhaps he could drink himself to death on a Shiraz.

⌁

He met Rosalind at a "faith convention," a residential weekend of workshops where they were enjoined to take part in circle dances and trust exercises, although what he mostly remembered about the event was the worthy food—wholewheat macaroni cheese, served up from enormous metal trays, and a dreadful gas-inducing vegetable curry. Equally memorable was the surprise he had when Rosalind slipped between his sheets in the middle of the night in the monkishly austere single room he had been assigned in the convention centre.

Rosalind was a vicar's daughter, her father was a rector in the Cotswolds, so she knew the ropes, it was a bit like having an arranged marriage really. They had pursued their courtship at a leisurely pace, perhaps from lack of enthusiasm on both sides, and Rosalind took a long time to fall pregnant once they were married. In fact, they'd almost given up when Isaac bawled his way into the world. They called him Isaac because Rosalind joked that she was "as old as Sarah" when she conceived (she would have been ninety if that were the case, so a bit of an exaggeration), and Simon responded in an amused, knowing way and then had to look up the Old Testament to check the story of Sarah and Abraham because his Bible knowledge left something to be desired, especially the Old Testament, which, apart from Genesis and the Psalms, he tended to ignore. Rosalind was well versed from childhood, although she said she didn't really believe in any of it, not literally. The faith convention was just "a way to meet people."

Rosalind—she had two sisters—belonged to the sort of family that Simon had longed for in his childhood. Her mother, Sibylla, played the piano in the evenings or led them all in a game of Scrabble or Charades, at which the whole family excelled. This was a particular torture for Simon, hobbled as he was by acute self-consciousness in their presence, especially as they delighted in baiting his incompetence with an unchristian lack of charity.

The Rectory had a huge garden, herbaceous borders, a big vegetable bed that Rosalind's mother referred to as a *"potagerie,"* as well as a small orchard with pears and apples and plums. "Our own little Eden," Sibylla said. The Rectory's bookshelves were weighed down by the classics, all of which had been read and were referred to with surprising frequency, so that Simon was always finding himself murmuring, "Mm, yes, of course, *Humphry Clinker,*" or "Ah, yes, *Amos Barton*, remind me again which one of the Brontës wrote that?" So that they laughed at him, not always kindly.

Rosalind's father, Desmond, did the *Telegraph* crossword every morning over his toast and homemade marmalade. The family dinner table strained with conversations about Nietzsche and Hume and Beatrice Webb and Rilke, so that Simon, who had previously got by with paddling in the intellectual shallows, felt permanently out of his depth.

They were married by Rosalind's father, conducting the service in his own church. The bride wore a simple white broderie anglaise dress and her head was adorned with flowers picked that morning from the Rectory garden and woven into a coronet by Sibylla. Simon thought his bride looked like a virgin sacrifice, although she was neither of those things.

Desmond's flourishing congregation packed the aisles and afterwards the reception was held on the cricket ground so that there was room for everyone. Simon's own parents were dead by then, toppled one after the other by different but equally fast-acting cancers. Their rapid decline had taken Simon by surprise. He had relied on their continuing existence as an excuse for his own ongoing sense of inadequacy. The loss of the house in Bromley—always there, rarely visited—left him feeling surprisingly unanchored.

Nowadays, he didn't think of Rosalind as dead, just as someone he didn't see any more. But that was the definition of dead, wasn't it?

It was at Beryl Sillitoe's house last week that "it" had happened. After he had worked his way through an enormous mug ("Best Grandma Ever") of milky coffee and half a packet of chocolate digestives (he had had no breakfast), Beryl said, "Shall we pray, Reverend Cate?"

Beryl always insisted on kneeling on the carpet. He had put his back out more than once helping her up again. He sighed and said, "Yes, Beryl, of course, but you don't need to get down on your knees, you know. I'm sure God's quite happy with you on the sofa."

Too late, she was already in the act of lowering her considerable bulk on to the patterned fitted carpet. He sighed again and joined her.

"What shall we pray for, Reverend Cate?"

"Do call me Simon, Beryl. I don't know—you choose, Beryl." You could pray for my soul, he thought. Did he have one? Good question.

She rattled off a series of supplications. All good stuff—suffering animals and children, the runners training for the Burton Makepeace 5K in a couple of weeks, Beryl's granddaughter's grade-three piano exam.

"Amen," she said solemnly. Simon had opened his mouth to echo the word. No sound came out, not even a squeak. The root of the word "amen," they had been taught at theological college, was the Hebrew for truth. Was that significant? Because his life was a lie? You had to wonder.

He nodded and smiled and mouthed soundlessly in a manner that made it seem as if he had somehow been humbled by the prayer, and then (as swiftly as he was able) he cranked them both up to standing and made his escape.

He had lost his voice! The voice that intoned the Eucharist, married the optimistic, comforted the bereaved. The one that "nattered" or quietly pleaded for his own salvation in the middle of the night.

Not blinded on the road to Damascus, but struck dumb on Beryl Sillitoe's Axminster. Speechless.

Hysterical aphonia, the ENT consultant concluded after a battery of tests when Simon took a trip to A&E in Bradford, although he used the word "psychological" rather than "hysterical." (Naturally, Simon had looked up his diagnosis on Google.) Hysteria implied an unmanly weakness. "Has something happened in your life recently?" the consultant asked. "Something different? Or in the past?" It seemed absurd to ask a question of a man who couldn't speak. The consultant handed him a notepad. "You can write it down." Yes, of course, Simon thought. Where to start? How to stop?

The Weight of a Weasel

Ghirlandaio, Pisanello, Vasari, Veronese. The names hardly tripped off the tongue. Jackson knew a good deal more about Renaissance portrait painters than he had previously as he was now in possession of Melanie Hope's copy of *Renaissance Portraiture*, plus the entire fecund hinterland of the internet was at his disposal.

Jackson was sitting with his laptop in a café in the centre of Leeds. So far he had spent three coffees' worth of time investigating the mustelids, as he'd learnt to call them, a family that covered stoats, weasels, minks, polecats and pine martens at the smaller end, otters at the bigger end. In the Renaissance, "weasel" seemed to cover all of them. Not an otter on the woman's lap—too small— and centuries before minks were imported and factory-farmed for their fur. (And look where that had led.) He had settled on a stoat, but he had grown used to *Woman with a Weasel* and found it difficult to rename it. It couldn't have been painted from life. There was no way you could get a weasel to pose for any length of time. If at all.

There was a surprising number of paintings of women clutching small animals, furry and otherwise. Squirrels, cats, lapdogs, stoats, ermine (stoats in winter coats), bigger dogs, rabbits and, in the case of one Raphael painting, a badly executed unicorn, clearly not drawn from life. (Yes, he did know unicorns didn't exist.) The animals were usually symbolic. A unicorn indicated a woman's purity, apparently. No comment, Jackson thought, or he would be up before the Court of Women, Judge Julia, his ex, presiding. Dogs for fidelity, peacocks for immortality, rabbits for lust. No animal got to be just an animal.

Weasels were high in the popularity stakes, they were everywhere and a lot of the time they were dead, carried by women like a tippet. To encourage fertility, apparently. Often their heads—the weasels, not the women's—had been replaced by a kind of jewelled helmet. Weird. There really was no other word for it.

He phoned Julia, always his go-to for any cultural question. "Well, of course, you know, it's a stoat in Leonardo's famous painting *Lady with an Ermine*," Julia said, middle-class ease in the way she said "Leonardo" as if he were a family friend. "Your portrait is more likely than not a young woman painted on the occasion of her betrothal or marriage."

The girl in the portrait was about, what—sixteen? Probably younger. Jackson thought of eighteen-year-old Dorothy Padgett. Unlike Dorothy, the woman with the weasel probably had no say in the choice of her husband. It would have been a mutually beneficial alliance between two families. Sold to the highest bidder, like any other object, except that she had to bring her own payment with her as a dowry. It wasn't that long ago in the greater scheme of things that women were the powerless property of their husband. Pawns in a greater game. Still were in lots of places in the world, of course. Jackson was surprised that more women hadn't simply killed their husbands. Maybe they had, maybe women were better at covering up murder than people knew.

At first, he had judged the woman's expression to be enigmatic, indecipherable even, but on closer scrutiny he could make out the little frown lines across the bridge of her nose, as if she might be perplexed as to why she was sitting in an artist's studio with a ruddy weasel on her knee. The weasel, on the other hand, looked inscrutable.

He contemplated a fourth coffee, voted against it, and got the bill. On the way out, he accidentally bumped into a woman who was coming in. She was muffled in winter clothing—a big scarf and a woollen hat—but nonetheless he could see that she was attractive. They performed an awkward little dance trying to get past each other. She laughed. She had an alluring, throaty laugh, which was one of Jackson's weaknesses where women were concerned. Although not the only one. Eventually they resolved the dance and she slid past him. They locked eyes for a brief second. Had she been flirting with him? he wondered. Yes, she had, he decided. His male ego was burnished. He had climbed to the wrong side of sixty, but he wasn't over the hill yet.

He might be learning more about Renaissance portraits, but Jackson felt as though he knew even less about Melanie Hope. She seemed to have as little provenance as the missing portrait. Provenance was just an evidence chain of custody by any other name, wasn't it?

Her phone—another big clue to criminal intent—was a burner. There were a couple of Melanie Hopes around, in the phone book and on the electoral roll, but neither of them fitted with the one he was looking for. He had paid a visit to both, as well as to the Grove Bookshop in Ilkley, where they testified that *Renaissance Portraiture* had not been bought there.

There might not have been any CCTV at the Willows, but it was a well-off neighbourhood so surely, Jackson reasoned, most of the other houses would have a security system. Plenty of the houses had alarms, he found, but not many had anything else. Dorothy's neighbour to the left had a doorbell camera, but there was no reply when he rang it. The house opposite had a sign saying "CCTV in Operation" and a "Beware of the Dog" sign, but the owner cheerfully admitted that they had neither. Further along the street, the occupants said their camera hadn't been working on the day in question. The security company had arrived later that afternoon to fix it. Convenient for Melanie Hope.

He struck luckier with a house four doors down, where the owner after some initial reluctance said Jackson could stand on his doorstep and scroll through the camera app on his iPad looking for that day's activity. Quite right, Jackson thought, I would be wary of me as well. Let's face it, a card that claimed you were a "private investigator" wasn't worth the paper it was printed on.

It was a laborious process—he knew from experience that if you fast-forwarded you inevitably missed the thing you were looking for. He found Melanie Hope eventually, or at least he was pretty sure it was her. She used the bus, according to Hazel, so no car and no handy numberplate. There wasn't a lot of foot traffic on this street, and she was the only person around at midday on the day that Dorothy Padgett died who passed in front of the security camera. She was wearing jeans and boots and a padded winter jacket, but he couldn't identify the maker's logo on it. A woollen hat was pulled down low and he couldn't see her face at all. She was indeed carrying a big bag. And then she was gone. Up the road into the thin air of nowhere, as mythical as Raphael's unicorn. He was chasing a phantom. *Phantom with a Weasel.*

⟶

Naturally, one of the first things he had done was to visit the address in Harehills that Hazel and Ian had given him. "Sixty-four" was the number written in the address book but there were only fifty-two houses in the street. Jackson knocked on doors, went into shops, even stopped passers-by to ask if anyone knew a Melanie Hope or anyone fitting her description. It felt rather like being a policeman on the beat again. He got the feeling that she had plucked the address out of nowhere and she probably didn't come from around here at all. "Did she have an accent?" he had asked Hazel. "Yorkshire? Northern? Anything?"

"Very neutral," she said. "She could have been from anywhere." Came from anywhere, went to nowhere, and everywhere he went he drew a blank. It did briefly cross his mind that Misleading Mel might be related to Treacherous Tessa, the woman he had been married to just long enough for her to relieve him of all his money. It was funny because although he had stopped looking for his fraudulent wife long ago, he still somehow expected to come across her again one day. But not, he suspected, in the person of Melanie Hope. Caring for an elderly invalid just didn't seem Tessa's style. Plus, she was a good deal taller than the five-foot-three that Jackson estimated Melanie's height to be. Unless Tessa had chopped a few inches from her legs, she was out of the picture.

What if Melanie Hope had never existed? What if she was a figment dreamt up by Ian and Hazel—an imaginary scapegoat to cover their own crime? All that "big bag" stuff that Hazel had introduced to give credence to the logistics of the crime, was that just made up? Dorothy's neighbours did, however, all testify that they had seen a woman (or a girl), about twenty (or forty), brown hair (or blonde), medium height (or quite tall), going regularly in and out of Dorothy Padgett's house. She took letters to the post, she came back with supermarket bags. She closed the curtains at night and opened them in the morning. She always said hello when they met her in the street. She seemed "very pleasant."

He wasn't surprised by the lack of solidarity over the physical description of Melanie. Witnesses, as every policeman knows, are completely terrible at remembering, but at least it proved that she had existed in one form or another, short or tall, young or old, and hadn't been invented as part of a devious plot on the part of Ian and Hazel. Of course, that didn't mean that she hadn't been *involved* in a devious plot with Ian and Hazel. (*Put it in a big bag and just walk out of the Willows. Hand the bag over later in the park and here's a hundred quid for your trouble, Melanie.*) But why? They already owned the portrait, why would they steal it?

At first, Jackson had been inclined to give Melanie Hope the benefit of the doubt, but as time wore on, he had to admit that innocent people tended not to have burner phones and false addresses and what was almost certainly a false name. What other explanation was there? That she was on the run from something? That she was in witness protection? To his knowledge, even when he was in the police he had never come across anyone in witness protection, but wasn't that the point? You weren't supposed to know. He sighed with frustration. He was over-complicating things. What was it they said—if you hear hoofbeats, look for a horse, not a zebra? But what if Melanie Hope *was* a zebra—what then?

~

Ottershall House no longer existed. It had been in Northumberland, thirty or so miles from Newcastle, and had burned to the ground in 1945. That really was the sum of what the internet had to say about it. Nowadays, you expected everything to be available at a keystroke, but the internet was fallible and sometimes things really were lost for ever.

The month of the fire was unspecified, along with the cause. The family that owned the house—the Cadsbys—had long since died out. Did the fire occur after the auction due to take place in September? Or before? If it was before, then perhaps some things were saved and still went to auction. One of those things being the portrait. But then if it was a legitimate purchase why were Ian and Hazel being so shifty about it?

Not a brick remained of Ottershall House, Jackson discovered when he drove there. Where it had once stood there was now a new-build commuter village servicing Newcastle. The streets remembered—Ottershall Drive, Ottershall Close, Ottershall Crescent—but the residents themselves knew nothing about the ground they lived on.

Jackson went in search of the nearest old pub, always a good source of information in his experience, and after some rooting around amongst the regulars found an old man, Ken, who had been a boy at the time of the fire. He had been an eager witness to the blaze and had returned later to see the smouldering remains of Ottershall House. "Everything gone," Ken testified, "not a stick of furniture left." Every last thing consumed by the fire. Did he remember what month that was? "September, definitely, it was the beginning of a new school year and I was skiving. I was a bad lad," he said, chuckling at the memory.

Probably not that bad, Jackson thought. "You don't remember the date, I suppose?"

"No, but we always went back to school in the first week of September, so it wouldn't have been any later than that."

And the proposed auction had been scheduled for the twentieth. "There was no auction of the contents later?"

"Nae, lad, everything had gone."

Jackson left a twenty-pound note behind the bar for Ken. As he was taking his wallet out, he felt the nub of something else in his pocket. A silver disc, smooth and rounded like a mint. It was a tracker, an air-tag, the kind you put in your luggage so you could trace it if the airline lost it. How had that got in his pocket? He put it back again. No doubt in the fullness of time it would reveal its purpose.

He drove back to Leeds. No one seemed to be following him. The tracker was silent, no little rinky-dink noise that indicated someone was looking for it. There was a pile-up on the A1. By the time he was back in Leeds he was exhausted.

"Find anything?" his "girlfriend" Tatiana asked.

"I have no idea."

"Some detective," she said.

To illustrate the journey from the sublime to the ridiculous, as well as *Renaissance Portraiture* Jackson had purloined the Nancy Styles novel *Hark! Hark! The Dogs Do Bark* from Melanie's room in the Willows and was reading it in bed. Its rolling cast of retired Army majors, befuddled vicars and posh aristos made for a very speedy nightcap.

Tatiana, an unlikely crime-novel connoisseur, was dismissive. According to her, Styles was "a poor woman's Agatha Christie." Most of her books were out of print now, although there was still a stage show, *The Body Walks*, famous for its longevity rather than its artistic content. The novel seemed like oddly anachronistic reading matter for Melanie Hope as well. Or perhaps it had belonged to Dorothy Padgett, it seemed more her era. The Willows had been pretty much a book-free zone, just some old copies of *The People's Friend* and the *Dalesman* and a couple of Maeve Binchys. It seemed that Dorothy wrote romantic stories but didn't read them.

Tatiana's current bedtime reading was a book about poisons. Should he be worried? "Hobby?" he enquired mildly.

"Opposite," she said cryptically. "Why are you asking?"

"Just curious," Jackson said.

"Good job you're not a cat, then."

And yes, he knew all about Tatiana's bedtime reading because he was usually to be found sharing a bed with her while she did that reading, as he was temporarily using her nest as a roost until he got somewhere of his own. (Don't judge me, he said to the now hastily convened Court of Women.)

In bed, Tatiana wore spectacles and a relatively modest pair of pyjamas and frequently drank Horlicks, something Jackson hadn't done since he was a child and wasn't about to start doing now. Given her unconventional CV—confirmed dominatrix, suspected assassin, ex-trapeze artist—none of this was what he had expected. Nonetheless, he was cautious around her. Tatiana was feral and getting close to her was like cosying up to a tiger. She might appear to be almost completely indifferent to him, but there was always the possibility that her claws would come out and she would savage him to death. "Yeah, just for fun," she said. "Ha, ha. In Russia my father was great clown, did I tell you that?"

"Yes," Jackson said, "many times." Many, many times.

—⌒—

Jackson had paid a second visit to the Willows the day after the first. Hazel had given him a set of keys, with instructions to post them back through the letterbox when he had finished. She couldn't accompany him, she said, she was "terrifically busy" as "there's so much to do when someone dies." Jackson had always found the opposite—when people had died in his life, there had been nothing to do but grieve.

"I have a funeral to arrange," Hazel said. She seemed to have a permanent aura of vexation around her. "Although of course Mum wanted everything to be very simple, she didn't like a fuss. She was a humble sort of woman." Humble or oppressed? Jackson wondered. *Dad was a bit of a bully.*

He was relieved to be unaccompanied this time as he wanted

to have another nose around without the claustrophobic presence of the Padgett twins on his shoulder. Jackson found himself wondering yet again why they hadn't chosen to go down the police route. Their reasoning—that they didn't want to cause Melanie any trouble—seemed specious, to say the least. Did they have something to hide? It seemed irrational to be suspicious of them, yet every time he tried to quell those suspicions they popped back up again. Whack-a-weasel.

Yes, Ian and Hazel made an odd couple, but surely neither of them fitted the profile of a criminal mastermind. And yet . . . Jackson's bedtime reading now also encompassed stolen art. There was a staggering amount of the stuff missing—more art seemed to have disappeared than was left still hanging on the walls of museums and galleries and stately homes. And there was one case that really made his little grey cells sit up and pay attention.

In 2017, in Arizona, the contents of a deceased couple's estate were bought by a local antique shop for two thousand dollars. The ("mild-mannered") couple had been retired schoolteachers and some of the contents of their house were put on display in the shop, including a painting that had been in their bedroom. Within days, eagle-eyed art lovers were identifying it as a de Kooning entitled *Woman-Ochre* that had been stolen thirty years previously from the University of Arizona Museum of Art. Once it was verified as genuine (provenance again), the shop owners returned it to the museum. All the evidence pointed to the dead couple having stolen it three decades earlier.

There were three things about this story that struck Jackson, none of which had to do with mild-mannered schoolteachers being the thieves. If it had been him investigating the theft they would have been at the head of his queue of suspects—they sounded far too innocent not to be guilty. He wondered if they taught Geography.

No, it was because, firstly, he had never heard of de Kooning ("I refer you to the aforesaid *Chinese Girl*, m'lady." His ex-wife was apparently now prosecution for the Crown.) Secondly, the couple in question had kept it behind their bedroom door, where they were *the only people who ever saw it,* and, thirdly, the painting was valued at a whopping one hundred and sixty-five million dollars. He had seen photographs of it. He wouldn't have paid a fiver for it in a car-boot sale. Emperor's new clothes came to mind.

"Jesus," he said to Tatiana. "One hundred and sixty-five million dollars. Who would pay that for a painting that looks like it was dashed off by a five-year-old?" ("I rest my case, m'lady.")

Jackson wouldn't have given a de Kooning the space on his wall. If he owned a wall. If he owned a de Kooning, he would sell it before you could say, "I could have painted that."

"Anyone die?" Tatiana asked, looking up from her bedtime book. She was reading a chapter on wolfbane. There was no way something called that could be good for you, Jackson thought.

"Only of old age," he said.

"Lucky death, then," she said, returning to her book.

It wasn't the value of the painting, of course, it was the fact that it had been kept where no one else could see it. Just like the woman with her weasel. Why would you do that unless you wanted to hide it? And why would you want to hide it unless there was something nefarious going on?

He'd found a site on the internet that detailed all the art that had once existed and was lost, whether by theft, fire or flood, but there was nothing listed from Ottershall House. And so here was a thought—what if the Padgetts didn't report the painting stolen last week because it was *already* stolen. And Hazel and Ian must know that, and that was why they hadn't involved the police. Ta-da!

⁓

It was only a couple of days since Dorothy Padgett had died, but when Jackson entered the hallway again he could feel the atmosphere of abandonment in her house, as if it had stood empty for months, not days. The central heating had been going full blast when he was here previously, but it was turned off now and the temperature in the house had already plummeted towards "nithering" on Jackson's personal temperature scale.

Ian and Hazel had not yet begun to clear the house of its contents—perhaps they'd started feuding over the placement of the red and blue dots. Everything was much the same as it had been yesterday, although he was glad to see that the covers had now been stripped from Dorothy Padgett's bed. There was something about the rumpled flowery bedding that had stayed with him. The spectacles were still there though.

He looked in every room. He'd executed enough search warrants in his life to know how to look for something incriminating without ripping everything to pieces. He fingertipped through every drawer and cupboard, beneath the faded sofa covers, on top of the kitchen cabinets, in the kitchen cabinets, beneath the kitchen cabinets. Some of the stuff at the back of the cupboards had sell-by dates from the Stone Age. There were gravy granules and instant coffee that had fossilized, dried herbs that looked as if they had been used just the once, and pickled red cabbage that had faded to an unhealthy pink.

In the bedroom he gingerly lifted the mattress of the recently deceased Dorothy, although he had no idea what he might discover there. Nothing, he was relieved to see.

On the surface, the house looked trim and tidy, but tucked away everywhere was the detritus of an entire life lived—old shopping lists, newspaper clippings, keys that no longer unlocked anything, buttons and paper-clips lying idle, even Dorothy Padgett's ration book from the war. Would Hazel and Ian sift through every last newsagent's receipt out of respect for their mother's memory or would the whole lot be swept into bin bags and carried to the tip without scrutiny or sentiment? Jackson was pretty sure he knew the answer to that question. Unfortunately, the debris resulted in no clue to either Melanie Hope or the painting.

And the woman with the weasel—what a shame she hadn't felt the need to leave something behind. But then she had, hadn't she? She had left an image of herself. Art was long, life was short. There was definitely Latin for that, but he couldn't remember it offhand. He went to the trouble of looking it up on his phone. *Ars longa, vita brevis. Ars longa* was the kind of thing that the boys at his school would have endlessly sniggered at. Jackson hadn't been to the kind of school where they studied Classics. He had been to the kind of school that prepared you for a working life down the pit. Much good that had done his classmates. Where were they now? He could barely remember any names. He didn't receive newsletters from his alma mater, had never gone on Facebook or Instagram to look. Not that he ever went on social media. They could be dead and he wouldn't know it. He didn't care, some bits of the past you carried with you for ever, other bits you jettisoned as quickly as possible.

Jackson closed his eyes and breathed in the house. The Willows had a secret, but he had no idea what it was. It was something to do with the painting, of that he was sure. Perhaps if he could find the woman in the portrait she might be able to tell him what it was. The weasel, he suspected, would keep its own counsel.

Time to go. Jackson had one last quick look around the house. He was beginning to feel like a prospective buyer. Or a thief casing the joint. He shut the front door quietly behind him so as not to disturb the ghost of Dorothy Padgett and posted the keys through the letterbox, as requested by Hazel. If he came back again he was going to have to break in.

—

The neighbour with the doorbell camera was at home this time. He had been at his lunch-club in town, he said, and was sorry to have missed Jackson. A minibus collected him and dropped him off again because his GP had advised him to stop driving. "So if you know anyone who wants a Vauxhall Corsa, ten years old, one careful driver," he chuckled. "Nothing like that beast you've got parked outside."

He was a sprightly man well into his eighties, in need of company. Longevity seemed to be on the menu around here. It must be the bracing air sweeping off the moors and down into Dorothy's street. The neighbour was called Bob Gordon ("Call me Bob") and seemed eager to pass time with Jackson. He was Scottish—

a Fifer, he said—and had the same accent as Jackson's father, but he was nothing like Jackson's father. He made them both robust tea in china mugs that were delicate and flowery and had probably been the choice of his wife, who had died last year. She was called Sheila, and Bob said he was determined to "stay positive." He wasn't about to go downhill, he said, no eating in front of the TV or "that sort of thing." Jackson ate almost every night in front of the TV. He'd let himself go downhill a long time ago.

They drank their tea in a conservatory that overlooked a garden that was very like Dorothy's next door. No willows though, Jackson noted. "You've probably got a million better things to do with your time than sitting here drinking tea with an old man," Bob said, bringing out a cake tin.

"I really don't," Jackson said, and it was true.

"Ginger cake," Bob said, cutting a slice and passing the plate to Jackson.

It was good cake, Jackson was impressed. "You made this, Bob?"

"Me, oh no, that's all Sheila's handiwork." The cake paused halfway up towards Jackson's open mouth. He thought of Dorothy Padgett—*she made a good steak pie,* but then she had been alive when she made her speciality, hadn't she? Had Sheila Gordon been baking from beyond the grave? Bob laughed. "Nae, son, it came out of the freezer. She stocked up before she went.

"So," he said, when Jackson had reduced the cake on his plate to crumbs. "What can I do for you?"

There was an app for the doorbell camera on Bob's phone. "The whole thing's a mystery to me," he said, "put in by one of my boys. They worry." He handed over his phone.

Too trusting, Jackson thought, his mouth still full of a dead woman's cake. "I'm looking for the day Dorothy died, to see if Mel passed by."

"Mel? Nice wee lassie. Used to pop in, ask if there was anything I needed when she was going to the shops." Which was she, Jackson wondered, Saint Teresa or a cunning thief? Perhaps she was both. He never ceased to be surprised by how complicated some people could be.

She wasn't only on Bob's doorbell camera, she also did Jackson the favour of turning towards it so he could finally see her face. She gave Bob a cheery wave as she passed. He must have been standing in the window of his front room. "Oh, yes, watching the world go by," he said. Bob's house and the Willows next door were the last two houses in the street, so hardly anyone passed by. Bob Gordon must spend a long time waiting for the world.

Jackson paused the playback and took a photograph. At last, Melanie Hope had a face. And it looked vaguely familiar. Had he seen her somewhere? But where?

"Why are you interested in Mel, Mr. Brodie?"

"Well, Hazel and Ian—"

"The twins?"

"Yes. They think that Melanie Hope stole something belonging to Dorothy."

"Do they now? And what would that be?"

"A painting."

"The one of the woman? With the wee animal?"

"Yes, that one."

"The one my grandson took a photo of for Dorothy?"

It turned out that Bob Gordon's grandson Matt was a photographer with the *Yorkshire Post,* and "some time before Covid" had taken the photograph of the painting for Dorothy so that she could send it off in the first step towards having it valued.

"She'd never had it valued before?"

"She said not. She wanted to find out what it added to her estate and so on. She was a nice woman, Dorothy. Kind, you know? Quite shy. Of course, Harold was still alive when we moved in here. Had Dorothy under his thumb. I didn't think it at the time, but now I wonder if he didn't knock her about. I should have paid more attention. Too late now. More cake, son?"

It was only when Jackson was preparing to leave that Bob said, "Have Hazel and Ian found out what's in the will yet?"

"Dorothy's estate's split down the middle, apparently," Jackson said. "Unless you know different?"

"No, no, I was just curious as to what was in the—what d'you call it?—codicil."

"Codicil?" Jackson echoed. His little grey cells were suddenly all ears. When he first met Hazel and Ian, they had just come back from the solicitors. What had Hazel said? *We knew what was in the will, of course. We just wanted to check everything was in order.* There was a late-added codicil to that will? Where possibly everything was not "split right down the middle," as Ian had said, but where the twins' inheritance was compromised. "Dorothy added a codicil to her will? How do you know that, Bob?"

"I witnessed it for Dorothy, the week before she died. She was as bright as a button right up to the end. I didn't read what was in it— it's a personal thing, a will, isn't it? The wee lassie was there as well. I was surprised that Dorothy didn't ask her to be a witness."

On more than one occasion in the past, Jackson had been called in to investigate a case where a "surprise" had been left by the deceased. A time-delay bomb that exploded in the faces of the heirs, punishment for perceived (probably real) neglect of the person when they were alive. The entire estate left to a cat or a cleaner. Or a carer. Dorothy Padgett didn't have a cat or a cleaner, but she had a carer.

Had Bob Gordon been brought in to witness the codicil because the "wee lassie" Melanie Hope couldn't be a beneficiary if she was also a witness? Had she been left *Woman with a Weasel* by Dorothy and simply jumped the gun on the probate and walked off with her inheritance? Or perhaps Dorothy hadn't really been "as bright as a button" and had been hoodwinked by Manipulative Mel and coerced into changing her will.

Where was the codicil? He had found nothing when he searched the Willows. Had Mel popped it into that big bag, along with the weasel and the woman? That big bag was getting pretty full. And was she then going to produce it later and scupper all of Hazel and

Ian's plans? Was that cheerful farewell wave to Bob on her way past his house simply a gesture of triumph at having pulled the wool over everyone's eyes?

⌒

It was a relief to return to the Defender. It asked no questions and had heated seats, not something even the most macho of men would turn his nose up at in the middle of a Yorkshire winter.

The Leg

"C an you feed the chickens?" Fran asked. "I haven't got round to
it yet."

"No problem," Ben said. "I'll chop some more wood while
I'm out there. They say there's snow coming."

"Thanks," his sister said. "I have to pop out to see to a dog."

Ben had been staying with his sister and her partner, George,
ever since he quit the Army. "Come and stay with us," Fran had
said. "A bit of R and R, as Daddy would say. It's lovely here—
home-grown veg, chickens, bees, fresh air, lots of things to do. You
can muck in—or not—and it'll give you some space to think about
what you want to do with the rest of your life."

Fran had been a vet in a busy Home Counties practice and
George a "galley slave" in a large London advertising agency when
they made the decision to move to Yorkshire and be more self-
sufficient. "The good life," Fran laughed. "Like that old sit-com."
They had bought the redundant dairyman's cottage from the Burton Makepeace estate, along with a few acres of land, and had set
about turning it into a smallholding—vegetables, fruit trees, a poly-
tunnel, chickens, a small flock of recalcitrant goats. Fran worked
part-time and peripatetically now, with pets rather than farm animals. Animal husbandry was "barbaric," in her opinion.

Fran and George had been married for several years and they
seemed happy. Ben was relieved as he knew his sister had been

through some dark times. "I've met someone that I want to spend the rest of my life with," she had written to him, "and I don't care what the family says. I know you'll support me, Ben."

"Congratulations," he wrote back, feeling it was his duty to be encouraging (sometimes it felt as if he did nothing *but* encourage other people). "Sounds like you're embarking on quite an adventure." It was ten years now since he had been in a helicopter over Helmand province, which at the time had been a different kind of "adventure." He had taken his mind off the danger by catching up on letter-writing, a soothingly old-fashioned analogue occupation. That was before, of course. There was "before" and "after," and in between was the Leg.

"Before" was when he was still in possession of the Leg. The Leg—it had a capital letter in his family, it was a proper noun. "How's the Leg?" his father asked gruffly whenever he saw Ben. The Leg didn't exist any more, so it seemed an odd thing to ask. "Managing all right without the Leg?" his mother asked. "Yes, absolutely!" he replied enthusiastically. He had respected the fact that no one really wanted to hear how bloody awful it was. Why would they? But eventually he had grown weary of maintaining this facade of cheerfulness.

Everyone in his family apart from Fran (who was quite the opposite) believed in stoicism as if it were a religion. They all spent an extraordinary amount of time straightening their backbones and stiffening their upper lips. It seemed quite exhausting. Ben couldn't do it any more. God knows he'd tried. "Oh, for heaven's sake, Benedict," his mother said. "Pull yourself together." She had run out of patience with him long ago. "Always look on the bright side," she had regularly (and rather relentlessly) counselled her offspring throughout their childhood, an injunction that made her seem warmer than she was. In Ben's opinion, if you spent too long trying to look on the bright side you eventually became dazzled and couldn't see anything properly at all.

"Poor old Ben," Fran said. "Poor old Leg," she added wistfully, as if it had been an old friend. To Ben it had been, of course. His sister had wept quietly when she visited him in hospital in Birmingham, hugging him as if he were made of thin, expensive glass. He had a lot of sisters. Too many for comfort. Fran was the gentle, fragile one, Ellie the practical one, Caroline the rather brutal one. There was another—Joanna—whom Ben always thought of as the enigmatic one, although she wasn't really, she just didn't talk as much as the others. They were all a mystery to him, one way or another. He was the baby, his father's longed-for son, and neither his sisters nor his mother had ever really accepted that he might have grown up.

"Oh, Benedict," his mother sighed when he was allowed visitors, "what have you done *now*?" as if he had always been accident-prone, which really wasn't the case at all. As if, in fact, he had somehow brought the whole thing on himself. And anyway, what had happened to him wasn't accidental, it was horribly deliberate.

His mother had been the first person to visit him. He had nearly died and was still experiencing surprise at finding himself alive. He remembered nothing about the explosion, nothing about being airlifted back to the UK. He wouldn't have survived at all if it hadn't been for his men. The guys had saved him. They had tied a tourniquet around his leg, or what was left of it, and then taken it in turns to run under enemy fire with him slung over their shoulders in order to reach the Chinook that had been sent to swoop down and casevac him back to Camp Bastion. He wanted to cry when he thought about it. His men loved him. He loved them. It was simple.

"Not dead, then?" he mumbled to his mother, his voice still thick with the morphine.

"No, not dead," his mother said, "just . . ." She gestured vaguely in the direction of the bedclothes.

"The Leg. I know," he said. Poor old broken Ben.

"At least it wasn't your face," his mother said. "You've still got your good looks and you're only thirty-four. You'll find a lovely girl somewhere, have children and be happy," neatly mapping out the trajectory of his future as if all his problems were over rather than just beginning. That's all right then, he thought, but didn't have the strength to voice his sarcasm. And anyway, he didn't need to find someone, he already had Jemima, didn't he? They had a date set for the wedding, the colour scheme was chosen (he hadn't realized weddings had colour schemes). The gift list was lodged with Selfridges, the choice of wedding dresses had been narrowed down to three. He was to wear the dress uniform of his regiment, the Royal Lancers. The altar was in sight. What his mother already knew and he didn't was that Jemima was already a renegade by the time he was coming round from the weeks of knock-out drugs he'd been given.

"Well, best foot forward and all that," his sister Joanna said when she visited, so faintly that he had to ask her to repeat herself and then regretted that she did.

"Where is it?" his nephew, Sam, asked, the only one interested in the gory minutiae of amputation. "Do you get to keep it?"

"Incinerated, I expect," Ben said. He hadn't thought too much about the Leg's whereabouts. He wondered idly if he would be reunited with it in the afterlife. Not that he believed in an afterlife. His heart had stopped in the Chinook and he'd been shocked back into the present by a defibrillator on board, but he had experienced nothing beyond. One foot in the grave. That was a joke, he explained to his mother. She had no sense of humour. She always referred to it as the "missing Leg," as though he had mislaid it somewhere. "Call a stump a stump, for God's sake," he said to her. He had been very irritable in those early days. It was a relatively new emotion for him.

"What will you do with only one leg?" Caroline had asked, demoting his remaining limb to the lower case.

"Limp, I expect," Ben said. Kindness to others, his greatest failing in his own eyes, forced him to put on a brave face, when what he really wanted to do was to punch someone, or find the Taliban bastard who had planted the roadside bomb that had robbed him of the Leg and hack the little shit's own limbs off one by one, his head last.

"We're commanded to love our enemies, Major Jennings," the chaplain said grimly, visiting him in hospital. "But it's not quite that easy, is it?"

"Well, you know, it's just a leg," Ben said, as if it were any old leg. (It wasn't, it was *the* Leg.) "People lose legs all the time."

"Well, not *all* the time," the chaplain demurred.

"Anyway, I've got another one," Ben said, feeling impelled to show Christian humour and forbearance in the face of the chaplain's lack of it.

"And prosthetics have improved so much, haven't they?" the chaplain said, cheering up.

⌒

Jemima had already been wobbly about the wedding before that last tour of duty, he just hadn't wanted to see it. She had even considered breaking off their engagement because she didn't want "to find myself being an Army widow."

"Thanks for the vote of confidence," he had said. "It's just what a chap needs when he's about to go over the top." He didn't know why he spoke like that sometimes. It was stupid. Old-fashioned books and comics in his childhood, he supposed. Perhaps it came from his father, or his grandfather. His father was a brigadier, his grandfather a lieutenant-colonel. They were an Army family—Waterloo, Alma, Isandlwana, Neuve Chapelle, El Alamein, Goose Green—the Jennings men had been fighting across the entire globe for centuries. Perhaps it was time to stop. If he had a son, Ben thought (if he could find the well-hidden lovely girl to be the mother of his son), he would encourage him into a less violent profession—law, architecture, accountancy—where people didn't routinely get blown up.

"You're not going 'over the top,'" Jemima had said irritably. "It's not the Somme."

"No, it's worse than the Somme," he said.

"Nothing's worse than the Somme." She was right. He conceded the Somme. The Somme was trumps.

He supposed in the end it had nothing to do with the Army—or the Somme—and that Jemima had simply called the whole thing off because she didn't like him any more. She never even came to see him in the hospital, never made any enquiries about the Leg. He understood. (No, he didn't.) Was it better or worse, he sometimes wondered, that it was about him and not the Leg? "I think a clean break is better," she wrote, which was an unfortunate use of language if you thought about it. Which he did, endlessly.

"Oh, poor old Ben, do you miss Jemima awfully?" Fran had said, her face almost collapsing beneath the sudden weight of sympathy. "Plenty more flowers in the field," she said encouragingly.

He had supposed that in principle sex would be much the same with one leg as it had been with two, although obviously etiquette demanded that the subject be brought up well in advance with the lovely girl. ("By the way, there's something I ought to mention . . .") And, of course, although his face was untouched, as his mother had been at pains to point out, the rest of his body was a sight, a lunar landscape, pitted and pockmarked with scars from the explosive.

He had wondered about paying for sex, just to get a bit of practice in, to be naked in front of a woman who probably wouldn't raise any objections.

"You can get it for free any Saturday night in any town," one of the guys from his platoon said, when they visited him in Headley Court. "Why pay an arm and a leg?" They roared with laughter. "Get your leg over, sir," one of them said. "Only if we get you legless first," another one said, and they all laughed their heads off, including Ben. "And it doesn't cost an arm and a leg!"

The guys had come back from their tour of duty, no more casualties. It had been unusual for him to go out on patrol, but the guys had lost a captain, killed a couple of weeks earlier, and they had become jittery, more jittery than usual. The land around their base was infested with IEDs. There would be something wrong with you if you weren't nervous. So he had led from the front, because that was what he believed in. That part of his life was over now. He hadn't seen any of his men for a long time. He never went to reunions because they would have made him feel even more low than he did on an everyday basis. "Death or Glory" was his regiment's motto, yet he had somehow been left stranded with neither.

He supposed Jemima's betrayal still felt so raw all these years later because there had been no buffer between then and now. He hadn't actually bedded a woman, paid or otherwise, since. He might as well have been castrated. ("But you weren't, were you, darling?" an alarmed Fran asked.) In fact, he was halfway to being a priest already—why not just join a holy order? At least he wouldn't have to keep explaining himself to everyone. Look at the vicar, Simon Cate, no one continually asked him whether he had "found" someone. If Ben were a priest, he would have a role, a purpose. If nothing else, he could be encouraging to others, which was probably the best one could expect from religion these days.

Perhaps in ten years' time people would stop fretting about his solitary status. And really—why should he inflict himself on some poor woman? He suffered from an appalling kind of mental lassitude, not to mention a never-ending premonition of doom and an ability to catastrophize everything under the sun. An unnamed dread stalked both his waking and sleeping hours. Why should anyone want to put up with that?

He had a very good artificial leg, the chaplain had been right. Landmines and IEDs had done wonders for advances in the world of prosthetics. ("Silver lining," his mother said. No, not really.) It had taken him a long time to feel competent with his prosthetic, longer than other people. This was because he was "so negative about it," his mother said. She had been right, he supposed. He'd sunk into a terrible depression after the amputation.

He'd learnt to be competent. Just a bit of a limp. He didn't like people knowing because it changed him from being a man with a limp who might, for example, have had a skiing accident or injured himself playing squash, to a disabled man whose life had changed for ever. The C word. Cripple. You shouldn't say that any more, but he did, in his head.

Ben knew that he should think of himself as one of the lucky ones. There had been guys at Headley Court who had lost a lot more than he had. There was a guardsman in the Grenadiers who had lost both legs and an arm. How could you go on like that? Yet the guy did, perversely cheerful, making Ben ashamed of his own melancholic response to his circumstances. "You're wallowing, dear," his mother said. "Indulging." (She was from an Army family too. Of course.) "You should be over it by now. Time to pull your socks up, Benedict, and move on."

"One sock," he murmured. Still, she was right really. He had expected his affliction, a kind of low-level nagging grief, to go away in time, but it seemed to have become his everyday state of mind.

"Clinical depression," Fran said sympathetically. "There are people who can help, darling. I know, trust me. I've been there." PTSD, he knew, but was surprised how reluctant he was to admit to it or to do anything about it. Counselling—and he'd had a lot of it in one form or another—had done nothing for him. "Perhaps you don't want to get better," his mother said.

After the hospital, after the rehabilitation at Headley Court, he had been forced to convalesce at his parents'. His mother spent her time recounting amputees who still rock-climbed, went skiing, mountaineered, ran marathons, played table-tennis. (When the Invictus Games came along, she could hardly contain herself.) Why wasn't he doing these things? Why wasn't he pushing himself? she would ask crossly as she pulled the bedsheets off him in the morning. (He went through a long period when all he wanted to do was sleep.) His mother had invented tough love, at least the tough part of it, not so much the love bit. But it wasn't really the Leg that was the problem. It was the rest of him.

⟶

"The Army will find you a desk job once you're back on your feet," his father said.

"Foot," Ben said.

"You'll spend the rest of your life at the MOD," his father continued gloomily. "I'm telling you now, you won't be able to hack it."

His father was right on both counts. Ben spent two years convalescing, followed by several years driving a desk, working mainly on logistics, which was hellishly boring, and now it was over—he had finally quit the Army. It had been his life and now it wasn't.

It had been a warm summer day and he had got up from his desk in Whitehall, limped along the bomb-proofed corridors past the blast-resistant windows of the MOD and out into the sour London air and thought, That's it, then. Can't do it any more. He walked around Trafalgar Square, warily scouting the surrounding rooftops in case there was a sniper concealed somewhere. Open spaces made him feel extraordinarily anxious, as if at any moment he might be blown up or shot at. It was not out of the question, after all. The great cities of the world could be almost as dangerous as war zones.

He went into the National Gallery, hoping to be somehow tranquillized by art, and devoted some time to two of his favourite paintings—*The Fighting Temeraire* and *The Rokeby Venus*—but they both made his spirits droop in different ways. They spoke of loss, he supposed. National pride, the soft naked flesh of a woman. Very different things, but both seemed equally out of his reach.

Going AWOL from his desk had been an uncharacteristic act of spontaneity. He had gone back to work eventually, of course, he hadn't wanted people to go to the bother of sending a search party for him, didn't want to make a fuss, which was the very worst thing a member of the Jennings family could do. He had a quiet word with HR and left in an orderly fashion.

Then he drove up here.

~

At his sister's small registry office wedding, delayed so that Ben could give her away, he had struggled awkwardly up the aisle on his new prosthetic, his parents sitting with their spines straight, their upper lips stiff and their socks pulled up while Fran took George to be her wife. ("Well, *you* married a woman," Ben pointed out to his father afterwards.)

"Poor old Mummy and Daddy," Fran said, "they're hopelessly prejudiced. They're like those caryatid things, trying to hold up the Establishment. Sooner or later it'll all be too much and they'll crack, or their necks will break." Ben thought that caryatids were always women, which was something that their father was clearly not. As for marrying George, they could barely bring themselves to speak about it without wincing. "They're silly old things but they'll come round," Fran said. She was a heroically non-judgemental person, and Ben both applauded her tolerance and despaired of it at the same time. He didn't know what that said about his own character. ("Indecisive," Jemima would have said.)

There was great relief all round when Fran and George decamped north to Burton Makepeace and everyone was more or less absolved from visiting them. "Allergies," their mother said, citing their old dogs. Their mother was robust, she had never succumbed to an allergy in her life.

Ben still hadn't done anything about the "rest of his life." He couldn't stay with his sister for ever. "Why not?" Fran said. He had tried to make himself useful—he had learnt about beekeeping and tended the hives that were kept in the field just over the garden hedge. By rights it was the goats' field, but bees and goats seemed to live in harmony. A rescue donkey, too, that had a tragic countenance. "If he could tell his tale . . ." Fran said sadly.

The bees liked Ben, according to Fran, although he couldn't see how she could tell, especially as they were forever stinging him— and dying in the process, something which seemed unfair. Yet it was the basis of warfare, wasn't it? Previously he had thought that bees loved their keeper, but he supposed in their eyes he was a slave-driving thief.

He "kept himself busy," which was the Jennings way, but a lot of that busyness was just marking time really. He was leading a cloistered life. Since he arrived here he had barely moved beyond a one-mile radius. He hadn't really driven either. If an armoured Scimitar hadn't protected him, then what chance was there for Fran's Volvo? Although sometimes he did go to Skipton or Halifax with his sister and once he had ventured as far as Bradford with her. He felt rather like a child, not allowed out unaccompanied. "The panic attacks," his sister said sympathetically. "Poor Ben, battling his demons."

Unknown dread stalked him during the day and at night it crawled into his dreams. It made no sense as surely he had been accident-proofed by the IED? The odds were against him encountering two disasters during his life. Nonetheless, he kept to Dairy Cottage, the village, the deer park. He liked the deer park. It was a place of safety. He felt almost a hundred per cent confident that there were no roadside bombs lurking beneath its greensward.

And the church. He often visited St. Martin's. It was very old and was nearly always empty, with the musty scent of history and chrysanthemums and candlewax. Its longevity was reassuring. Not that he was a churchgoer, but he liked the atmosphere. There were always a couple of votive candles flickering in a tiny side chapel that was dedicated to an English knight who had been in Edward I's retinue during the last Crusade. You could probably have found a Jennings from Ben's own family hacking away with his great-sword in Jerusalem or Acre, taking part in yet more senseless warfare.

"You've not become a pacifist, have you?" his horrified father had asked him the last time he phoned. No, of course not. He would defend his own country to the hilt of his great-sword, but all those foreign fields seemed so senseless to him now. He usually lit a candle, for the dead in general rather than any one individual (he would have had to light quite a few), grubbing a coin out of his pocket and listening to it rattling into the tin provided, startlingly loud in the echo chamber of the church. "No one has coins any more," Simon Cate, the vicar, had said to him. "A lot of places have put in card-reading machines. I find that a bit depressing somehow."

"Call me Simon," he always said. He seemed to mooch around a lot, rather like a shop assistant waiting to pounce, and said things like "Is there anything I can do for you?" or "Is there anything you need?" so that Ben almost expected him to produce a shirt or a cashmere sweater and ask if he'd like to try it on.

Ben supposed that what he really meant was prayer or confession, although as churches went St. Martin's was very low Anglican and there was no sign of a confessional. Ben might have needed both, but he didn't want either. What could he confess? Only a vague miasma of misery that he was unable to get over. Who wanted to hear that? His family were always dishing out advice—join a club, get a hobby, have you thought about a Ramblers group? A bridge club? On and on went the restorative menu. He could just imagine Simon saying, "Have you tried prayer?" although thankfully he didn't.

St. Benedict was the patron saint of beekeepers, something Ben didn't know until Simon told him. "Although just one of many," Simon had said. "Several vied for the position—Ambrose, Abigail, Bernard of Clairvaux, a couple of others. I suppose, as specialities go, beekeepers seemed more attractive than, say, ironworkers or charcoal-burners." Benedict had not been named for a saint—too Catholic for his hawkishly Anglican parents—but for a great-uncle killed during the assault at Monte Cassino. St. Benedict's day was sometime in July, something else Ben hadn't known until the vicar had turned up one morning and asked if they would like to have their hives blessed.

George was against religion in all forms (George was against almost everything, to be honest) but Fran thought it was a charming idea. It had been rather nice—a lot of murmuring about "Creation" and "gratitude" and "honouring all the animals"—and their numbers had been swelled by several of the locals who seemed very accepting of their vicar's odd ways. There was an abundance of Labradors. Apparently Simon had recently held a service for people's pets that had given him a new-found popularity in his parish and beyond.

Someone brought the tea urn from the village hall and Fran sold pots of honey and George relented and made several Victoria sponges that were dished out on paper plates.

Ben had worried for Simon during the blessing because he was in his cassock, which was black, and black was a colour that the bees had a particular dislike of. Also, he had wafted around in a way that seemed almost designed to annoy them, and yet the bees had behaved remarkably well.

"You know," Simon Cate had said, his mouth full of cake, "in

Celtic mythology the bees are intermediaries between this world and the world of the spirit. That's why we tell the bees when someone in the keeper's family is born or marries, or, perhaps more importantly, dies." The vicar was eyeing up another piece of cake. ("The poor man eats very badly in that horrible vicarage," Fran said.) "It's tradition in some parts to lay a black ribbon on the hive after a death. It's a nice idea, isn't it? Quite moving."

The vicar, Ben thought, knew more about bees than he did.

"Well, animals," Simon Cate said vaguely, "they're better than us, aren't they?"

Fran appeared at Ben's shoulder and asked, "More tea, Vicar?," pleased with herself for having found an opportunity to say the line.

"Yes, please," Simon said enthusiastically. "And is there any more of that delicious cake?"

He wasn't sure why exactly, but the little ceremony had left Ben feeling maudlin and he'd had to blink his tears away. It was surprising the (frequently mundane) things that could "set him off," as George put it. There was no greater crime for a Jennings man, of course. "Blubbing," his mother called it.

"Breathe," Fran had murmured, reaching over and patting him on the back as if she was bringing up a baby's wind. She was the only one of the entire Jennings clan who would make a good parent. "I think that ship's sailed, I'm afraid," she said ruefully. He understood why people offered to be surrogates. If he could have done, Ben would gladly have had a baby for his sister.

⤙

He heard his sister's car pulling up outside the house. When she said she was "popping out" to "see" to a dog (or a cat, a rabbit, a pony, or any number of small furry creatures), it was usually her delicate way of saying "killing," as Fran's job seemed to consist mainly of putting people's pets to sleep in their own homes. "Much less traumatic for them," she said.

Ben had made the mistake a few months ago of accompanying her when she had gone to someone's house to put down an old Border collie. Even though he was only a bystander, Ben had felt almost as bereft as the dog's owner. His sister, he discovered—hardly a surprise if you knew her—had a lovely bedside manner in the face of death.

"Another dog in dog heaven," she consoled Ben as they drove away. The fact that the dog had been a Border collie had made it all the worse somehow, although Ben had no idea why that should be. He supposed they were the soldiers of the dog world—stoic, loyal and obedient to orders. That had been him once. Still was, really.

Ben thought that if he was euthanized he would like it to be at the hand of his compassionate sister. Killed with kindness. He supposed she had quite good drugs to get the job done. "Pentobarbital," she said, "but I'm not going to put you down, Ben. So don't ask."

George, who devoted herself more or less full-time to the garden, was less easy-going than his sister. She didn't seem to like anyone, apart from Fran and the old dogs that they gave a home to—sad-eyed creatures whose owners had left the Earth before them. "You soon get a reputation when you take in waifs and strays," Fran said. "You take in one homeless Jack Russell and the next thing you know you've got a job lot of old terriers snoozing all over the house."

There were a couple of ancient moth-eaten cats as well, sleeping out the last of their days next to the Aga. Ben had thought they were rather poor examples of the taxidermist's art until one of them flicked an ear dismissively in his direction. He supposed he was one of the waifs and strays, too.

He had fed the chickens and collected any stray eggs. The birds didn't seem too keen on laying in the winter. They weren't that good at laying in the summer either—in fact they seemed to have pretty much retired from egg production. He didn't blame them. They had been rescued from a factory farm that had been closed down by the RSPCA after an investigation into cruelty. Ben had foolishly watched some undercover footage on YouTube. Tiny weightless chicks on conveyor belts, tumbling and falling like pom-poms. It burned his eyes. Was he always this sensitive? He had killed people and yet the sight of the helpless little chicks had made him cry. The Dairy Cottage hens seemed happy enough now. No PTSD in the henhouse.

He got out the axe and started to chop up the big logs that Burton Makepeace sold to them at a discount. He might not have made a very good lumberjack, but he could get the job done and he enjoyed doing something vigorous in the open air. He wasn't much good at digging (the Leg), but he'd got pretty competent at chopping wood, at picking things and pruning things, hauling things down, putting things up. Fixing things. He was very good at fixing things. Everything except himself really. He supposed there was always Fran's stash of Pentobarbital to fall back on. He hadn't found where she kept it, but he supposed he would if he kept looking.

〜

Ben spotted Simon Cate at the bottom of the garden, gazing benignly at the beehives like a latter-day St. Francis. Simon turned to go and didn't seem to hear Ben when he hailed him. He was halfway across the field by the time Ben reached the hives. It was very cold, and the bees were in a winter cluster inside, oblivious to visitors. A flint arrowhead had been left on top of one of the hives, like an offering.

Ars Longa, Vita Brevis

Jackson's reading had expanded beyond bedtime—there was so much of it to get through. Lost art, missing art, stolen art. From museums, from galleries, from private houses. Half a billion dollars' worth of art alone, including a Rembrandt and a Vermeer, from the Isabella Stewart Gardner Museum in Boston. A da Vinci from Drumlanrig Castle in Scotland. A Vermeer, amongst others, from Russborough House in Ireland. Another Vermeer from Kenwood House in Hampstead. Vermeers were popular obviously. And that wasn't even scraping the surface of what had been stolen during the war by the Nazis. Truckload after truckload, laid at Hitler's feet like tribute by functionaries and lackeys. Göring and von Ribbentrop systematically funnelling stolen artworks into their private collections, all the art and artefacts stripped from countries and individuals and intended for the "Führermuseum." Everything the Jews owned. Everything. Reparations weren't much good to you when you were dead. *Ars longa, vita brevis.*

Before the Willows, if he'd thought about it at all, Jackson had imagined modern-day art theft to have a touch of James Bond about it. Endlessly complicated security involving laser beams that needed to be disabled by black-clad SAS-type thieves dropping down from the ceiling on spiderweb harnesses. Not glamorous—he would never have assigned glamour to any crime—but in a different league to shoplifting or walking into a house and lifting car keys. And yet most art theft wasn't high-tech at all, just your basic smash-and-grab with a bit of violence on the side.

In his naivety, he might also have imagined some shadowy pluto-crat hungering for something that money could not buy—a Vermeer, for example. There were only thirty-six of them known to exist and they virtually never came up at auction, so the only way to get one for yourself would be to steal it. Or, rather, get someone else to steal it, like ordering takeaway—give your shopping list to a master thief, a secret mastermind, who would deliver the work of art to you for a fantastic sum. Then presumably the wealthy purchaser would keep his trophy in a hermetically sealed, temperature-controlled room at the heart of his lair, where he would drool over it in solitude. Per-haps in the company of a long-haired white cat.

Jackson now knew this was more or less a fantasy. In real life, stolen art functioned as underworld currency, used as collateral by organized crime syndicates, passed around to finance terrorism and drug-dealing. Cabals of criminals washing their money through a handy mid-range Monet.

And nor was the art likely to be in a room in a rich man's man-sion. It was probably stored in one of the world's so-called free-ports, in Geneva or Singapore or Luxembourg—tax-free havens within a country, like giant upmarket safe-deposit boxes where no questions were asked about the contents. That was where Jackson would put a painting if he really wanted to keep it away from the prying eyes of the law. Or, of course, he could just hang it behind his bedroom door.

The other thing that happened to art was that it was kidnapped and held to ransom. Sometimes the owners, but usually the insur-ance companies, quietly paid up in the form of a reward or a finder's fee via shadowy middlemen who negotiated the painting's return. After all, it was cheaper for an insurance company to ante up £100,000 in "reward" money on, say, a Cézanne or a Corot than it was to pay the millions of their market value. And easier for a thief who was never going to be able to sell a famous painting on the open market.

There were other motives as well—the demand for the release of prisoners or terrorists, the highlighting of a cause. The portrait of the Duke of Wellington stolen in the early Sixties from the National Gallery by the unlikely-named Kempton Bunton called attention to, of all things, his campaign for free television licences for pensioners. But really most works of art were taken for money, one way or another, and many if not most were never seen again. The world was still waiting for the plundered goods from the Isabella Stewart Gardner raid to resurface. The Vermeer—*The Concert*—was now valued at a mind-boggling three hundred million dollars.

"Anybody die?" Tatiana asked.

"No."

⁓

According to Ian, Harold Padgett had finished up the war attached to the 11th Hussars. The 11th Hussars were cavalry originally, mechanized by the Second World War, not swords into ploughshares but the opposite—horses turned into armoured vehicles. Their history was both illustrious and notorious. They had helped to relieve the Siege of Ladysmith, they had fought at Waterloo and, most famously of all, perhaps, they had been part of the Light Brigade, the six hundred who blundered blindly onward into Russian artillery at Balaklava in the Crimean War.

When Jackson was a boy, Balaklava had been spelled with a *c*, not a *k*. He had an unexpected flashback to the balaclava he had been forced to wear in his youth. It had been an uncomfortable, itchy grey thing, knitted by his mother and resembling a knight's chain-mail hood. She would pull it roughly over his protesting head every morning in winter before he set off for school. That was before she died, of course. He didn't remember wearing it after she died but he suspected he had, just to appease her spirit in case it had lingered. He shook off the memory, an extra unnecessary ounce of weight on the balance of history. Nowadays anyone in a balaclava was a thief on the job or a member of a SWAT team. (Melanie Hope hadn't worn one. Therefore, she wasn't a thief. Logical fallacy. Ta-da!)

The 11th Hussars had been at the head of the 7th Armoured Division when it entered Berlin. They carried the Union Jack that they had brought with them all the way from El Alamein. Ten thousand troops six-abreast along the Charlottenburger Chausee. And apparently one of those ten thousand had been Harold Padgett.

Was it completely outlandish to think that Harold Padgett might have acquired the portrait during his time with the Army in Berlin? A "souvenir," perhaps? Lots of guys took souvenirs of one kind or another. Harold Padgett certainly wouldn't have been the first soldier to take booty from the enemy. Conquering armies had always carted off the spoils of war, although Jackson couldn't imagine there'd been much left in Berlin in '45. A loaf of bread might have had as much value, if not more, in Berlin at the end of the war as a little Renaissance painting. That would certainly account for its lack of pedigree. But then why write "Ottershall" on it? Did Ian and Hazel know that there had been no auction at Ottershall because of the fire? And if they did, why pretend that there had been?

❧

Jackson went down several more black holes on the internet in terrier-like pursuit of the woman and her weasel. One of them led him to a theft from a house in the Highlands five years ago. A place called Mount Fernie from which a Rembrandt had disappeared along with a member of the cleaning staff, a woman called Cheryl McDaid. It was a private house owned by the same family for hundreds of years and had never been open to the public, its treasures hidden from view, with precious little in the way of modern security. A gang could have snaffled the lot, but a light-fingered cleaner could probably only have managed one painting, sliced neatly out of the frame. The Rembrandt was the most valuable thing in the house, so Cheryl probably knew what she was doing. Or had been instructed by someone else who knew.

Both house and family, not to mention Cheryl McDaid, seemed to have vanished back into the mists of Brigadoon. No one from the household would speak to Jackson on the phone. He wondered about driving up there but couldn't muster enthusiasm for the idea. Apart from the fact that snow had already closed several roads in the far north, Scotland was a place full of unfortunate memories for him. He had nearly died there, he had lied about a double murder (no regrets), and he had met a woman he really liked, possibly loved, although the word was difficult for him to pronounce, and he had slipped away in the night without so much as a goodbye, leaving a dog in his place. Louise Monroe had named the dog Jackson, thereby cementing the exchange. Out of all the women he'd ever known, Louise Monroe was the one he probably shouldn't have let go. (Regrets? Yes, he'd definitely had a few.) So, no, not keen on returning to Caledonia.

Luckily a wormhole in the internet spat him out somewhere much closer to home. Burton Makepeace House, not much more than an hour's drive from the café in Leeds in which he was seeking refuge from Tatiana.

A Turner had been filched from Burton Makepeace House a couple of years ago. It was valued at over thirty million. Not in the Vermeer or da Vinci stratosphere, but also not exactly pocket money. And perhaps easier to shift than something as well known as *The Concert*. It seemed like it might have been another inside job. The police wanted to question a housekeeper called Sophie Greenway in connection with the theft. Over two years later and they still didn't seem to have found either her or the Turner. And, yes, he had heard of Turner but would prefer not to be cross-examined on the subject.

Cheryl McDaid, Sophie Greenway, Melanie Hope—could it be the same woman in all three cases? A woman who seemed to like domestic duties as well as art. It was the perfect disguise, wasn't it? Whoever took any notice of a cleaner or a carer? It wasn't just a hi-vis jacket or a clipboard that gave you immunity from query, an overall and a service job would do just as well. Jackson thought of that ugly brown and yellow tabard that Melanie Hope had worn every day for four months in Dorothy Padgett's house—it was the only aspect of her that the neighbours remembered accurately. It might as well have been a cloak of invisibility.

Harold Padgett had died nearly thirty years ago, and Dorothy's bedroom bore no sign of him now, or of any manly presence. There were no photographs of Dorothy's lauded husband, instead she was shepherded into the Land of Nod every night by a small six-hundred-year-old painting of an unknown woman and a weasel. What did Jackson make of that? Not a lot, unfortunately. Without resurrecting the Widow Padgett, there was no hope of finding out what her feelings had been. And resurrection would be difficult anyway as she was being cremated. Without an autopsy. Who needed an autopsy when your friendly GP was only too happy to confirm that you had expired peacefully of a heart that had run out of beats? A "lucky death," as Tatiana called it. Or was it?

"Nephew," Jackson said, when asked his relation to Dorothy Padgett by the woman who came scurrying to greet him some time after he entered the funeral home in Halifax. J. W. Jessop, Undertakers ("A Family Company Who Care"). It seemed wrong somehow that you could just walk in off the street as if you were looking to buy light bulbs or cheese. Why Halifax and not Ilkley? Presumably it was more convenient for Hazel as this was where she lived. Not so convenient for anyone who had known Dorothy in Ilkley.

There was a seating area in reception where a coffee table carried what looked like a thick brochure—or a catalogue. His sister used to shop from catalogues, paying off her debt every month. He surprised himself with the memory, buried for decades, as was his sister. He began to leaf idly through the catalogue until he realized it was for coffins. He placed it back on the coffee table.

The place was deserted. Where was everyone? He was tempted to shout, "Shop!" but then a woman came hurrying along a corridor towards him. "Moira Jessop, very nice to meet you," she said, brushing crumbs off her skirt. It seemed as if she might have been eating her lunch in the back somewhere, perhaps using a coffin as a picnic table. She had the look of a woman who brought her own sandwiches from home.

"And your name?" she prompted gently.

"Patrick Padgett," Jackson said, immediately regretting his choice of name—the first one that had entered his head. He was improvising. He should have rehearsed his role. It sounded like it belonged in a tongue-twister. Patrick Padgett picked a peck of pickled peppers. "Pat," he amended. He had an Uncle Pat, lived in Dublin, never met him. ("How is that possible?" Marlee had puzzled. She had a new family, she didn't understand old ones.)

He had come to visit the deceased, he told Moira Jessop. "Visit" was perhaps not the right word, it implied a two-way transaction. It was unlikely he was going to have a conversation with Dorothy Padgett. He sincerely hoped not. "Here to pay my respects," he amended. "To a beloved aunt. Ian and Hazel's cousin," he added for clarification.

"Of course," Moira said. Neat and smiley, she seemed intent on taking the sting out of death, like a good nurse. She wasn't distressed by the ordeal of others, instead she brought straightforward acceptance to the table.

There seemed to be no one else around, it surely wasn't a one-woman operation? "Goodness, no," she said. "I'm just front-of-house, as it were. We have quite a few staff. There's a lot going on behind the scenes, but grieving relatives don't want to see that." No, they didn't, Jackson agreed. They wanted death sanitized, the practicalities of being a corpse swept out of sight.

When his sister died—when his sister was *murdered,* he corrected himself—his Irish mother had insisted on a wake, but as none of the mourners were themselves Irish they didn't know how to be comfortable in the presence of the open coffin in which his sister was on display, like a Disneyfied Snow White. Adding to this effect was the fact that her lips had been painted red by the mortician, a colour of lipstick she would never have used.

Jackson had had many dealings with funeral directors over the years, a direct consequence of having had many dealings with the dead, and had always found them to be the most pleasant, most non-judgemental of people. There was nothing you could say that seemed capable of either surprising or alarming them. Moira Jessop was too trusting. He could be a necrophile for all she knew. At the very least, he thought she should ask for ID—a passport or a driving licence—before saying, "The Chapel of Rest is this way, Mr. Padgett," and leading him down a brightly lit corridor to a dimly lit room where the tiny figure of Dorothy Padgett was nesting in a padded satin coffin.

Mum didn't like a fuss, Hazel had said, but for all anyone knew Dorothy might well have liked a fuss, she might have liked a New Orleans jazz band marching in front of a red velvet coffin smothered in roses, but what she got was a bottom-of-the-range oak-veneer job. At least it wasn't cardboard, which in Jackson's opinion was like being put in a box to be sent off by parcel post to the next life. (*Was there another one? Wasn't this one enough?*)

"But it makes environmental sense," Marlee had said. "Much better for the planet. What do *you* want, Dad, when your time comes? I know, I know, miles to go before you sleep yet, but it doesn't do any harm to know. If you got knocked over by the proverbial bus tomorrow."

Well, not a cardboard box, he thought. Not one of those woven ones that reminded him of laundry baskets and made it seem as if you were about to go in the washing machine along with the rest of the dirty washing. He wanted solid English oak. Proper brass handles. The handles on Dorothy Padgett's coffin were plastic covered in fake brass. Still, what did it matter? It was all going up in smoke, wasn't it? Dorothy herself was going up in smoke.

"Not cremated," he said to Marlee. He had a horror of coming round as the gas jets were being fired up. And not buried either, finding yourself suffocating helplessly beneath the earth. "You will be dead," Marlee reminded him. But what if he wasn't?

"You can leave me out for the wolves," he said. "Failing that, burial at sea," he concluded. "The fish can feast on me. Hire a fishing boat and tip me over the side."

"It's not quite as simple as that. You need a permit and there are designated areas." Sometimes he forgot that his daughter was a lawyer.

"You'll manage. Dying man's wishes and all that. Make sure you stick a needle through my nose first. Old sailor's trick."

"Can we stop talking about this now, Dad?"

"It was you that brought the subject up."

⟶

"I'll leave you here, Mr. Padgett," Moira said, when they reached the Chapel of Rest. "Stay for as long as you like with your aunt. I won't be far away."

As well as the obvious centrepiece of the coffin, there were real flowers in a vase and an artificial candle flickering surprisingly realistically on the sill of a stained-glass window. The chapel had eschewed religion in favour of an abstract jigsaw in primary colours that disguised the fact that the window looked on to nothing. There were several chairs, like dining chairs, and Jackson carried one nearer the coffin and took a seat. He had thought a lot about Dorothy Padgett in the past few days, but he hadn't expected to meet her face to face. And yet here she was. And here he was.

"Hello, Mrs. Padgett—Dorothy," he said quietly. Nothing wrong with displaying good manners towards the dead. Who was to say they couldn't hear you? And she was definitely dead—even this was something he had begun to doubt. Spending time with Ian and Hazel in the Willows had been a bit like being with people playing Charades, and he wouldn't have been totally surprised to find that the corpse of Dorothy Padgett had been playing her part too.

She had a light sheen of make-up on her face, to make her look less dead, Jackson supposed. No spectacles though. The Ancient Egyptians would have buried them with her so she could see her way in the underworld. He sat in silence with his new acquaintance.

Had Dorothy Padgett had a good life? It was hard to say from this vantage point. She had enjoyed dancing and been married to a man with two left feet. She had wanted to travel and been married to a man who couldn't even bring himself to visit the country's capital. She had learnt to cook French food and been married to a man who liked meat and two veg. She had married at eighteen. Harold with his motorbikes, his war stories, his entrepreneurial dreams that must have butchered hers.

Dorothy's husband had been *a bit of a bully*, a description that could cover a multitude of sins. When the black bile came on him, usually caused by drink, Jackson's father used to knock his mother about. It was a family where casual violence was acceptable. Jackson, impelled to defend his mother, always paid the consequences. If he chose to remember, which he didn't usually, he could still feel what it was like to be hit by someone much bigger. You were allowed to hit men—sometimes it was wrong not to—but not women, children or dogs.

At least Dorothy Padgett was beyond caring about all that now. Jackson leant over the coffin and said, "Sorry about this, Dorothy," before taking a pair of scissors from his pocket. She didn't seem to mind.

～

Moira Jessop was waiting patiently for him in the reception area when he came out of the chapel. He clocked a security camera ahead of him. Had there been any in the Chapel of Rest? He hoped not. She offered him a cup of tea. "Or coffee?" He demurred as he was beginning to get a headache. Perhaps it was caused by the faint aroma of air freshener that permeated the funeral home, something that he should be grateful for, he supposed.

"Your daughter was here just before you," Moira Jessop said.

"My daughter?" Jackson was so surprised that for a moment he found himself wondering why Marlee would have visited Dorothy Padgett. Or perhaps he had a second daughter that he'd forgotten about.

"Sorry, I just presumed," Moira said. "Perhaps not your daughter, she said she was Mrs. Padgett's great-niece. I know it's a small family. Mr. Padgett—Ian—told me in great detail." Jackson congratulated her silently for keeping the sarcasm out of her voice.

"What did she look like?"

"Your daughter?" He commended her for barely raising an eyebrow. "Let me think. Blonde hair, I think, but she wore a woollen hat that covered most of her head. Brown eyes, possibly green—I'll settle for hazel. About the same height as me, I'm five foot four. Boots, leggings, puffer jacket." She was a better witness than most, but really she could have been describing every other woman on the high street.

"Oh, and a nice manicure," Moira Jessop added. "Pale-pink varnish. I noticed because I do the ladies' nails." For a moment Jackson thought she meant she had a side-hustle working in a nail salon and then he realized who the "ladies" were. Dorothy was one of them. Her nails had been neat and short. Too short to take a clipping from.

"Hannah," she added, just in case he might have forgotten his daughter's name.

"Ah, *that* daughter. Hannah did say she might pop in. She's home from university at the moment." ("Remember—less is more," Julia said, directing him from off-stage. Jackson chose to ignore the note.) He had done an inventory of all the Padgetts. There were no Hannahs.

"Nice girl, you should be proud of her," Moira said.

"Oh, I am, believe me. Tell me, just out of curiosity (*good job you're not a cat*), did she have a big bag with her?"

❧

On his way out, he noticed something he hadn't seen on the way in—a small patch of ground at the side that had been fenced off and contained headstones, all in different styles. It took Jackson a moment to realize that this was a display rather than a graveyard— Jessop's offered the full service, right down to the stonemason. It was rather like exiting through the gift shop. He hurried on without purchasing. A man buried at sea didn't need a headstone. *His name was writ in water.* Who said that? And about whom? He had no idea, but it was as good an epitaph as any. Better than *She made a good steak pie.* But what did it matter anyway? It only took a couple of generations for you to be no more than an entry on Ancestry.com, a withered twig on the family tree.

Perhaps he should pay a visit to Burton Makepeace House and see if any of the nabobs recognized Melanie Hope. He was, after all, a bona fide private detective, and if there was one fertile feeding ground for his profession, he had discovered, it was that of stolen art. And it wasn't just private investigators that were feasting at the table, there was a dodgy network—security experts, undercover informants and lawyers, not to mention the swarms who worked in the insurance field—all looking for finders' fees. He might claim one himself if he ever found the woman and her weasel.

It was a good bet that a fair few of the mercenaries on the above list had already chanced their arm at Burton Makepeace, so although he could just turn up unannounced on the (undoubtedly magnificent) doorstep without a legitimate introduction of some kind, he would probably be sent away with a flea in his ear. It didn't matter, help was close to hand. He dialled a number on his phone. It was a while since they had spoken. She was probably still mad at him.

Last Rites

Isaac, Simon and Rosalind's son, had been born early and was angry from the start, as if he'd been kicked out of paradise. Night and day, his howls echoed through the house. Trailing clouds of fury, Rosalind said. They thought he would improve as the weeks went by, but he got worse, as if he was possessed by a demon or was a child of the devil. *Rosalind's Baby*, they joked, and Simon laughed and said he was considering exorcism. "Good idea," Rosalind said. It was terrible to joke about a child in that way. He knew that now, but at the time it felt as though they had invited an angry alien into their home and had no idea how to placate him.

The sleeplessness was the worst thing. Isaac never slept, day or night, so they never slept either, all three of them trapped in the wretched stranglehold of wakefulness. Everyone around them was so nonchalant about it, telling them he'd settle down, that was babies for you, you never had a good night's sleep again once you were a parent. And so on.

"It's not too late to take him back and get another one," Rosalind said. If only, Simon thought. *Respice in me et miserere mei, Domine.*

Then, when Isaac was six months old, Simon woke up one morning and realized he'd slept for the whole night for the first time since his son was born. They had fed him at midnight, and he had slept through. They had weathered the storm. It was like a miracle. With the silence came an overwhelming sense of relief. Simon turned and looked at Rosalind's peaceful face. A bar of sunshine had found its way through the curtains and was warming her cheek. He suddenly felt very fond of her. He had a wife and a son. He was a Man of God. "All shall be well," he murmured. (For years he had thought Julian of Norwich was a man.)

He rolled out of bed, went into the kitchen and put the kettle on. It was seven thirty according to the clock on the wall. He took two cups of tea through to the bedroom and said to Rosalind, "Come on, sleepyhead. The Kraken is yet to wake, let's make the most of it." It was odd how he remembered those words.

They didn't go through to Isaac's room for another hour. *Quoniam unicus et pauper sum ego.* (The Introit was a Catholic prayer, of course, but the Romans did these things better. "Are you thinking of going over to the dark side?" his bishop queried mildly when Simon had said something about the attraction of absolution.)

⤙

Isaac was dead, of course, as cold as clay. He had died sometime in the night, while they were blissfully asleep. "Cot death," the coroner said, no one was to blame, they couldn't have known. God had tested Abraham, saving his Isaac from sacrifice at the last moment. This time around he hadn't stepped in.

There was all the horror that attends a sudden death—the funeral, held at the Rectory and conducted by Desmond, was like a negative image of Isaac's christening. If Simon had loved his son more, if he had loved him as he should have loved him, perhaps the boy would have lived. How offhand they had been about him, how resentful.

He supposed everything deteriorated after that. *Vide humilitatem meam et laborem meum.* Simon found himself mourning in reverse. What was acceptance in the beginning was nowadays raw grief for that little lost life. His love for his son had a ferocity that frightened him sometimes. There was no comfort to be had. All manner of things shall never be well.

⤙

Simon had been pleasantly surprised at how well he could get along without a voice. Perhaps he could return to the College of the Resurrection in Mirfield and offer himself anew for candidature as a monk. Or join the Trappists. The imposition of silence would no longer be a problem for him. It had already been imposed. The Trappists were a flagellant kind of order—hair shirts and thorns in the clogs—doing penance to redeem the sins of the world. Was that what this speechlessness was? An enforced penance?

He had lost his family, his faith, his voice—what would be next? he wondered. Eyesight? (Please, God, no.) Or his hair? His hair had always had character.

A limb, perhaps. Ben, the retired Army officer whom he sometimes came across in the church, had lost a leg in Afghanistan. Ben had lost a leg, Simon had lost his faith—in his mind it put them on an equal footing (wrong word!) because although they were two very different things, they left you with an ache at their absence. Not that he'd spoken about it with Ben, he had hardly talked to him at all, but Simon knew Ben's sister Fran, and on a few occasions she had shared her concerns about her brother with him. PTSD, apparently. And chronic depression. "Oh, and just a quiet sadness, you know?" Fran said to Simon.

"I do," he said.

Fran had moved here with her wife not long after Simon arrived, and they had bonded over their outsider status. She was a vet and on a few occasions he had taken injured or lost animals to her— a couple of hedgehogs, a fox cub, a duckling that had come adrift. Lots of dogs, too, of course.

He thought often about getting a dog and Fran Jennings certainly had a panoply of the halt and the lame that needed a home, but he hesitated. Despite the coroner's assertion that no one was to blame for Isaac's death, Simon blamed himself every day. He wasn't fit to look after anything, even a dog, perhaps especially not a dog. He was supposed to believe in redemption and forgiveness, in salvation, but he was not St. Paul. He would not regain his voice. He would not be saved. He would not be forgiven. *Domine, dimitte peccata mea.*

At first, after losing his voice, when he visited parishioners Simon had wrapped a woollen scarf around his throat and rattled a box of throat pastilles to indicate a problem, but that led them to shun him as if he were a victim of the Black Death ringing a plague bell ("Unclean!"), so he had learnt to carry a little notebook around with him, whipping it out the moment they opened their front doors. In it, Simon had written "Not Covid! Laryngitis! Not infectious!," which seemed to do the trick.

Exclamation marks, he had discovered, made even the most calamitous things sound as if they might be fun or, at worst, a precursor to a joke. "Lost my faith!" "Very tired!" "My son died!"

Once he was deemed to be safely non-contagious he was welcomed into the fold and invariably offered a hot toddy made from whatever dregs of alcohol were left over from Christmas. He was reminded of the kinds of concoctions he had made as a teenager with his friends, raiding parental cocktail cabinets across Bromley for an unholy mix of advocaat, cherry brandy and gin.

He had finally unearthed a rather theatrical flair for Charades—too late, sadly, for Rosalind's parents' Rectory games. Unexpectedly liberated from the self-consciousness that had dogged him his entire life, Simon discovered that he could negotiate the passage of the day quite successfully with his own rough-and-ready repertoire of signing. Hands together for "thank you" (handily doubling up for "let us pray"). Bowing from the waist, Japanese-style, filled in very satisfactorily for "hello" and "goodbye" and a more formal sign of gratitude if required. A series of facial gestures covered sadness, sympathy, puzzlement and (less frequently, if at all) happiness. A thumbs-up was by its nature necessarily cheerful. Perhaps he should get on Amazon (there wasn't a bookshop for miles) and order a book on sign language. Or buy a set of signal flags and learn semaphore.

He had dealt with the problem of the Sunday service by directing his thin congregation to hold it themselves, to gather their chairs round in a circle and imagine they were in the days of the

Early Church before priests hijacked God. No wonder Rosalind had been attracted to the Society of Friends. So much more egalitarian than expecting one man—or woman—to shoulder all the burden.

He had a funeral to conduct on Monday, but perhaps that could be held Quaker-style, as Rosalind's had been so long ago. Some weeks after his visit from her partner, Neil, he had received a little card in the post informing him that a "Meeting for Worship in Thanksgiving for the Grace of God, as shown in the life of Rosalind Wells" was to take place. She had reverted to her maiden name, he noticed. He had felt duty-bound to attend. The event had the flavour of a memorial rather than a funeral, as the reason it was taking place "somewhat after the fact," as Neil put it, was because there had been a lot of bureaucratic rigmarole in returning her "remains" from abroad. Simon couldn't help but wonder what those remains consisted of.

It had not been a funeral that Rosalind's father, Desmond, would have recognized from the Anglican Church, but nonetheless he sat stoically through it, staring straight ahead, bracing himself with his hands on his knees. As was the custom, if the spirit moved them, various members of the Meeting stood up and said things about Rosalind—nice things, obviously. It was hardly the forum for grievances, although it might have been interesting. Rosalind never, for example, turned the light off when she left a room, and she forgot her door key *all the time*. She was never the first one to get up in the morning, it was always Simon who brought her a cup of tea in bed. Of course, for a long time after Isaac died she never got up at all, but he could hardly hold that against her.

Desmond had eventually roused himself to standing and said his daughter was a "good woman" and her price was "above rubies." Sibylla let out a tremendous sob at that. One of Rosalind's sisters was the next to get up. She recited Henry Vaughan's poem "They Are All Gone into the World of Light." Simon knew the first verse (vaguely), but he hadn't realized the whole thing was quite so *long*, especially the way that her sister declaimed it. Very slowly.

He was surprised to learn from other Friends that in the years since their divorce Rosalind had become both an ardent bird-watcher and a keen member of an amateur operatic society, neither of which she had previously shown any interest in. (He had wondered idly if they might be burying the wrong person.) He couldn't remember ever hearing her sing, although he supposed she must have crooned lullabies to Isaac. Why didn't he remember that? There was so much he seemed to have blanked out of his life. The good bits, mostly.

~

After Rosalind left, he had pursued a few other relationships in a half-hearted manner. The only women he met were parishioners, so he had joined a secular dating site—there were religious ones, but he gave them a wide berth. In fact, he gave any woman he met a wide berth if they admitted to having a faith. He was surprised how many were allured by the dog collar. (Indeed the entire priestly vesture—he suspected it was a mild form of fetish.) He couldn't commit, of course. He knew he was incapable of truly pledging his faith to anyone or anything again.

He didn't miss sex, not at all. He hadn't really had any desires of the flesh since the summer of 2008 (an encounter that had been just on the decorous side of embarrassing). As with so many other aspects of his life, sex had been killed by religion. Nowadays he was awkward in the social company of women and used his cassock as a shield.

Sophie Greenway had been an exception, of course. Not where sex was concerned, God forbid, she was almost young enough to be his daughter. He had really liked Sophie, in an entirely non-licentious way. She was someone you could talk to, even though she, like Rosalind, was the daughter of a vicar. Or, at least, she said she was. They rarely conversed about religion—the spirit, yes, but that was something else. They understood each other. (She was an "empath," she laughed.) They used to take long rambling walks around the deer park together, pointing out birds and trees to each other, in thrall to nature.

He had felt an immense hurt when she disappeared, a betrayal really. He didn't care that she was supposedly a thief. (And what proof did they have? It was all circumstantial, wasn't it? Innocent until proven guilty.) Nor did he care that she appeared to be a first-class liar. What wounded him was that she had left without saying goodbye, as if their friendship was as false as her name. Another little rent in his soul, so torn now that it was nothing but rags.

Simon checked his watch. He had a dying woman—Edna Gibson—to visit. It would get him out of the vicarage. Any excuse.

As he was leaving, accompanied by his portable Communion kit, his eye was caught by something in the deer park. Not something but someone—a woman. A fleeting moment later and she was gone, vanishing through a gate and into the wood. He could have sworn it was Sophie Greenway. He was thinking about her and then he conjured her out of the air. The mind was a funny thing, full of tricks.

When the Turner was still in residence, Simon had stood in front of it with Sophie while she told him about it. He could remember very little that she had said—something about Turner using oil paints like watercolours to create his atmospheric effects and how he purposefully chose pigments that weren't durable, so all his works had faded. "He didn't care," she said, "so that must have meant he also wasn't bothered about posterity, or his legacy. You have to admire that. It's about the art, in the moment. The creative moment. Like God making the world."

He could appreciate a medieval stained-glass window, but that was about as far as his knowledge of "art" went. Sophie, on the other hand, seemed to know a great deal. She said she had studied Art History at St. Andrews, was in the same year as the Prince and Princess of Wales, as they now were, but, laughing ruefully, said that their "paths had diverged" after graduation. Now he was led to doubt everything she had ever told him. She was a con artist "of the first order," the police had told Lady Milton. Simon still found it difficult to believe. She had struck him as transparently honest. Could you be both?

Sophie had shown him the Turner on a day when the Miltons were all elsewhere, taking him on a tour of the house, pausing before some of her favourite paintings and talking expertly to him about them. Although Simon knew embarrassingly little about the subject, he had heard that the Miltons owned a famous Raphael, yet it was nowhere to be found as they went round the house and Sophie laughed sardonically when he mentioned it. *"The Madonna and Child?* Gone," she scoffed, "along with all the rest of their Old Masters, sold off piecemeal to pay bills. The Turner's probably the most valuable thing they have left." The Raphael, she said, had been traded by Cosmo "on the QT" to a friend of a friend of a friend of a Russian oligarch, who had seen it when he was invited to a shooting party at Burton Makepeace. "He decided he couldn't live without it and made an offer for it on the spot. He paid squillions for it—cash, can you believe? The sale was under the table, as they say, so no one had to pay tax."

"It sounds like money-laundering," Simon said.

"Call it what you will, but it was highly illegal. And, of course, now the Miltons are forced to pretend they're still in possession of it. They've managed to alter the house's inventory—God knows how—so that the Raphael isn't on it any more and when Lord Milton dies it won't enter probate and they won't have to pay inheritance tax on it. They're a parcel of rogues." (And yet it had turned out that she was the greatest rogue of all!) "Cosmo's been in the doghouse ever since. I would have loved to have seen it," she sighed.

Simon wondered where the Raphael was now. Had the cash-laden oligarch been sanctioned and the painting confiscated? Or perhaps he had escaped censure and the painting was now hanging unashamedly in the state room of his fugitive yacht, cruising around the oceans of the world. Was that where Sophie was? Lying on a lounger on the sun deck of a yacht somewhere, or beside a tropical pool, sipping a cocktail and laughing at what fools they had all been. The Turner notwithstanding, Simon thought he had possibly been the biggest fool of all.

He missed her. Lady Milton did too, he knew. "Bereft," she had murmured to him not long after Lord Milton's demise, when he unexpectedly came across her standing before the altar in St. Martin's. "One looks to the Church in times like this," she said to him. He felt like telling her that she would be better off looking to the brandy bottle, but he supposed it was not the kind of advice she was seeking. At the time, he thought that she felt grief because of her husband's sudden exit, but now he was sure it was Sophie's departure that had bruised her heart, perhaps even broken it.

He had conducted the funeral for Lord Milton. It had been simple—a short sermon on the transcendency of death, followed by a eulogy given by Piers, during which Lady Milton could be heard occasionally snorting derisively. Simon wasn't sure if this was a testy response to the new Lord Milton's plodding style or a dismissal of the excessively complimentary contents of the eulogy itself. Piers made his father sound like a saint, when Simon knew for a fact that Lord Milton had been a nasty so-and-so who loathed both his sons, a feeling that was mutual.

Only the alarmingly brusque Arabella had escaped her father's contempt. Arabella who had sat in the front pew, with the straight spine of a lifelong horsewoman (she had mounted her first pony at the tender age of two). She shed no tears, and when Derek Truitt had squeezed out the final notes of "O Lord, our help in ages past" on the church organ, Simon heard her mutter, "That's the old bugger really gone, then."

They all trooped out to the graveyard for the committal, where the family stood around the open grave, impatiently watching the coffin being lowered. Piers had pushed for cremation, but Lady Milton insisted on burial and, after some wrangling, the new widow's wishes trumped the new heir's. Simon wondered if it was because she believed the body needed to be intact for the Last Judgement. "No," she said, out of earshot of Piers, "in case Johnny needs to be exhumed."

Simon lit a votive candle for Edna's soul before he left the church. Not a candle, a tea-light. They were displayed on a rickety metal stand in the small side chapel that was dedicated to a Crusader who had been made a saint. The Crusades always struck Simon as being a particularly awful period in history, but then, was there any point in the past that hadn't been?

Simon liked to keep a few of the votives burning all the time, light in the darkness and so on. A rebuttal against the awfulness. He bought them by the job lot from Ikea online. The only other person who ever seemed to light one was Fran's brother, Ben.

There you go, Edna, he thought. A pre-emptive guiding light, in case her soul had already left her body by the time he reached her.

It hadn't. Not quite. Edna weighed little more than a sparrow and was so ancient that she already appeared to have been mummified. Simon placed the Communion cup on her bedside table amongst a clutter of pill packets and plastic cups and used tissues that were strewn across its surface. Death was never tidy in his experience.

Simon was called to a lot of deathbeds, resigned to being more popular with the dying than the living. He rejected many of the Anglican guidelines on what to say on this unique occasion—they contained a good deal of beseeching mercy and begging forgiveness of sins. You wanted something cheerful, something comforting, for the endgame. And perhaps not *We will see God as he is* from the Gospel of John, also recommended. It was an ambiguous statement at best. What if the true nature of God turned out to be a mollusc or a hyena? "I really don't think that's what it means, Simon," his bishop said. He saw more of the bishop than he would have liked, certainly more than any other humble rural incumbents of the diocese did, as the vicarage provided a convenient stopping-off place on the bishop's way to a cottage he owned on the outskirts of Heptonstall. Could bishops have second homes?

"Of course they can."

Simon provided coffee and a "bathroom break" for the bishop, and in return the bishop dispensed lofty advice to this most lowly of his charges.

Apart from these sporadic stopovers, the Church hierarchy left Simon alone to putter on to the end of his career. He hoped he would die in service, otherwise he would probably end up in a retirement home for clergy. He couldn't imagine anything worse.

Unable to provide vocal comfort to Edna, Simon contrived to mouth the words silently. *The Lord Jesus says, today you will be with me in Paradise.* Edna was almost bald, just a few wispy white hairs across her pate. He stroked her forehead.

"And what if," Sophie had said to him on one occasion (for they had talked about the mollusc possibility), "God was one of us, like that song."

What if *Edna* was God? An alarming idea that dissipated when a district nurse popped her head round the door and said, "It's going to be a while yet, Vicar. I'd come back later, if I were you."

Simon shrugged exaggeratedly, which the district nurse rightly interpreted to mean that he didn't have anything better to do with his time. "I'll put the kettle on, then," she said. "I've got chocolate digestives."

He gave her a thumbs-up sign.

Law and Order

Reggie had just come off shift, driving back from Keighley, when he phoned. She'd been doing some follow-ups in the aftermath of a double stabbing in the centre of town last week. She'd driven out there with a DC called Tiffany Sellars who griped all the way about it being something that uniforms could have been tasked with. She hadn't been on the case and Reggie had no idea why she'd suddenly said she wanted to ride along with her this afternoon. "Avoiding paperwork," she said shamelessly. Reggie liked paperwork, it tidied everything up in the permanent war against chaos.

"Dot the *is* and cross the *ts*," she said cheerfully to Tiffany, who was keeping a keen eye out for the next Greggs. You never had to go far.

"Interesting fact," Reggie said to Tiffany. "Did you know that not only was the first Spiritualist church started in Keighley, but it was also the first place to receive a Carnegie library?"

"And?"

"And nothing, it's just a fact."

"Right."

"Do you know what a Carnegie library is?"

"What is this? School?"

"Sorry. Can't help it. I like facts. They're reliable." Not like people, Reggie thought. She was determined to remain steadfastly good-humoured in the face of Tiffany's ongoing negativity. She had recently decided to practise being as serene as a Zen nun. It was a daily—nay, hourly—challenge. With Tiffany, it was every minute.

They had parked outside a neat Sixties semi, the home of one of the boys who had been stabbed. Big green pom-poms of artificial privet hung either side of the front door. Reggie tried not to be judgemental, but she just couldn't see the point, although in the chart of things she couldn't see the point of there were, let's face it, many entries that outranked artificial-privet pom-poms.

Two fifteen-year-old boys. Callum and Rusel. "Friends," according to people who knew them. Strange friendship. "That's not how you spell Russell," Tiffany said, looking over Reggie's shoulder. (Annoying!)

"It is, it's a Muslim name."

Tiffany made a kind of snorting noise that Reggie chose not to interpret.

No one else seemed to be involved, they had stabbed each other—clear as day on CCTV in the town centre. Not much for anyone to do really, apart from mop up the blood and decide whether it had been premeditated. One lived, one died. One was lucky, one was unlucky. Rusel was the unlucky one. It was about "something and nothing," Callum said, when Reggie interviewed him in his hospital bed.

"What a pair of muppets," Tiffany said. "What did they think would happen if they went at each other with blades?"

"You don't understand consequences at that age," Reggie said. Well, you did, but somehow they didn't apply to you. Reggie was different, she had always understood consequences. It had made her old before her time.

The neat Sixties semi was the home of Rusel's family. The one that lived, Callum—the only one who would now be charged—was still in hospital. Callum had brought his mother's kitchen knife to the fight. It had sliced between his best friend's ribs as slick as a butcher's knife. "We were just laiking," Callum had moaned to Reggie when she first interviewed him. "He means larking about," someone back at the station interpreted for her. She was still thrown when she came across the Yorkshire language. She had her own Scottish lexicon—hackit, bogging, bowfing, scunnered, numpty, gowk, crabbit, peely-wally—all suppressed when she was around her colleagues so they didn't think she was weird.

"Callum's a good boy," Callum's mother had said many times.

"They all say that," Tiffany sneered. They *were* all good boys once, Reggie thought. Even her brother had been a good boy once. He was dead now. He had lived the kind of ramshackle life that ended in a ramshackle death.

Rusel's autopsy had got stuck in a queue behind a horrible murder-suicide. It had involved small kids and was not Reggie's case, thank goodness. The delay was distressing to Rusel's family, and Reggie had wanted to visit them today to reassure them that the release of his body was a priority.

Bad enough that they couldn't bury him within twenty-four hours, but that he would be cut up before going to the next life was troubling them deeply.

"Muslims believe the body should be whole in order to be resurrected," Reggie said. "So no cremation either."

Tiffany sighed, suffering more *school*. She was an empathy-free zone, she should be working with objects not people, in Reggie's opinion.

There was one of John Donne's Holy Sonnets that Reggie had learnt for her Highers. *At the round earth's imagin'd corners.* The angels blew their trumpets to signal the Resurrection and all the "scattered souls" returned to their bodies. Reggie imagined it to be like getting into a rather awkward coat. What if it was true? What if you couldn't find your coat? She had once known a woman who believed in "the Rapture," who expected to be amongst those chosen believers who would ascend to heaven at the end of days. Reggie didn't care about the afterlife, she just wanted to stay alive in this one. She had outlasted everyone she was related to. Sometimes she worried that she was on borrowed time.

"You're quiet," Tiffany said.

⌒

She dropped Tiffany off in Huddersfield, where she lived in a house very like the one they had just come from. She had privet pom-

poms too and Reggie was relieved that she hadn't voiced her feelings on their aesthetic.

Reggie had a large mortgage on a small flat—modern, painted in neutral colours, purposefully impersonal because she didn't want anyone judging her by her décor. No clutter either (more Zen). She went all Marie Kondo when she moved in. Life out there on the mean streets was messy and Reggie wanted to stop the mess seeping over her doorstep and into her home.

She'd maybe gone a bit far. She was living with a bed, a sofa, a coffee machine and a toaster—which pretty much meant she lived off coffee and toast, but that was okay because she liked coffee and toast. The coffee machine had cost an arm and a leg but was worth it. She had a fridge, too, a freestanding Siemens bought at a knockdown price in Currys' sale, and her aspiration when she bought it had been to stuff it with healthy food, but sadly more often than not the most it contained was a bowl of leftover baked beans and a carton of almond milk with a dodgy sell-by date.

➤

Reggie took a roundabout route home, a back road across the moors. Brontë country. *The wiley, windy moors.* It made her think of Ronnie. She missed Ronnie. Reggie had worked with her for only a few weeks a couple of years ago, but the two of them had been a perfect fit. Two peas in a pod. Sisters of Mercy. Ronnie was in a different league to Tiffany.

Ronnie had moved south and was working with the Met in London. "You should think about it," she said. No way, Reggie thought. And besides, here was okay, and okay was something that Reggie could handle. She was on the up. She had ambition. She was fast-tracking and had already put in for her sergeant's exams.

"Bright girl," the Chief Superintendent had said to her. Reggie couldn't help preening just a little bit, but she tried very hard not to let it show. She valued the Chief Superintendent's opinion. "I was a bright girl once," she had said. "Now look at me, a boring old battle-axe." She wasn't, of course, she was handsome and whip-smart and about to be promoted to ACC, she'd probably retire as Chief Constable. A great role model. Reggie wanted to be her in thirty years' time.

"Thirty years? Jesus, you make me feel old," the Chief Superintendent had said.

It was true she could be a bit of a battle-axe, but that was the kind of sexist terminology you were supposed to avoid. Words like fishwife, harridan, crone, virago, vixen, witch, harpy, shrew. There were a lot of them. The male equivalent was just "man." "Termagant," Reggie supplied enthusiastically. "Did you know that word has a really interesting etymology? It's essentially Anglo-Norman, but it relates improbably to—"

"As I said, bright girl," Chief Superintendent Louise Monroe had said, cutting her off.

"Heard you were brown-nosing with the big guns," Tiffany had said to her at the time.

"I wouldn't call it that. We happen to belong to the same running group."

"*We happen to belong to the same running group*," Tiffany had mocked, waggling her head from side to side. She reminded Reggie of the worst bullies at school, girls who had taken delight in Reggie's orphan status, her lack of height, her secondhand uniform—anything they could latch on to. Unkind girls.

In fact, Reggie and Chief Superintendent Monroe were very good at keeping a professional distance. Reggie wanted to be on the up because of merit, not favouritism. Of course, they had some history, going way back, that neither of them ever mentioned, because at the heart of that history was a great big fat lie. The big fat lie involved Jackson Brodie. Of course it did! He was like an infection that got everywhere, tilting truth off its axis. Reggie had helped him cover up a double murder ("lawful killing," he said) right under Louise Monroe's nose. At least Reggie hadn't been in the police at the time, not like last year when she helped him "reassign" the identity of a murderer. ("Redistribution of justice—we assigned blame to a guiltier person.")

Reggie was never sure whether Jackson Brodie and Louise Monroe had been "an item" (she hated that word!), but there had certainly been a lot of what you might call yearning between them. Louise had probably had a lucky escape.

Jackson Brodie's MO was disruption. His attitude to the law was like that of a Wild West sheriff. All that coincidence-being-an-explanation-waiting-to-happen baloney was just a cover for not following procedure. Procedure was good, you knew where you were with procedure.

Reggie hated running, but it was the only thing she could do that didn't involve sweaty, germ-laden gyms or the slow, mind-numbing tedium of Pilates or yoga. At least with running you didn't have to think, you just threw on a pair of trainers and went. It was okay.

She didn't have a boyfriend, hadn't had one since Sai upped and left. Perhaps she should have told Tiffany that her only serious boyfriend had been Pakistani, seen if she snorted at that. Reggie had only recently started thinking about him in the past tense. "Time to move on," Ronnie said. But really Reggie wouldn't be able to spare enough time to make a relationship work and then she would just feel guilty all the time, whereas this way she felt lonely only some of the time.

It wasn't that she didn't want someone, in fact Reggie considered herself to be an arch-Romantic. Her favourite film was *The Last of the Mohicans*, and when Daniel Day-Lewis said to Madeleine Stowe, *No matter how long it takes, no matter how far . . . I will find you*, it sent shivers down her spine every time. She had the DVD and had watched it so many times she almost knew the dialogue off by heart. But that was how high and deep it would have to be to make it worthwhile—not just a Chinese takeaway and a bottle of wine in front of *Succession*. Plus, she wanted him to be handsome. Reggie hardly ever came across a handsome man. There must be at least twenty good-looking women for every barely decent-looking man. And it would really help too if he looked like Daniel Day-Lewis, or at any rate Daniel Day-Lewis in his Nathaniel Poe incarnation. So, yes, for now . . . Zen nun.

"You know," she had said to Tiffany, "that in the film *The Last of the Mohicans,* the main character is called Nathaniel Poe, but in the original book by James Fenimore Cooper he's called Natty Bumppo. You can see why they changed it, can't you?"

"Jesus, Reggie, you *really* don't get out enough," Tiffany had said.

Zen, Reggie had reminded herself. *Zenzenzen.* She should work on feeling sorry for Tiffany, the woman was thick as mince, was Ms. Plod, sticking out for the pension and early retirement.

∼

She reached the top of the moors and passed the turning for Burton Makepeace. For a moment she was tempted to take it, to drop in and find out how Lady Milton was faring. Reggie had been one of the first on the scene after the Miltons noticed that their Turner was no longer hanging on the wall. It had been cut from the frame, leaving a melancholic rectangle of wallpaper behind. Quite a big rectangle. Reggie couldn't imagine how you would go about cutting the canvas out of the frame. Sophie Greenway wasn't tall, and she would have needed, at the very least, a sturdy stepladder. Had it been a two-person job? Had she sneaked in a comrade-in-arms in the middle of the night? Or were they already there? Another person on the inside? And why the Turner, come to that? You could still pick up a Turner on the open market, and for a lot less than some other artists. Da Vinci's *Salvator Mundi* and de Kooning's *Interchange* were worth more than ten times the Turner. But of course they weren't just hanging on a wall in a remote part of Yorkshire, waiting to be plucked. The security at Burton Makepeace was minimal, just one camera on the front door and one at the back. Sophie Greenway showed up on neither.

At the end of a long day, Reggie had been tasked with conducting a final interview with Lady Milton. Dotting *i*s and crossing *t*s. Lady Milton was quite batty. Reggie had never come across any members of her class before, certainly not in their native habitat, so it was interesting from an anthropological perspective, if nothing else.

Most of the rest of that long day had been spent going door to door in the village with the uniforms. No one had seen or heard anything, apart from a woman called Janet Teller who claimed to have heard a "very loud motorbike" in the middle of the night. No one in the village had CCTV or alarm systems. "We trust each other," Janet Teller said. Perhaps they shouldn't.

"It's probably the most valuable painting we had left," Lady Milton said. "We've already sold the Rembrandts and the Titian. And a small da Vinci, although its provenance was disputed. And a Constable and the Canalettos. And all the Stubbs, of course. The Gainsboroughs, too," she added, lost now in this mournful inventory. Reggie had been brought up by a widowed mother who regularly pawned her engagement ring on a Friday to put fish fingers on the tea-table. But everything was relative to your circumstances, she supposed. The suffering of the rich was known only to the rich.

"We are an endangered species," Lady Milton had sighed, although it seemed to Reggie that they were thriving compared to most people. "But no cash, you see," Lady Milton said. "Not two farthings to rub together." A bit of an exaggeration, in Reggie's opinion, when there was an entire gallery full of portraits of the Milton family. You could tell they were Miltons because they all bore an uncanny resemblance to Piers Milton, even the women.

Why hadn't Sophie Greenway taken the Raphael? Reggie asked. Burton Makepeace was known to have a stonking Raphael, but Lady Milton seemed confused by the question. "It's away being cleaned," Piers interrupted, as if he'd been eavesdropping. "Very lengthy process, you know."

❧

As Reggie and Lady Milton were gazing at the absence of the Turner on the wall that day, the vicar had "popped in" to offer his condolences, as if there had been a death in the family.

"Oh, dear, the Reverend Cate," Lady Milton whispered loudly as he approached. The room they were in was enormous ("the Red Room," Lady Milton said) and it took the vicar some time to traverse the vast space. Of course, most of the rooms at Burton Makepeace were enormous—Reggie's entire flat would have fitted into the Red Room several times over, probably—although the room was not so large that it prevented the vicar from hearing Lady Milton say, "He's a bit wet, I'm afraid."

"She's not entirely wrong," he said to Reggie. "Do call me Simon."

He joined them in contemplating the pictureless frame as if they were at a Surrealist exhibition.

"It's strangely symbolic, isn't it?" he said. "After all, isn't something that is lost also something that is waiting to be found?" Oh, God, Reggie thought, he was from the Jackson Brodie school of aphorisms.

The case had been handed over pretty much wholesale to the Met's Art and Antiques unit. There had been no subsequent ransom demand for the Turner and, despite the insurance company offering a hefty reward, no reward had been claimed. It was on the Lost Art Registry as well as Interpol's Stolen Works of Art database, but it had never resurfaced. It had simply disappeared into thin air.

It was the first time that Reggie had thought about Burton Makepeace in a while and then, as if her very thinking had conjured it up out of the same thin air that the Turner had disappeared into, her phone rang and the voice on the other end was asking her about it. Reggie really, really hated coincidences, especially when they involved the person on the phone.

"What do you know about that art theft at Burton Makepeace, Reggie?"

"And hello to you too, Mr. Brodie."

❧

She agreed to meet him the next day on neutral ground, a vegan café in town with a pared-down Scandinavian feel about it.

"Ah, a clean, well-lighted place, as Hemingway would have said," Jackson said when he sat down. He could quote Hemingway? It seemed unlikely but Reggie didn't query it.

"So," she said instead, "what is it that you want, Mr. B?"

"Can't I just want to have a catch-up—see how you are?"

"Unlikely."

He looked put out, as if she had impugned his virtue in some way. "There's this case that I'm on—"

"Jings, a 'case'? Like a real detective?"

"Very funny."

She was reluctant to let him back into her life. He constituted part of the mess out there on the mean streets. Whenever she saw him, he brought a tsunami of it in his wake that would have defeated Marie Kondo. And now it transpired that he had moved to this side of the county—*her* side of the county—so there would no doubt be more mess and he would try to drag her into it.

"Go on, then," she sighed. "What's the scoop? Give me the headlines. It's counter service, by the way. You're buying. I'll have an almond latte and a brownie, please. And this place is vegan, in case you hadn't noticed, so don't go asking for a full English."

"As if," he said.

━━━◝━━━

"Okay," he said, when he'd ferried her requests back to the table. "Headlines it is. A few days ago a ninety-six-year-old woman called Dorothy Padgett died, and a painting she owned went missing the same day. The painting was a small Renaissance portrait of a woman, sitter and artist both unknown. Dorothy Padgett's carer, Melanie Hope, went missing at the same time as the painting. The heirs—Dorothy's son and daughter, Ian and Hazel—seem convinced that she took it. I haven't been able to find any trace of Melanie Hope since then. She gave them a false address and her phone was a burner."

"Why haven't the heirs called the real police?"

"Could you not use that word?"

"What word?" Reggie said, feigning innocence. " 'Police'?"

"I don't know why they haven't gone through official channels, some poppycock about not wanting to get Melanie Hope into trouble."

"Oh, 'poppycock'!" Reggie said, feeling a surge of lexical delight. "Do you know where that word comes from?"

"Not really."

What is this? School? Reggie heard Tiffany's voice in her head. It wasn't that Reggie wanted to teach people, she just wanted them to understand the pleasure of learning and the satisfaction of knowing. She'd fought against horrible odds herself to get an education. She loved quizzes, loved knowing the answers to questions. *In what year did ITV commence broadcasting? What is the deepest lake in the world? Who won the Battle of Naseby?* Why wouldn't you want to know this stuff? ("Because it's boring?" Tiffany offered.) And wasn't that why she had become a detective? To have answers. It was certainly why this annoying person sitting opposite her went into the police.

He took a photograph out of an envelope and pushed it across the table towards her. *"Woman with a Weasel,"* he said. "That's what the heirs call it anyway."

Reggie picked up the photograph and gazed into the eyes of the unknown woman. There was a gulf of centuries between her and this lovely woman, but Reggie was moved by an unexpected feeling— not kinship exactly, but a kind of nod to the continuum of existence. She took out her phone and took a photograph. An image of an image of an image. Somewhere at the end of that meta chain had been a real woman. It could give a girl existential angst if she wasn't careful. "An insurance fraud?" she hazarded, back in her professional jacket.

"Not an insurance fraud," he said. "Ian and Hazel say it wasn't insured. And even if they're lying about that, they won't be able to claim anything without the insurance company involving the police. They insist it's of sentimental value."

"And you don't believe them?"

"Call it instinct, but I can't help feeling there's something a bit fishy about the whole thing. Hazel and Ian seemed like people playing parts."

"They could be pulling a scam and you're just their useful idiot, helping them unwittingly."

"Useful idiot?"

"Yeah. Go on."

"Ian and Hazel claim their father bought it at a house-clearance auction in 1945, but the auction never took place because the house in question burned down."

"And they don't know who painted it? It doesn't have a provenance?" Reggie knew all about provenance since the Miltons' Turner was stolen. *Sunset over Fountains Abbey* had a shedload of it, right back to the original purchase, with receipt, from the artist's studio in 1824. That, Reggie knew, was the year Beethoven's "Choral" was first performed. She had been to a performance by the Hallé in Manchester just before lockdown. She knew about a lot of other things but she hadn't known about music, and she had been alarmed to find herself in tears long before the end. Reggie wondered what other worlds were waiting to be discovered and whether she was strong enough for them.

"No, none," he said. "And do you know why I think it doesn't have the all-important provenance?"

"Hold me back."

He launched into a convoluted story about the 11th Hussars during the Second World War, a story that seemed to wander all the way to the Crimea and back, via Arizona and a stolen de Kooning. (No way he knew de Kooning—that was even less likely than him having read Hemingway's stories.)

"And do you know what I think?"

"You're going to tell me anyway."

"The painting wasn't reported stolen because it was *already* stolen. Ta-da!"

"*Ta-da*—is that gumshoe-speak?"

"And that would explain why it was never insured, because then it would have had to be authenticated and somewhere in that process its questionable ownership would have been revealed. But—and this is interesting—"

"Are you sure?"

"Yes. Dorothy's next-door neighbour Bob—Bob Gordon—told me that one of his grandsons—he has three, Lucas, Ewan and Matt—Matt's a photographer with the *Yorkshire Post*—"

"Losing the will to live here, Mr. B, just so you know."

"Before lockdown, Dorothy asked Matt to take a photo of the painting because she wanted to send it off to have it valued."

"And?"

"The first time this painting's seen the light of day in over seventy years and a few months later it's stolen?"

"Stolen by a photographer from the *Yorkshire Post*?" she puzzled.

"*No,* from whoever she sent the photo to for valuation."

"Seems an outlandish conclusion to me. You have no proof she ever sent it anywhere. You've developed a very vivid imagination since I last saw you. And all this conjecture relates to Burton Makepeace exactly how?"

"Come on, Reggie, you're a smart girl." (Irritatingly, she felt flattered.) "You worked on the Burton Makepeace case, didn't you? Make the connection—trusted housekeeper steals painting, trusted carer steals painting. And wasn't there something similar at Mount Fernie?"

"Trusted cleaner steals painting?"

"Did you look for similarities?"

"We looked, but there didn't seem to be any. The family weren't very cooperative. That was ages ago."

"Five years—not that long," he said.

"It seems unlikely they're all the same woman," she said.

"Does it? I think it makes it *more* likely. Of course, if I could check Melanie's fingerprints," Jackson said, "or any forensics at all, it would help. You know, 'real police' stuff. I don't suppose you could have a quick shufti at the PNC, could you, Reggie?"

Oh, here we go, she thought. "You can't just use me because you don't have access to official resources," she said crossly. "We're not a partnership, we're not 'Brodie and Chase, Detectives.'"

"That has quite a good ring to it though, don't you think?"

"Sounds more like a couple of grave-robbers to me, Mr. B."

"Are you growling, Reggie? I don't remember you being so hostile previously."

"Maybe you weren't paying attention."

He wanted to use her, or rather the resources she had access to.

She wasn't going to play that game. Absolutely not. There'd been too many blurred boundaries in her short life. Nowadays she was trying to stick to clear guidelines and was determined not to ask him a single question, because one question led to another and then the questions led to a discussion and then before she knew it they'd be Brodie and Chase. Or Chase and Brodie, which sounded much better to Reggie's ears.

"Melanie Hope," he said. "Five foot four-ish, slim, in her thirties. Brownish hair, brown eyes, or possibly green. There's some debate about the eye colour. Indeed, about everything to do with Melanie Hope. What did your housekeeper look like? What was she called?"

"Sophie Greenway, you know perfectly well that was her name. Five foot four, slim, brown hair, blue eyes," she admitted reluctantly. A wig and a pair of contact lenses and she could have been transformed, they both knew that.

He took out his phone and showed her a photograph. "Something like her?"

"Is that Melanie Hope?" She could have kicked herself for sounding so eager.

"Yes, it's from the next-door neighbour's security camera on the day that Dorothy died. Hair and eyes can change," he mused, "but you're pretty much stuck with the biometrics—fingerprints and so on. And I presume you managed to lift some prints. Was Sophie Greenway on record?"

"No. And there were surprisingly few prints. You would think they'd have been all over the place. She moved through that house like a ghost."

"I don't suppose she left a fancy coffee-table book behind about Turner, like a big fat clue?"

"No. Stop asking me questions." Sophie *had* left a book behind though, hadn't she? Reggie remembered an old Nancy Styles novel, something with "clock" in the title. Hang on a minute. What had he said? *Of course, if I could check Melanie's fingerprints.* Check them against what?

From his pocket he produced a battered paperback in a plastic bag. "Mine are all over this," he said, "but hers should be, too."

Reggie stared at the book. Her heart gave a little bump of excitement.

Hark! Hark! The Dogs Do Bark. "Nancy Styles?" she murmured, more to herself than Jackson, as she gingerly took it from him.

"Don't worry, it won't explode. I read it, it's a bit rubbish. I guessed the ending. Weird title and there aren't any beggars in it and only one dog, and it doesn't bark."

Reggie recognized the nursery rhyme as one that Dr. Hunter used to recite to the baby. That "baby" was at secondary school now, in New Zealand. Time was the biggest thief of all. "The doyenne of cosy crime," she said thoughtfully, looking at the rather lurid artwork on the cover.

"Doyenne? That's a fancy word."

"Queen was already taken by Agatha Christie, apparently." She was *not* going to tell him about the Nancy Styles novel left behind by Sophie Greenway. He would come out with his usual catchphrase. *A coincidence is just an explanation waiting to happen.* And, infuriatingly, he might be right. She was not going to give him the satisfaction. *She* was police, not him, not any more. If there was a connection, *she* would be the one to find it, she thought grimly.

"Are you all right?"

"Yes."

"You'll break your jaw if you clench it any tighter. It's odd though, isn't it? I mean, thieves are usually in and out as quickly as possible. They don't embed themselves with their victims. Unless they're relatives. Did you eliminate the family at Burton Makepeace? Yes, of course you did, you're not the Keystone Cops. And, you know, two thefts with the same MO less than twenty miles and two years apart—bit of a co—"

She put a hand up as if stopping traffic. "Don't say it!"

❧

Art, war, pillage, false identity, he certainly knew how to tell a good story. One designed to reel her in. And it worked. Damn him!

The first thing she did when she got back in her car was to google "Keystone Cops." She'd heard the term but didn't know where it came from. Reggie hated it when there were things that she didn't know. Especially when Mr. Know-it-all Brodie knew them.

The second thing she did, when she got back to the station, was to drop off Melanie Hope's book, *Hark! Hark! The Dogs Do Bark,* with a fingerprint officer in Forensics called Josh who belonged to the same taekwondo dojang that she did. She found him with his eyes glued to a screen displaying a hugely magnified print, its patterns of furrows and ridges and loops like the contour map of a country. He was carefully tracing a characteristic in red on the screen. Reggie would never have the patience for his job.

She asked him to do a fast cross-check with fingerprints taken from Burton Makepeace. He baulked at the word "fast" because she ought to know by now that it wasn't like it was on television, something he had lectured her about several times. She mollified him with a promise of pizza. "You already owe me three pizzas," he grumbled. "*And* dough balls."

The third thing she did was to send the photo of *Woman with a Weasel* to Ronnie, accompanied by a quick text saying, "I know it's not your beat, but . . ." Ronnie's current girlfriend, Ginny, worked at the Courtauld Institute and Reggie guessed that she might know someone who knew someone who knew someone. "Speak later!" she added jauntily, in case it sounded as though she was just using Ronnie for her contacts. Ever since Ginny had come on the scene, Ronnie had communicated a lot less with Reggie.

The fourth thing Reggie did was to go to Evidence and check out the box labelled "Burton Makepeace—Sophie Greenway." Perhaps it was time to revisit the mysterious housekeeper.

There indeed was *The Secret of the Clock Cabinet,* first published in 1938, "this edition reprinted in 1982." It seemed like a close relative of the book that Melanie Hope had left behind. They both had a creased, charity-shop air about them, the pages yellowing and felty with age. She signed the book out and castigated herself for having overlooked it at the time. It just hadn't struck anyone that it was an *i* that needed dotting, let alone a *t* that should have been crossed.

The fifth thing Reggie did was to spend the evening reading

The Secret of the Clock Cabinet. As far as she was aware, all Styles' novels followed the same pattern. They took place in a large house with a big cast of characters, hierarchical class divisions firmly in place and everyone a suspect until they were bumped off. *Downton* with daggers. And poison and rope and blunt instruments, like a tortuous game of Clue. She had fallen asleep before reaching the dénouement.

Just as she was dropping off, she jerked awake again. She had forgotten to get that photo of Melanie Hope off Jackson Brodie's phone. A photo of a potential suspect and she'd failed to get hold of it! Detective School 101. If she asked him, he would be smug about it. Eventually, after a good deal more fretting, she dropped into the relief of sleep.

Not for long. She was woken by her phone dinging. It was a text with the screenshot of Melanie Hope attached. *You forgot to ask for this. Jx*

Another ding. Another text. *Fancy going to a funeral tomorrow?*

Dearly Beloved

You're early," Reggie said. They had arranged that he would pick her up and they would drive together to the crematorium for Dorothy Padgett's funeral. Jackson was surprised that Reggie was letting him come to her place, she seemed so determined to keep him at arm's length. Although he wouldn't have said it to her, because she was very prickly with him at the moment for some reason, Reggie came under the umbrella of "family" for Jackson. Not the intimate family of Marlee and Nathan and Niamh, but close enough for her to be beneath its shelter.

"Nice to see you too, Reggie. Are you going to keep me standing on the doorstep?" She let him in, rather reluctantly. "Just moved in?" he said, looking around.

"I've been here six months actually."

"Minimalist approach, then."

"I have everything I need," Reggie said defensively.

"You don't even have a television."

"I see your powers of observation are undimmed, Mr. B. I watch stuff on my laptop. That's what the young people do these days."

Jackson ignored the jibe and said, "Are you going to offer me a coffee? We've got a while before the main attraction's due to begin."

Reggie sighed and switched on the coffee machine.

"Nice piece of German kit," he said, admiring the coffee machine's shiny surfaces. Appreciation, not envy. After all, he was living with a woman who had a machine that would have fuelled an espresso bar in Milan station. "Police salaries must have gone up since I was in the force."

"Everything you say is annoying."

"So I've been told. You didn't give that Nancy Styles novel to Forensics, by any chance, did you?"

"No," Reggie said. She had a terrible poker face, but he didn't challenge her and instead said, "It's okay, Reggie, I know you don't want to get involved. No more of that Brodie and Chase stuff from me."

"I know you don't mean that, so don't pretend, Mr. B."

"Me?" he said innocently.

She ignored him while the coffee machine went through its noisy, dramatic performance in order to make a thimbleful of espresso. "You don't have any surprises up your sleeve, do you?" she asked.

"Surprises? Me? No. No surprises." He drained his cup and said, "Better get going, we don't want to miss all the fun, do we?"

➤

"Wow," Reggie said when she saw the Defender. This, Jackson was learning, was turning out to be the usual female reaction to his new vehicle. Not a good "wow," as in, "Wow, what an amazing set of wheels, I wish I had one." No, it was "wow" more in the line of Marlee's "Wow, so the male menopause isn't a myth, then," or Julia's "Wow—a manifestation of your existential dread." Or in Reggie's case, "Wow, Mr. B, flash motor. That's a lot of meals on wheels."

"It's just a jeep," he said, silently apologizing to the Defender. Defender of the faith. Of course it wasn't just a jeep! It was a really covetable off-road vehicle. He'd been flush, he'd had a couple of very good years, and he would have liked to pay cash on the nail for it like a drug dealer or a money-launderer, but Land Rover dealers tended to be suspicious of men who wanted to hand over not much short of £100,000 in folding money. Thanks to Tatiana and her connections, he'd done a lot of work for Russians when the Russians had still been around, and Russians loved cash. They weren't oligarchs, just ordinary people (or at least he had liked to think they were), but even ordinary people if they were Russian made everything seem illegal, even when it wasn't. Or perhaps it was. Lately though, hardly surprisingly, they had melted back into the woodwork. Or Switzerland, perhaps. Or the Caymans. Probably not Russia.

The sensible part of him knew that the Defender might have been a mistake, now that his clients had mostly dried up and he was reduced to the Ians and Hazels of this world for work, but the sensible part of him had some communication problems with the rest of his brain. Wisely, he didn't mention any of this to Reggie, but instead gave her a boost up into the passenger seat. She was short, the Defender was tall. Her own car was a Mini.

"Makes sense," Jackson said.

He started the engine and said to Reggie, "Nothing like a funeral for a good day out, is there?"

"Depends on who's dead," she said.

Dorothy Padgett's funeral was a small, muted affair that took place in the chapel of a crematorium in Halifax. The family comprised the bulk of the mourners. Jackson supposed that by the time you got to Dorothy Padgett's age the Grim Reaper had scythed a swathe through your address book.

If the funeral had been in her home town, Dorothy's neighbour Bob Gordon would have come, but Halifax was a crematorium too far. Jackson remonstrated with himself. He should have offered the man a lift. He might go and visit him when all this was over, take him out to tea at Bettys, buy him a cake made by the hand of a living woman.

Ian and Hazel were present, of course, along with their two-of-each children, some of whom looked as if they thought they had better things to do with their time. A sharp-suited, fortysomething man surreptitiously texted throughout a Katherine Jenkins recording of "Abide with Me" that, thankfully, no one was expected to sing along to. The grandchildren fidgeted uncontrollably until they were quietened by being allowed to play on their phones. Dear God, Jackson thought. Was there nothing left of decorum in this world?

He spotted Moira Jessop keeping a discreet eye on the proceedings and acknowledged her with a little salute. She returned it with a smile.

Ian turned and nodded in recognition at Jackson. Hazel, however, was completely focussed on the cheap coffin, adorned now with a modest spray of white lilies. She was clutching a handkerchief and dabbed her eyes with it occasionally, although it didn't look as if she was managing to produce any tears. The only person who seemed genuinely upset was sitting next to the sharp-suited texting man. The toddler on her knee was asleep and she was weeping quietly so as not to wake him. The texting man frowned occasionally at her show of emotion, as if a funeral wasn't the right place for it. The husband, Jackson thought.

The eulogy was unremarkable. A female vicar, whose claim to have known Dorothy seemed tenuous at best, came out with some bland platitudes about "a life well lived" and "a close, loving family" that she probably recycled for every funeral. Was that better than *She made a good steak pie*? Probably not. Jackson sighed. He had attended too many of these things. Reggie had as well, he supposed. She looked around the chapel and whispered, "Are you thinking that Melanie Hope might come?"

"Don't know," Jackson whispered back. "But she'd have to be in disguise. Although it seems like she might be pretty good at that."

"Let us pray for the soul of Dorothy Padgett," the vicar concluded, and the coffin slid silently behind a pair of royal-blue velvet curtains to begin its journey to the oven, like baggage on an airport carousel. Yeah, Jackson was definitely ticking the box marked "burial at sea."

⌒

They made their way to a local carvery where a perfunctory buffet of sandwiches and sausage rolls was on offer, the celebration of Dorothy Padgett's life not even meriting a joint of beef and a Yorkshire pudding. If Greggs did funerals, Hazel would probably have booked them.

"I'm a vegan," Reggie said, surveying the sad smorgasbord on offer.

"Mm, me too," Jackson said, after inspecting the unappetizing grey filling in a sausage roll. "Today, anyway."

As well as this cold collation ("funeral baked meats," Jackson thought. Where did that phrase come from?), Dorothy Padgett's memory was dispatched with cheap white wine and a whole load more banalities, culminating in Ian raising a glass "To Mum," adding, "At least she's with Dad now." Jackson couldn't help but wonder if Dorothy Padgett would have chosen to spend eternity in the company of Harold Padgett.

Hazel circulated round the room, receiving condolences like a bride accepting congratulations. "Mr. Brodie," she said, eventually acknowledging him. "Nice of you to come. Although I don't recollect inviting you."

"You don't really need an invitation to a funeral. Anyone can come."

Hazel raised an eyebrow at Reggie. "Is this your daughter?"

"No," Reggie said.

"Yes," Jackson said. "Stepdaughter," he modified.

"Yeah," Reggie confirmed grudgingly after he gave her a prod in the back.

"What was that about?" she asked when Hazel had moved on to the next group of mourners.

"Obviously I don't want to highlight the fact that I've brought a 'real' police officer to the funeral."

"Why not?"

"The Padgetts might think I was suspicious of them."

"You *are* suspicious of them."

"I'm suspicious of everyone."

The grieving woman with the toddler from the front row wandered past, the child now hefted over one shoulder. She was trying to deposit a plate that had an empty glass balanced on it. The woman was an accident waiting to happen. Jackson relieved her of the plate and the glass, left her with the toddler. She was almost too grateful.

"Jackson Brodie," he introduced himself. He didn't elaborate. No "used to be a policeman" stuff. Didn't want to scare her away. She had wept in the front row, so she must have cared for her grandmother, and perhaps she might have something useful to say.

"Alice, Alice Smithson. Hazel's daughter," she said.

Alice Smithson didn't look anything like her mother, but interestingly she was quite a good fit for Moira Jessop's description of Jackson's supposed daughter, "Hannah." She was very . . . he tried to think of the word. "Groomed," he decided. Right down to her pale-pink nail varnish. *Nice manicure,* Moira Jessop had said.

She seemed nervy, but maybe it was just the enervation of motherhood. She was stick-thin, but put a bulky puffer jacket on her, pull a woollen hat on her head and get her to step out of her skyscraper heels and she could definitely have passed as the mysterious Hannah, although he couldn't imagine why she would want to do that. Why claim to be a mythical great-niece when you were a genuine granddaughter? Jackson attempted to embark on small talk—*So, how close were you to your gran?*—but the toddler started mewling and Alice said, "I should get going, Freddie's tired."

"You've got a funny look on your face," Reggie said when Alice Smithson had moved on. Would it be a mistake to tell her about his suspicions? he wondered. He hesitated before confessing reluctantly, "I went to visit Dorothy in the funeral home."

"Dorothy? Dead Dorothy? Dead Dorothy Padgett?"

"Yes, that Dorothy."

"Visit?"

"Said I was her nephew."

"Her nephew?"

"Are you going to repeat *everything* I say?"

"Probably."

"There was no post-mortem, so I wanted to have a look at the body."

"Tell me you didn't."

"I did."

"You think there was something fishy about her death?"

"You don't need to sound so thrilled, Reggie."

"Oh, look who's talking. Was there? Something fishy? What on earth were you looking for?"

"I don't know—signs of petechial haemorrhaging?"

"You think she was *smothered*?"

"Shush, keep your voice down," he murmured as several people cast curious glances in their direction. "I tried to take some scrapings from beneath her fingernails, but they'd been cut short by Moira Jessop, the funeral director." He paused for a decent amount of time before adding, "But I managed to get a hair sample."

Reggie stared at him as if he'd just grown a second head. "You think she was poisoned?" she hissed.

Yes, it had been a mistake to tell her, he could see that now. "You're not going to ask if I found any evidence of foul play?"

"Me?" Reggie said. "Oh no, sorry—I was so busy totting up how many crimes you've just admitted to, beginning with impersonating someone and escalating upwards."

"It isn't actually a crime to pretend to be someone else."

"It is if you're doing it for nefarious purposes."

"Nefarious in a good cause, and to answer the question you're dying to ask, no, there were no signs of petechial haemorrhaging."

"And the hair you took from a dead woman's head without anyone's permission? What are you planning to do with it? And please don't say you're going to ask me to have it analysed."

Jackson thought it probably best not to say, "I'm going to give it to my dodgy Russian so-called girlfriend who, it turns out, is studying for a Masters in toxicology." God help mankind when she graduated.

Reggie was practically jumping up and down with indignation, but at that moment Ian Padgett appeared at her shoulder, glass in hand, in bloke-in-a-pub mode. Jackson half expected him to order half a lager top off him. "Did you come on the A65?" he asked. "Traffic was a nightmare. I took the A59 instead. Much better. This your dad?" he said amicably to Reggie.

"Yes," she said. "Best dad in the world."

"No need to overdo it," Jackson murmured.

"Sorry for your loss," she said to Ian. He looked confused for a moment, as if he couldn't remember what it was he was supposed to have lost.

"Your mother," Reggie prompted.

"Er, yeah, thank you. You haven't got a plate, you should have a sausage roll," he said to Reggie. "You look like you could do with putting some meat on your bones. They're paid for."

"Tell me," Jackson said, "do you have anyone called Hannah in the family?"

Ian's face contorted as he seemed to mentally tick off the Padgetts. "Well, let's see, there's an Emily, a Chelsea, a Robin—girl, not boy—a Liam. I've got a nephew by marriage called Sam and a niece the same called Mabel—who thought that name would come back into fashion, eh? And then in my wife's family there's a Haylee with two es, but that's not the same, is it? And then—"

"Thanks, Mr. P," Reggie said, putting them all out of their misery.

"No problem," Ian said. "Any leads?" he asked Jackson.

"A few I'm following up on. Early days still. I'll be in touch." Jackson could do clichés as well as anyone, if necessary.

⌒

"Do you have anything to eat?" Reggie asked, raking through the Defender's glove compartment.

"No eating allowed in the car," Jackson said.

"You must be a fun dad. And *grandad*. Does that make you feel old?"

"Only the way you say it."

He took the little silver disc from his pocket and showed it to her. "A tracker."

"I know what it is. We had a case a few weeks ago—a guy slipped one of these into a girl's handbag at a nightclub. Used it to follow her home. You can imagine the rest. Who would be tracking you? Ian and Hazel? Or one of the thousands of people you've annoyed over the course of your life? Or how about the Russian girlfriend that you think I don't know about?"

"She wouldn't bother with a tracker. She'd send a pack of wolves."

"Perhaps you should get rid of it."

"And not know who's got me in their sights?"

⤐

"Well, thanks, I've had a lovely time," Reggie said when Jackson dropped her back at her flat. "You certainly know how to put the fun into funeral, Mr. B."

"Oh, by the way," he said (a lasso designed to rope her back into the corral), "I thought you might like to know that I wasn't the only one who visited the deceased in the funeral home. Someone called Hannah went to visit Dorothy. Claimed to be a Padgett, but as you heard Ian say, there are no Hannahs in the family."

"Just a Haylee with two *es*. So poor old Dorothy was visited by at least two fraudulent relatives. We know why you went—to steal from and mutilate a corpse—but what did the mysterious Hannah want, do you suppose? Do you think Hannah was Melanie Hope? Saying goodbye to a woman she'd grown fond of? Or perhaps, like you, she was stealing something from her coffin, although what I can't imagine. Perhaps she was putting something *in* her coffin," Reggie mused. "Something she wanted to go up in smoke along with Dorothy."

"I was wondering about Alice Smithson—Hazel's daughter. She fits the description. Of course, it would help if someone could get a look at the CCTV at the funeral home—Jessop's, do you know it? Only the *real* police would be able to access that, though. Day before yesterday, somewhere between three and four in the afternoon. But I've involved you enough, Reggie. Do you want a hand getting out of the car? Or a ladder, maybe?"

"No, I do not," she said crossly, dismounting awkwardly from the Defender, sliding rather gracelessly down to the ground.

"Good to see you, Reggie."

"Mr. Brodie, hang on—"

"Mind how you go. They say it's going to snow later."

Reduced Circumstances

Luncheon had been a sparse meal of cold ham alongside a Russian salad made with the potatoes from last night's dinner, which were now an unappetizing grey colour. Despite Lady Milton's expectation that she would die in harness, Cook had in fact left them in the lurch to go and live in Thirsk with her daughter, and now they had a woman called Mrs. Bradfield who came up from the village every day and who couldn't even make a decent egg custard, let alone pluck a pheasant. No point in feeling sorry for yourself, Lady Milton thought. At least she was still here, unlike poor Johnny. ("Still here, Ma?" was Cosmo's way of greeting her whenever he turned up.)

Nowadays, Lady Milton usually ate in solitary silence from a tray on her lap. It was at times like this that she was surprised to find herself missing Johnny. He must have been more of a companion than she had realized. He did not last long after the Turner was stolen, dropping head first into a plate of soup at dinner like a character in an old-fashioned farce. Indeed, Andrew the footman had barked with laughter before understanding he was witnessing a tragedy rather than a comedy. He had become quite hysterical when he grasped that Johnny was dead.

In the intermission between the theft of the Turner and Johnny's death, Piers had decided to appoint a replacement for Chalmers, their old butler. The new man, Henderson, was cut from a very different cloth to Chalmers. He claimed to have a qualification in "butlerdom," something that Lady Milton had never heard of and which sounded rather absurd. After Sophie's false reference she was less inclined to trust such things.

Henderson did more or less everything now, none of it terribly well. He knew very little about claret. Sometimes Lady Milton would come across him gazing thoughtfully at a painting or a bit of Meissen or the pair of battered old Canova lions at the front door and he would say to her, "How much do you think that's worth, then?" And he was from Australia! Whoever had ever heard of an Antipodean butler? Irish at a pinch, perhaps, but Australian? "Breath of fresh air," Piers said. Lady Milton preferred the old stale air. Also, Henderson had an unnerving habit of entering a room very quietly, as if he had paws for feet. He seemed to think it was a butler's duty to glide around silently, but Lady Milton preferred her servants to give her plenty of warning when they were arriving. ("Staff, Ma," Piers reminded her. "They don't like the word 'servants.' ")

Still, Henderson had been a good deal more help than Andrew when Johnny died, running in to give him the kiss of life, or whatever it was called now. May as well have been the kiss of death for all the good it did. By the time Lady Milton got there it was all over.

Mushroom, as it happened, was a soup Johnny had been fond of, so at least his last meal had been something he liked. Trudi had picked the mushrooms herself. Being European, she claimed to know about these things. Piers, lunching with his father, had been the sole family witness to his father's demise. Johnny was the only one to eat the soup, but the pathologist was confident his death had nothing to do with what he had eaten. He was an old pal of Piers from Cambridge, it turned out. A stroke, he pronounced. "The stress of the burglary, probably." It was true, Johnny had been apoplectic over the loss of the Turner, more so than he had been when Cosmo sold the Raphael. They had almost *expected* Cosmo to betray them, but Sophie was an outsider, worming her way into the heart of the family, eating their trust.

The two events—the robbery and Johnny's death—the one following so close on the other, were now entwined in Lady Milton's mind. It was a tangled thicket at the best of times, but sometimes it felt as though Sophie had stolen not the Turner but Johnny himself.

The Turner had been placed on something called the Lost Art Registry, a name that struck Lady Milton as rather poignant. Poignancy was a new emotion for her. It was uncomfortable. And now poor old Johnny was on a lost registry too.

The Art and Antiques unit of the Metropolitan Police reported back to them occasionally, but no progress seemed to have been made. The chances of getting the painting back, especially after all this time, were virtually nil, according to them. The Turner, like Johnny, had disappeared without a trace.

The money from the insurance still hadn't come through, but Piers had recklessly borrowed against it to turn the Rookery into Rook Hall and fulfil his madcap scheme to become a hotelier. (How could you have a hotel *in* a house? It made no sense.) And now more money had been soaked up by his divorce from Trudi. Nothing to do with the mushrooms, of course. Although things had turned rather frosty after Lady Milton had suggested—just a suggestion, not an accusation—that they might have been responsible for Johnny's downfall.

Since then, Trudi had decamped with a pop singer. "A hip-hop artist, Ma," Cosmo corrected her. Lady Milton couldn't even *begin* to imagine what that meant. She still had her own hips. She intended to die with them. Trudi had taken all the poppets with her, didn't even say goodbye, and now she was living in a gated community in California, spending all the Milton money, according to Cosmo. The roof would never be fixed properly now. It would cave in eventually and crush them all in their beds. "The Fall of the House of Milton," Cosmo said, making it sound like a horror story.

Cosmo was living at Burton Makepeace at the moment, lying low because of a "four in a bed" scandal in the *Sun* newspaper. It was not a reference to the television programme of the same name where people stayed in each other's bed-and-breakfast establishments, which Lady Milton had found herself accidentally watching recently. She had never stayed in a B&B and supposed she never would now.

Cosmo told her that he was hoping to revive his fortunes with something called *Made in Chelsea*. Lady Milton thought he said "maid" and presumed it was something pornographic. "It is," Arabella said. "Besides, they're only interested in twentysomethings." ("I *am* twentysomething," Cosmo said. "You're forty-two," Arabella said caustically.) Perhaps Cosmo took after his grandfather, the Old Marquess, who had a collection that Lady Milton avoided by never opening a book in the Library in case it was one of his "special" ones.

⁓

Before his untimely death, Johnny had put up a rear-guard fight with Piers over the hotel, but Piers had been determined to plough ahead with it. Johnny had spent his last weeks on this Earth closeted in his study, plotting to disinherit both Piers and Cosmo. He had tried to persuade Arabella to have a sex change (it wouldn't take much) so that she could inherit the title instead, but she wasn't accommodating. Then, of course, poor Johnny handily succumbed to the mushrooms.

Inocybe rimosa. It was a mushroom whose effect mimicked the signs of a stroke. Lady Milton had found it "on line." She loved saying, "I have been on line." It made her sound so modern. She had bought an iPad and signed up for a "Get to Know the Internet" class held at the local village hall. There were six of them in the class, all of a certain age, including Marian Forster and the church organist, Derek Truitt, who was extremely gallant. He called her Lady, as if that was her Christian name. Or perhaps he thought it was. He might have been teasing, she couldn't be sure. He was fond of the Labradors. Before the class, Lady Milton had never touched a keyboard, not once! It was really quite thrilling. Sophie would have been proud of her.

Their little group had become friendly, they had even come to take tea at the house and endured Mrs. Bradfield's baking—scones that could have been substituted for cannonballs. They had several cannons up on the crenellated roof—the battlements. Johnny always used to say they would come in useful if they ever found themselves under siege. They were always under siege, mostly from the Inland Revenue.

Lady Milton missed her new friends. Perhaps she could invite them to tea again. They had asked her if she would like to come to their prayer group, "at Janet's, every Thursday morning, but really it's just a social gathering." She had demurred. Prayer wasn't really Lady Milton's thing; nor were social gatherings, for that matter. Although it would be an excuse to spend some time with Derek—oh, stop it, Honoria! Really, what was the good of harbouring feelings. Look where they had got her last time. (Cosmo. Exactly.)

Lady Milton had hoped to have been banished to the Dower House by now, but instead Piers had let it out as an "Airbnb," which was just a badly spelled bed and breakfast without the breakfast, as far as she could see. The shepherd's cottage had gone the same way, ditto the forester's. The dairy cottage had been sold to two pleasant women from London who now called it Dairy Cottage with capitals. One, Fran, was a vet—which was handy as the poppets had left behind their attention-seeking ponies.

Although still in its infancy, Rook Hall was not proving to be quite the unmitigated success that Piers had hoped for. People came, but not in droves. They booked mainly for the "Country House Weekend package," which involved things like an early-morning shooting party (in season, but sometimes, Lady Milton had noticed, just a little bit *out* of season. Her father would have shot Piers for treason). The shoots were for game birds, but sometimes Piers transported a few deer from the deer park on to the moors. They were so tame that they provided easy targets for the hotel's guests, most of whom had never seen a shotgun, let alone fired one. The weekend package also included a "private, behind-the-scenes" tour of the main house that Piers himself conducted, lecturing grandiosely on the "artefacts" in the house. They weren't artefacts, they were their belongings!

Lady Milton herself was occasionally wheeled out for "pre-dinner drinks with the family." Piers always introduced her to the guests with, "May I present the Dowager Marchioness Lady Milton," and then they all expected her to behave as if she were a member of the cast of *Downton Abbey* and to say pithy things. They were nice enough, nicer than her own family anyway. She never used the term "dowager" herself. Daughters-in-law may come and go—mostly go—but there could only ever be one Lady Milton and it was herself. "Perfect, Ma," Piers said. "Maggie Smith couldn't have said it better herself."

〜

The house had closed early today—there had been hardly any visitors because of the weather forecast. The guides all wanted to get home before they got stuck, but so far only a few flakes of snow had fallen. Mrs. Bradfield reported to Lady Milton that she was off (like old game), and had put aside some soup and cold salmon for supper. Lady Milton thought that when she said "off" Mrs. Bradfield meant that she was going home, but it turned out she was merely crossing the velvet rope that formed the barrier between the private quarters of the house and the hotel. "Going to help with the cooking over there," she said. "They're short-handed." God help the guests, Lady Milton thought, if they were hoping to survive on Mrs. Bradfield's cuisine.

It was all hands on deck, apparently, even Cosmo's, because Piers was hosting a new enterprise—a Murder Mystery Weekend. Piers was in a stew because the hotel manager, a man called Glen, had "gone AWOL." Lady Milton had had one or two hostile encounters with Glen, who seemed to regard her as an object to be removed, like unwanted furniture. He had requested, via Piers, that she not wander into the hotel as though she owned it. She startled the guests, apparently. The cheek of the man! Glen's absence wasn't the only problem. Piers was facing wholesale rebellion on the part of the hotel staff, due to the meagreness of their wages and the length of their working day. "Pathetic" was Piers' judgement on this dereliction of duty. He had bussed in agency staff for the Murder Mystery tonight. "Come and join us, Ma," he said. "We could do with an extra corpse and you're not far off qualifying."

Flora and Fauna, Arabella's twins, had also been off-loaded on them for half-term. The entire family—apart from Arabella, thank God—was now squashed into the small part of the house that contained their private quarters. It was ridiculous, like an awful game of Sardines—which was something that Lady Milton's sisters used to like to play. The objective of the game being to suffocate the littlest one. Honoria, needless to say. "The runt of the litter," their mother called her.

The Murder Mystery Weekend was indeed a mystery to Lady Milton.

"Actors," Piers said.

"Actors?"

"Yes, actors. Acting. They'll be arriving soon. Hopefully. It's like a whodunit. They act out a series of murders, *en promenade*—ambulatory, as it were—in the house, and the guests must work out who the murderer is."

"Why?" Lady Milton puzzled.

"Fun," Piers said, frowning. "I'm worried they're not going to get through this snow, though. I'd better go and phone them and check on their progress." He hurried off.

Was it possible that he had poisoned his father? There was no way it could be proved, of course, unless you exhumed poor old Johnny from the family plot in the local graveyard. Piers had pushed for cremation. Lady Milton had resisted. Miltons didn't go up in flames, they rotted slowly, giving themselves back to the earth in exchange for everything they had plundered from it over the centuries. Best not to think too much about it. And avoid the mushrooms.

—

Lady Milton was currently taking tea in the small sitting room that she had been relegated to since Rook Hall opened. An unwilling waitress from the hotel had brought the tray, laid not with the Miltons' lovely, ancient Crown Derby but the bland white catering service that Rook Hall employed. Tea-bags in the teapot and a plate with a pair of custard creams that were pre-wrapped and branded with the hotel's "logo" (a new word to Lady Milton), which was just a bastardization of the family crest. Lady Milton sighed with disappointment. The waitress reported that this was her last day in "this miserable dump" and then she flounced off, nearly knocking over (possibly on purpose) one of the Worcester plates that sat on the upright Bechstein that had been shoehorned into the room. It hadn't been played since Sophie left. She occasionally used to laugh and say, "Shall I tickle the ivories for you, Lady Milton? Nothing too challenging—a bit of Liszt, perhaps?" She knew Lady Milton's tastes were lightweight. (Nothing to be ashamed of in that.)

Before she could unwrap the biscuits on the tea-tray, Lady Milton was startled by a disturbingly loud *thud-thud-thud*, climaxing in a tremendous crash. It was exactly the kind of noise that Nanny would make if she fell down the stairs.

A few moments later, Flora and Fauna appeared in the doorway of her sitting room, looking unusually wide-eyed and attentive. Lady Milton braced herself for disaster.

"Is it Nanny?" she hazarded.

Both girls nodded mutely.

"Is she dead?" Lady Milton asked hopefully.

This was exactly the kind of crisis that Sophie would have managed so well. Nanny was quite clearly dead—Lady Milton had seen enough dead people to know one when she saw one—so she didn't know why Piers was fretting that the phone lines were down and he couldn't conjure up an ambulance. What Nanny needed was an undertaker.

The twins were now sitting at the foot of the main staircase, gazing in fascination at Nanny, like ghouls waiting for the signal to start feasting. "It's our first dead body," one of them said. "Well, it won't be your last," Lady Milton said briskly. It did cross her mind that Flora and Fauna might have pushed Nanny downstairs, heaven knows she had wanted to do it herself often enough.

"Why don't you try and move her to somewhere more convenient?" she said to the twins. It would be good for them to have a task as they were astonishingly lazy. They certainly didn't get that from Arabella. "She can't stay here. People will have to step over her. It's extremely awkward." They made no effort to move either themselves or Nanny. Lady Milton abdicated her duty. Let someone else deal with it for once, she thought. "Come on," she said to the dogs. "Let's go." They were alarmed and excited in equal measure by the tone of her voice.

She heard a faint cry ("Ma, where are you going?") from the innards of the house as she pulled on her old Barbour and dragged her Hunters out from where they lived in the Boot Room. Last of all, she took a shotgun and cartridges from the Gun Room. Always best to be prepared. Nanny was so resilient it wouldn't have surprised Lady Milton if she hadn't already turned up as a ghost in the yew.

Outside, the yard was already covered in a deep layer of snow. Not enough to deter the ancient Land Rover. The heating, such as it was, never worked properly and its insides always smelt of diesel and wet dog, laid over the scent of generations of dead game birds. It was a vehicle that Lady Milton was unreasonably fond of. Her father had always driven a Land Rover on his estate and it had never occurred to her to do otherwise. Her father, the Duke, had killed himself in his vehicle, firing off a shotgun into his mouth, an awkward thing to do at the best of times, let alone in a Land Rover. Lady Milton had rehearsed it, just to see.

Her father had never really become comfortable with being the head of the family. "Not born to it, you see," he said to her once. He'd had two older brothers, both killed in the First World War when he was still at school. And he'd had no sons himself. The line had ended in daughters, as it said in Debrett's. Girls, let's face it, were a curse on a family.

The snow seemed to turn from benign to blizzard in a moment and was suddenly so fierce that she was driving almost blind. The Land Rover's engine, usually so robust, was complaining in a way that sounded rather threatening. In the back, the dogs, disturbed by the weather, were sitting up, alert, fighting to keep their balance. Lady Milton was also beginning to feel a little nervous, although she wouldn't have admitted it, not even to herself. Certainly not to the dogs.

She pushed on stubbornly past the point of no return. It was only snow, she reminded herself. People made such a fuss these days about the weather. About everything! In the old days you just got on with things. Nobody got on with anything any more.

Without warning, the faithful Land Rover began to drift slowly, almost carefully, into a bank of snow and came to a gentle but decisive halt. "Bugger," Lady Milton said.

She struggled out of the vehicle and retrieved the spade from its customary place in the back. "Never be without a spade," her father used to say. "You can never tell when it might come in handy." Lady Milton felt the same about hip flasks. She had a lovely engraved one, given to her by Johnny on their silver wedding anniversary. She could feel the comforting weight of it in the Barbour's pocket.

The dogs would usually have jumped out and bounded around excitedly, but they stuck their heads out cautiously to inspect the snow and decided against it. They were going soft in their old age, Lady Milton thought. She had no intention of doing the same.

The snow was blowing almost horizontally and she felt her face icing up immediately. The snowflakes seemed to be sticking to her eyeballs. Lady Milton had come out *sans* gloves and with only an old silk head square for protection up top. If it had been good enough for the Queen, it was good enough for her, although perhaps not in a blizzard.

She persisted, shovelling snow from in front of the Land Rover. It took less than a minute for her to realize what a hopeless task this was. Beaten by the elements, she fought her way back inside the

Land Rover and took a long draught of Johnny's best cognac from the hip flask. Now what? she wondered.

If she stayed with the Land Rover she might be buried alive. No one was going to find her here. No vehicle would make it through behind her and no one at home had any idea where she was anyway. It would take for ever for a search party to come across her. All she had with her was the hip flask and the little packet of custard creams that she'd absent-mindedly thrust in her pocket when Nanny had fallen downstairs. She could be here until the spring, when someone stumbled across her frozen corpse thawing out.

She took another swig of the cognac. She would have to walk, there was nothing else for it. Probably die out here, but nothing ventured, nothing gained. The Milton family's piratical motto, more or less. *Fortuna fortes adiuvat*. Latin had not been on the syllabus at Lady Milton's girls' school. It was a small establishment that had concentrated on subjects like deportment and the correct way to address a viscount. And French, of course. They made a point of how useful an accomplishment French would be to the girls in their future lives. Not true!

The snow was already piling up against the Land Rover and for an awful moment Lady Milton thought she might be trapped inside. She pushed hard against the door and tumbled straight out on to the ground, landing with a painful bump on her tail-bone. Really, she thought, this was becoming absurd. She was glad no one could see her, only the dogs, and they probably thought it was a game. Unusually, she found herself wishing that Arabella was here. Out of everyone in the family, she was the most likely one to get them out of this dilemma, if only through sheer brute strength.

The shovel had long since been swallowed by the snow, but Lady Milton took the shotgun from the Land Rover. She wasn't entirely sure why. Perhaps she would need to find something to kill and eat. (Raw? Could she? Like a savage? Probably.) Or the dogs. Would she eat the dogs if it came to it? That was always the question, wasn't it? She supposed she would die of hypothermia long before hunger and she wouldn't have to face that particular problem.

"Out," she said to the laggardly dogs. "No dissension in the ranks. Come on."

～

What seemed like days passed as she flailed and floundered in the snow. Lady Milton had no idea where she was. There was no sign of a road or a path or a fence, just endless uncorrupted snow. Then suddenly there was a light in the distance. A lovely warm yellow light gleaming faintly through the thick curtain of white that was falling all around. Was it a mirage? You got them in the desert, did you get them in the snow, too? Was she imagining this heart-warming beacon? She must get a grip, mustn't fall prey to hallucinations. That had been Ariadne, Piers' first wife. Always seeing things that weren't there. Said she was being "gaslit" by Piers, which was ridiculous, there'd been no gas lamps in the house since long before the war.

The light seemed to shimmer in a halo of snow. Was it the church? There was always a light on in the church—dreadful waste of electricity. The Reverend Cate said it was important that there always be "a light burning in the darkness." Previously she would have dismissed this as his usual feeble nonsense, but now she was glad of it because she knew where she was—she must have strayed into the deer park. Just as she made up her mind to set out and follow the light, it disappeared and a figure loomed into view. It was a wraith-like creature that seemed to be made from snow. For an awful moment she thought it might be Nanny. Out here anything seemed suddenly possible, even a snow-woman version of Nanny lumbering towards her.

The light returned just as suddenly as it had disappeared, on the move, approaching, nearer and nearer.

"Steady the buffs," Lady Milton said to herself, lifting the barrel of the shotgun and talking into the snow. "Halt!" she said in the voice she had to use sometimes to the dogs. "Who goes there?"

Jeopardy

George had gone to forage for Seville oranges in Hebden Bridge to make marmalade later and Fran was out somewhere, killing some poor creature, so Ben spent a pleasantly solitary morning chopping more logs.

Chop, chop, chop. There was something satisfyingly brutal about chopping wood—the primitive act of slamming an axe into an adversary, even if that adversary was only innocent pine, had an air of revenge about it. Displaced, obviously. These days, if Ben were ever actually to come face to face with the man who had planted the IED that had blown up his life, he suspected he would probably shake his hand and say something about letting bygones be bygones. The Jennings were unfailingly polite, even to their enemies, unless they were actually killing them. *Chop, chop, chop.*

It was a brilliantly cold morning, the sky a bright winter blue, and he was having a hard time believing the forecast of heavy snow later. George and Fran had been less sceptical, they had grown used to the capricious nature of the weather here. Fran returned in time for lunch and said that she had been up at Burton Makepeace as one of the ponies needed an injection.

"Not a lethal one?" Ben said. The idea of killing a horse seemed particularly horrible to him.

"No, no. God, no. Just an antibiotic. Did you know they're having a Murder Mystery thing up at Rook Hall this weekend? Could be fun," she added, looking rather wistful. Was his sister getting enough fun? Ben wondered. She spent most of her time euthanizing creatures with fur, and on the home front George could be rather dour, to put it mildly.

Jemima had once dragged him along to a play by the crime novelist Nancy Styles. Jemima was a theatrical agent, and it was her job, she said, to go along and effuse over the performances of her clients. The Styles was a long-running play, the audience mainly consisting of tourists and coachloads of pensioners bussed in from the provinces. *The Body Walks*—that was the title, he remembered now—had an endlessly revolving cast and Jemima always seemed to have at least one of her clients in it. Which probably explained why as soon as she was settled in her seat she closed her eyes and fell fast asleep. She woke up for the ice-cream he fetched her in the interval and then promptly fell back asleep, waking again just before the dénouement so that she could reveal to Ben, and half the stalls, the identity of the murderer. He had feared that the audience was going to lynch her.

The Body Walks had been peopled with all the stock characters that usually appeared in Nancy Styles' bloodless plots. Ben had read the entire oeuvre during the course of the rainy afternoons of his school holidays. The novels belonged to his father, who was a surprising devotee of crime fiction. The books, all first-edition hardbacks that might be worth something now, contained a cast of retired majors, country vicars and amateur sleuths, not to mention English and foreign aristocrats, mysterious strangers, lovely young girls and slinky temptresses. Would Burton Makepeace's Murder Mystery Weekend take its inspiration from Styles? "I believe so," Fran said. "Butlers and corpses everywhere, I should think."

～

Lunch was a rehash of last night's supper, indeterminate hearty vegetarian fare, composed mainly of lentils and turnips. Ben didn't mind, in fact he was quite relieved not to be eating something that had lived its life blithely unaware that it was heading towards the slaughterhouse. He thought of Waterloo, Culloden, the Somme—what were they, if not abattoirs? He had studied them all at Sandhurst. He still conceded the Somme to Jemima.

Jemima wouldn't have given a lentil the time of day. She liked "fine dining." She had always been dragging him off to new restaurants. She took him once to some two-star Michelin place in London where he'd been served a roast woodcock that had been neatly split down the middle and opened like a book. Handing him a teaspoon, the waiter said, "For scooping the brains out with, sir." He hadn't. Sometimes the image came back to him—the small head, a couple of tiny charred feathers still stuck to the beak. It gave a whole new meaning to "bird brain."

"Well, you know, Ben," Jemima had said, in her "reasonable" voice, "if you feel queasy at the prospect, perhaps you should become a vegetarian. Meat's meat, you can't pick and choose the bits that seem more *acceptable*." She was eating rabbit. Its liver and kidneys had been made into a little parcel, tied with a string bean. "And anyway," she said, "you *shoot* people, for heaven's sake." (As if that was a logical sequitur!)

"I don't eat them though," he pointed out.

Could he eat a person? he wondered. The plane crash in the frozen wastes, the last days of Earth after Armageddon? Probably not. Although, if push came to shove, he was prepared to fine-dine on Jemima.

"Good God, Benedict," his mother had said, "are you not over that girl yet?"

Apparently not.

⌒

The sky had turned from blue to grey and small flakes of snow began to flutter about. Within a short space of time they began to look more purposeful.

They battened down the hatches—George shut the hens in, Fran the goats, and Ben went to check on the bees. Somewhere in the mountain of literature on beekeeping that he had worked his way through he had read that the brightness of snow could fool them into thinking it was warm enough to leave the hive. He had already prepared some small pieces of wood to block the entrances and now he placed them like little doors on the hives. Ever since Simon Cate's blessing of the bees in the summer, Ben found that his emotions seemed to be dependent on the bees' welfare, if not their actual happiness. When they harvested the honey, George complained that he had left too much of it for the bees themselves, but how could it be right to rob them of the fruits of their industry? "Christ, he'll be a vegan next," George said.

George and Fran embarked on their marathon marmalade-making session with the crate of gnarled Sevilles, and Ben, having run out of anything useful to do, made a fire and sat by it, listening to *The Marriage of Figaro* on his headphones, his hand resting lightly on the head of a big old toffee-coloured Labrador that had quietly collapsed against his thigh. He had a book about Buddhist meditation open on his lap, but he was having trouble concentrating on the words. Fran had given it to him, saying it might help him simply to accept what had happened and stop trying to make sense of it. "I mean the IED," she said quietly, as if it might still explode in their faces even after all this time. "It wasn't *personal*, Ben." Of course it was personal! It had blown him up. You didn't get more personal than that. "Anyway," she said, "I just thought, you know . . . meditation, maybe." The very idea of meditation made him feel irritable—he would rather be smashing axes into things—but he said, "Thanks. Thanks a lot, I'll certainly give it a try."

The Labrador gave an immense sigh and Ben thought, I know, I know, me too. The Countess had embarked on *"Dove Sono."* Too sad, he thought, and felt a sudden overwhelming need to be moving, to be outside. Not to feel so *trapped* all the time. Trapped by himself, by "poor old Ben."

"All right?" Fran asked, putting her head round the door and letting in great wafts of warm, sugary, orange-scented air. He removed his headphones, hoping she wasn't going to suggest something up-lifting. "Enjoying the book?"

"Absolutely!"

"The kettle's on, do you want a cuppa?"

"No, thanks. I'm going to pop out for a bit," he said, gently dis-lodging the Labrador's head from his thigh.

"Walking? In this snow?"

"I've done cold-weather training in northern Norway in minus twenty-five, Fran, a bit of Yorkshire snow doesn't bother me. And I like snow."

"Sorry, sorry, sweetheart, I was just thinking, you know . . ."

"The Leg? It might be gammy, but it can manage a bit of snow. Thought I'd go round the deer park. It'll be pretty. I could take a dog," he offered. "Do you think any of them are up to it?" He cast a doubtful eye around the ragbag assortment on offer. Fran picked out a small, sad-eyed spaniel. "Take Holly," she said. The dog looked entirely unsuitable to Ben, who usually took a (slightly) more robust retriever. His sister pulled a jumper over the dog's head. The jumper was a cheerful, stripy garment, knitted (very badly) by George. "You know, knitting's supposed to be good for depression," Fran had said to him the other day. "Perhaps you should give it a go." He added it to the list of good ideas. Meditation, wild swimming, climbing Mount Kilimanjaro, gong baths. It seemed unlikely that he would take up any of them. Ever.

"Keep her on a lead," Fran said. "The Miltons will shoot if they think she's going after the deer. They're a trigger-happy lot. And take your phone. And be careful, Ben."

I was one of the youngest majors in the Army, he thought, shrugging on his big Arctic parka and pulling on his watch cap. I've led men into battle. I've watched people die. I've killed people, for God's sake. I think I'll be all right. He didn't say any of those things, of course, because they sounded petulant and ungrateful, although he did shut the back door with unnecessary force, something he regretted afterwards, but it was too late to apologize.

The snow on his face felt good, icy and fresh. It had already settled on the ground, meaning business now. When they reached the gates to the deer park Ben dutifully clipped the lead on the dog, even though she didn't look capable of chasing anything, let alone a deer. She gazed at him with big, trusting eyes. "Just a quick walk, old girl," he reassured her.

The deer park belonged to the Milton family, but the public were allowed access to it. Ben had never met any of the Miltons, never been inside Burton Makepeace House. The Miltons were all "mad as hatters," according to Fran.

He followed what was still visible of the path that threaded its way through an avenue of old limes before crossing the deer park and ending up at the church on the far side. There was an other-worldly silence, everything muffled and muted by the snow. No sign of any deer, no sign of anyone. He was beginning to wish that his sister hadn't used the phrase "trigger-happy." The two words had made the deer park suddenly seem less of a place of safety and more of a firing range. "Pull yourself together, Ben," he admonished him-self. "This is the last place anyone's going to pull a gun on you."

Ben was relieved when he reached the church. It was like a refrig-erator inside its walls, but his leg—or what was left of it—was ach-ing. He had chopped logs this morning like a maniac and now he was paying the price for it.

He took a seat in a pew near the back and parked the dog next to him, as the flagstones were too brutal with cold. Closing his eyes, he relented and attempted to meditate so that he could truthfully tell his sister that he had given it a go. ("Didn't really work for me, Fran. Sorry.") Not prayer. Prayer always felt like begging. He had attended a Church of England boarding school that catered for the sons of military officers along with the minor aristocracy. The chaplain was forever walloping the boys as if they were large dogs or roaring at them to run faster. He coached the Lower School at rugby, which although it was treated as a religion was as far from spirituality as it was possible to be.

When Ben opened his eyes, he nearly jumped out of his skin at the sight of Simon Cate, who had materialized from nowhere and was standing as silent as an apparition in front of the altar, regarding him with equal alarm. He probably wasn't expecting to find anyone in the church in this weather (or any weather, to be honest).

Simon Cate mimed his surprise by making his eyes comically wide and beating a little tom-tom on his chest with one hand as if to demonstrate how fast his heart was going. He nodded and grinned, and when Ben said, "Hello, Vicar—Simon—how are you?" he nodded and grinned even more vigorously and gave Ben a thumbs-up sign. Then he pointed at Ben and raised his eyebrows enquiringly, which Ben interpreted as a reciprocal enquiry into his own state of happiness or otherwise. Without really meaning to, Ben began to participate in the dumbshow, giving the vicar two thumbs back, as if raising the ante. The vicar seemed so pleased by this that Ben thought if he could have done, he would have trumped him with a third thumb.

Perhaps he was afflicted in some way. Laryngitis maybe, or a throat operation. Ben said, rather more loudly than he'd intended, "Well, I'd best be off, Vicar, before we get trapped here by the snow."

Simon Cate made a clown-face of horror at the idea and then grinned again. Should Ben offer to squire him home to the vicarage? As if reading his mind, the antic Simon made a pantomime of shaking his head and pretended to shoo Ben out of the church.

Ben woke the dog. She had not been a participant in the mummery and looked as surprised to see Simon Cate as Ben had been. The vicar did a little jig of delight when he saw the dog, as if they were old acquaintances. The dog was more restrained.

"Well, goodbye again," Ben said and was rewarded with another sad clown-face from Simon Cate. He put his hand up as if in benediction, but then moved it from side to side like a puppet. A gesture of farewell, Ben understood. He gave a little wave back. Simon Cate was still grinning like a loon. The man had gone mad, Ben thought.

He must have been inside the church for longer than he thought, as outside the light was fading fast and a blizzard was raging, visibility no more than a few inches in front of him. "Capricious" hardly described the mutant change in the weather.

Ben had a small torch, he never left home without a torch, a knife and a length of thin rope in his pocket. Be prepared. None of those things were much good in the snow. All the torch did was illuminate a world pixelated by snowflakes. "Shit," he murmured to the dog, who was floundering helplessly in the snow. She was shivering and there were already lumps of ice clinging to her fur. Ben picked her up and tucked her awkwardly inside his parka, leaving her head free in case she thought he was trying to suffocate her. How long-suffering dogs were, how uncomplaining. He would try to be more like a dog in future. A purposeful collie, perhaps. Or a big, easy-going Leonberger.

They would have to return to the church, but as soon as Ben had that thought he realized that the church and the deranged Simon Cate within it had already been swallowed up by the snow. Still, Ben had faith in his orienteering skills. He knew that the church nestled on the east side of the deer park, so all he had to do was to find the guideline of the perimeter fence and he would—inevitably—end up back at Dairy Cottage.

Or not.

He had no idea how, but the fence also disappeared almost immediately, leaving him lost in the middle of a giant snow globe that was being shaken incessantly by an unseen hand. ("Don't be fanciful, Benedict," he could hear his mother saying.) The compass on his phone was no use as the phone had seized up in the cold. If we walk in a straight line, he reasoned to the dog, then eventually logic dictated that they would come to a boundary. Of course, he had no way of knowing if he was walking in a straight line, and after he had trudged on for what seemed for ever it was hard to avoid the conclusion that he was probably just going round in circles. So much for Arctic warfare training. He was only too aware of the absurdity of the situation. He couldn't be more than a couple of hundred yards from shelter of one kind or another. And that was exactly how people died.

He yomped on though, trying to conjure the spirit of Shackleton. Ben admired Shackleton enormously. He had cared about the survival of his men more than he had cared for himself or for glittering prizes. Ben no longer had men, of course, all he had was a small, cold dog, but nonetheless she represented as much of an obligation as the entire crew of the *Endurance*.

How much time had passed? Hours? Minutes? Ben was completely disorientated by now, his vision blurred from continually trying to make sense of nothing but a veil of snowflakes. Shapes occasionally seemed to start to emerge out of the veil like wraiths, but then failed to resolve into anything tangible. He supposed he was beginning to hallucinate. Perhaps it was time to accept his fate—lie down somewhere and fade upon the midnight with no pain. Everyone said hypothermia was an easy death, like falling asleep. Would he really be missed? He certainly wouldn't miss himself. His frozen corpse would be found in the morning and there'd be a few "poor old Bens," but people would soon get over it. But then, he had the dog to consider. It hardly seemed fair to subject it to an icy death in the snow when it had been promised a gentle end at a friendly fireside. Shackleton would not have lain down in the snow, he reminded himself.

He could feel the little dog's heartbeat, a fast pulse against his own surprisingly strong and steady beat. It was a long time—since Jemima, in fact—since he had felt a heartbeat next to his. He felt a sudden surge of compassion for the world in general, for the dog in particular. "Come on, now," he said softly in the dog's frozen ear, "best paw forward."

His leg hurt like blazes. Just when he had reached the point where it seemed physically impossible, when the snow was no longer a veil but a solid wall, he was suddenly assaulted by a high-pitched, strident voice shouting at him, "Halt! Who goes there?" Had he somehow wandered on to MOD land? But did anyone say, "Halt! Who goes there?" outside of old Second World War films? He had never heard anyone say it when he was in the Army.

"Identify yourself," the voice commanded.

"I'm Ben Jennings," he said. "Major Benedict Jennings," he added, in case it *was* MOD land.

He waited for an introduction, but the next thing he knew, there was a gun being shoved into his stomach.

Peril

R eggie was sitting in a café that was neither clean nor particularly well lit, finishing *The Secret of the Clock Cabinet* in the company of an underwhelming hummus wrap. The lack of anything that might be called edible at Dorothy Padgett's funeral earlier meant that she had had nothing but coffee all day. She was beginning to feel quite bilious, although that might equally be as a result of reading Nancy Styles' novel.

The murderer in *The Secret of the Clock Cabinet* wasn't revealed until the very final page and, infuriatingly, Reggie had failed to work out who it was. It was a case of: think of the most unlikely character to have committed the murder—several murders, in fact—and then right at the end suddenly reveal their identity, without ever really having seeded them into the plot or written a convincing narrative journey for them.

She could hear Jackson Brodie's voice in her head saying, "Bit of an over-reaction there, don't you think?" That made her even more irritated—she didn't want him as an inner commentator, didn't want to be measuring her conduct against the yardstick of his opinion. Damn him. He had reignited her curiosity about the Burton Makepeace case. She wouldn't rest until she had gone back there and shown the Miltons the photo of Melanie Hope that he had given her, to see if they thought it might be Sophie Greenway.

Was there a connection between the theft at the Willows and that at Burton Makepeace? If there was, she wanted to be the one who discovered it, not Jackson Brodie. She phoned Josh in Forensics and asked if he had retrieved any fingerprints off *Hark! Hark! The Dogs Do Bark* from Dorothy Padgett's and if he could match them to anything at Burton Makepeace.

Sophie Greenway's *The Secret of the Clock Cabinet* had been dusted for fingerprints at the time of the Turner theft, along with much else. Reggie remembered only too clearly the farcical fight the police had had trying to garner everyone's prints for elimination. Lady Milton had been particularly intransigent.

"Fingerprinted like a common criminal," she complained. "Why don't you just put me in handcuffs and throw me in an *oubliette*?" (All of the Miltons displayed a flair for over-dramatizing.)

"Normal police procedure," Reggie kept saying patiently, until Lady Milton finally agreed to getting her fingers inked.

And then, of course, there were the staff, or "the servants" as Lady Milton referred to them, as if they were flunkies from the court of Ruritania. They all kicked up a fuss as well, particularly Andrew Baker, whom Lady Milton referred to as the "head footman" although actually he was the only footman. Andrew wasn't even his real name, he was called Kyle, but Lady Milton said their head footman had been called Andrew from time immemorial and anyway she didn't like the name Kyle. Cook had no name at all other than Cook, as far as Lady Milton was concerned. "It's Linda Bagshaw actually," Reggie informed her.

"Well, she'll always be Cook to me."

Fingerprinting had been no help at all, except to reveal that there wasn't a single member of staff, apart from the butler, who didn't have a conviction of one kind or another, even Cook. It was as if the entire class of petty criminals had at one time or another heard a siren call from Burton Makepeace.

Cosmo, the younger son of Lord and Lady Milton, was the worst of the lot—drink, drugs, and an upper-class brawl at a club in Chelsea that had put the doorman in a coma. One of the uniforms, who had come across him several times, informed her that in his professional opinion Cosmo was a "total twat."

Reggie knew that you could get out on the roof and so she had asked Cosmo to show her up there. There was always a possibility that Sophie had stashed the Turner somewhere to retrieve later, although the logistics of that seemed pretty near impossible.

"The roof?" Cosmo said. "Okay, your funeral, I suppose." (What did that mean?) He led her on a twisty-turny route that ended up as a narrow spiral staircase that messed with her balance, so that when she finally reached the top she staggered out like a drunk. "Steady on," Cosmo said, "we don't want you falling off the battlements. I'd get blamed, no doubt."

"Battlements?"

"Yeah, that's what we call them. There are cannons, in case we have to shoot the revolting peasants. Joke," he said, when he noted the look of disapproval on her face. "There's a ghost up here, the Grey Lady—some Milton woman who jumped off the battlements after her fiancé died. She wanders around looking for him."

"You've *seen* her?" she asked cynically.

"Me? No. It's a bitch if you see her, because it means that you're about to die."

Reggie didn't believe in ghosts, not one bit, but she was finding it slightly unnerving being up here all alone with Cosmo. "Right, well, Grey Lady or no Grey Lady," she said, "we should have a look for the Turner."

They had done a circuit of the roof. The place was a mess, stones and slates lying around everywhere, piles of bricks, as though some-one had started trying to fix it and then given up. There was even a cement-mixer, heaven knows how they got it up there. "Yeah, roof repairs," Cosmo said. "They never stop. We had to sell all the Stubbs, but the work's still not finished. Those chimneys are prob-ably going to fall down soon." There were a lot of chimneys, Reg-gie thought apprehensively as she checked there were no paintings hidden behind them. She couldn't shake off the feeling that the Grey Lady was going to jump out from behind one of them and frighten her to death.

She had peered cautiously over the edge of the "battlements." It really was an awfully long way down. She suddenly realized that

Cosmo was behind her and was gripped by the paranoid idea that he was going to push her off.

"You're a funny little thing, aren't you?" he said, his voice alarmingly close to her ear. It took her a moment to understand that he was making a pass at her.

"*Really?*" she said. "I've got a black belt in taekwondo. You're lucky I'm not chopping you in two."

"Worth a try," he said, backing off, hands in the air. "Arrest me."

The Grey Lady nodded encouragingly but Reggie said, "I've better things to do with my time." She was overcome with relief to get back down to earth again and vowed never to go up on the Miltons' battlements again.

⌐

Also in the mix at Burton Makepeace, of course, was the steady stream of visitors who, despite the endless signs exhorting them not to touch anything, seemed to have put their grubby paws on everything in the house. Reggie wondered how much went missing every year. There were so many little things (*objets d'art* would be the term, she supposed) that could be easily slipped into a pocket—the enamelled snuff boxes, the ivory netsukes, the little bronze dogs, the silver coasters. Temptation everywhere.

There had been no reliable inventory for the contents of Burton Makepeace, there were just too many impediments for anyone to have catalogued it all. The place was stuffed to the gunnels with objects of every shape and size. It would have taken a hundred Marie Kondos to sort out the Red Room—she would probably have been galvanized by the amount of joy sparked in that room alone. For although Burton Makepeace and its inhabitants stirred the *sans-culotte* in Reggie's soul, she couldn't deny that the house contained an incredible number of lovely things that she found herself coveting. Perhaps that was why Sophie Greenway had run off with the Turner, perhaps it wasn't about the money, perhaps the painting had spoken to her soul. Reggie had seen photographs of it, of course. Painted somewhere in the middle of Turner's life, before

he made sky and land melt elusively into each other for ever. Reggie
had gone to Fountains Abbey and sat where Turner must have sat,
to try to capture the view for herself.

~

Apart from the Nancy Styles novel, there had been surprisingly
little in Sophie Greenway's evidence box. There were the clothes
that she had left behind and a notebook. She seemed to have been
an admirably organized woman with very neat, nice handwriting.
Unfortunately, she had not chosen to write something helpful like
"20th November—steal the Turner." The notebook was clean, no
sign of fingerprints having been lifted from it. Why not? An over-
sight? Or was Sophie Greenway a ghost who didn't leave a trace of
herself?

Instead, the notebook contained entries such as—*Thurs, July 6
FitzRoberts for lunch. Riesling (the Egon Müller? Too expensive for the
FitzRs? If not, what?) Order salmon trout from fshmgr (ask Tom for peas
and rasps from gdn). The wife (Suzanne) has celery allergy. Remind Lady
M not to mention South Africa.* There were more prosaic entries—
Buy E45 cream for Nanny and *Ask Tom for peonies for the Stbs rm.* and
Arabella arriving Friday! Was that a joyous exclamation mark or a
minatory one? Reggie had not met Lady Milton's daughter, who
had stayed away after the robbery. ("Thank goodness," Lady Milton said.) The theft seemed to engender despair in the Miltons: one
more thing that had disappeared into the maw of oblivion.

("Maw of oblivion?" Jackson queried. Yes, exactly that.)

The maw of oblivion was where all the lost things were kept. It
would be discovered at the end of time. The walls (it was a room,
in Reggie's imagination) would be boarded with the panels from
the Amber Room in Catherine the Great's palace, Tsarskoye Selo,
and hanging on that amber there would be Rembrandt's *The Storm
on the Sea of Galilee* and Vermeer's *The Concert* as well as a lovely
portrait of his wife by Jean-François Millet, stolen in Montreal fifty
years ago, which most people seemed to have forgotten about—but
not Reggie. It was unlike anything else he had painted, no sign of

peasants in the field, of earth and mud and toil. There was love in every brushstroke. Or so it seemed to Reggie anyway. At the time some people called the burglary the "Skylight Caper" because the thieves had gained entrance to the gallery through a skylight. Caper! Reggie hated that word, it was so *Thomas Crown Affair*. Theft was theft. At least that was one subject on which Jackson Brodie was in agreement with her.

Also in the maw of oblivion, piled haphazardly like the grave goods in the antechamber of Tutankhamun's tomb, there would be the enormous Bamiyan Buddhas from Afghanistan that the Taliban destroyed, the missing bronze animal heads from the Zodiac Water Clock in the old Imperial Palace in Beijing, the seven Fabergé eggs still unaccounted for, the whole of the Baalshamin Temple from Palmyra . . . the list could go on for ever.

"Pretty big room," Jackson said. "What about Shergar, you missed him off your list. Plus I'd like to find *Woman with a Weasel* before 'the end of time,' as you so apocalyptically put it."

This conversation had taken place in the "clean, well-lighted" café and, looking back, Reggie wished she had never agreed to meet him, to have her soul bought with an almond latte and a brownie (very good brownie though). What if his Melanie and her Sophie did turn out to be the same person, how was she going to explain to DCS Louise Monroe the complicated and non-procedural route that had led her to that conclusion? And that it involved her *bête noire*, Jackson Brodie? She decided to wait for the fingerprints to come back and then, if there was anything, she would come clean about his involvement.

Reading *The Secret of the Clock Cabinet*, Reggie wondered if there was a clue hidden in the pages, if the Nancy Styles books were even perhaps decryptors for a code. No, she had to remind herself, that was patently ridiculous, she wasn't going to go all Dan Brown over this. (See how Jackson Brodie messed with a person's head?) Reggie liked codes though. She had kept a diary when she was young, written using the Caesar shift to stop her brother reading it. She had no idea why as he had never shown the slightest interest in her diary.

The diary was an incredibly laborious way to record the dull quo-tidian of "Got an A in History" or "Missed the bus this morning." Reggie stopped recording her daily life when her mother died. It had taken a long period of grief before she had any days she wanted to document.

No secret clues, no code in the Nancy Styles novels, at least noth-ing that Reggie could see. Despite her reservations, she had taken a "quick shufti" at the Police National Computer yesterday, not because Jackson had requested her to but because she wanted to find out for herself whether there was a Melanie Hope in there, or anyone whose speciality was looking after someone really well for weeks, even months, before quietly disappearing with the most valuable thing in the house under their arm. No. Melanie and the theft of the Rembrandt from Mount Fernie in Scotland seemed to have reached a dead-end some time ago now.

It took for ever to get through on the phone to Josh. When she eventually did, he seemed irritable. "It's not exactly top of my list, you know," he said. Seemed like sooner or later she was going to have to come good on those pizzas. There was a lot of noise in the background, the kind of noise you got when a station was gear-ing up to something. "It sounds like something's kicking off there," Reggie said, but Josh said, "Sorry, Reggie, got to go." Was she miss-ing out on something? Reggie hated missing out, especially on ex-citement, of which there was precious little in her life.

She abandoned the remains of the hummus wrap and retrieved her car. She sat for a while and stared at the windscreen. Did she really want to spend the rest of her day off, already blighted by a funeral, trying to get any sense out of the residents of Burton Make-peace? She sighed and started the engine. Yes, apparently she did.

～

The turning for Halifax was coming up. Reggie resolved to ignore it. *It would help if someone could get a look at the CCTV at the funeral home—Jessop's, do you know it?* "Drive on," she muttered to herself. "Do not in any circumstances take the road to Halifax."

〜

It was on the outskirts of the town. A tasteful sign at the foot of the drive—burgundy with gold lettering—that announced J. W. Jessop, Undertakers ("A Family Company Who Care").

"Yes, of course we have CCTV," Moira Jessop said, rather taken aback by the production of Reggie's warrant card. Reggie wondered aloud if anyone had ever tried to steal a body ("Chase and Brodie— Bodysnatchers"). Necrophiliacs might be a problem, she supposed. She thought of Jimmy Savile. Shook the thought vigorously out of her head.

"No, just a bit of vandalism," Moira Jessop said.

Reggie was led into an office that looked like any office anywhere and was shown a small array of screens displaying the reception area, a yard that must be at the back, a garage where a hearse was parked and, rather alarmingly, the mortuary itself, the "fridge," as Moira Jessop referred to it, which would make Reggie think twice the next time she went rooting around for something—anything—to eat in her own fridge.

"The cameras are monitored remotely twenty-four hours a day by a company, but you can take a look for yourself," Moira Jessop said. "I'll leave you to it, shall I? I've got a delivery to see to."

A delivery of what? Reggie wondered. On the camera in the "fridge" Reggie could see a closed coffin as well as a body on a mortuary tray, covered, thankfully, by a sheet.

Day before yesterday, somewhere between three and four in the afternoon, Jackson had been at pains to tell her.

He was right. At 15:10 on the time stamp a woman entered and talked to Moira Jessop, who then led her away down a corridor. There was no surveillance camera in the Chapel of Rest, which seemed like an omission to Reggie. (Savile again.)

To anyone else it might have seemed unlikely that the woman had come to put something in Dorothy's coffin, but Reggie had once tucked a kilo of heroin into a coffin and sent it blazing into the next world. It had been a good deed, the kind of thing that Jackson himself would do. He was always making the distinction between justice and the law. She was always trying not to. *Was* it a crime? She had never thought to find out. People put all sorts of things in coffins—teddy bears and photographs, anything that might help the dead person's journey to the next world. Jackson had said something about Dorothy Padgett not having her spectacles with her, but surely in an afterlife you would have perfect eyesight. Although it went against all her rational beliefs, Reggie liked to think there might be some sort of life after this one, if only so that she could place her mother in it, waiting patiently for Reggie to join her.

This place was making her morbid. She returned her attention to the CCTV and the woman on the screen. She was keeping her head down as if she knew there were cameras watching her. Her hair was pulled up beneath a hat and she was sporting a shiny black puffer jacket that made Reggie think of a beetle's undercarriage.

She was good. She never once let the cameras capture her face.

The tape ran on. Jackson Brodie appeared and was greeted by Moira Jessop. It gave Reggie a funny feeling seeing him on camera. It was like catching sight of someone you hadn't seen for a very long time, and yet it was only a handful of hours since she'd been at the funeral with him. Her heart had, undeniably, warmed when he had introduced her as his daughter at Dorothy Padgett's funeral. It unsettled her more than she would ever be prepared to let on.

He left Jessop's a few minutes later. Reggie could see him checking out the camera as he walked towards it. She almost expected him to wave at her, but he didn't.

Reggie returned the camera to the live feed. Time to get back on track. Burton Makepeace here I come, she thought.

Reggie stopped to fill up at a petrol station. She realized her phone was still on airplane mode after the funeral and when she switched it back on she found the airwaves alive with drama. "Two-Cop Killer Carl Carter" was loose and on the rampage on the moors.

She had heard of Carl Carter, of course. Also known as "Mad

Dog Carter" by the tabloids, but if he'd been a dog you would have put him down. He was a legend—a bad one—doing life in Wakefield for killing two police officers during a post-office raid ten years ago, and now it seemed he had escaped while on a visit to hospital. For an MRI, the paper said. No handcuffs in an MRI, Reggie supposed. You just had to get off the thing before you went into the tunnel, batter a couple of prison wardens and the odd nurse, and you were off. It was probably a ruse—faking an illness. It would be easy to fake anything if you knew the symptoms.

Carter had carjacked a vehicle in the hospital car park, dragging out the driver—an eighty-two-year-old woman who was now in A&E. Carter's mother wasn't so lucky when he went to her house. It seemed that before he was jailed he had had the forethought to stash a couple of guns there. What kind of police sloppiness had overlooked them at the time? No is dotted and ts crossed. Now he had retrieved the guns and driven off, but not before battering his mother over the head with one of them. It had been his mother who turned him in, so from his point of view it was a justified grievance, Reggie supposed. "Armed and extremely dangerous," the news said, relishing the excitement.

And all this—*real* life-and-death stuff—had been happening while she had been reading that stupid Nancy Styles book. Now she knew why there had been such a buzz in the station when she called. She tried phoning again but the line was engaged. She should go back instead of wasting time chasing the wild goose that was Sophie Greenway.

"They should bring back hanging," the gloomy man at the counter said, indicating the rolling news on the TV screen behind him.

"Well," Reggie demurred. She didn't agree with hanging, she much preferred the idea of criminals roasting in the fires of hell twenty-four hours a day. Did they have day and night in hell? Did they damp down the fires in the evening and stoke them up again in the morning?

"Are you paying?" the man asked, looking at the Twix she was clutching.

"Sorry," Reggie said. "Miles away."

⌒

She got back in the car and ate one of the fingers of Twix while she tried to get through to the station again. No luck. Ten miles further on she stopped again and ate the other finger. Regretted not buying a KitKat as well. She finally managed to get through to a sergeant at the station. Carter had a Heckler & Koch handgun and a sawn-off shotgun, he was heading west, last sighted in Oakworth. "You coming in?" the sergeant asked. "It's all hands on deck here."

"As a matter of fact, I'm quite close to Oakworth," she said.

"Well, wait there," he told her sternly. "Don't play silly buggers and go looking for the bastard on your own."

"As if. I'm on my way to Burton Makepeace House, some new evidence has come to light. You know—about the painting that was stolen."

He was indifferent to this news, having bigger fish to fry. "Be careful," he said.

"Always," she replied.

She wasn't an idiot, she wasn't about to go rogue. She wasn't some maverick cop in a TV show, like *Collier*. Nor was she a lawless lawman like Jackson Brodie. Wasn't planning to bring in single-handedly a man who had now killed three people and was probably intending to add to his tally very shortly. No, little Reggie Chase, orphan of the parish and harbourer of great expectations, was too sensible for that. And if Carter happened to be in the same area— well, it was nothing to do with her, was it? And yet her heart was beating just a little bit faster at the idea that she might become the heroine of the day.

⌒

A few miles further along the road, Reggie's phone rang and she pulled over into a lay-by that declared itself a "viewpoint." From here you could contemplate the moorland rolled out below, the heather now sifted with snow like icing-sugar. Shards of papery white were beginning to fall. No sign of alliterative killers at the viewpoint. Reggie was secretly relieved—her initial enthusiasm for confronting Carl Carter had begun to evaporate.

The phone call was from Ronnie, who said, "So I showed the photo of the painting to Ginny, and she contacted someone she knows who's an expert in Italian Renaissance portraiture. He's very excited, he thinks it . . ." The signal started to stutter. Of course it did, because it was obeying Sod's law and several other laws that the hidden powers-that-be had passed when they thought no one was looking. ". . . There is a painting that's known to have . . . by . . . 1512 . . . pinks in her hand like the Madonna of the . . . betrothal . . . fertility . . . coral . . . traced back . . . lost since . . . it would be ama— . . . weas—"

Gone. It didn't matter how many times Reggie tried phoning her back, Ronnie had disappeared into the ether. The thin air. Along with the woman and her dratted weasel.

The car was warm, maybe too warm, and Reggie could feel herself beginning to nod off. It suddenly struck her how tired she was, she shouldn't have stayed up trying to finish that stupid Styles book. Dorothy Padgett's funeral already seemed days ago, even though it was only this morning. Five minutes of shut-eye, that was all she needed. The better part of valour and all that, she said to the Mini. She had seen what happened when people fell asleep at the wheel and it was not a fate she wanted for herself.

$$\sim$$

What had happened to the world while she'd been asleep? (How *long* had she been asleep, for goodness' sake?) The car was now at the centre of a ferocious white-out. There was no way she could drive in this. She wouldn't last ten minutes outside the cocoon of the car. But, equally, there was no way she could stay here, being slowly buried alive by the snow. The wiley, windy moors were going to be the death of her.

Reggie experienced a little frisson of fear at the shroud of snow that was covering her car. Quite a big frisson. Could a frisson be big? It always seemed like it should be a little thing, and this seemed like a very big thing indeed. She tried to remember what you were supposed to do if you were stranded in a blizzard. Should you turn the engine off so that you didn't die of carbon monoxide poisoning if the exhaust got covered? But then without the engine there'd be no heating and you'd die of cold, wouldn't you? It wasn't a dilemma that she had been expecting when she woke up this morning.

Her thoughts strayed of their own accord to Moira Jessop's fridge (not helpful!). She was disappearing into the snow. What if she was never found? Her thoughts now turned to Pompeii (even less helpful!), sending her heartbeat rocketing.

The should-I-stay-or-should-I-go dilemma was resolved when the Mini refused to start. She was going to freeze to death.

One small miracle was offered by the universe—her phone signal kicked back in. A weak kick, it was true, but maybe strong enough to get help. Who did you call when you'd got yourself into this kind of trouble? The AA? The traffic cops? Ghostbusters?

~

"Brodie and Chase, Detectives. How may I help you?"

"I've got a bit of a problem, Mr. B."

Janet's

Earlier today, Simon had found himself writing, "I would like to come back as a tree when I die." He had been (mutely) taking part in a lively discussion about reincarnation at a meeting that was held every Thursday in Janet Teller's living room. Janet was one of the more able-bodied—no walker, no stick, no Sholley trolley. She had been a schools-champion hockey player when she was young, she still had her hockey stick, kept behind the bedroom door in case she needed "to repel boarders." Simon imagined that she would quite cheerfully bash an intruder's brains out. She could still touch her toes, something she found it necessary to demonstrate whenever possible. It gave her an inflated sense of self.

When it was first inaugurated, the little knot of people—four women, one man, all over the age of seventy-five—had called it a prayer meeting, but so little praying went on—it was mostly rival baking and "a topic for discussion"—that now they didn't call it anything, it was just "Janet's." "Are you going to Janet's?," "I'll see you at Janet's" and so on. Simon didn't usually attend, they seemed to prefer his absence to his presence, but today it gave him a useful opportunity to announce—as it were—his newly speechless state to several people at one time. Kill several birds with one stone.

He had killed a bird with a catapult when he was a boy. A blackbird. It was just bad luck because he wasn't a good shot and hadn't expected to hit it. He was eleven at the time, consumed with horror afterwards. He told no one. It was silly, but it still weighed heavily on his heart all these years later. His heart was the repository of guilt. It was crammed now, painfully swollen with sins and misdemeanours. He fully expected it to burst any day. They could put "guilt" on his death certificate rather than "myocardial infarction." His first job in TV all those years ago had been on a hospital drama. He had retained a surprising amount of medical knowledge. It wouldn't really matter whether he had hit the blackbird or not (it mattered to the bird itself, obviously) because the point was—he had aimed at it. Therein lay the sin.

Sometimes he fantasized about moving to India and becoming a Jain monk, carefully considering every step for fear of treading on an ant, wearing a mask in case he inhaled a midge. And apparently no alcohol for fear of destroying the microorganisms it contained. It would be an exhausting penance. Perhaps he could be reincarnated as a microorganism, humble and useful, brewing beer, maturing cheese, more like a diligent monk than a microorganism. Indeed, you might say—

"Sherry, Vicar?"

He mimed a regretful "no." Surely no microorganism could survive the process that Janet Teller's Bristol Cream must have gone through in its journey from grapevine to cut-glass schooner. It was still relatively early. Did they always start drinking at this time of the day? A Jenga-type tower of cherry Genoa fingers was placed carefully on the coffee table. "Shop-bought," Shirley Havers murmured under her breath to Simon. There was no greater affront.

There was some chat about Edna Gibson's "passing." Why not just say "death"? he thought. Marian Forster suggested they say a short prayer "for the deliverance of Edna Gibson's soul," a rather churchy phrase for a laywoman. Given his affliction, she volunteered to say it herself, resulting in a short tussle between her and Shirley Havers, who also wanted to "lead the congregation in prayer." Simon remained polite. It turned out to be quite a long prayer. "Amen," Marian finally intoned solemnly, and they all shifted in their seats and after a few seconds of decorous silence made a move on the cherry Genoa.

During lockdown, "Janet's" had been held on the village green. They masked up and hauled chairs out from their houses. Like the early saints, Simon thought. *For where two or three are gathered in my name.* Simon's offer of St. Martin's had gone unheeded. They were a law-abiding generation. Derek Truitt brought his tape measure and meticulously mapped out the required distance between them.

"If you believe in the Resurrection," Barbara Levitt said earnestly, cake crumbs moustaching her top lip along with her actual moustache, "then there's no reason not to believe in reincarnation. Is there, Vicar?" This was going to be a testing sort of morning, wasn't it? Simon made a gesture of helplessness, as if the question was too great for a simple answer.

They had spent a considerable amount of time discussing their future manifestations over the sherry and cake (instant coffee for Marian Forster, a supercilious teetotaller). Barbara Levitt wanted, predictably, to come back as a cat. Her own cat, fat on tinned sardines and tuna from Aldi in Skipton, was an indulged creature. Simon wanted to say to her, "Be careful what you wish for," because only yesterday he had come across a feral cat in the graveyard that had tried to take his hand off when he bent down to stroke it.

Despite its lack of manners, he had placed a saucer of cat food on the flat stone of *Ambrose Belling, 1790–1880*. He admired the longevity of one born in an age of disease and infection. Ambrose had been a "sailing master," although Simon didn't know what that entailed. He had enjoyed the Master and Commander series, perhaps it was the same thing. (It wasn't, he looked it up later.) What was Ambrose doing beached so far inland? Simon wondered. He would often wander around the graveyard, nodding greetings to the inhabitants, reassuring them that they had not been forgotten— although, of course, they had been. The cat, growing impatient at being kept from its free meal, had arched its back and hissed theatrically. If a dumb animal could communicate so effectively, then really there was nothing to inhibit himself, was there?

Barbara Levitt had taken "meek and mild" as her life's motto, so perhaps she would enjoy a rambunctious afterlife, slaughtering the weak and helpless. Janet Teller wished to come back as a dolphin.

In the wilds of an ocean presumably, not in the confines of a tank in some marine park where she would be expected to spin a hula hoop round her snout three times a day. (Simon had recently signed a petition.)

Also nominated as afterlives by the group were: a rose bush (Marian Forster, variety not specified), a dog (Derek Truitt, specifically a Labrador; Simon suspected it was one of Lady Milton's Labs, Derek was rather taken with her—or with her dogs, Simon wasn't sure which) and Mount Everest (Shirley Havers, hubris in Simon's opinion—better to be a self-effacing daisy).

Simon had to write down his choice, as if it were a party game. "What kind of tree?" was the immediate urgent question from the group. It didn't matter, he would take whatever he was given, but wrote "Oak!" and that seemed to satisfy them all. "How apt," Marian Forster said. Why? How was it apt that he would be an oak tree? He had none of an oak's admirable qualities—they were steadfast, true and honourable trees.

"Nature is sentient, don't you think?" he wrote laboriously. (Decades of keyboard use had mangled his handwriting.) Simon was so used to thinking this that he didn't realize it might be a provocative idea. The group were startled but also, he was pleased to note, open to a small symposium on the subject. In his old London days his liberal artsy friends had been far less tolerant (and less liberal) than the little group at Janet's.

Janet Teller's bungalow was hot and airless, and Simon felt himself beginning to wilt. The village of Burton Makepeace didn't fall under the edicts of the Clean Air Act, so many of the older villagers still had open fires. Janet not only had a coal fire burning in her hearth but also appeared to have the thermostat on her central heating hiked up to the equatorial setting.

"Snow's coming," she said, as if girding up for an epic battle in *Game of Thrones*. (Yes, he watched far too much television.) The rest of the group murmured agreement. There had been much fearful chat about the weather forecast as they nested snugly amongst the squishy cushions of Janet's three-piece suite. Simon, an unexpected latecomer, was marooned on a folding sun-lounger that was dragged through from the conservatory.

They had moved on to discussing the "Big House." The comings and goings at Burton Makepeace always provided them with endless speculation. Derek Truitt had insider information as it was known that he had "got close" to Lady Milton and there had been some teasing about him becoming Lord of the Manor. They were holding a Murder Mystery Weekend at the hotel this weekend, Derek informed them. "People paying to dress up and pretend to solve a murder."

It was generally agreed that this was a complete waste of money when people could more easily stay at home and watch the same kind of thing on television. What did the elderly and infirm do before the invention of television? Simon wondered. (What did *he* do?) As well as his evening viewing, Simon watched quite a lot of daytime television these days. A guilty pleasure, although it did help him to keep up with his congregants' own viewing habits, around which many of their conversations were centred. They mostly seemed to watch programmes about buying property abroad, which was the last thing they would ever do themselves. If he had never gone to York for that wedding, never been infected by the Holy Ghost, he might have been the Director General of the BBC by now.

"Aye, well, there's nowt so queer as rich folk," Derek said.

Simon felt awfully tired suddenly and close to fainting with the heat in Janet's living room. He wrote down, "Have to go—sermon to prepare!"

None of them queried this statement, even though they knew that his sermons these days were mostly improvisations on whatever random subject had inspired him on the walk from vicarage to church. Primroses! The first swallow! Picking apples! Holy white birds flying after!

"Good for you, Vicar," Derek said encouragingly. "I'm sure you'll have your voice back tomorrow. Nothing like a bit of positive thinking." They all murmured in agreement.

Simon stood up, rather too quickly, and mimed an extended

farewell, tapping his wristwatch, prayer hands, hand on heart with gratitude for the cherry Genoa. He mimed eating the cake and suspected he looked like a crocodile flapping its jaws.

"Get well soon," they all chirped.

"See you on Sunday, Vicar," Barbara Levitt said as he battled through the crowded furniture to the front door.

"Call me Simon!" he shouted cheerfully (in his head). They never would, he accepted that.

He had left with gifts—a quarter (opened) bottle of brandy for his throat and a Tupperware container of scratchy coconut macaroons that were homemade and not "shop-bought"—Simon could tell by the way they scraped his gullet like a cheese grater.

Anyone who genuinely had a sore throat would have avoided them, but Simon was ravenous and scoffed the lot on the trek back to the vicarage, throwing the crumbs to the rooks that trailed him everywhere knowing he always fed them at some point during the day. They had an astonishing collective memory and got quite aggressive with him if he didn't provide for them. They had been exiled from the East Wing of Burton Makepeace when it was converted into a hotel and seemed to hold him personally responsible for their diaspora.

The chill of the vicarage enveloped him when he entered it. The place felt very unloved, as did Simon. He mustn't indulge in self-pity, he was in a better place than most of the world's population, he reminded himself. No real comfort in thinking that, of course. Marian Forster came once a week and did some elementary cleaning, but otherwise the vicarage was untended. No aproned housekeeper, bossy but with his best interests at heart, cooked or fussed over him the way they did in TV vicarages.

It was just as well that he had eaten the coconut macaroons as it was short commons for lunch. Honey on toast—the honey scoured from the bottom of the jar that Fran Jennings had given him in the summer, and the toast from the heel of a loaf in the old chest freezer that lived in a neglected scullery off the kitchen. He felt guilty about eating the honey—the hard-working bees made it for themselves, not him. Did he have any right to take it? He had given an entire sermon recently on the tricky subject of dominion. "Food for thought, Vicar," Shirley Havers said to him afterwards. "Not *everything* in life has to be a moral dilemma," he heard someone complain *sotto voce* as the organ wheezed into "All Creatures of Our God and King."

He sighed. He would have to do some food shopping, he supposed. He should probably get out before the weather moved in. This morning's blue sky had turned leaden, about to fulfil its earlier unlikely promise of snow. He could go to Burton Makepeace's farm shop to see if they had anything he could make a meal from (doubtful). But then, on the other hand, maybe his foraging could wait until tomorrow. He excavated a Tesco ready meal (mushroom risotto) from a lost corner in the freezer. It would do. Was that Christian acceptance or just laziness? It was a fine line.

⌒

Simon was just thinking about settling down for *Pointless*, Beryl Sillitoe's favourite (they sometimes watched it together), when he realized that he'd left his phone somewhere. At Beryl's? Or at Janet's? The last time he remembered having it was in the church, first thing that morning. He had looked at the BBC news site while he was drinking his coffee. He should probably start the hunt there. The landline in the vicarage had stopped working several weeks ago and he hadn't bothered reporting it as everyone phoned him on his mobile anyway. He felt obliged to find it. Someone might have a spiritual emergency or (more likely) a burst pipe.

He sighed and retrieved his coat.

⌒

The chrysanthemums had been changed since this morning, so Marian Forster must have been in the church. Did she find his phone? Wouldn't she have said so when he saw her at Janet's?

He did a sweep of the pews, lifted the kneelers, shifted the piles of hymnals and prayer books. Nothing. Perhaps Marian had left it in the vestry for him and forgotten to say. He got distracted in the vestry by the piles of paper that needed filing. A shredder would be a useful thing to have, he might apply to the diocese for the money for one. He could go mad and shred everything. How satisfying that would be.

He was standing in front of the altar, gazing rather mindlessly at the simple crucifix—the Resurrection felt more like a threat than a promise—when he had the sudden feeling that he was being watched. For a moment he hoped it might be a deer, but when he turned round he discovered that it was Ben Jennings, Fran's brother, sitting quietly unnoticed in one of the pews, Marian Forster's sister's old spaniel, Holly, asleep by his side. Of course, Fran had taken the dog in when the sister died, hadn't she?

Lacking words, Simon worked his way through his ever-expanding gamut of clowning. He was rather pleased with how well the exchange seemed to go.

After Ben left, Simon returned to the vestry, and on the way he accidentally kicked something that was poking out a little way from beneath the altar as if it was trying to get his attention. Underneath its snowy linen cloth—Barbara Levitt saw to the church laundry, she had the soul of a washerwoman—and its brocade runner, the altar was a simple table from IKEA, assembled by Derek Truitt. Simon could have managed, he was surprisingly good at DIY, but his little platoon of parishioners were all exceptionally eager to be useful and who was he to deny them simple pleasures?

The old altar had succumbed to woodworm some time ago, causing a flurry of Rentokil visits to investigate the ancient church's timbers. Thankfully, from a financial point of view anyway, they were worm-free. But would it really have mattered if St. Martin's had slowly crumbled into dust? Wouldn't that have been a fitting metaphor for the Church itself?

Why would anyone hide something beneath the altar? Simon lifted the linen cloth (actually a large tablecloth—much cheaper than anything on a Church supplies website) and found a square package, a parcel really, wrapped in old-fashioned brown paper and string. His first thought was "bomb," a paranoid thought but excusable, he reckoned, given the manner of Rosalind's death. Fran Jennings said Ben worried about being blown up again. All part of PTSD, he supposed.

Warily, he plucked the package—heavier than he had expected—from beneath the altar and laid it on the cloth. After some rooting around he found Marian Forster's florist's scissors and cut the string, because he'd seen bomb-disposal officers do that on TV programmes when dealing with parcel bombs. He felt a little thrill of nerves as he slowly unfolded the brown paper and found—not a bomb, but a painting. A small oil painting—a portrait—in a deep, gilded frame. Normally he worried about someone carrying off the church silver, but this felt like a theft in reverse.

Was it a gift? To Simon? Towards church funds? The roof! he thought. Perhaps Lady Milton had wanted to give a discreet, rather underhand donation to make up for all the ones that the Miltons had failed to give over the years. Though they would have denied it, there were enough paintings still hanging on the walls of Burton Makepeace to re-roof every church in England. The Long Gallery was lined with family portraits by Reynolds and Romney and Kneller, there was even a Holbein. Why didn't they sell them?

"But they're *family*," Lady Milton protested. "You don't sell family. One can't sell *everything*."

Or, better still, the money from selling the Miltons' portraits could be used to feed the starving and house the homeless. He didn't say that. No point.

An odd thought struck him as he carried the painting into the vestry. He had the sudden distinct feeling that it was seeking sanctuary. He should probably keep that thought to himself. Of course, since he'd been struck dumb, all of his thoughts were kept to himself.

He propped the painting in front of the vestry's computer and examined it. The light in the church had been too dim to appreciate it, but now he could see that it was old—fourteenth or fifteenth century, he reckoned—and was rather lovely. A thing of beauty. A woman, attractive and with a sympathetic gaze, as if she understood you. He doubted that she was a Milton. But who was she and where had she come from? Should he take it to a police station? But what if it *was* a gift from Lady Milton? She would be horrified that he had involved the police. Humiliating for everyone. A bit of a dilemma.

At first, in the gloom of the church, he hadn't noticed the small animal on the woman's knee. A pine marten, by the look of it. Rare in Yorkshire, it was true, but he thought he had seen one once in the deer park. He returned home, carrying the painting awkwardly under his arm to protect it from the elements.

Back in the vicarage, he found an ancient Morrisons plastic "bag for life" in the scullery that was just the right size for the picture. It might not be a gift, of course. Its uncertain status made him cautious—who was to say a thief hadn't parked it temporarily in the church and wouldn't come back for it? He decided he'd better keep it close and take it with him to Janet's, that being the most likely place he would find his phone.

He set off into the snow yet again.

———

The front door of Janet Teller's bungalow was ajar. Janet wasn't the sort to let the cold bluff its way into her home. Had she slipped out? Perhaps to fetch more coal to keep the fire stoked? But her coal shed was at the back of her house. He knew because he had filled the heavy scuttle for her on more than one occasion. Or perhaps the last person to leave this morning's group had accidentally left the front door open. Unlikely—ever since the theft of the Turner from Burton Makepeace they all locked, barred and bolted their houses as if they were preparing for a siege.

He stepped cautiously into the hall, mindful of the hockey stick Janet kept as a defensive weapon. He shut the door behind him and put the Morrisons bag down next to the umbrella stand in the hallway before advancing through the house, wishing he could call out Janet's name to warn her of his presence in case his unexpected appearance gave her a heart attack.

In the living room everything seemed untouched from when he had been here earlier. There was an unsettling atmosphere about the place, a touch of the *Marie Celeste*. The remains of the cherry Genoa and the empty sherry glasses were still on the coffee table, the folding sun-lounger Simon had perched on had not made its way back to the conservatory. The bottle of Harvey's Bristol Cream lay on its side, empty. Surely they hadn't finished the whole bottle. It wasn't like Janet not to clear up. She usually started hoovering around him before he was even out of the door.

The kitchen was orderly, the bathroom with its pink suite and matching towels was gleaming. He felt envious of its warmth. The vicarage bathroom was not a place you would ever want to linger in. He pushed open another door and found it was a bedroom—white crocheted bedspread, old-fashioned furniture. Janet's bedroom, from the look of it. It felt like trespassing, and he wondered nervously if a scared Janet, fearing he was an intruder, was hiding and was about to jump out from somewhere and whack him over the head with her hockey stick.

He found her eventually in a second bedroom—the guest bedroom, he supposed, although as far as he knew no overnight guest had ever crossed Janet's threshold. She had no family and all her friends lived close by. The spare bedroom was indeed spare, furnished with nothing more than an old divan bed, a chest of drawers and a pair of thin curtains. No heat had been wasted in here.

She was in a sitting position, her back against the cold radiator, beneath an amateur watercolour of what looked like Helvellyn. Her hockey stick lay on the carpet, the curved end sticky with what was almost certainly blood. It didn't seem to be Janet's blood and, if you thought about it (which he did), it was probably logistically impossible to hit yourself on the head with a hockey stick. No, what Janet had was a hole in the middle of her forehead, like a stigma. Simon's finger would have fitted neatly into it. It was so unexpected that it took him a few befuddled moments to conclude that it must be a bullet hole. She had been shot in the head. His stomach heaved at the sight of Janet Teller's blood and brains spattered beneath Helvellyn. She would not be touching her toes again.

Simon might have readily dismissed the idea that Janet Teller had
been shot as a fanciful flight of his imagination if there hadn't also
been a gun in the room. It was lying on the other side of Janet, near
the window. Simon's first thought was that she must have shot herself, but where would Janet Teller, seventy-eight years old, spinster
of the parish, have acquired a gun? It was unlikely in the extreme,
even more unlikely that she would have used it on herself. And if
she had, why had it ended up on the other side of the room? Had
her unknown assailant dropped it when she had hit him with the
hockey stick?

It was a proper gun, not a wartime relic, it looked like something
you would see in an American TV police drama. He picked it up,
very cautiously. "Heckler & Koch," it said on the stock. He put the
safety catch on. Television was a useful tutor in these matters.

What on earth had happened here? Did Janet have a secret past
as a Russian spy—or a British one come to that—and had that past
caught up with her? Or was this a break-in that had gone wrong?
There'd been burglaries in the village in the past—apart from the
Miltons' Turner, of course—but usually they were petty, ad hoc
affairs. He must phone the police, but his own phone was still missing. Of course! Janet had a house phone in the hallway. He slipped
the gun into the copious pocket in his cassock, where it hung heavily
by his side, and headed to the phone. He dialled 999 and the operator asked him which service he required. She repeated the question.
And again.

He had forgotten he had no voice. Irritated, the dispatcher dismissed him as a crank caller. It was surprising to Simon that in the
heat of such an extreme emergency he hadn't been able to conjure
up a voice. If his muteness was psychological, as the ENT specialist
had suggested, then surely coming across a murder victim would be
enough to jolt you out of your silence? But no. The line went dead.
(Like Janet, he thought.) He wasn't sure if the operator had hung up
on him or if perhaps the murderer had cut the phone line.

It suddenly struck him that whoever had shot Janet might still be
in the house, and there was nothing to say that this had been their

only gun. And if it was their only gun, perhaps they were about to come back and retrieve it and would shoot him with it if they found him here. Simon's heart *boom-boom-boom*ed with fear. He must get out of here, he must find help, although it was clearly too late for poor Janet.

Feeling more of an obligation than ever to the portrait, he picked up the Morrisons bag and walked out into the blizzard. He went astray immediately.

That's the Way to Do It!

I t was a while since Jackson had undertaken surveillance and he had almost forgotten what it felt like—the full bladder, the empty coffee cup, the need to stay focussed, even though at the moment he would have appreciated a little siesta. When he had been looking after his granddaughter they used to take a nap together every afternoon. No one would have judged him for it then, but now he would, let's face it, just be an old man snoozing in a car. He could imagine the police officer's rap on the window. ("Everything all right here, sir?")

He was listening to an old Nanci Griffith album, *Last of the True Believers*. That was him, in some ways. Not in others. Nanci still sounded good, he was pleased to note. She was dead now, outlived by her music. *Ars longa,* or whatever. He took comfort in things that had stood the test of time. Had he himself? Good question.

He was parked down the road from Alice Smithson's house. Hazel's daughter lived in an upmarket enclave of new houses in Leeds. According to the property website he'd consulted after Dorothy's funeral, the average house price in this street was over a million. The source of the money seemed to be Alice's husband, the texting man at the funeral. He was called Mark and he was the director of a financial services company, something Jackson had discovered after another internet search. He was never entirely sure what "financial services" meant—it seemed to cover a spectrum from innocent to guilty and then extremely guilty with knobs on. Did Alice herself have a job? She gave the appearance of being a lady of leisure. A pop-up Court of Women assembled themselves in the back seat of the Defender and gave a collective sigh.

At the funeral this morning, Alice had been attired in sombre black. "Designer," according to Reggie. One black dress looked much like another to Jackson, but what did he know? ("Nothing," the Court of Women declared predictably.) Hazel, Alice's mother, on the other hand, had only committed to a halfway-house kind of mourning—a grey coat and a purple dress.

Now Alice had changed into sporty leggings and a padded winter coat. Jackson could make out the Moncler logo. He might not know black dresses, but he knew pricy warm winter jackets. Melanie Hope had not been wearing Moncler when she left the Willows for the final time. Of course, for all he knew, once she was out of sight of the neighbourhood CCTV she might have ripped off a wig, stuffed her cheap clothes in her infamous "big bag" and pulled on her expensive coat, while congratulating herself at the way she had managed to hoodwink the Padgetts and laugh all the way to the Bank of Lost Art.

He put his binoculars down. He was due an eye test. He should probably have a hearing test as well. He'd feared recently that he was growing hard of hearing. He supposed that was what happened when you hit your seventh decade. (Seventh! Jesus, how did *that* happen?) *Vita longa.* His Scottish father had been in possession of an ancient aunt who visited them occasionally and, heaving her bulk up from their sagging sofa, used to croak, "Aye, old age disnae come by itsel." At the time Jackson had had no idea what she meant, even once he'd deciphered her Fife accent, but now he was beginning to understand. The so-called "golden years" (really should be called the "rust years") came attended by a retinue of unfriendly ailments. Sooner or later, Jackson supposed—if he was spared long enough—he would make the acquaintance of them all.

Alice Smithson was pottering about in her garden, a trowel in hand. She was being followed around by her snow-suited toddler

(Freddie, Jackson recalled after some effort), who was clutching a toy fire engine and pretending to fly it through the air. The sky was already a strange lemon colour, pregnant with snow, so Alice must be getting a bit of work in while she could.

Jackson had never been a gardener, even when he had a "proper" life—wife, child, house, job—he had been possessed of neither the time nor the inclination. Heaving the big, petrol-driven lawnmower out of the garage once a week had been his macho limit. When he moved out, after his marriage had disintegrated, his wife had bought a Flymo, one of the many (many) ways in which she demonstrated her independence of him.

Jackson wasn't entirely convinced that Alice Smithson was the mysterious Hannah from the funeral home, but he had the feeling that she might be more inclined to tell the truth than her mother. And to be honest, he didn't really have anything else to occupy his time. He thought of Harold Padgett, the pillar of his community— filling his time with golf, snooker, Masonic ritual. It sounded exhausting, but perhaps he *should* get a hobby for himself. Was it too late? You were supposed to fight the atrophy of your little grey cells, weren't you? Learn a new language, do sudoku, take up ballroom dancing, to stop them ossifying. It wasn't going to happen, especially not the ballroom dancing. "*Goin' Gone,*" Nanci was singing. It was about falling in love, but it could be applied to anything. Now it applied to poor Nanci herself. RIP. He yawned. Must stay awake, he warned himself.

⌒

He woke with a brutal start. He was surprised his heart didn't go into a convulsion. Someone knocking on the window of the car. Not the police, but Alice Smithson. When he opened the window she said, "What are you doing? Are you *spying* on me?"

⌒

Finally, it had begun to snow as if it just couldn't hold back any longer. The Smithsons' living room had big patio doors, beyond which was an extensive garden with all the accessories—a trampoline, a fire pit, decking, and a massive barbecue rig that you could have grilled an ox on if you were so inclined. Mark Smithson's preserve, no doubt. Jackson had never found it necessary to barbecue so much as a sausage to prove his masculine credentials. The snow had started to settle on the garden. Lots of greenery out there, despite the season.

"Shrubs," Alice Smithson said, and Jackson nodded knowledgeably as if that meant something to him. "Evergreen," she added. "Something to look at in the winter. Do you have a garden?"

Polite chit-chat was not beyond Jackson's capabilities, but really, could he be bothered with small talk? Especially if it was going to be on soporific subjects like shrubs. He was more interested in big talk, big talk like *Did you visit your grandmother in the funeral parlour using a false name?* And *If so, why?* Not to mention *Did you know about a codicil?*

Alice made coffee and brought out a plate of Rich Tea biscuits, the plainest biscuit in the biscuit tin. "Hardly any calories," she said, by way of explanation. She looked as if she might count the calories in oxygen.

The place was spotless. Jackson perched tentatively on one of a pair of enormous cream leather sofas, the upholstery of which must have required the hides of an entire herd of cattle. They were separated by a sea of carpet, the same colour as the sofas. Seriously? With a two-year-old? She must spend half her life cleaning. Or, more likely, another woman did. The snow-suited Freddie had disappeared—the only sign that he existed was the toy fire engine sitting on the coffee table. Where was he? It was late for a nap and early for bedtime. Perhaps there was a nanny or an au pair somewhere. The cream décor was making Jackson nervous, he felt he was almost destined to spill his black coffee on it. He held his mug very carefully, two hands, Trump-style.

He put the mug down and bit into a Rich Tea. They were stale and he quietly placed the uneaten half back on the plate. The plate sat on the big glass coffee table that bridged the breach between the sofas. Its heavily brass-bound corners were at toddler head height. The Health and Safety officer in him was taken aback—it was not just Alice Smithson who seemed like an accident waiting to happen, her whole house did too.

While still in the car, he had shown her his card. "A private investigator?" she had said doubtfully. It had, naturally, made her even more convinced that he was spying on her, but he had managed to convince her that he was here on an entirely innocent mission. Nonetheless, he was surprised that she let him over the threshold. Perhaps she was bored, and he looked like entertainment. Perhaps she had a confession to make. There was something about Alice Smithson that was off, but he couldn't quite put his finger on it. He had sensed it at the funeral, he was sensing it now. The brittle, jittery aura that indicated not so much a lady of leisure but a woman walking on eggshells, waiting for the sound of the first crack. Was it guilt that she was feeling?

He had been hired, he told her, by her mother and uncle to find Melanie Hope because they thought that she had taken something valuable from Dorothy.

"From Gran?"

"Yes. The painting that hung in her bedroom."

"The woman with the weasel? That old thing, she's welcome to it."

"You don't think it's worth anything?"

She shrugged. "I doubt it. I don't know why Mel would want it."

"Did you know that Dorothy had made a codicil to her will?"

"Codicil? What was in it?"

"No idea. I thought you might know something about it."

"*Me?* No, why should I know anything?" She seemed genuinely baffled, the very face of innocence. He was reminded of the woman in the portrait. A woman holding a secret to herself.

They both heard the ugly roar of a bombastic car swaggering up the driveway. A Ferrari, if Jackson wasn't mistaken. He was closely attuned to the nuances of the internal combustion engine. Mark Smithson, he supposed—just the kind of car that texting-man would drive.

Alice jumped at the sound and managed to drop her mug of coffee on to the glass coffee table, where it smashed dramatically, hurling the coffee far and wide over the sofas and carpet, besmirching the pristine cream. Worse, the crash was so unexpected that Jackson jumped off his sofa as well, thus, as he had feared, spilling his own coffee on the cream carpet. They stared at each other in horror for a second—from the expression on Alice's face you would think she'd just smashed a priceless piece of Ming porcelain. It seemed to be the cream carpet that was the most distressing victim of the upset, and she startled him by ripping off the hoodie she was wearing, oblivious to the skimpy little tank top that was exposed beneath. Her collarbone protruded in an unhealthy fashion. He could see her ribcage outlined beneath the thin cotton.

She started mopping and sponging with the hoodie like someone possessed by the spirit of an ancient charwoman. He was alarmed by the ferocity of her reaction.

"I'll get a cloth," he said, but before he could, they heard the front door opening and then being slammed shut. Jackson thought that you could tell a lot about a person by the way they entered and exited a room.

"Alice?" her husband shouted from the hallway, as if calling a recalcitrant dog.

She froze where she was, on her knees on the carpet, looking very much like someone who would like to follow her namesake through the looking glass and disappear. Her face displayed the bleak, helpless expression of the abused. So at least now he knew why she was so nervy.

Mark Smithson made a rather stagey entrance at the door of the living room and said, "What the fuck's going on here, Al?" Jackson had to concede that it was an understandable reaction, given that there was a strange man in his house and his half-undressed wife on her knees amid the debris from a coffee explosion. It wasn't the homecoming he would have been expecting.

"Mark!" Alice said brightly, scrambling quickly to her feet. "You're home! This is Mr. Brodie—he was at the funeral, remember?"

Mark Smithson ignored the introduction, instead wrenching his jacket off and tossing it towards his wife, saying, "Put something on, for Christ's sake, Al." Rather than attempting to catch the jacket, Alice ducked. She was either terrible at catching or she was used to having things thrown at her.

"What the fuck happened here?" Mark Smithson asked, surveying the mess. "Christ, you know how much this carpet cost, Al."

A spasm of something—horror, perhaps—passed over Alice's face. She knew what was coming.

"It was all my fault, Mr. Smithson," Jackson intervened smoothly. "I'd be happy to pay for the cost of cleaning."

"It's going to take more than cleaning," Mark Smithson said churlishly.

"Whatever it takes," Jackson assuaged. He had no intention of paying for anything in this house, but this man was a simmering volcano looking for an excuse to erupt and Alice Smithson would be the one caught by the boiling lava. His little grey cells high-fived. It wasn't often they pulled off a metaphor.

You could tell just by looking at Mark Smithson that he was one of those flashy City types, but northern, which was worse somehow in Jackson's book. Real men (i.e. northern) did not have well-honed muscles that came from the gym rather than honest labour. Smithson's face was positively polished—he must have facials, Jackson thought. This was all justified prejudice, in Jackson's opinion, although *Justified Prejudice* did sound like the title of an Arnold Schwarzenegger movie.

Mark Smithson had bully written all over him. Perhaps he would have got on well with Alice's grandfather, Harold Padgett. He looked as though he was squaring up to a fight. Jackson reckoned that he could take him on if necessary. His own muscles had never seen the inside of a gym, but they knew what it took to be a street-fighter. However, he'd rather not have to prove that.

"What are you doing here?" Mark Smithson asked.

"Giving my condolences," Jackson said.

"Mr. Brodie was just leaving," Alice said hastily. "I'll see him out."

Luckily, Mark Smithson seemed to have lost interest in him and was already booming on the phone to a specialist cleaning company.

"Get the fucker's address off him for the bill!" he shouted after Alice.

"Are you going to be all right?" Jackson asked when they were out of earshot of her husband.

"Don't worry, he'll calm down," she said. They spoke in the hushed tones of conspirators. She was a woman who needed an escape exit from her life.

"You could come with me," he offered. "Grab your kid, get in my car, I can take you somewhere safe."

"Don't be silly. It's you that needs to go," she said.

"No, Alice, you need to leave, you really do." He put his hand on her arm, ready to pull her into another life.

"Alice!" her husband bellowed. They both flinched. He dropped his hand.

"It's fine, don't worry," she said, pushing Jackson out of the house.

He dug in, searching for something in his pocket. His card. "Here," he said, thrusting it into Alice's hand. "Call me. I'll come and get you. Any time."

"Alice!"

"Go. Now," she hissed. "Please."

The door was shut firmly behind him. He could hardly kidnap her, could he? (Could he?) He guessed not. Dragging a resistant woman into the Defender wouldn't look good. (*Everything all right here, sir?*) Should he call the police? (The "real" ones.) He tried Reggie's number but got no reply. 999? Too dramatic?

He sat in the car and waited a while, and was relieved when a few minutes later Mark Smithson came through the front door and roared away like a rally driver in the canary-yellow Ferrari that had been parked in the driveway. A vulgar colour for a vulgar car, in Jackson's opinion. What a wanker.

Something was nagging at the corners of his brain. An omission. Something he hadn't asked. His detecting antennae wiggled around, trying to pull it from the ether. He drove back to Ilkley, even though the snow was getting heavier now. He stopped on the way to pick up a bottle of good malt.

———

He was welcomed warmly by Dorothy's old neighbour, and not just because of the fifteen-year-old Glenfiddich. Bob Gordon offered him a glass, but he plumped for water and sobriety. Bob poured himself a generous measure of the whisky and said, "*Slàinte mhath.*"

"*Slàinte,*" Jackson said, raising his water. He let a decent interval pass. He didn't want Bob thinking that he was just here for information. Although he was.

"So," Bob said, "have you found your painting yet?"

"No, I haven't, I'm afraid, but I just wanted to clarify something, Bob. When you witnessed the codicil to Dorothy's will, you said 'the wee lassie' was present as well."

"I did. Alice often popped in to see her gran, with the bairn. None of the others ever bothered."

"Alice Smithson was there when the codicil was signed? Alice was the 'wee lassie,' not Melanie Hope?"

"Well, they're both wee lassies, but yes, it was Alice."

Alice. The face of innocence my arse, Jackson thought. She said she knew nothing about the codicil and yet she'd been standing right there at her grandmother's shoulder while she was signing. And, again, not witnessing it—so did she inherit something? The painting? (*That old thing?*)

Did Hazel and Ian know about the codicil? Had Melanie Hope taken that as well? *We just want to find Mel and get back what she stole from us,* Ian said. Was the painting a ruse—a red herring—when it was the codicil they wanted to get their hands on? And destroy, presumably.

Had he missed something at the Willows because he didn't know what he was looking for? What *was* he looking for? Several cats dropped dead from an overdose of curiosity. Or perhaps boredom.

He poured Bob another whisky and said, "Best be off, Bob. I'm just going to pop next door and have one last look around."

It took less than a minute to pick the lock on the back door, because yes, of course he had a set of lock-pickers, because—why wouldn't you? This was why people should have alarms and security cameras—to protect themselves from people like him, Jackson thought.

The back door opened straight on to the kitchen. It smelt slightly fetid, as if decades of frying mince and simmering stew had come out of the walls to try to reclaim their source. The place was in chaos, drawers upended, papers scattered everywhere. Somebody had been very keen to find something. Hazel and Ian searching for the codicil, perhaps.

He stopped in his tracks when he thought he heard a noise coming from upstairs. He was jumpy and picked up the nearest handy weapon—a rolling pin on the draining board—and made his way warily into the hallway, feeling rather like Mr. Punch about to cosh someone. He had seen a Punch and Judy show as a boy, during a week in Scarborough, a trip organized by the Salvation Army for kids from families too poor to give them a holiday. He had been struck by the internecine violence of Punch and his wife, so like his own family. His father had also once hit his mother with a rolling pin. ("A glancing blow," he'd excused himself.) The dog, the sausages, the crocodile—to the seven-year-old Jackson it had seemed the highest form of theatre. Still did.

He was on the upstairs landing when he heard the noise again. Coming from above his head somewhere. The house had an attic, he had asked Ian about it and he had claimed that it wasn't an attic, "just a loft, really. Never converted, no one's been up there in years." Someone was up there now, someone with small, skittery feet. A rat or a squirrel, by the sound of it. Or mice, moving into the Willows the moment the previous occupant had been exfiltrated by the Grim Reaper. There was a little trapdoor just above his head that presumably was the way in. Should he look? Of course, once you'd posed that question there was only one answer. Go on, open the box, Pandora. Kill another cat. What's the worst that could happen? Jackson sighed at the inevitability of it.

To access the loft there was a ring set into the trapdoor, like the
ring-pull on a beer can. It seemed to require a hook to catch it and
after some searching he found it, on a wooden pole that appeared
to have been designed specifically for the job. It was at the back of
a cupboard on the upstairs landing. As soon as he opened the door
of the cupboard, more of the detritus of Dorothy Padgett's long life
tumbled out in a heap on the carpet. Jackson could see why Reggie
had chosen to go all minimalist. Less stuff for people to throw out
when you die.

The trapdoor was stiff, and he had to heave and pull on the hook.
It opened abruptly and an old wooden ladder shot halfway down,
nearly hitting him on the head. It proceeded to unfold slowly and
creakily under its own weight, like an unwieldy stick insect. He put
an apprehensive foot on the first rung, the idea of woodworm flash-
ing uninvited before his eyes. This was probably not a good idea,
although when had that ever stopped him?

He reached the top of the ladder and poked his head cautiously
through the open hatch. Whack-a-weasel popped unnecessarily
into his mind. He dismissed it and pulled the rest of his body up.
Nothing attacked him. There was a musty, mouldy atmosphere in
the loft, the dust of neglect everywhere. Ian Padgett seemed to have
been right, no one had breathed this air for a long time. There was
no electric light, just a small skylight, although much good it did as
the afternoon had ceded early to the evening and snow had already
started getting a purchase on the little window. He used the torch
on his phone like a searchlight. Shrivelled cobwebs were strung up
everywhere like Halloween decorations. There was a make-do floor
of sorts, just some boards placed across the joists, but at least he
didn't have to crawl along the beams and risk crashing through the
ceiling below.

There was no ancient chest bound with iron hoops, inside which
you would find treasure when you lifted the lid (a boyhood fantasy
of Jackson's). No corpses, no skeletons. No madwomen in this attic.
No Renaissance paintings or mysterious codicils. Only a large rat,
surprised by Jackson's unexpected presence. It swiftly disappeared

into a hole in the wall that looked far too small for it to fit in. Rats didn't worry Jackson, not animal ones anyway. If it had been a weasel he would have tried to capture it and have a polite chit-chat with it on the whereabouts of its fugitive woman friend.

Before he could begin to clamber back down the ladder, Jackson heard voices. A woman's voice, drawing nearer. For an unlikely moment—she had been on his mind so much—he thought it might be Melanie Hope. Because—and here was a thought—what if the painting or the codicil (or both) was still in the house, hiding in plain sight? Sleight of hand on Melanie Hope's part, to come back and retrieve her loot later? She still had her keys to the Willows.

He pulled the ladder up as quietly as he could and closed the trapdoor, leaving just enough room to spy on whoever was there. His heart sank when he recognized the rather peevish tones of Hazel. The more subdued voice of Ian joined in. Jackson wondered if they had returned to scatter more of the red and blue dots of ownership around. Their voices grew louder as they mounted the staircase.

"Come on, let's go," Ian said. "We've looked everywhere, it's not here."

"Look at that," Hazel said. "You left the hatch to the loft open."

"Me?"

"Yes, you, Ian," Hazel harangued. "You were the last one up there. You *did* look up there, didn't you? You didn't just *say* you had?"

Ian must have lied to his sister, there was no sign of him having been up here. Maybe he had decided that he couldn't face the creepy-crawlies.

"I don't trust him," Hazel said.

"Who?"

"Mr. so-called private detective."

"Brodie? Why not?"

"I think he's keeping things from us."

The cheek! Jackson thought. He suspected it was much more likely to be the other way round.

"Close it, will you?"

"*Jawohl, mein Führer.*"

"Don't be so stupid, Ian."

Jackson caught the gist of a grumbled conversation about the whereabouts of the necessary hooked pole. Right in front of your eyes, he felt like saying, only obviously he didn't because he would rather they didn't find it and imprison him up here. He contemplated the small skylight. It had clearly not been touched in years, and even if he had been able to force it open the chances of him squeezing weasel-like out of it were non-existent. Not to mention that he'd be three storeys up with no way down.

There was nothing else for it. He was going to have to stick his head through the hatch and give Ian and Hazel the fright of their lives (*Evening, all*), but they caught him off-guard and the trapdoor was suddenly slammed shut before he could say or do anything.

Another fine mess he'd gotten into.

"I've got to go out again," he said to Tatiana. "There's a damsel in distress in need of rescue."

"Up your alley," she said. Her grasp of English sayings was slippery at best. Tatiana was the only woman he had ever shared living-space with who didn't ask him where he'd been the minute he walked through the door. At first, he had appreciated the lack of interest, but recently he had begun to wonder—if he slipped his leash and never came home at all, would she care enough to go around the streets whistling for him, or would she just go out and get a new dog? ("New dog," she said with a nonchalant shrug. "Bigger dog.")

What Houdini-like trickery, you might ask, did Jackson employ to escape from his confinement in the attic of the Willows? No trickery at all, because, although it took him an embarrassingly long time to realize, it turned out that the ring in the trapdoor was a two-way gizmo with a matching ring on the loft side, and by dint of sliding a pen into it and then pulling heroically he was able to dislodge it. *Open, sesame.* It was almost disappointing in its simplicity. Almost.

On his return to Leeds, he had scarcely crossed the threshold of Tatiana's flat when his phone rang, trumpeting an emergency.

~

The snow in Leeds had been manageable, but up here on the moors it was a different story entirely. No wonder Reggie had run into trouble, her car was the size of a shoe and just about as much use, whereas the Defender pushed through the weather as sturdy as a snow-plough.

Glancing in his rear-view mirror, Jackson spotted a white Skoda. Just the kind of car a retired geography teacher would drive. Although he knew it was Hazel's because he had clocked her getting out of it when he first went to the Willows and no one had a better memory (a policeman's memory) for a car and a number-plate. Was she *following* him?

~

He was relieved when he finally came across Reggie. He knew she had been scared, so he didn't mention her previous disparagement of his "flash motor," nor did he point out that without its valiant specs she might have disappeared for good in a snowdrift. Instead he helped her into the vehicle and wrapped his jacket round her, and the Defender did its bit with its heated seats.

They had long passed the tipping point and would never make it back to Leeds in these conditions. They were orphans of the storm, seeking shelter. And there was only one place to go once you were up here.

"Burton Makepeace," Reggie said. "It was where I was heading, actually."

"So you weren't in pursuit of a mad axe murderer who'd escaped from prison and whose last known sighting was a couple of miles from here?"

"Don't be ridiculous. And Carl Carter's never used an axe."

"First time for everything," Jackson said.

~

It took the best part of an hour to travel the five miles to Burton Makepeace and there were moments when Jackson doubted that they were going to make it at all. "Phew," Reggie said (an understatement) as the lights of the long drive finally came into view, glimmering dimly ahead of them like a flare-path welcoming a World War Two bomber home (an overstatement).

"Welcome, welcome," the man who opened the door to them said. "Your fellow sleuths are having drinks in the Library."

"Sleuths?" Jackson puzzled.

The Body Walks

No, Lady Milton informed Ben, he had not been wandering around on MOD land, he had been in Burton Makepeace's deer park all along. Luckily she hadn't shot him but instead said, "Follow me," which he was only too relieved to do.

After he had persuaded her that he was not the enemy, she had offered him "a snifter" from a hip flask and they had drained the whole contents while on the freezing-cold trek back to the House (unlike other people's houses, Ben realized that Lady Milton's had a capital H). She seemed to have the stomach of a camel, whereas Ben was feeling exceptionally inebriated.

He had drunk surprisingly little since leaving the Army (the Leg—fear of falling, fear of looking like an idiot). In fact, he felt himself embarrassingly lacking in vices these days. Not that he had ever really had any to begin with. Perhaps that was where he had gone wrong in life. He had been too moral and upstanding. Although he had killed quite a few people in his time, he supposed that redressed the balance a bit.

"Keep up," Lady Milton said to him, in the same tone that she addressed the dogs.

"Yes, sir," he murmured.

⟳

Burton Makepeace had eventually appeared out of the snow, all lights ablaze like a splendid ocean-going liner ploughing through the blizzard. "Lost my way for a bit back there," Lady Milton said. Me too, Ben thought, although for him it felt more like a metaphor. They entered through a side door—the Boot Room, according to Lady Milton—and divested themselves of their snow-boltered outerwear. Holly was released from Ben's jacket, apparently unscarred by her adventures. She looked quite rejuvenated, in fact, and went pitter-pattering off after Lady Milton's Labradors, excited to have new friends. Ben himself was feeling far from refreshed.

"We'd better get you warmed up," Lady Milton said, and she proceeded to lead him on what seemed like a long, complicated route through the basement of the house. "Shortcut," she said. It didn't seem like a shortcut to Ben. The journey caused an unfortunate flashback to an Afghani compound he had entered on one occasion with his men. It had proved to be more of a warren than they'd been led to expect, danger seemingly concealed round every corner. All they had found in the end were the women and children of the village, huddled against a wall in the furthest reaches of the place, but that hadn't made it any less unnerving. In their jitteriness they had almost shot them. It was the near-misses—of which there were too many—that haunted Ben in the long, dark watches of the night.

"All right?" Lady Milton asked, perhaps divining his disquiet. They had ascended again, via a back staircase and a servants' green door, into a vast marble entrance hall that possessed the bleak quality of a mausoleum. "I wouldn't worry—she's quite harmless now."

"She?" Ben puzzled. Lady Milton seemed to be referring to the large heap of clothing that was lying at the foot of an operatic staircase. The heap of clothing had feet. And arms. And probably a head there somewhere.

"It's only Nanny," Lady Milton said. "I was hoping someone would have moved her before I got back."

Ben remembered his sister saying a Murder Mystery was taking place here tonight. Nanny must be one of the victims, he thought. An actress pretending to be a corpse. She was very good at it. Not an eyelid flickered, not a breath rose in her chest. He frowned.

"Is she real?" he asked. "Is Nanny real?"

"Real? Of course she's real."

"Not an actress?"

"An actress? *Nanny?*"

"I just thought . . ." What had he thought? "Shouldn't we help her?" he asked, edging towards the heap of clothes as if it might rear up at any moment like an unwieldy golem. Someone should take a pulse and it didn't seem as if that someone was going to be Lady Milton. Ben crouched warily down next to Nanny.

"She won't bite," Lady Milton said. "But I'm afraid that we're going to have to move her ourselves. If you want a job doing well, do it . . ." She trailed off, clearly perplexed by the logistics of the task.

"Perhaps it's more of a job for an undertaker?" Ben suggested, standing up again and almost falling over from dizziness. Lady Milton was right—Nanny appeared to be quite dead. He felt queasy. The cold, the alcohol, the corpse. Not to mention the combat flashbacks.

"The undertaker would never get through," Lady Milton said. "Not in this weather. The last time we were snowed in, we were stuck here for two weeks. We had better find somewhere cold to store her."

Best to be practical in the face of madness, Ben thought. "Let's find something to move her with, then," he said.

～

Ben retrieved his coat, still stiff with snow, and went to search the outbuildings for a suitable bier with which to transport Nanny. Despite having worked in Army logistics in the MOD for several years, he couldn't think of anything that would do for the task in hand. The wheelbarrow he was currently looking to requisition was Lady Milton's suggestion. It was, at least, better than some of the other ideas she had come up with, such as "rolling pins." He didn't enquire further, but it seemed to have something to do with her having watched a documentary on television about how the slaves in Ancient Egypt had moved the stones that built the Pyramids.

The wheelbarrow was eventually unearthed in the stables, whose three occupants, small, rotund ponies, regarded him with indifference verging on hostility.

Back outside in the cobbled courtyard, the snow seemed even heavier than it had done moments before. *Last time we were snowed in, we were stuck here for two weeks.* He glanced around. There was an awful lot of snow. He felt his heartbeat getting fiercer. He was both claustrophobic and agoraphobic at the same time. Just "phobic" would cover it, he supposed. Phobia, from the Greek via Latin. He had done both at school.

When he needed to shut out fear, he would recite the alphabet in Ancient Greek. As well as the Seven Wonders of the Ancient World, the periodic table (Actinium, Aluminium, Americium and so on, all the way to Zirconium), Kings and Queens of England starting with Anglo-Saxon Egbert, and the names of the Seven Dwarves, which were, for some reason, the most difficult of all to remember. Also English Test Match captains, starting with James Lillywhite in 1876. There were a lot of them, he hadn't conquered that list yet. If all that failed, he turned to poetry, scraps and oddments. *Your shadow at evening rising to meet you. Devouring Time, blunt thou the lion's paws. That will be England gone.* "Breathe," he imagined his sister soothing him.

He breathed. He stood up straight. He picked up the wheelbarrow's handles.

⌒

It felt as if hours had gone by when Ben finally made it back to the entrance hall. He went by the overground route, through the part of the house that was open to the public, navigating by the floorplans that were fixed to lecterns in each room along with a guide to the highlights of whichever room you were in. ("Note the inlaid patera in the oak and mahogany floor . . . the grand neo-Gothic fireplace in the Red Room.") Ever-obedient to instruction, he noted it.

He passed no one on the way to what he now learnt, courtesy of the visitors' guides, was called the Great Hall. In fact, the entire house seemed to be deserted, like an enormous sepulchre. Were they all hiding, biding their time until they jumped out at him (*Surprise!*) and sent him into shock?

No sign of the living, but no sign of the dead either. Nanny had disappeared. He put the empty wheelbarrow down and stared for a long time at the spot on the marble floor that had previously been occupied by the heap of clothes. It must have taken a considerable feat of engineering to move her. Or sleight of hand—now you see her, now you don't. Or had she, as he had first suspected, just been *playing* dead? *The Body Walks.* Was Nanny, after all, an actress? Once he had been sent on his ludicrous errand, had she heaved herself off the floor and shared a good laugh with Lady Milton at his expense? "Lady Milton," who was herself probably one of the Murder Mystery company pretending to be the real Lady Milton. Perhaps the entire house was just one big theatrical set. And here he was on stage, a solitary man with his prop, an empty wheelbarrow, like a character in a farce, or a play by Brecht—both equally unappetizing theatrical experiences in Ben's view. One of the upsides of no longer being with Jemima was that he would never have to sit through a performance of *Mother Courage* again.

Ben felt suddenly tremendously, horribly tired, and he would have lain down right where he was on the cold marble and gone to sleep if at that moment the doorbell hadn't rung. It was insistent and, as no one else was rushing to answer it, apparently the task fell to him.

What seemed like an army of people was carried in on a great whirlwind of snowflakes. Ben thought of Napoleon's retreat from Moscow and wondered why he felt it necessary to relate everything in his life to the battlefield.

These people were not Napoleonic, nor were they on retreat from anything—quite the opposite. They were in dramatic high spirits, laughing and stamping snow off their shoes and already breathlessly relaying their shared adventures to each other like people just rescued from near-death—*Nearly stranded out there! . . . Oh my God, the snow, I thought we were going to die! . . . Remember that funny little man at the motorway services?* And so on.

Actors, Ben thought glumly. He had been around enough of them when he had been with Jemima. When they eventually spotted him, they introduced themselves in a flurry of names—*Titus-Zelda-Dom-Camilla-Max-Robin.* The woman called Zelda was wearing a turban. Ben wondered if it was a way of making an impression on people—important if you were an actress, he supposed. *Oh, yes, Zelda, she's the one who always wears a turban.* Jemima was never seen without her bright red lipstick for the same reason. *People always know who I am.* She was a terrible narcissist. He was always blotted with that lipstick, as if she were putting her mark on him.

The oldest of them, and clearly the leader, was a big, piratically bearded man who advanced on Ben with his sword arm outstretched. "Titus North, artistic director," he boomed, ready to pump Ben's hand. Ben thrust his hands in his pockets. Titus North looked as if he'd just walked off-stage in a production of *Treasure Island.* Long John Silver—that was one of the nicknames the men had given Ben after he lost the Leg. And Jake the Peg and the One-Legged Bandit and just plain Stumpy (the Eighth Dwarf—he had no trouble remembering that one). Silly stuff, really. Offensive in the civilian world, of course. The entire Army was offensive in the civilian world. God, he missed it.

"You must be Piers, I presume," Titus said, before Ben had a chance to introduce himself. "My Lord Milton," he went on, making a stupid exaggerated bow and doffing a large imaginary hat with a flourish. The rest of them laughed, delighted, and when he said, "May I present the Red Herrings Theatre Company, who are, for one night only, the Makepeace Players, here to perform *Death Comes to Rook Hall* for your delectation and delight."

The rest of them copied his over-inflated gestures, the men almost genuflecting, the women sinking into curtseys as though they were at the court of the Sun King. They looked ridiculous. Ben thought that they weren't just actors, they were playing the part of being actors. Perhaps they thought that was what was expected of them. He didn't care enough to correct them about his identity, he just wanted to locate the little dog he'd been put in charge of and find a way to escape from this Bedlam.

"Where shall we go?" Titus North asked sonorously. "Where do you want to put us?"

Hell, preferably, Ben thought, scanning the hall's icy acreage of marble for somewhere to square the actors away. There were many doors to choose from, like a nerve-racking game show or perhaps Russian roulette. Every time he opened one and peeked in a room he could feel the odds shortening against him. Sooner or later, he supposed, he was going to be confronted by something ghastly. ("Surprise!")

The most hospitable room appeared to be the Library—a fire burning in the fireplace, big armchairs, lots of books, obviously, although they gave the impression that they had not been removed from their shelves for several centuries. There was a table set with decanters and glasses and bottles that gleamed in the firelight. Perhaps this was where Lady Milton had been taking him to thaw out when they had been waylaid by the inanimate Nanny. It looked inviting. No dead body on the hearthrug, he was relieved to note. "In here, ladies and gentlemen," he said, ushering them inside.

Lady Milton made a sudden appearance from behind another door in the hall. It was going to be all exits and entrances, wasn't it? Ben thought. He tried to remember the rooms on a Clue board—conservatory, study, billiard room. What else? Ballroom? Was there a kitchen? They played a lot of board games at Dairy Cottage. And some fiendish card games. He was constantly berated by George for his "wimpish" lack of competitive spirit, but he actually enjoyed seeing other people's pleasure at winning. "Something wrong with you, then," George said. She could be very blunt. "Lots of things wrong with me," he agreed, more cheerfully than he felt, perhaps.

"The actors are here," he warned Lady Milton. "They're quite excitable. I put them in the Library."

"The Library?" Lady Milton said, in the same tone that Lady Bracknell might have queried a handbag. "Oh, they can't be in there. That's for the welcome drinks for the guests." She steamed off before Ben could ask her what she'd done with Nanny. And, come to think of it—rather late in the day, perhaps—how had Nanny ended up dead? Ben took up his burden and was beginning to trundle the wheelbarrow away when the doorbell rang again. It wasn't a regular doorbell sounding an inoffensive two-note chime, but rather it tolled a despondent fanfare somewhere in the depths of the house. Like a death knell, Ben thought. For Nanny, perhaps.

"Get that, will you?" Lady Milton said to him as she came out of the Library, herding the recalcitrant actors in front of her. "It must be the first of the guests. Can you see to them?"

Ben sighed and put the wheelbarrow down.

"And organize drinks in the Library for them, will you?"

"Yes, of course," he said, because it was so much easier to say yes than to say no.

At least people were still getting through the snow, he thought. That was good, that meant it would still be possible to leave. All he had to do was find Nanny, and the dog—don't forget the dog, no dog shall be left behind. He felt slightly hysterical. Hardly surprising.

Lady Milton found the actors remarkably resistant to being turned out of the Library. "But we need a tiring-house," the one who seemed to be in charge objected. "Titus North," he introduced himself, placing his hand on his heart to denote sincerity, apparently. Sincerity was overrated, in Lady Milton's opinion. Piers' wife, Trudi, had been very sincere. Forthright, even. Perhaps it was a Teutonic thing.

"And you are?" Titus North said to Lady Milton, rather gracelessly, she thought.

"I'm Lady Milton," Lady Milton said stoutly. She felt her identity challenged. Something which, to be honest, she had been experiencing more and more recently. Off-kilter, that was how she thought of it. Was she really Honoria Milton? She had woken up the other day and for a few seconds she hadn't been able to remember who she was. Going ga-ga, she presumed. (Bound to happen eventually.) "Lady Ga-Ga," Cosmo had sniggered. That was a real person, apparently. Not in *Debrett's*.

"Ah," Titus North said obsequiously, he even bowed, which was ridiculous. "I am *so* sorry, enchanted to make your acquaintance, Lady Milton." He attempted to take her hand and kiss it, but she snatched it away. She had never met an actor before, but he fulfilled all her expectations of what one might be like. What was a "tiring-house"? Burton Makepeace was a very tiring house, positively exhausting, but it seemed unlikely he meant that.

"A green room," Titus North explained. "Where the company may prepare themselves. Get into costume and so on."

"Well, the Library's hardly the place for that. We do have a *Green* Room, if that's what you want," she offered. They also had a Blue Room, a Yellow Room and a Red Room, which Cosmo always referred to as "the bloody chamber," although in fact it was the formal drawing room, the previous home of the Turner.

In anticipation of a visit from Edward VII, when he was still the Prince of Wales, the Miltons had decided to instal a new fireplace in the Red Room to impress their royal visitor. The fireplace was a monstrous Gothic affair, a massive marble inglenook—very ugly. There was a family rumour that the Prince had impregnated one of the Milton girls, an aunt of the Old Marquess. If it were true it was quietly covered up, as one did in those days, and the baby shipped off to the colonies somewhere. If there had been a liaison it must have occurred elsewhere, as the Prince of Wales had cancelled the visit for some unsubstantiated reason (heirs to the throne did not need to substantiate, apparently), leaving them lumbered with the godawful fireplace.

The Yellow Room was also known as the Chinese Room and Lady Milton recalled Sophie wondering if that wasn't "rather racist." Lady Milton was baffled, the Miltons were very much not a racist family. It was called the Chinese Room because it was stuffed with the spoils a Milton had brought home during the First Opium War. Although it *was* yellow—the walls hung with silk that had transformed over the years from gold to a dirty nicotine. Lady Milton felt an unwelcome pang of loneliness at the memory of Sophie.

She succeeded in chivvying the actors out of the Library and decided that it would be better to show them the way to the Green Room rather than tell them. It was very easy to get lost in Burton Makepeace. It had taken Lady Milton a good five years after she moved here to find her way around. Even now she had a sneaking suspicion that there was a passage or a suite of rooms somewhere that she didn't know about. Sometimes she dreamt about it. It was very unsettling.

"The Green Room is at the other end of the house," she said to the actors as she herded them across the hall. "It's rather out of the way, I'm afraid." With any luck, Lady Milton thought, they might not find their way back.

"All the better," Titus North said. "We wouldn't want our audience to come upon us unawares. Lay on, Macduff!"

⌒

The Green Room had no particular function and was rarely used and never heated, although fortunately this wasn't something the actors realized until they had been penned inside it.

"I'm sure you'll be very comfortable in here," Lady Milton mollified once they were all gathered in. She employed the kind of agreeable tone with them that Sophie would have used. Perhaps, Lady Milton thought, she should have pretended to be a housekeeper, the chatelaine of Burton Makepeace. It would, after all, not be so very unpleasant to be relieved of the burden of being oneself. "Just ring the bell if you need anything," she said, still channelling Sophie. There was no bell, as she knew very well.

She shut the door of the Green Room behind her. If there had been a key in the lock she would have been tempted to turn it and keep them in there all evening, but all the keys had been removed years ago after Cosmo had locked everyone in their rooms and a footman had had to climb down a rope out of a window to free them. A search party discovered Cosmo in the Milton Arms trying to buy crème de menthe on Johnny's credit card. He was just thirteen.

Where *was* Cosmo? Or Piers, for that matter. Cosmo would be much better suited to looking after these people. Lady Milton hadn't seen him since she had dragooned him into hauling Nanny into Johnny's old wheelchair, after she had suddenly recalled that it was in the neglected half of the attic in the West Wing. The East Wing attic that had once housed the servants was now part of the hotel. "The cheaper rooms," Piers said. To make them en-suite, oddly shaped shower cabinets had been wedged beneath the eaves. There was barely room to stand up in them. Lady Milton failed to understand the modern obsession with en-suites. Nothing wrong with walking down a hallway with your sponge-bag in your hand.

Cosmo had been unfazed by Nanny. "Ding-dong! The witch is dead," he said. Lady Milton was surprised to find herself feeling almost sorry for Nanny. "Yeah," Cosmo said, "I suppose she must have been human once." Perhaps it was Cosmo who had given her the fatal shove into the next world. "My hands are clean," he insisted.

He reported that he had "parked" Nanny in one of the pantries, of which they had several for various comestibles—cheese, meat and so on. Now they had one for Nanny. Not that Nanny was a comestible. Not yet.

The doorbell rang. Lady Milton ignored it. One never opened one's own front door. "Get that, will you, Major?"

―――

"Welcome to Burton Makepeace," Ben said to the shivering couple on the doorstep.

"Roy, Roy Nelson, and this is my wife, Anita. We're from Idaho," Roy added.

"Splendid stuff," Ben said. He was from Wiltshire himself but had never felt the need to introduce himself with his point of origin. The Idahos were in their sixties, maybe seventies—Ben wasn't very good at guessing ages, particularly when it came to women. Jemima's mother, an alarmingly coquettish woman hard-wired to flirt with men and dogs, had asked him how old he thought she was when he was first introduced to her.

"Um," he said helplessly, "forty-eight?" He thought he was erring generously on the flattering end of the age spectrum, but she was extremely vexed by his calculations. "Nearly forty," he hastily amended, but it was too late. It was absurd, as she was fifty-six.

"I'm afraid we're a bit late," Anita said. "My Lord Milton," she added uncertainly.

"I'm not Lord Mi—" Ben began, but why bother? "Not at all," he said, adopting the gracious demeanour of a host or a particularly superior butler. (Did the Miltons have a butler? Or anyone who did the dog-work of answering the door or carting away corpses?) "The weather's atrocious," he continued pleasantly. "I'm surprised you made it at all. Why don't you come into the Library, there's a nice fire going in there. Maybe a drink to warm you up?" Ben was not someone who had previously done much in the way of role-playing—it wasn't exactly the Army's way—but now he was beginning to rather enjoy this adopted persona. Perhaps this was the way out of depression—simply to become someone else? It made sense.

Roy Nelson rubbed his hands and said, "Wonderful." He looked around the entrance hall appreciatively. "Lead on, My Lord."

"*Is* that the correct way to address you?" his wife fretted. She was all angles and bones with the scrag-end look of the Duchess of Windsor. " 'My Lord?' Or should it be 'Your Grace?' "

"I think 'Your Grace' is for archbishops," Ben said. "And dukes and duchesses," he added, "but not the ones that are members of the Royal Family, so for the Duke of Westminster but not for the Duke of Kent." He had been at school with several members of the minor aristocracy, their parents all keenly aware of the nuances of title and address. Both Idahos regarded him quizzically, as if they were trying to translate an obscure, long-dead language. He felt feverish, maybe he was coming down with something.

Ben shepherded the Idahos into the Library and said, "Back in a jiff. Help yourselves to anything."

The doorbell pealed its mournful note again. Ben didn't need to be asked this time. Pavlov would have had a field day with him.

～

"Emma and Gavin Hutchins. Here for the Murder Mystery Weekend?"

"Of course, welcome to Burton Makepeace." Ben was getting into the swing of it now. "Follow me to the Library. There's a nice fire going in there. You look half-frozen. Where are you from? Your fellow sleuths are from Idaho." Rather reluctantly, they admitted to Basingstoke. "Super," Ben said (not a word he recollected ever using before, not in this context anyway). They were younger than the American couple and less eager.

"We were given this 'experience' for Christmas," Emma explained, making the word sound vaguely threatening. "We thought we'd better get it over with."

"More fellow sleuths to pit your wits against!" Ben announced cheerfully to the Idahos in the Library. "Drinks all round?" he offered. For himself, he chose a forty-year-old Macallan from the drinks tray. (Cost a few bob, he thought.) "Water of life," he said to no one in particular. He clinked glasses with everyone and said, "Here's to a fun evening." (Who *was* this person? Ben liked him. He might keep him.) He downed the expensive Macallan like a shot. It landed comfortably in his stomach on the cushion of Lady Milton's cognac, extinguishing his previous nausea and replacing it with an unfamiliar sense of well-being.

"I'm afraid it looks as though you're the only four guests who've managed to make it through," Ben said. "We're going to be snowed in, by the looks of it. Might be here for days, weeks even." A look of horror passed over the faces in the Library. "Better make the best of it," he said cheerfully, pouring another whisky. He raised his glass and said, "Bottoms up!" which was something else that he'd never said before.

~

Dinner was a lacklustre affair, held in the Stubbs Room, although there were no pictures hanging on the walls, Ben noticed, by Stubbs or anyone else. A handwritten menu promised pheasant, but an understudy of meagre, shrivelled duck appeared in its place. A "luscious" strawberry cheesecake was still half-frozen. The general paucity of everything, the icy temperature in the room, the awful food, the shambolic arrangements, seemed to more than satisfy the Idahos' preconceptions of life in Britain.

After dinner, Lady Milton charged Ben with marshalling the guests and showing them to their rooms. He tried to point out to her that he had no idea where any of the rooms were, but his initial success in finding the Library seemed to have convinced her of his capabilities. Either that or—and this, in fact, seemed more likely—she was under the impression that he had joined the staff of Burton Makepeace. So be it, he thought. Private Dogsbody had been promoted to Major Domo, or perhaps even to General Factotum.

"This seems like a nice room," he said to the Basingstokes, opening a door blindly and bracing himself for whatever might be lurking inside. They seemed grateful to find only banality in their room. Perhaps they had been fearful of being overwhelmed by "inlaid patera" and "neo-Gothic fireplaces" but here there were only neutral colours and the sole adornment on the bare walls was an uninspiring landscape print. "A top-notch en-suite, as you can see," Ben said, opening the door to the tiny shower room. "And tea- and coffee-making facilities over here. Biscuits, too—custard creams, how lovely." He quietly pocketed one of the small cellophane-wrapped packets. Battlefield rations. He had eaten hardly anything at dinner, although the waitress had slipped him an extra bread roll. "Tilda," she had murmured huskily in his ear. Ben found her very attractive, something he tried to conceal in case it made her uncomfortable. Women were a minefield that you had to pick your way through.

~

"Blind leading the blind," he said sportively to the Idahos as he led them up the histrionic staircase to their room. It wasn't a sentiment they seemed to appreciate. "My brother is blind," Anita said. "It's not something we jest about."

"I'm so sorry," Ben said. "I don't have a leg to stand on in my defence." He couldn't help himself, he burst out laughing.

"I don't know what's funny," Anita said. Anita, and to a slightly lesser extent Roy, had been aggrieved with Ben ever since discovering that it was in fact Piers who was the "real Lord Milton" and that Ben was a mere imposter, the Perkin Warbeck of Burton Makepeace.

"I'm *so* sorry," Ben apologized. "We seem to have got off on the wrong foot." He creased with laughter. "Just can't help myself."

"Something wrong with the guy," Roy said to his wife.

You have no idea, Ben thought.

"So, if you're ready," he said, "we're to gather in the Library again for the start of the Murder Mystery." He checked his watch. Twenty-one-hundred hours. Far too late to be starting such ridiculous antics. Ben himself was usually to be found getting ready for bed at this time. A child's bedtime, he thought. He slept a lot. ("Depression does that to you," Fran said. As if he didn't know that.) He gave himself a little shake and jumped back into his Major Domo skin.

He was dispatched by Piers to fetch the actors and drive them through the maze of rooms back to the Library, where Titus directed them to wait outside the door. "We shall make an entrance," he said pompously.

The doorbell rang again. Ben waited to see if the snooty butler who had appeared at dinner was going to see to it. It rang again. No, no butler scurried to answer. He wondered if perhaps he had died of hypothermia out in the deer park and now was stuck here as a punishment for past sins. Even by his own estimate, he had led a relatively blameless life, so it seemed a harsh kind of retribution.

A man and a younger woman this time, difficult to work out their exact relationship. Father and daughter, perhaps. Rather antagonistic with each other.

"Welcome, welcome," Ben said exuberantly. "Your fellow sleuths are already here."

"Sleuths?" the man puzzled.

Dramatis Personae

DEATH COMES TO ROOK HALL

A Murder Mystery devised, written and directed by Titus North and performed for one night only by the Makepeace Players.

Dramatis Personae

SIR LANCELOT HARDWICK, owner of Rook Hall .... Clifford Haig

LADY MADELEINE HARDWICK (née Merchant) .... Camilla Debord

OLIVIA HARDWICK, Sir Lancelot's daughter .... Amy Ripley

CARO MILES, Sir Lancelot's sister .... Stella Pickard

CHARLIE MILES, Caro's son .... Max Naismith

GUY BURROUGHS, friend of Madeleine .... Dominic Lester

MAJOR ROGER LIVERSEDGE, friend of Sir Lancelot .... Max Naismith

DR. BERNARD DANKWORTH .... Robin Chester

THE REVEREND ST. JOHN SMALLBONES .... Clifford Haig

COUNTESS IRINA VORANSKAYA .... Zelda Naismith

RENÉ ARMAND .... Titus North

ADDISON, the butler .... Robin Chester

LETTICE, a maid .... Amy Ripley

⌒

Titus North regarded the dramatis personae with something akin to despair. Even with a full complement of actors (if you could call them that) they had to double up, but now they were not one, not two, but three men down. One man and two women, to be exact. Clifford Haig, Stella Pickard and Amy Ripley all *hors de combat*.

The list formed part of the flimsy "notebooks" that were handed out with every Murder Mystery, although to call them notebooks was wishful thinking as really they were just pieces of paper that had been photocopied and then folded and stapled together. The list of the characters was on the first page, followed by a *mise en scène*. There were blank pages for the audience to write down the clues they had acquired. For this evening's play, Piers Milton had provided a hastily scribbled map of the ground floor of Burton Makepeace.

"It's fucking freezing in here, Titus," Zelda complained. "I think I've got frostbite."

"And it's not a green room, far from it," Dominic Lester added. "Not even a glass of water or a wee oatcake to nibble on." (Dominic was Scottish but usually hid it well.)

"Yes, you said there'd be food and drink," the brattish Max Naismith said. He was Zelda's eighteen-year-old son, foisted on them by her so he could get an Equity card.

"Come on now, Blitz spirit, everyone," Titus said, trying to summon his inner Churchill. (He had played him on stage once, a one-man show, just missed out on an award.) "I'm afraid we're going to have to sing for our supper." Much rebellious muttering ensued. Much Muttering—that would be a rather good name for a fictional village, Titus thought. He filed it away in his head. He was writing the screenplay for a TV series—hard-boiled London detective retires to sleepy, picture-perfect village, uncovers a murder, solves the murder, investigates another murder, and so on. Eight episodes, immediate option on a second season. BritBox might take it, although there was no sign of a commission yet, but it was just a matter of time. Titus North was nothing if not optimistic.

Titus North (real name Nigel Jubb) used to have a sideline in corporate-bonding weekends where he would orchestrate role-playing scenarios for middle-management, all of whom were more interested in anticipating the evening bar and whether Susie from Purchasing was really as wild as rumour would have it. It had been stultifying stuff. And then, of course, he'd inevitably fallen foul of the woke brigade and ended up being cancelled by a large soft-drinks manufacturer, at which point he decided it was safer to stick to the Red Herrings.

The Murder Mysteries were set in some mythical pre-war England (yes, just like his proposed TV series) where vicars came to tea and jolly girls played tennis and the hierarchy of the class system was firmly in place. You could get away with a lot in this kind of fictional England without being blackballed. People hankered after it, they just didn't like to admit it. He had "borrowed" most of his plots from Nancy Styles' old novels. No one read them any more, if people recognized her name it was only from that long-running play. Even Titus had been in it, straight out of RADA. It had ended badly, both for his character and Titus himself. "Mustn't dwell," he murmured to himself.

They performed mostly in hotels, the odd luxury train, tailor-made site-specific stuff like tonight. ("You don't have to go to the theatre—the theatre comes to you!") They'd done one for a cruise line (*Murder at Sea*). Being on board a cruise ship just added an extra layer of horror to the whole affair. (No escape! Passengers hounded you!) Every year quite a lot of people disappeared from cruise ships in mysterious circumstances. Unfortunately, Camilla Debord's fiancé, Damien, had been one of them. Tragic. Especially as it left them without a Dr. Dankworth from Dubrovnik to Southampton. Titus had called Robin Chester up for service on their return to dry land. Robin was ancient but still game. He "trod the boards" with Olivier, something he mentioned frequently. Dementia, possibly.

They'd performed a Murder Mystery in Leeds last summer, in Roundhay (*Murder in the Park*), but it had descended into pandemonium. The audience got lost and wandered all over the place, accosting members of the public in the mistaken belief that they were actors. The police turned up eventually, just to add to the confusion. Apparently Roundhay Park had been a favourite hunting ground of the Yorkshire Ripper, something that was pointed out to Titus by several police officers and some angry women. (But then, weren't they all? Certainly the ones he encountered.)

And what to do about Lettice, the maid? It was a small part but

crucial to the "business" and had been played by their *soi-disant* ingé-
nue Amy Ripley, until she had phoned him late last night and jumped
ship (not literally, not like Camilla Debord's fiancé). Amy had been a
pain in the *derrière*, always trying to make comic entrances and exits,
rolling her eyes like a mad horse to signify humour and making a
mockery of her few lines ("More tea, Lady Hardwick?"). Although,
let's face it, no one chewed the scenery like Zelda. Chewed it, swallowed it, regurgitated it, and then chewed it some more before spit-
ting it out. She may as well have been a cow.

And the turban! What a ridiculous affectation, she was neither
bald nor a cancer patient. It made her look like a mad fortune-teller.
The only work Zelda had had in years was the occasional voice-
over, purring about chocolate or soap powder or, recently, saving for
your funeral plan ("Peace of mind for you and your loved ones").
Could she play Lettice the maid as well as Countess Voranskaya?
Subtract the letter *o* from Countess and you got the measure of
Zelda's personality. ("And take the *us* out of Titus," she responded,
"and see what you're left with.")

He read over his introductory notes.

> Sir Lancelot Hardwick, the owner of Rook Hall, has recently
> returned home from his honeymoon in Antibes, bringing with
> him his new young wife, the American actress Madeleine Mer-
> chant. Sir Lancelot's first wife, Rowena, died three years ago when
> she fell from a bedroom window, a death ruled by the coroner as
> "accidental."

(He wondered about those inverted commas—did they give
the game away?) Clifford Haig played Sir Lancelot's corpse, a brief
appearance that allowed him to double up as the Reverend Smallbones later. Clifford was now, ironically, an actual dead body. Titus
had watched as his coffin was lowered into his grave just two days
ago. No play-acting there.

Titus had been with Clifford Haig when he died (by accident
rather than design). Clifford had reported himself unwell and Titus
had gone to visit him in his poky flat in Wandsworth, above a Chi-

nese takeaway, a lesson in how far you could fall. He'd taken the invalid a half-bottle of Johnnie Walker and a pack of Rothmans, Clifford's cigarette of choice, announcing, "I come bearing gifts," when Clifford answered the door.

"Nice to have visitors," Clifford said, leading him inside. "My niece is coming by later as well. I am blessed." He'd turned to religion, apparently, since "the diagnosis."

"Diagnosis?"

"Terminal, stage four," he said, shrugging. "What can you do? I'm afraid I have heard the chimes at midnight, old boy. Time to leave the great stage to go to that 'undiscovered country from whose bourn no traveller returns,' as Hamlet would have it."

"Jesus, Clifford," Titus said. "I didn't know. I thought you had shingles." He probably wouldn't have come if he had known. It was difficult to know what to say, so he offered some saccharine platitudes: "Might not be as bad as you think," "Miracles do happen" and so on. It certainly would take a miracle, Clifford was obviously at death's door—one foot over the threshold, in fact. Nonetheless, he had insisted on making coffee for them both, wobbling through to the tiny kitchenette that looked as though it hadn't been cleaned since Thatcher was dethroned. "No milk, I'm afraid," he said.

"Don't bother," Titus said, fearful of Clifford's idea of "coffee." He suggested they crack open the Johnnie Walker instead.

They drank the whisky side by side on the sofa—it was the only seating—and then Clifford stubbed his cigarette out, leant back on the cushions, emitted an enormous, theatrically morose sigh and closed his eyes.

Naturally, Titus thought Clifford had simply fallen asleep, but then it dawned on him rather slowly that he was, in fact, dead. No other word for it. Not much point in calling an ambulance, it would just be a waste of resources. He had no idea who Clifford's GP was. He could have phoned the NHS helpline, he supposed, but what advice could they have given other than praying for a miracle or sending for an undertaker?

In the end, Titus toasted the departed Clifford with another whisky and smoked one of his Rothmans, inhaling deeply. Titus had given up smoking years ago (to save the voice) but he missed it every day. He recalled that Clifford had said his niece was coming by later, so he stubbed out his cigarette and, remembering the plot of their current murder mystery, took his empty glass through to the kitchenette and washed and dried it, just in case the police thought he might have somehow poisoned Clifford Haig. (His fingerprints were on file, unfortunately.) Then he pocketed the Rothmans before exiting quietly, stage left, pursued by Death.

It was tragic, he reported back to the other cast members—they had lost their Reverend Smallbones. The rewrites, needless to say, were a nightmare.

Guy Burroughs, a film star and friend of Madeleine, is visiting from California. Caro, Sir Lancelot's sister, also lives at the Hall, following a bitter divorce. Charlie, her ne'er-do-well son, recently sent down from Oxford, is visiting her.

The part of Caro Miles had gone because Stella Pickard, who played her, had simply walked out on them with no apology, mid-performance in Basildon. *Christmas Is Murder,* for a party in a church hall. Toned down a bit for the kiddies. Father Christmas was the murderer. A very unpopular choice, it turned out. The way the company was dropping like flies, Titus would soon be the only one left. A monologue. *Then There Was One.*

A polite knock at the door of the makeshift green room announced the entrance of a woman in a black dress and a white apron, carrying a tray. For a brief, delusional moment Titus thought she must have arrived to play Lettice, but it turned out she wasn't an actress, she was an actual maid, or a waitress, which was the same thing really, wasn't it? The tray was piled with sandwiches ("I thought you might be hungry"), which were descended on by what remained of the company like hyenas.

Could a civilian be roped in to play Lettice? It was a thought. The waitress ("Tilda," she said with the ghost of a curtsey) wore thick-rimmed spectacles, and her black hair was cut in a sharp bob—very Louise Brooks. She was going for a *look,* Titus thought. At least it didn't involve a turban. Before he could audition her she was gone, with a cheery "Break a leg!" (No one *said* that.)

They had to endure the Arctic conditions of the green room for another hour before the man who had greeted them when they first arrived came to fetch them. ("The Major"—a questionable rank.) "That's where you've been hiding," he said. "I was looking everywhere for you. Everyone's waiting in the Library."

"Showtime," Titus North said gloomily.

———

Titus took up a commanding position in front of the fire. "Ladies and gentlemen and everyone in between," he greeted in his best *basso profundo*. He could have been trying to reach the back of the stalls in the Palladium rather than the confines of Burton Makepeace's Library. The pack in front of him shuffled restlessly. They were a meagre audience—a motley crew of Miltons had been conscripted by Piers to make up the numbers.

"I am Titus North, Artistic Director of the Red Herrings Theatre Company, and this evening—under the soubriquet of the Makepeace Players—we are proud to present for your delight a little offering entitled *Death Comes to Rook Hall*. The notebooks that are currently being handed to you by the Major will enable you to write down the evidence that you come across during your promenade through the rooms. Lord Milton" (a necessarily deferential nod in Piers' direction) "has kindly allowed us the freedom of several rooms on the ground floor of his magnificent house. He has kindly asked you to remain within the designated areas."

"And not to touch anything!" Lady Milton squawked.

"Of course, m'lady," Titus said, bowing vaguely in the direction of her voice. "As you roam through the various rooms," he continued, "you will discover members of the company acting out little tableaux. These will help to give you the evidence needed to solve the murder—or should I say 'murders' in the plural?"

"Is there a prize at the end of it?" the American woman asked. "For finding the murderer?"

"*Au contraire*," Titus said. "The prize is knowing you are the cleverest person in the room." Not an answer that seemed to satisfy anyone. What a fractious bunch they were. "You may ask the characters anything you like," he pressed on. "Are their alibis watertight? Do they have motives? Will they accidentally incriminate themselves? Et cetera, et cetera. Anything that will help you to piece together the puzzle and crack the case. We shall begin here in the Library, where our characters have been forced together by external circumstances."

"Bloody hell," he heard someone mutter. "How long is this going to last?"

Titus was unfazed, he'd been heckled by the best. "Come, come," he said, gesturing to the actors hovering in the doorway. "Come and be introduced to your audience." The Library was not large and was now considerably overcrowded. "Black hole of Calcutta," someone complained.

Titus gave a little cough to oil his vocal cords and then took a majestic breath before saying, "Picture the scene. It is a dark and stormy night . . ."

Marooned

Reggie's heart had given an utterly unexpected little lurch when the front door of Burton Makepeace opened. She had been expecting the po-faced butler who had previously always let her in—with, it had to be said, an unnecessary amount of pomp and circumstance, unusual in an Aussie. *And who shall I say is calling, miss?* Even though he knew perfectly well who she was. "It's not 'miss,'" she said caustically, "it's *Detective* Chase to you." She hadn't said that, only in her head. She was Zen.

The man who greeted them this time, however, was cut from a different cloth—definitely not a butler, unless butlers had started to dress in old Army fatigues. "Welcome, welcome," he said. "Your fellow sleuths are already here. In you come, out of the cold. It's biting, isn't it? I'm surprised that you made it at all." He was so full of bonhomie you could have lit a candle off him. Or manic, perhaps. It was hard to tell.

And who cared, because he was good-looking! Really good-looking! And, as a bonus, he didn't look vain, rather he was ruggedly handsome, like an explorer, or an adventurer. And yes, "ruggedly handsome" was a clichéd term that belonged in her mother's old Mills & Boon books, but really Reggie couldn't think of another way to describe him. He looked like someone who would trek across the Antarctic or man a lifeboat or captain a submarine. He was the sheriff riding into town. Someone who would save you from a Huron war party. Be still, my beating heart, she thought. She felt slightly sick.

"You all right, Reggie?" Jackson said.

"Yes, of course I am," she said crossly.

"You look a bit flushed, that's all."

The good-looking man ushered them across the enormous hallway. (Did he have a name? He must have a name. Everyone had a name.) "I'm afraid you've missed dinner—no great loss, truth be told. I could probably rustle up a sandwich for you, if you want. The revels haven't started yet."

"Revels?"

"I must warn you, I'm afraid it's theatre. This way, just follow me. Mind that wheelbarrow. Let's get a drink to warm you up. Everyone's in the Library."

The good-looking man had a slight limp. It made him even more handsome. Perhaps he had injured himself climbing the Matterhorn or traversing an ice crevasse.

They hadn't got very far when they were ambushed by Lady Milton. Frowning at them, she said to the good-looking man, "Are they also actors, Major?," unwilling apparently to address them directly. (Major!)

"Don't think so," he said. "*Are* you?" he asked.

"Actors? God, no," Jackson said.

"No," the handsome Major conveyed to Lady Milton, in his role of go-between. "They're not actors."

"It's me, Lady Milton," Reggie intervened.

"Me?"

"Reggie Chase." (Little Reggie, orphan of the storm, she of the great expectations.) "From when the Turner was stolen. I've been here a couple of times since then."

Lady Milton peered at Reggie as if she were looking at a specimen through a microscope. "Ah," she said. "Regina, isn't it? I would have thought you would have enough murder on your hands without all this play-acting."

"Murder?" Jackson asked, perking up. "*Has* there been a murder?"

"Not yet," Lady Milton said. "Although . . ." she trailed off, staring at the huge staircase as if captivated by the colossal size of it.

"Nanny, perhaps?" the good-looking Major prompted her.

"Possibly."

Burton Makepeace had always been teetering on the edge of being a madhouse, but now, Reggie thought, it had gone into full Bedlam mode. Lady Milton flapped her hand, half Royal wave, half Nazi salute, as if dismissing herself. She walked off and disappeared behind a door. And then reappeared a second later, a disembodied head that said to the Major, "Someone should move that wheelbarrow," before disappearing again.

"As before, follow me," the Major said, ignoring the wheelbarrow.

They set off again, Reggie trotting behind him, increasing her pace to draw level with him. "I don't think we've been introduced," she said. "My name's Reggie Chase." She hoped he hadn't deduced from her exchange with Lady Milton that she was a police officer, she wanted him to think of her as a civilian.

"Ben Jennings," he said as they skirted the incongruous wheelbarrow in the middle of the floor. "Very nice to meet you." Ben Jennings. Ben. Ben, rhymes with Zen. Glancing behind her, Reggie saw Jackson Brodie sauntering after them, a big grin on his face. He was laughing at her, wasn't he? He would be the one being murdered soon if he wasn't careful. *Zenzenzen*, she reminded herself.

"I'm sorry, did you say something?" the Major asked her.

"No, nothing," Reggie said.

"I think we're in for a frolicsome evening," Ben (as Reggie now familiarly thought of him) said. "That's a rather lovely word, isn't it?" Reggie felt her heart skip a beat (yes, she did!) and thought—a man who enjoyed words! A handsome man who enjoyed words. A handsome man who enjoyed words who would also drag you out from a house on fire, pull you from the water if you were drowning, find you on the side of a mountain if you were lost. Of course, a good dog would also do all those things. ("So would a good woman," Ronnie's voice in her head said.)

"Drink?" he offered when they reached the Library. He poured something into a glass and pushed it into her hands. Normally, she would have refused, Reggie wasn't much of a drinker at the best of times, but it had been a difficult day, stranded in the snow and so on. Plus, a very handsome man was offering it to her, like a libation, so Reggie said, "Why not?"

"Are you sure?" a voice behind her said. Jackson Brodie, naturally. She turned and glared at him, but that didn't stop him from saying to Ben Jennings, "I'm her dad." *Zenzenzenzenzen.* More a swarm of angry wasps than Buddhist serenity.

There were four people already in the Library (their "fellow sleuths"). Two couples, Jackson guessed from the way the twosomes were sticking like glue to each other. The weather meant that most people had failed to turn up for the weekend, or perhaps the sheer horror of being voluntarily stuck with a bunch of strangers playing make-believe murder had made them think twice about coming. Some reluctant small talk ensued. Apparently Idaho grew more potatoes than any other state.

They were joined eventually by a big, rather bloated man, gussied up in an evening jacket that was beginning to stretch at the seams to accommodate his girth. "Lord Milton," Reggie whispered to Jackson, behaving rather like one of those flunkies who murmur the names of people in the monarch's ear when they're being introduced ("Alan Watson, sir—owns a confectionery-distribution company in Walsall").

When someone addressed him as "My Lord" Piers said, "No standing on ceremony here, call me Piers." It was a touch of egalitarianism that seemed to disappoint the American guests.

Although he liked to think of himself as the tolerant sort, Jackson had to suppress his latent working-class bile from rising whenever he rubbed shoulders with the upper classes. "Come the revolution . . ." he muttered to Reggie.

"Calm down, Trotsky."

"Picture the scene," Titus North said. "It is a dark and stormy night. A fierce snowstorm has left several people stranded at Rook Hall until the morning—René Armand, the famed Swiss detective, his friend Dr. Bernard Dankworth, Irina Voranskaya, a mysterious Russian countess, and the Reverend St. John Smallbones, the vicar of the local church, St. Botolph's."

"Have you read this rubbish?" Jackson murmured to Reggie as the actors made stagy entrances into the room. He was leafing through one of the notebooks that Titus had just distributed. "It asks more questions than it answers."

"That's the whole idea, I think," Reggie said.

"For example, what was bitter about sister Caro's divorce? What did Charlie, the ne'er-do-well nephew, do to get sent down from Oxford? Why is Guy Burroughs here—is he relevant to the plot or does it just provide an out-of-work actor with a job? And who is Countess Voranskaya and why is she mysterious?

"Plus," Jackson continued (in the face of theatrical yawning on Reggie's part), "is 'the famous Swiss detective René Armand' here by chance, or does he have suspicions that have led him here? And why is the point made that Lettice, the maid, was hired while the happy couple were on honeymoon? Is that relevant? And, perhaps most important of all, the first wife—what was her name?"

"Rowena," Reggie supplied with a sigh.

"Rowena, thanks—did she really fall or was she pushed?"

"Wow. You should solve crimes for a living."

"I'm good at asking questions."

"Not so good at answering them," Reggie said.

Jackson ignored this slight. "I'm guessing that it's going to be Sir Lancelot who bites the dust first."

"Correct," Reggie said. "Sir Lancelot is going to die from drinking a brandy that's been poisoned—spoiler alert—by the first wife, Rowena, because, thanks to some extremely unlikely plot manipulation, it turns out Rowena's not actually dead and is out to wreak vengeance on the person who tried to murder her."

"And you know all this because?" Jackson asked.

"Because the plot and characters are lifted straight from *The*

Mystery at Folly Abbey—another out-of-print Nancy Styles. Some of the characters even have the same names. I skimmed the plots of all her novels online, because, oh, you know, I don't have anything better to do than be your assistant."

"You love it, admit it."

"Anyway—blatant plagiarism," Reggie said. "And illegal—Nancy Styles died in 1975. She might be dead but her copyright lives on."

"You know what I think?"

"I'm on tenterhooks."

"Think about it," Jackson said. "Who benefits from Sir Lancelot's death? Charlie's the next in line to the title and all the money that goes with it. If Sir Lancelot were to have a child with the new Lady Hardwick then Charlie loses out, so to inherit he needs to kill his uncle before that can happen. Although he could equally well knock off Lady Hardwick—unless, of course, he *married* her. There's an idea."

"It's not real, you know," Reggie said wearily.

"I know that. If it was real, I would have arrested all of them for bringing murder into disrepute."

"You can't arrest anyone, you're not police any more."

"Citizen's arrest."

"Whatever."

Against the odds, Jackson was beginning to enjoy himself. "Ey up, we're on the move," he said when Titus started goading them out of the Library. "An inspector calls."

⌒

"And so we leave the Library," Titus announced, "and make our way to the Morning Room, also known as the Blue Room. Follow me, please . . . Yes, all of you, that means you as well," he said to the two teenage girls—identical twins—who were lagging behind. They were Miltons by the look of them, strong genes or inbred, it was hard to say. They had clearly been co-opted unwillingly into the evening's revels.

"No, not that way, not *that* door, *this* one here." Each room in the house had at least two doors, Titus had counted four in the Red Room. It was like the stage set of a farce, rigged for endless comings and goings.

"The Blue Room, in which we are standing, is where the body of Sir Lancelot Hardwick has just been discovered by the house-maid, Lettice." Of course, Titus thought ruefully, there was no actual body, only unoccupied carpet where an inanimate Sir Lance-lot should be. That didn't stop Camilla Debord, playing Lady Hard-wick, from sticking to the script and gazing in horror at the empty air, moaning "Oh my God, is he dead?" to no one in particular. She hadn't been herself since her fiancé jettisoned himself off the QM2—when, in fact, these had been her very words. Art imitating life. Or was it the other way round?

"The body of Sir Lancelot has already been removed," Titus said to his audience. "Grief is causing his new widow to hallucinate." Dr. Bernard Dankworth, played by Robin Chester, tottered into the room. "I have examined the body," he said, "and I believe it to have been a heart attack, m'lady."

"But he was as fit as a fiddle!" Camilla exclaimed. And so on. It was a tedious scene, but necessary. Dominic Lester, in the guise of Guy Burroughs, burst into the room and growled, "What the hell happened here?" Very Bogart for someone who was originally from Troon. "You okay, baby?" he said to Lady Hardwick. Camilla, in her role as herself (she was incapable of playing anyone else), did look a little green around the gills.

"All three characters are available for questioning," Titus said to his audience. Everyone gazed at the floor. "By *you*, questioned by *you*," he clarified. More floor-gazing. "You may notice, for exam-ple," he prompted, "that a glass has fallen to the carpet. Did Sir Lancelot drink from it before collapsing and dying? Who gave the drink to Lord Hardwick? Why don't you ask *that*, for God's sake?"

"Poisoned," Lady Milton said, rather loudly, "like poor Johnny."

"Who's Johnny?" someone asked.

"Not a character," Titus snapped. "What was in the glass?" he persisted. "Could it have caused a heart attack?"

"That's unlikely," the American woman said. (She claimed to be a retired cardiologist.)

"And where's the body?" someone else piped up. Emma, from Basingstoke, Titus forced himself to remember. "You said that Sir Lancelot had just been killed, so where is he?"

Six feet under in Highgate Cemetery, Titus thought. "As I said, the body has already been removed," he explained patiently. He mustn't lose his temper, he reminded himself. He shuddered at the uninvited memory of an away weekend in Leicestershire with a publishing company. They had turned on him like feral dogs at the end of it.

"But where is it?"

"In the pantry," Lady Milton said.

"Thank you," Titus said. "The body's in the pantry."

"But surely you shouldn't have moved the body?" someone else said. "The pathologist needs to examine it *in situ*. You can't just take this Dr. Dankworth's word for the cause of death without a post-mortem. And has anyone taken witness statements? What about the housemaid, Lettice—has she been interviewed? She seems like a crucial witness to me."

"Lettice is tied up at the moment," Titus said.

"Really?" Piers asked, perking up.

"And what about forensics?" the same person as before said. "People have walked all over this crime scene, haven't they? All the evidence will have been compromised."

Oh *him*. Titus sighed. The one who said he used to be a policeman. "Let us move on," he said hastily. "Leaving the Blue Room for the Yellow Room, also known as the Chinese Room, and as you can—"

The doorbell interrupted him. The restive audience seemed to think it was part of the plot and turned towards the door to see who was about to make an entrance.

"Pay no attention," Titus said irritably. "It is not part of the evening's entertainment." The bell rang again. "Is anyone going to answer that? Major, isn't that your job?"

"Absolutely," Ben said.

"Welcome, Welcome. Your fellow sleuths are— Oh my God, are you all right? What on earth happened to you?"

The latecomer looked as though he had been astray in the snow for hours. He was wearing a grubby grey tracksuit, sported a bad cut on his hand, and a large bruise was blooming on his temple. Added to that, his nose looked as though it might be broken and his eye was already blackening. He was limping, too, and Ben felt an immediate comradeship. The halt and the lame.

"Slipped," the man said gruffly with no elaboration when Ben enquired how he had injured himself.

"Yeah, it's pretty awful out there, isn't it?" Ben said, shepherding him inside. "We need to get you warmed up. Why don't we find you a room?"

Had the man been simply stranded on the moors or was he here for the Murder Mystery? He seemed too truculent to enjoy playing games. The tracksuit, for one thing, indicated a different purpose, but then it took all sorts, as Ben's sister was always telling him. "Are you here for this evening's shenanigans?" he asked. "For murder most foul?"

"What?" The question seemed to knock the newcomer off balance.

"No, clearly not," Ben said hastily. "Sorry. My name's Ben, by the way," he added. "And yours?" he prompted when there was yet more silence. The man took some time to consider the question. Did he have amnesia? Ben wondered.

"Adam," the man said eventually, seemingly plucking the name from the air. He didn't seem convinced by it.

"The first man, eh?" Ben said. A ridiculous thing to say, he supposed. It wasn't as though he believed in the Bible. Creation was a lovely idea, but preferably without any people attached. It was a point of view also held by Simon, the vicar. "The Fall of Man," he had said to Ben, apropos of nothing on the afternoon when he came to bless the bees. "You never hear anyone say the Fall of Elephants, do you? Or the Fall of Sloths, or robins, or even hornets and hyenas, for that matter, or—" Ben had interrupted with an offer of another slice of George's Victoria sponge before the vicar had a chance to work his way through the entire ark. But he had been right, of course. Man had fallen and had kept on falling and there was no sign of him stopping. The abyss was bottomless, apparently.

"Anyway, this way, follow me," Ben said as he led the man over to the hotel side of the house. No response. Poor guy must be traumatized, Ben thought. No existential dread for the jovial Major Domo though, only good cheer as he ushered Adam into a room. "Fully ensuite, as you can see. Minibar, too," he added, looking inside the tiny fridge and finding a meagre supply of miniatures. "Tell you what, you get cleaned up and I'll go downstairs and find a first-aid box and something decent to drink." Adam grunted. Ben took it as assent. "Righty-ho. Back in a jiffy, then."

It took some time to locate either of the aforesaid items, but eventually the kitchen provided both. A rusted white tin with a red cross on it was located beneath the kitchen sink and a bottle of good brandy was winkled from the back of a cupboard by Tilda, the waitress from dinner. "Have you hurt yourself?" she asked solicitously when he grubbed out the first-aid tin from its hiding place.

"No, no, not me, it's a guy who's just arrived. He was in a bit of a state from struggling through the snow. Lucky he made it here."

All the kitchen staff seemed to have disappeared now, but Tilda was getting on with the clearing-up—rinsing plates, loading the dishwasher, wiping down the counters. Of course, Ben was genetically hard-wired to admire people who simply got on with things, so it wasn't just the dark bobbed hair and the blue eyes behind the spectacles and the petite figure that he found beguiling, although they certainly played their part. He helped ferry some dishes to her at the sink and asked, "Have you worked here long?"

"Oh, I don't work here, thank God," she said. "I'm with an agency, hired for the evening."

"I don't suppose that you'll get home tonight with all the snow. Do you live locally? When you're not stuck here?"

"Questions, questions," she said and laughed.

"Sorry."

"You'd better go and see to your wayfaring stranger."

"Yes, of course, duty calls."

⌁

There was no answer to his polite knock. He knocked again and then began to fret that Adam had succumbed to concussion or hypothermia. He knocked a third time before making a hesitant entrance into the room. There was no sign of anyone. Adam had gone walkabout, a chancy activity in this place. He might be wandering about for hours or collapse unconscious somewhere and never be found. Ben left the first-aid box behind, but took the brandy bottle with him when he set off again. A St. Bernard on a rescue mission.

⌁

"In the Yellow Room," Titus said, "we discover Charlie Miles, the ne'er-do-well son of Lord Hardwick's sister Caro, talking to Dr. Dankworth."

"But that's the guy who played the butler," one of the twins objected.

"Yeah," the other said. "He's taken his moustache off, that's all."

Titus heroically ignored them. He was feeling the absence of Stella Pickard, who played Caro Miles, Lord Hardwick's sister, and was vital to this scene. "But why, you may ask, is Charlie rifling through this chinoiserie chest? And where is the—"

"I'm going to check on Lady M," Reggie whispered to Jackson. "I think she got left behind somewhere."

The Reverend Smallbones

Simon had blundered on awkwardly through the snow, handicapped by the gun in his pocket bumping uncomfortably against his leg. He was still lugging the painting in the Morrisons bag, weightier by the minute. More than anything, he wanted to stop moving and sit down. He wondered how much more trudging he had in him before he quit trying and embraced hypothermia.

The never-ending yomping gave him a flashback to his one attempt at pilgrimage. He had planned to walk the Camino de Santiago—the Way of St. James. It was when his faith had started to dim and he thought a pilgrimage might sort it out somehow, as if it was old grouting or earwax. All that walking (over five hundred miles!) would be a test of his endurance, both physical and spiritual, and he would return with strong calf muscles and his faith a shield, polished to a dazzling brightness.

Of course, the hardships would be tempered by the promise of "sociable lunches" along the way and some pretty decent food in the evenings—a lot of "the Way" was in France, after all—but he had eschewed the premium package with its luggage assistance and overnight stays in "converted water mills and stylish farmhouses," opting instead to rest his weary limbs in humble hostels and—big mistake—to carry his own backpack. Jesus, after all, had carried his own cross.

He had begun the journey jauntily enough, unintentionally falling in with a group of enthusiastic (and alarmingly fit) young Americans from Texas, who were delighted to be accompanied by a Man of God. He soon regretted revealing to them the fact that he was a vicar (they insisted on referring to him as Pastor Simon), as they all knew the Scriptures backward and presumed he did, too. It was like taking an exam while on a forced march beneath an unforgiving continental sun.

While he was grunting and sweating from the exertion of heaving himself and his heavy pack up some hill or other, they gambolled around him like baby goats, forever reeling off great chunks of the Bible—"In James 2:14–26 it says, 'What does it profit, my brothers, though a man say he has faith, and have not works? Can faith save him?' Can it, Pastor Simon? Can faith alone save us?"

Nothing can save us, he thought gloomily. Certainly not faith. "What do *you* think?" was his usual breathless response.

Of course, the Americans were especially fond of quoting St. James as they were walking "his" Way. The authorship of James was in doubt—"Not really in the canon," he said to them one evening at dinner (no alcohol, not even a light ale, they were all brashly teetotal). And by all accounts it was pseudepigraphic, he continued, written not as a letter but as a moral treatise, several centuries after Christ. He lost them at "canon," long before "pseudepigraphic."

Nor did they doubt for a minute that James's relics were lying in the cathedral in Santiago de Compostela waiting to greet them. Simon thought anyone who claimed to be in possession of saints' bones or bits of the "True Cross" had been duped by medieval con artists. But what did it matter? Nothing mattered, did it?

By the end of the first day his face was tight with sunburn because he had stupidly forgotten to pack a hat, even though it was highlighted on the extensive list he had been given by the company that arranged his trip. One of the girls—Amanda, all hair and metal retainers—supplied him with her spare baseball cap. It was pink and emblazoned with the name of her college cheerleading squad. He didn't care. He still had it at the bottom of a drawer somewhere, his very own relic for whoever came after him to find. No doubt his own reliquary would be the waste bin.

For the first few days he managed (a true miracle) to match their long limbs stride for stride (twenty-five miles a day!), while the pilgrim's scallop shell they had given him bounced rhythmically on his backpack. He quoted Sir Walter Raleigh's "The Passionate Man's Pilgrimage" to them. *Give me my scallop shell of quiet, my staff of faith to walk upon.* They regarded him amiably, their faces blank.

He hadn't even got as far as Chartres when he had to admit defeat, overwhelmed by a rotator-cuff injury to his shoulder and blistered, bleeding feet (he had not thought to wear in his new hiking boots). His legs had turned to string, each step more impossible than the last. Those people inclined towards sanctimonious cliché said it was the journey, not the destination, didn't they? They were wrong. It was all about the end.

The young Americans romped on, leaving him in their wake. "Or the hands of God," as they put it. Very unchristian on their part, he thought, as he limped into the outskirts of Chartres, where he recuperated for several days in the welcome luxury of the five-star Maison Blanche. He made sure no one found out that he was a Man of God, because, let's face it, he wasn't, was he? Not really.

～

The house finally loomed out of the snow ahead of him. He had been lost and now he was found. Geographically, anyway. He had prayed for deliverance and here he was, delivered, if only to the back door of Burton Makepeace. The house had been built with its back to the church, as if the ancestral Miltons had preferred not to look religion in the face. The back door was the one that Lady Milton had long ago made it clear she preferred that he use. The "servants' entrance" as she called it, and when he (mildly) queried this she said, "Well, you're a servant of the Lord, aren't you?"

And then suddenly, just when safety was in sight, he found himself falling through empty air, his legs and arms flailing in a way that would have looked comical to an onlooker. He landed on his back with a heavy thump. He had hit the back of his head, too, and spent some moments simply staring into the night sky, icy snow-flakes landing on his eyeballs, wondering if he was all right or if he'd given himself a brain haemorrhage that was going to slowly leak blood into his skull until he quietly died.

No, not dying, not a bleed on the brain, he decided as he strug-gled to sit up. Where was he? He seemed to have fallen into a trench of some kind. Everything was snow, no contours visible anywhere. Was it a trap? Some of the locals set rabbit traps but they were wire contraptions, designed to snare a small, innocent leg. He had found a cat caught in one in the woods once. It had been dead for several weeks, dried out and flattened like an old mat. He had released its little corpse and buried it at the back of the churchyard, murmur-ing a funeral prayer as he did so. *Grant to the souls of all our faithful departed, your mercy, light and peace.*

He was gripped by a spasm of guilt. He had said nothing over Janet Teller's body, no prayers to light her way into the darkness. Janet's Way. It was unlikely she would be canonized, but perhaps she was already a dolphin, swimming in the warm waters of the Pacific. The odds seemed against it. He had been cowardly, of course, he had run in fear from her killer rather than staying to give comfort to her soul. And this was his punishment, he thought, as he attempted to climb out of whatever he was in. He slipped back down, landing painfully on his coccyx this time.

Oh, of course—he knew where he was now—he was in the Miltons' ha-ha. (A ludicrous name for what was basically a ditch.) Beyond was the lawn (once a parterre, long abandoned). Behind him was simply landscape—an artificially created pastoral that Marie Antoinette might have coveted. The rolling hills had once been dotted with old-fashioned ornamental livestock—prize-winning Red Lincoln cows and Wensleydale sheep. Lady Milton had relent-lessly catalogued them for him one afternoon over weak tea and stale scones, while lamenting the desertion of her cook.

Beasts of the field. Simon thought of Genesis, for some reason. God brought "every beast of the field and every fowl of the air" to

Adam to be named. It must have started off as a novelty and ended up being mind-numbingly boring, like working for Farrow & Ball and having to find yet another name for a new shade of grey.

The ha-ha had been sunk invisibly into the land to keep the farm animals at bay and prevent them from wandering into the garden and eating up the parterre, but now the Miltons had sold the farmland and the animals were long gone, and where once Gainsborough had painted *The Marquess of Milton and His Wife, Aurelia* with the vista of their acreage behind them, an industrial field of rape glared radioactively in the summer.

The gun was still in his pocket, but it took some time for him to find the Morrisons bag as the snow had already started to cover it. He was committed now to saving it. Finally, with an almost superhuman effort, he got himself and the painting out of the ha-ha. He had been reduced to praying for help in the end, but he doubted that was the reason for his liberation. He supposed coincidence was at the root of many people being led into thinking that their prayers had been answered. Ha ha.

Trapped!

Burton Makepeace was a warren, as puzzling as an Escher drawing or a fun house (with no fun), and, in pursuit of Ben, Reggie somehow ended up on a lower floor, in a bleak scullery that didn't seem to have changed since the house was built. The scullery led to a small room that she supposed was a pantry, not that Reggie had ever actually encountered one before because no one had pantries any more. From the Old French *paneterie*, a place to store bread, she knew. (*What is this? School?*)

In the pantry there was a deep stone shelf on which sat an enormous drum of Stilton, parts of which had been gouged out—by the silver spoon that sat next to it, Reggie presumed, unless rats with a taste for blue cheese had been pillaging in here. On one side, the Stilton was neighboured by a rather glossy roasted chicken that indeed looked more like a stage prop than actual food. On the other side was a big leg of cured ham. A small, delicate trotter remained attached to the leg, as if to authenticate its origins. Provenance, Reggie thought, a word that Jackson was obsessed with.

A door led to another pantry, this one even chillier than the last. Here the stone slab displayed a joint of raw beef and an enormous uncooked goose. Rabbits, hares and feathery game birds, still unplucked, were hanging from hooks. The butcher's-shop smell made Reggie feel squeamish.

Was that yet another door? Leading to yet another pantry? How many pantries did a house need? And was there going to be something even more unappetizing in the next one?

Yes, there was. Another big stone shelf, but on this one there was no goose-pimpled goose or bloody baron of beef. No, on this shelf there was a woman. A large woman. A large, old woman. A large, old, dead woman.

She *was* dead, wasn't she? Or could she possibly be part of the Murder Mystery that was taking place upstairs? An ersatz corpse. Or a waxwork figure, perhaps. Reggie steeled herself for a closer inspection.

Yes, dead. So not part of the Murder Mystery, unless it was not the innocent parlour game it appeared to be and was actually some kind of nightmarish *Squid Game* "experience" with actual murder victims.

Then, as if it had taken a walk-on part in a horror film, the heavy door behind Reggie closed with a loud clash, and when she tried to open it she found that it was stuck fast, and no matter how much she pulled and pushed, it remained stubbornly closed. Had someone locked her in? Was she walled up alive? In a crypt disguised as a pantry? With a corpse? Where was a handsome Major when you needed one?

Reggie hadn't felt this kind of fear since she was told about her mother's death. Her mother had drowned in a swimming pool—her hair caught in a drain—on a holiday abroad when Reggie was a teenager, and Reggie spent a lot of time afterwards imagining the terror her mother must have felt. It had taken her years to learn how to block those awful images. Give me a swift death, she thought—a hammer blow to the head, the sudden aneurism, the proverbial bus. Not drowning at the bottom of a swimming pool, not suffocating slowly in a shared tomb.

The house of Usher, the fortress of Udolpho, the castle of Otranto—she thought of all those Gothic texts she had read when she was doing her English Literature A-Level, even though they weren't on the syllabus and none of her teachers had recommended that she read them. "Leave no book unread" could have been Reggie's motto when she was younger.

Oubliette. Lady Milton's word echoed unnecessarily in her brain. She would be forgotten. Perhaps years from now someone would find her corpse, shrivelled and mummified, and wonder how this had happened. Would they find her police ID and say, "Oh, Reggie Chase, wasn't she that detective who went missing years ago? So *this* is what happened to her!"

And then, just to complete the nightmare, the lights went out in the house of Gothic fiction. She had found herself in a real-life Hammer Horror.

Drenched in panic, Reggie had forgotten for a moment that there was a torch on her phone. She fumbled in her pocket, but couldn't find it. Was it in her bag? Where was her bag? Did she even have a bag? Had she ever had one? What was a bag? And then the door that was stuck fast began to creak slowly open, relishing its part in the nightmare.

"What the fuck?" Cosmo said when he saw Reggie. "You nearly gave me a heart attack. I came down to get something to eat." He waved the large chicken drumstick in his hand in the direction of the dead body. "I heard noises, I thought Nanny might have turned into a zombie. I wouldn't put it past her. What are you doing in here in the dark?" He reached for a switch next to the door and the light came on. "The magic of electricity," he said.

"The lights went out."

"Yeah, they're on a timer."

"I couldn't open the door."

"It's sticky. You've got to give it a good old heave."

"Nanny?" Reggie said faintly. Was there a rational explanation for her, too?

"The old goat, the bearded lady, the war horse."

"She's dead," Reggie pointed out.

"Very. Not by my hand though. The story is that she fell downstairs."

"Story?"

"Yeah. Want some?" he said, offering her the drumstick.

"God, no."

"Anyway, lovely to chat, but Nanny's beginning to reek so I'm going back upstairs to see if anyone's been murdered yet. Coming?"

"There you are," Jackson said when she caught up with him. "Where have you been?"

"Nowhere," Reggie said weakly. She wasn't going to give him the satisfaction of making a joke about her predicament. Nor was she going to tell him about the body in the pantry. (*The Body in the Pantry*. It could be the title of a Nancy Styles novel.) He would only get excited and want to play detective. Nanny had died of natural causes, if Cosmo was to be believed. She was being "kept on ice," he said, until the undertaker could get through. And Reggie certainly wasn't going to tell Jackson Brodie how she had bleated with fear when she thought she was immured with the dead nanny.

"You've missed some dramatic developments," he said. "The Major—not your Major—claims that he overheard Dr. Dankworth talking to Charlie Miles, Sir Lancelot's ne'er-do-well nephew. The Major's a little deaf—not like yours, I'm sure—but he thought he caught the words 'inheritance' and 'poison.' Pretty big clues, huh? And *then* the body of Dr. Dankworth was discovered in the Red Room, dead as a dodo with a knife in his chest."

Reggie couldn't stop herself from asking, "What kind of knife?"

"That's what *I* asked. Great detective minds think alike. A kitchen knife last used by Lettice, the maid, to slice lemons for Lady Hardwick's gin and tonic. Make of that what you will. Did you find your Major?"

"Who said I was looking for him?" Reggie said indignantly. "And he's not mine." (He was!) Did Jackson Brodie know she'd been in trouble? Or suspect that she had been? But what was the difference really?

"You left this in the Library, by the way," he said, digging in his pocket and handing over her phone. "Easy, tiger," he added when she snatched it off him.

Annoying though it was, and handsome as the Major might be, Reggie knew that the one person who could be guaranteed never to leave her behind if she was in trouble was standing right next to her with a big, annoying smirk on his face.

The Red Room

Lady Milton had remained in the Red Room after everyone else had moved on. She dropped gratefully on to one of the ancient, sagging sofas, of which there were several in the room. The house had so many sofas that you had to question whether they were quietly breeding when no one was looking. In the Red Room they were all covered in the same red damask silk that dressed the walls. The silk on the sofas had been so ravaged by moths that it had almost ceased to exist in places. Lady Milton expected that when the moths eventually ran out of sofas, they would start on her.

She was not alone. The actor who played the doctor was still lying on one of the sofas, a dagger sticking out of his chest. "Don't worry, it's not real," he said, pulling it out. "Nodded off there for a minute. I'm too old for this malarkey."

"Me too," Lady Milton said.

"Robin," he said, tipping an imaginary hat. "Robin Chester."

"Lady Milton," Lady Milton said.

After a minute or so, Robin Chester hauled himself off the sofa and said, "Better get going. I'm playing the butler as well."

"I'm sure you'll do it very well," Lady Milton said encouragingly. He looked much more suitable for the part than their own Henderson.

She really was quite exhausted. It had been such a long day that she couldn't even remember how it had begun. All days seemed long now, and at the same time terrifyingly short. She closed her eyes and quickly dropped straight into a dream where she was stalking on the moors with her father. She was young in the dream. She hadn't particularly liked shooting, but none of her sisters were interested so it meant that she could spend some precious time alone with her father. Their parents had been very remote. The only time the children saw them really was after their nursery tea, when, in their nightclothes and on their best behaviour, they were taken downstairs to say goodnight and then whisked away by their nanny as soon as their parents began to grow bored with the novelty of their offspring. That was the way it was, of course. She had tried to show more enthusiasm for her own children, but to be honest, they hadn't been very interesting.

⤚

When she woke, she felt even more befuddled than usual. While she had slept, she was surprised to find, an unknown hand had covered her with a blanket. She was grateful for this caring gesture (unlikely to be one of her family), as it was freezing in the Red Room. She had to put up quite a struggle to escape the worn-out innards of the sofa, which seemed to have tried to swallow her up. Eventually she managed to wrestle herself free of its clutches and ratcheted her vertebrae one by one until she was upright.

Lady Milton had nearly traversed the interminable length of the Red Room when a man appeared in the doorway in front of her. He was carrying a shotgun and for a moment her dream came back to her and she wondered if it was her father, which was an absurd thought as the man was wearing a tracksuit. Her father wouldn't have even known what a tracksuit was. Lady Milton did, however, because Derek Truitt wore one when he went out jogging. She had seen him occasionally doing a slow lap around the deer park. Sometimes he looked up and spotted her at a window, and once on the battlements, where she had gone to consider whether she would be able to throw herself off them if her mind gave out entirely. Miltons didn't commit suicide, of course, but she was only a Milton by marriage, not blood. She was, in the end, her father's daughter.

Derek was very slow at the jogging, but nonetheless Lady Milton found it commendable. She had never jogged, nor had she even run, unless it was away from her sisters.

The man took aim and Lady Milton gave a little cry of horror and her hands flew instinctively to her chest as if she might somehow protect her heart from a bullet. She immediately regretted her actions, they smacked of cowardice. And probably fulfilled the man's expectations that she would quake in her shoes like a weak old woman. Oh, come on, Honoria, she thought to herself. Show some pluck, for heaven's sake.

Would it be so bad to be shot? After all, before the new vet came to live on the estate they used to shoot their horses and dogs when they could no longer manage their lives. You didn't want to watch them suffer a lingering, painful death, did you? It was not a bad way to go. She'd had a good innings, after all. She felt emboldened.

"Come on, then," she taunted the tracksuit man. "Why don't you shoot me? Go on—shoot!"

He did.

⌒

The tracksuited man was rather slow (he had already been winged himself, she noticed) and not a terribly good shot, and so Lady Milton, who was backed up against a handy little Sheraton escritoire, had time to reach behind her to try to find a weapon of her own before he had a second go at her. She had seen someone do this on *Midsomer Murders*. They had kept the killer talking while surreptitiously rummaging on a table behind them for something to throw at him. What Lady Milton found was a "Bleu Céleste" Sèvres dish. It was a kind of fat banana shape, and no one had any idea what it was for. Most of the objects at Burton Makepeace were without purpose. The Sèvres had come from Versailles, after the Revolution, spirited away as a souvenir.

She sliced the dish through the air like a boomerang or a frisbee. Before they became galumphing adolescents, Flora and Fauna used to play with a frisbee on the lawn when they visited, shrieking like banshees. Lady Milton had never actually heard a banshee, but she felt sure that if she did it would sound exactly like Flora and Fauna. The dish found the tracksuited man's head, knocking him off balance and resulting in him discharging the gun into the air. It hit the Chippendale display cabinet, taking with it nearly all the Chelsea and Bow figurines that the Old Marquess had collected. No great loss, Lady Milton had never liked them.

The man slunk off, blood pouring down his face. Lady Milton was rather proud of herself, and it was not often that she felt she could say that.

Another intruder! She looked around for a handy piece of priceless porcelain and found a Meissen sweetmeat dish. Not an intruder, she realized just before she lobbed it at Piers. The itch to throw the Meissen was no less.

Harlequinade

Simon had imagined himself walking into the house and announcing, "There's been a murder," but it sounded a bit too much like *Taggart* and it would involve him finding his voice, which seemed irretrievably lost. His discreet vicar-cough wasn't of much use here in the vastness of Burton Makepeace. He regretted not getting a whistle—or a klaxon, like a circus clown. The antic Man of God.

The place was as quiet as a morgue. Where was everyone? He caught a distant murmur of voices somewhere and began to trail through the enormous rooms, following the sound. It was a curious thing, but whenever he felt he was growing closer to the voices they immediately began to fade away. He knew that the acoustics in the house were aberrant. Sophie had told him that you could stand in the kitchen downstairs and hear Nanny in the attic, and yet when standing at one end of the Red Room you would be unable to hear someone at the other end.

He began to feel that he had been condemned to wander helplessly through the empty house, his terrible news unvoiced and unheard, a kind of dumb Cassandra—although, of course, Cassandra had been foretelling future events, whereas Simon wished to relay the past. Janet Teller qualified now as history. Oh, do be quiet, he said to himself. The endless *nattering* his dead wife had accused him of still went on, trapped in his head now instead of escaping through his mouth.

In the kitchen, which he came across by chance, he was able to lay down the burden of the painting on the big wooden table that dominated the room. He was feeling weak with hunger and was disappointed to find that there was no food lying around. The fact that he had recently come across the corpse of a murdered parishioner didn't seem to have diminished his appetite. He had imagined that Burton Makepeace would be a place of plenty—deep-crusted game pies and big slabs of gammon (he was hungry enough to relinquish temporarily all thoughts of veganism). All he could find, however, was the melted slop that seemed to be the remains of a cheesecake. He spooned it up, as greedy as Goldilocks.

He plodded on and discovered the Library. A room—one of many—he had never been invited into by Lady Milton. He was usually taken into the conservatory by her, the rest of the house off-limits to him. The conservatory was in a dreadful state of disrepair. He suspected that Lady Milton was trying to prove to him that the Miltons were "virtually destitute," something she had said to him on more than one occasion, forestalling his requests for alms. It was interesting now to have the freedom of all the rooms.

In the Library, as you would expect, the walls were lined with shelves that were crammed with old leather-bound books. Animal skins, he thought, stripped from the bodies of innocent creatures. Lambskin. Was there a sadder word? Well, yes, many. He must stop thinking like this. They were just books, for heaven's sake, and be thankful for paperbacks. But then—trees. Pulping the world's precious forests. Oh, shut *up*, Simon.

He wondered when the last time was that a Milton had taken a book down and opened its pages. ("They're functionally illiterate," Sophie told him once.) Not that he wished to see it, but it was rumoured that Piers' grandfather, the Old Marquess as he was known, had a huge collection of pornography, from ancient to modern.

Simon removed the weighty gun from his pocket and placed it on a little side table that was next to an inviting armchair. The fire in the Library was dying down, but was still radiating a glorious warmth compared to the ice-box that was the rest of the house. He experienced an unexpected wave of desire at the sight of a large drinks tray in the corner. He probably shouldn't drink. Concussion and so on, not to mention years of priestly restraint. Bugger that, he thought rebelliously, pouring himself a large tumbler of malt.

He sank into the armchair and felt the smoky, medicinal burn of the whisky hitting his insides. He couldn't remember when he last drank whisky. The Millennium, possibly. His head still hurt where he had banged it in the ha-ha. It had been an awful day and it was a long way from over yet.

***

"In this room we discover Countess Voranskaya and Lady Madeleine Hardwick deep in conversation. What, you may ask, are they talking about? Is it the piece of paper the mysterious Countess is holding in her hand?" Out of the corner of his eye, Titus saw Piers Milton deserting, peeling off and disappearing through a side door that was disguised as part of the wall. He had already lost Gavin Hutchins, who claimed he had food poisoning. The more stalwart Emma said that she was prepared "to see this thing through to the end." He hadn't seen Lady Milton since they were in the Red Room, and he'd barely become acquainted with the Scottish girl before she disappeared, although she had deigned to come back now. How many more were going to abandon ship? Although he wouldn't mind if those dratted twins were pushed overboard.

They had moved on from the Red Room, where Dr. Dankworth's body had been discovered, and now they were in one of the less grand rooms in the house, its function unclear. Following the usual logic, it should be called the Beige Room. Like the other rooms, it contained a profusion of sofas, as if the inhabitants of Burton Makepeace were continually overwhelmed by the need to sit down and rest. All the sofas in the room were currently occupied. The American couple seemed to have fallen asleep on one.

"Is the mysterious Countess harbouring a SECRET?" This last word bellowed to wake the sleepers.

"Where is 'the famous detective René Armand'?" someone asked. "Shouldn't he be the one asking questions? Solving the murder?"

Titus North sighed. Brodie. That was his name, Titus remembered. He doubted very much that he had been in the police, like he said. "He's here now," he said.

"Where?"

"*Here.* It is I. *I* am René Armand. And I will be questioning the suspects shortly, if you would just be quiet and let us get on."

"You've left it a bit late."

He ignored him and addressed the sofas instead. "You should ask to see the letter. Perhaps someone would like to read out what it says. Anyone. You," he said, pointing at one of the twins.

"Me?"

"Yes. You," he said, handing her the letter.

Flora took it, slowly and reluctantly.

"*Dearest Guy,*" she read (appallingly). "*What we have had has been everything to me. Yours undyingly, M.*"

"Madeleine!" the other twin howled. "M must be Madeleine. Lady Fucking Whatever. She must be shagging fucking Guy Whatsisname."

"Undyingly?" the American woman queried. "Is there such a word?"

"Yes, of course there is," Titus snapped. "It's part of the English language. Perhaps you are not fluent in it."

"Excuse me?"

"Continue, please," he said to Camilla.

She proceeded rather shakily. "I thought I saw someone in the passage outside the Library. I thought it was Charlie—"

"Hang on, back up a bit, Lady Hardwick," Brodie said. "This person you thought you saw outside the Library just before Sir Lancelot was killed, you're saying that you think it was Charlie. Why did you think it was Charlie?"

"Well . . ." Camilla hesitated, she was not one for extemporizing. Titus mouthed "Improvise" to her. "Well," she said again, taking a cleansing breath, "I don't know. The way he walked, perhaps?"

"Was there something distinctive about his walk?"

"Um, a limp?"

Dear God, Camilla was going off-script, losing the plot, literally. She was on enough tranquillizers to fell a horse, but that was no excuse.

"Doesn't Major Liversedge have a limp? Do they *both* limp?" Brodie was relentless.

"Well, everyone limps, don't they?" Camilla said.

"Aren't they played by the same actor?"

"Jesus Christ."

Guy Burroughs entered the room, the two fingers and thumb of one hand forming a pretend gun as if he were a child playing Cops and Robbers. Under his breath he muttered, "The fucking prop gun's gone walkabout again, Titus." He aimed his "gun" at Countess Voranskaya and pulled his thumb "trigger." Titus almost expected him to say *Bang!*

"The gun obviously has a silencer," Titus said smoothly to the sofas. "It still works," he added. "The woman is still *shot*." This aimed at the Countess, who after a few seconds of delay clutched her breast and fell, very cautiously, to the floor, where she writhed and twitched for a long time before finally becoming still. In her death throes she dislodged her turban. It made her less mysterious.

"Finished?" Titus murmured to her. She gave a tiny nod. "Sure?" Another tiny nod.

"Line!" Titus roared at Lady Hardwick, making everyone jump.

The new widow gasped melodramatically, "Are you going to kill me too, Guy?"

Yes, go on, shoot them all, Titus urged silently. They had brought the theatrical profession to a new low, something that even he hadn't previously thought was possible.

He was enormously relieved when he overheard Brodie say, "I'm off to do some real sleuthing," before sloping off through one of the many exits. Thank God for that, at least.

Simon woke with a start. He immediately felt horribly guilty—here he was indulging in warmth and whisky while poor Janet's corpse grew colder by the minute and her killer roamed free. What if someone else had been murdered while he was lazing around in the Library? He heaved himself out of the comfort of the armchair and set off again.

This time, although no thanks to the whisky, he had more success following the thread of voices. They were coming from the room ahead of him. The door was ajar, and he caught sight of a woman lying lifelessly on the carpet. She was wearing a turban that had been knocked askew. Another, younger woman moved into view. She looked to be in the grip of terror and was staring at someone or something Simon couldn't see, concealed from his view by the half-open door. "Please, Guy," she begged. "Put the gun down. Don't kill me as well!"

Who else had this unseen person—Guy—killed? Was this Janet Teller's murderer—traipsing around the village shooting people whenever and wherever it took his fancy? A man on a rampage. A spree killer, a term he had learnt from television. Different from a serial killer. Useless knowledge in the circumstances.

He hesitated, but only briefly. It was time for him to show that he was no coward. He had fled the scene of a crime once today, he would not do it a second time. He would redeem himself. He reached for the gun in his pocket and remembered that he had taken it out when he sat down in the Library. Never mind. He picked up a large brass poker from an overwrought fireside and advanced. The time for turning the other cheek had passed.

Simon had been under the impression that the room contained only the two women and this Guy person, but when he stepped over the threshold he was flummoxed to find that there was in fact quite a crowd inside.

"Ah, the Reverend Smallbones, I presume," a man with an American drawl said to him. "We wondered when you were going to make your entrance."

And then the dead woman on the floor sat up and adjusted her turban before saying to him, "Who the fuck are you, darling?"

A dishevelled Reverend Smallbones charged into the room, brandishing a large brass poker like a weapon and wearing a stagy look of horror on his face. Yet another bad actor, Reggie concluded. He was saying nothing (had he forgotten his lines?), just gesticulating wildly like someone who was very poor at Charades. He was going to do some damage with that poker if he wasn't careful.

"That man is not the Reverend Smallbones!" Titus North declared loudly. "He is an imposter!" The other actors murmured agreement. The imposter shook his head vigorously, tugging on his dog collar and impatiently making the sign of the cross several times. Was this part of the plot? Apparently not, for when Reggie looked more closely at the Reverend Smallbones, she saw that he was in fact Simon Cate. A real vicar. She had met him here after the Turner theft. "Call me Simon." Fact and fiction were now hopelessly entangled.

Simon Cate spotted the "evidence" notebook that one of the twins was holding and snatched it off her. He scribbled furiously on one of the pages and then thrust the book into Reggie's hands.

"A murder? Who? Who's been murdered? Sir Lancelot Hardwick? Dr. Dankworth?"

Simon Cate looked puzzled and shook his head, equally vigorously. He grabbed the notebook back in order to write something else. He showed it to Reggie again.

"Janet Teller? Janet Teller's been *murdered*?"

Yet more vigorous nodding.

Reggie remembered taking Janet Teller's witness statement after the Turner theft. She was a real person, not a fictional character. The vicar mimed shooting a gun. He followed this with a pantomime of being shot.

"Janet Teller's been shot?" Reggie hazarded. More eager nodding. "Who shot her?"

Despite his deranged countenance, it seemed unlikely he was lying—after all, he was a vicar—but further one-sided dialogue was scuppered when they all heard the startling crack of a gun going off. A real one, by the sound of it.

It was possible, Reggie supposed, that one of the Miltons had fired a shotgun by accident. It was the kind of reckless prank that Cosmo would indulge in, but he was lolling on a sofa not two yards away from her. Someone had shot Janet Teller less than a mile away and now a gun had been discharged in the house? It didn't take a mathematical genius to put two and two together and come up with four. Perhaps that was an explanation waiting for a coincidence. (No, it didn't work that way round, did it?)

What if it was Carl Carter? Carl Carter who was last spotted two miles away, coming in this direction. Had he gone to ground *here*? Reggie's stomach swooped with fear. She had set off on the road to Burton Makepeace full of bravado at the idea that she might be the one to find Carl Carter, and now it really was the very last thing she wanted to do. There was no one else, just little Reggie Chase, orphan of the parish and the sole official representative of law and order. She couldn't wait for the sheriff to come to town, she *was* the sheriff.

"I'm a police officer," she said to the unruly pack. She heard some murmurs of disbelief. "Yes, I am," she said, pulling out her warrant card and holding it aloft. "I am not part of the Murder Mystery," she added. "I'm going to go and investigate. I expect it's just someone being stupid." She could have done with a sidekick in this venture. Jackson Brodie would have objected to the word "sidekick," of course. (Where was he? He said he was going to do some "real sleuthing." What did that mean?) Reggie took out her phone and looked at it hopefully, even though she knew there was no signal. She sighed. Carl Carter had at least one gun, according to the news. *Armed and extremely dangerous. Do not approach without back-up.* And here she was, no back-up. Approaching. "Give me that poker," she said to Simon Cate.

Portrait of an Unknown Woman

Burton Makepeace was enormous, bigger on the inside than it was on the outside. Jackson didn't encounter anyone on his odyssey around the house, just a dog, a small old spaniel wearing a badly knitted jumper. The dog was sleeping contentedly on a sofa.

Before long, Jackson found himself in the kitchen. A large table dominated the room, and laid flat on the table was an old plastic supermarket carrier bag. Poking out from the bag was the top of a picture frame. *Fancy—gold,* Jackson recalled Ian Padgett's description. He tugged the painting out of the bag.

He gazed at the woman, trapped inside her gilded frame. The woman gazed back at him. The weasel, its eyes shining with malevolence, was the clincher.

"Oh, that's where I left it," she said, breezing in and taking the portrait from his hands. "Thank you for finding it." She was slim, early forties rather than late thirties by Jackson's reckoning, dressed in biker leathers, which was not something he'd predicted. Was there a motorbike nearby that she was going to make her escape on? Greenish eyes, blondish hair tied up carelessly. A woman rendered in flesh and blood rather than oil paints. Put a short black wig and spectacles on her and she was the waitress who had cleared away the drinks in the Library before the start of the Murder Mystery. Put a sensible skirt and blouse on her and brush her hair and she was Sophie Greenway. Give her a brown and yellow tabard and she was Melanie Hope. And stick a woollen hat on her and she might bump into you in a café in Leeds and slip a tracker in your jacket pocket. Unlike everyone else in the world, Jackson was an exceptionally good witness.

He had been biding his time since he first noticed her in the Library. You could tell that, if nothing else, she savoured slipping into a role. He could see it now in the amused little moue at the corner of her mouth. She was enjoying her duplicity, changing chameleon-like before his eyes, recalibrating her thinking, deciding who to be for him.

Of all the stately homes in all the villages in all of Britain, Melanie Hope walked into his. Well, not his, he wouldn't have thanked you for the encumbrance of Burton Makepeace, but he liked the quote. Even for Jackson it was stretching the Law of Coincidence, already so thin it was at breaking point. And, yes, there was a law. It was codified in the Book of Coincidences, an obscure part of the biblical Apocrypha.

"It's a lovely painting," Jackson said. "Who is it a portrait of?"

"I've no idea. No one seems to know."

"What do you call it?"

"Call it? I don't really call it anything," she said. "*Portrait of an Unknown Woman*, I suppose."

"Not *Woman with a Weasel*? Melanie? Or is it Sophie?"

She gave him a long, cool look and after a thoughtful silence said, "It's a pine marten. *La Donna con Martora*, thought to have been painted by Raphael but never conclusively attributed to him. Not yet, anyway. Presumed lost since 1945. Shall we have a drink? There's a good malt around here somewhere. The kitchen staff are drinking the place dry." She extracted a bottle of whisky from a cupboard. "Balvenie, fourteen years old," she said, pouring two glasses and handing him one. "Cheers," she said, clinking her glass against his. Jackson didn't reciprocate. "Why don't you sit down, Mr. Brodie?"

She knew who he was. Of course she did.

He was surprised that Melanie Hope and the portrait were still together, even more surprised—completely baffled, in fact—that she would be with it in Burton Makepeace, but it seemed she had cached it in the local church for safekeeping. Of course she knew the area well from when she had been pretending to be the housekeeper here. This was her old stamping ground (or perhaps hunting ground would be a more appropriate term). Only someone with supreme confidence in their powers of deception would return to "the scene of the crime," as Ian Padgett would have called it, and insert themselves back into it so blatantly. Wasn't she worried about being recognized?

"The Miltons never look at their staff," she said. "Or at least they might look, but they never see. And Tilda was rather a good disguise. I had to come back to get the *Donna* from the church, so I thought I would visit an old haunt. Then I heard they'd put out a call for agency staff and—*voilà*. I thought it would be fun."

Fun? It was an odd word to use, but it wasn't about theft, was it? It was about playing a game, fooling people. She was a serial liar who loved a long con, loved taking risks. A charming sociopath.

"And the Turner?"

"Oh, long gone. I was supposed to take the Raphael, but Cosmo sold it on the QT just before I arrived. Very naughty boy, Cosmo. The Turner was all that was left of any real value, so Piers said to take that instead."

"Piers? Lord Milton was behind the theft?"

"He needed money."

"But wouldn't it have been simpler just to sell the Turner, instead of the whole charade of the fake housekeeper stealing it?"

"Questions, questions. Piers was greedy—and stupid, that goes without saying—he wanted the insurance money as well as the sale money. It had to be the black market, of course."

"No provenance."

"Yes, a fraction of its value, but still a lot of money."

"And people like stories."

"Exactly. Smoke and mirrors and misdirection. Everyone was looking at 'Sophie Greenway,'" she said, making rabbit ears. "No one was looking at Piers. I enjoyed being Sophie," she added wistfully (she was an actress par excellence, Jackson reminded himself). "She was *nice*, it was a pleasant interlude, inhabiting her. And it was interesting being part of this . . ." she waved a hand vaguely around the room, searching for a way to describe Burton Makepeace, "this white elephant," she concluded. "They've been bred to be superfluous. It was fascinating. But for the record, I was genuinely fond of Lady Milton. Dorothy Padgett, as well. I was a good friend to her."

"Such a good friend that you robbed her blind. So what happened to the Turner?"

She laughed. "Turned out it was a fake. I couldn't sell it. Piers still owes me for that."

"So that's why you came back?"

"No, I came back to catch up with old friends."

Jackson stood up abruptly, the whisky untouched. He'd had enough of play-acting. "Melanie Hope, or whoever you are—"

"Beatrice."

"Whatever. I'm arresting you on suspicion of the theft of—"

"You're not in the police any more."

"Citizen's arrest."

She stood up and made a move to pick up the painting, but Jackson grabbed it first.

"Oh, for heaven's sake, give it to me," she said. "It *is* mine. Dorothy left it to me in a codicil in her will."

"You'll never be able to sell it."

"Who said I was going to sell it? Give it to me."

"No."

And then, to his astonishment, he was looking at a gun pointing at him. "A gun?" he said incredulously. This was a woman who lived on her wits, who was kind to old ladies, not someone who resorted to weaponry. "You must be joking," he said. "It's the missing prop from the Murder Mystery, isn't it?"

She laughed again and said, "You've got me bang to rights, guv," and placed the gun on the table between them. "Sit down and I'll tell you about the *Donna con Martora*. That's what you want to hear, isn't it?"

He sat.

It felt like a trick somehow, as if she was going to put him under a spell. But, on the other hand, he really wanted to know what she had to say for herself before the "real" police got involved. She was a criminal and a liar. Let's face it, Jackson thought, that was his kind of woman.

"In your dreams, old man," a woman's voice in his head said. Probably hers.

"Come on," she said. "You haven't touched your whisky. Drink with me."

He sighed. He drank.

"So—*The Woman with a Weasel*?" Jackson said. "It was stolen, wasn't it?"

"Got it in one, Mr. Brodie."

"I had a theory that maybe Harold looted it when he was in Berlin at the end of the war and that's why Hazel and Ian are being so shifty about it."

"Not even close. Good try on your part, though. You should be a detective."

"There's something incriminating in one of the stories she wrote, isn't there?"

"You see, you're improving at this lark already."

"A story about how Hazel and Ian's parents came to acquire the portrait?"

"Hazel was convinced that Dorothy was hiding something from her. She found the story in a drawer, mixed in with all the others that Dorothy had written over the years. Dorothy had given it a title—'The Portrait'—and to Hazel it looked like all the others.

"Poor Dorothy, she was a dreadful writer, a purveyor of deathless prose. Near the end, she asked me to burn everything that she'd written over the years. I think she was embarrassed. She was a nice old soul. We got on well with each other. She'd had a rotten marriage. It's an old story, Mr. Brodie—timid young girl marries older, dominating man. It was a great relief for her when Harold died. You know he caught gonorrhoea in Cairo during the war but didn't tell his new bride? She was an innocent. When her GP told her, Dorothy thought Gonorrhoea was a girl's name. It made her infertile, hence the adoption of the twins."

"Does this have *anything* to do with the painting? Can we just cut to the chase?"

"Very well. After Dorothy died, Hazel remembered the story about the portrait and realized that it might not be one of her mother's fantasies after all. Ian and Hazel had always expected the painting to be worth something when they eventually came to sell it, but they would need to prove some provenance for it. Unfortunately, the provenance turned out to be . . ."

"Dodgy?"

"Exactly. And 'The Portrait'—the story—was proof of that. I expect Hazel went crazy looking for it after Dorothy died."

"*You* took it?"

"The Padgetts wanted the story *and* the painting returned. To have any hope of making money from the painting, they had to get rid of the story."

"And—say what? That they bought it in a car boot sale?"

"Something like that. I can just see Hazel on *Fake or Fortune*— 'stunning discovery as Raphael thought lost for ever resurfaces.' It would have to be authenticated by an expert, of course, but there are no Cadsbys left to claim ownership."

"Where's the story now?"

"Ash on the wind."

"You put it in Dorothy's coffin," Jackson said. "You were Hannah." (How many other identities was she going to spawn?)

"Dorothy asked me to. You can't go against a dying woman's wishes. She wanted her confession to go with her to the grave."

The light dawned (admittedly rather slowly) in Jackson's brain. "It was *Dorothy* who stole the portrait?"

"Well done, you got there in the end, Mr. Brodie."

⌒

"Shall I tell you the real story, the one that Dorothy told me?"

"Please."

"Well, Dorothy's honeymoon was a week touring the north on Harold's motorbike, staying in farmhouses that offered bed and breakfast. Harold had bought a sidecar for the bike as a concession to marriage. On one very hot afternoon—the north was having an Indian summer—they were drawn by a sign at the side of the road that promised refreshments, and found themselves bumping along a neglected side road and riding through the gates of Ottershall House. 'Two shillings entrance fee and a shilling for the tea,' Dorothy wrote. Dorothy liked an afternoon tea.

"The house had been owned for centuries by a family called Cadsby. The Cadsbys' fortunes had fallen—no money and two sons lost in the war. They were about to sell the contents of the house and rent the building to a boys' boarding school.

"The housekeeper had been instructed to offer cream teas on the lawn and a tour of the house to any visitors, but when Harold and Dorothy arrived she said she was too busy packing up for the forthcoming auction. She served them tea on the lawn though, and Dorothy goes into great detail about the quality of the scones, if you're interested. No? Anyway, after all that tea she needed to answer 'a call of nature,' as she termed it. There was no sign of the housekeeper, so Dorothy wandered around the house in search of a cloakroom. And on her way back she came across the portrait."

"At last."

She ignored him. "It was 'a thing of beauty,' Dorothy said. Perhaps she divined that there would not be many things of beauty in her future. 'My heart beat faster at the sight of it,' she said."

"Don't tell me, she just unhooked it off the wall and scarpered?"

"In a nutshell. Put it in the sidecar and went back to tell Harold she wasn't well and needed to leave. He was 'fuming' when he realized later that his new bride was light-fingered. The next day, Dorothy found out that Ottershall House had gone up in flames. And this is the interesting part—in the middle of the night Harold had left their bed in the farmhouse where they were staying. Dorothy got up and looked out of the window and saw him disappearing on his motorbike. When he returned an hour later she pretended to be asleep rather than asking him where he'd been. 'He didn't like being questioned about things,' she said. It was only later that she put two and two together. Was he protecting his wife or was he protecting himself?"

"He couldn't just have returned it? Left it on the doorstep rather than burning the entire place down?"

"Sometimes arson is the easiest option, although the Cadsbys were slapdash about record-keeping and any paper trail that might have authenticated the painting went up in smoke. It wasn't long before both Cadsby and his wife were dead. Natural causes, I hasten to add. There was always a rumour in the art world that they'd had a Raphael portrait, but even that rumour faded with time. Dorothy had her thing of beauty. *Chapeau,* Dorothy."

She gave a sudden start. "Did you hear that? It sounded like a gunshot."

Jackson hadn't heard anything. He wasn't about to admit to a shortcoming in his hearing to the leather-clad siren in front of him. "The Murder Mystery, I expect," he said. In his defence (one Jackson resorted to afterwards with Reggie several times), the kitchen was quite a long way from where the shot was fired. If Jackson had thought for a second that there was someone letting off a gun in the house, he wouldn't have stayed there listening to Scheherazade spinning her tales.

Call of Duty

Reggie was crossing the oceanic expanse of the entrance hall when her nightmare was made real, because there he was, there was the shooter, walking towards her, gun in hand. Fear scooped out her insides, her legs trembled and gave way, plonking her down on the marble floor. This was it, then, she thought. A poker wasn't much of a defence against a gun.

"Are you okay? It's Reggie, isn't it?"

"Ben? Major?"

"Yes." He held out a hand to help her up.

"You were pointing a gun at me," she said crossly, embarrassed by her faint-heartedness. He would think she was a complete wimp.

"Not at *you*," he said. "Just pointing it in general. Sorry if I scared you. I'm pretty drunk actually," he added cheerfully. "Been drinking." He had a bottle of brandy in his other hand, a long way from full. "Want some?" he offered.

"No. Did you fire that gun just now?"

"Me? God, no. See," he said, holding the gun out towards her. She shrank away from it. "'S okay. Know what I'm doing. I found it in the Library just now, can you believe? Just lying there. Thought I'd better not leave it there, you don't know who might find it."

"Is it real?" Reggie asked.

"Pretty real. A Heckler & Koch. Not Army issue, the Army has Glocks these days. I thought that perhaps the theatre people might have misplaced a replica, but replicas are made of a lighter metal and the firing pin would be removed and the barrel blocked in some way. The bullets look *very* real. And if that shot just now *was* just a sound effect, it was convincing enough to give half of them a heart attack, I should think."

Reggie was disquieted to realize that Ben with a weapon in his hand was even more attractive than Ben without one. And that his knowledge of weapons was—she could hardly bring herself to think the word—sexy. She had hitherto thought of herself—essentially— as a pacifist, and furthermore untroubled by the idea of a man in uniform. Not that he was in a uniform, but he probably had one somewhere. And a dress uniform for reunion dinners and so on. She wondered what he looked like in it. Devastatingly handsome. She was being reduced to a quivering heap of cliché. She had to get a grip, she really did.

"You're sure you're okay . . . ?"

"Reggie," she reminded him. "Yes, I'm good," she said, clambering back into her brain. "I know that shot wasn't the Murder Mystery. I was there when we heard it."

"Commiserations."

"Thanks."

"Have you been in the Library? It's a lovely room," he said, sounding like a tour guide. "Plasterwork by Robert Adam, apparently. There's a fire in there, do you want to come and see?"

"Yes, I know, I've been in the Library and it's a wonderful idea," she said. "But I think if someone's firing a gun we ought to look for him. I'm a police officer—"

"Really?"

"Yes, really," she said patiently. "And there's an escaped prisoner on the run, near here, quite possibly in this house. A psychopathic killer, to be exact. Very dangerous," she coaxed, because Ben looked as though he was still thinking about the Library and its plasterwork.

"Dangerous, huh?"

"Very. Put the bullets back in the gun."

"Sure?"

"Yes."

"Okay, if you say so." He reloaded the gun. Drunk or not, he did it with the ease of a professional. "Right, then, let's go and find this villain. I'm must warn you though, I'm pretty drunk."

"Yes, you said that."

They didn't have much looking to do. He was suddenly right there, materializing in the hall, a sawn-off shotgun in his hands. Carl Carter, snarling at them like the mad dog that he was.

"Adam?" Ben said.

～

"Adam?" Ben repeated, keeping his voice pleasant. He stepped quickly in front of Reggie to shield her.

The man had acquired a new head wound since he had last seen him. Ben tried to put an optimistic spin on why Adam would have a shotgun. Burton Makepeace was probably full of them. His sister said the Miltons shot anything that moved. Adam had probably stumbled across one of their guns and, bewildered by a blow to his head, was now wandering around looking for someone to hand it over to.

"That's him, Carl Carter," a little voice whispered behind him. "You've got a gun, just shoot him," the little voice urged, surprisingly militant. But surely it would be better to try to negotiate with him, rather than going full *High Noon*? Ben had hoped to live out the rest of his life without ever shooting anyone again. On this basis, he said to Adam, "I won't shoot if you don't. That's fair, isn't it?"

Apparently not, because Adam—or Carl Carter—aimed the gun at them anyway. Ben pushed Reggie to the floor and threw himself on top of her. The sound of the gun going off was deafening as the bullet ricocheted ruthlessly around the hard marble surfaces of the Great Hall. Ben had been very drunk, now he was very sober. The bullet failed to meet its target and Ben waited helplessly for a fatal second shot, but instead all he heard was an ineffective clicking sound. When he lifted his head it was to see Adam loping away, the shotgun abandoned.

"Gun jammed," Ben said to Reggie. "He can't shoot anyone now."

"He might have another gun," she said, struggling breathlessly out from beneath him. "He had an arsenal stashed at his mother's house. We have to stop him."

"No 'we' here," Ben said. "I'll go after him, you go and fetch what reinforcements you can find—your dad, maybe, and Piers and the big bloke who's in charge of the Murder Mystery—no, maybe not him." She started to protest, but he held his hand up and said, "No time to argue."

Interestingly the Major Domo had not cowered mentally at the threat of being shot, nor had he experienced any flashbacks to the field of battle. In fact, he was quite energized by the thought of a firefight. Could just be the alcohol bolstering him, of course. He held his gun-toting arm out straight. Not a tremor. He was good to go. He set off in search of Carter. The war dog reporting for duty.

———

Carter had injured his ankle, bashed his head, broken his nose. Ben's quarry was a wounded stag, he shouldn't be difficult to bring down. And also, it seemed unlikely that he would understand the layout of the house when even the people who lived in it seemed sketchy about its geography. Ben, on the other hand, had been mapping the place unconsciously all evening. Always know where the exits are. Never go in somewhere without knowing how to get out.

He spotted Carter disappearing through a doorway. The door led straight on to a staircase, an old servants' one, uncarpeted and narrow. It came out in a picture gallery where the portraits of the Miltons over the centuries were displayed. Carter hobbled along the Long Gallery, Ben not doing much better. His leg was complaining bitterly. If he'd been at home he would have taken it off several hours ago. If he was at home, he would be in bed asleep, instead of hobbling with a gun after a madman.

For a moment he had a clear shot, but he was reluctant to shoot an unarmed man in the back. Reggie said that Carter might have another gun, but his hands appeared empty. He had already vanished around a corner at the end of the gallery. And then it was up more stairs—and then, dear God, a stone spiral, corkscrewing so blindly and narrowly that Ben was surprised his ribs weren't squeezed. They were heading for the roof. Ben didn't see how that could end well. There would be no escape for either of them. His leg *hurt*.

He felt the first stirrings of unnamed dread in his gut. Anything could be waiting at the top. He gripped the handle of the gun tighter and took a deep breath and summoned the soldier within. Whether he liked it or not, it was his job to fight the enemy. No, not a job, a vocation. He was a Jennings.

He was relieved when he finally made it out on to the roof and found that no one had laid an ambush. It had stopped snowing now, thank goodness, but the snow lay thickly on the roof, shrouding any obstacles in his way. There was no sign of Carter, but there was an endless array of chimney stacks to provide cover for the man. Ben remembered that his sister said the Miltons referred to the roof as their battlements. He supposed they meant the crenellated wall that ran the length of the building. Perfect spot for an archer. Or a sniper. He must remember that the next time he was in the deer park.

He spotted a movement further along the wall, a figure, but difficult to make out in the dark, no more than a grey shape, and for a moment he thought it was a woman. "Carter?" Ben shouted. "It'll be much better for you if you give up. They'll shoot you if you don't. They think you're armed." There was no "they," of course, just Ben.

Carter suddenly stepped into view from behind one of the chimney stacks. He did have a weapon, after all, there was a brick in his hand, which he lobbed with surprising accuracy, catching Ben off-guard and hitting him square on the forehead. The gun in Ben's hand went flying off into the ether. The crack of brick on bone made him feel sick and, dazed by the force of the blow, he had to grab on to the battlements for support. And then—*douf!*—he was rammed from behind by Carter, and the next thing he knew he was hanging halfway over the wall and Carter had got hold of his ankle and was trying to use it as a lever to tip him over the edge. He heard Carter mutter, "What the fuck?" when he discovered the ankle wasn't flesh and blood. "Fucking bionic man," he growled, tugging harder.

Could Carter yank off his prosthetic? Hanging over a wall while a deranged killer tried to tip him into the void wasn't a scenario Ben had ever explored with his prosthetist. He imagined the leg coming away from his stump, the suck and pop of the vacuum that wedded the two together as it uncoupled. He would slip over the battlements into thin air—a clownish sort of death. (*Oh, Benedict, what have you done now?*)

He just needed to get more of his body back over the wall, away from the vertiginous drop. It was simple physics really, the wall was the fulcrum, his body the see-saw. The thought spurred him on to greater effort, kicking backwards with his good leg. He thought that he'd failed to make contact, but Carter gave a grunt and loosened his grip. Ben torqued himself round and dropped heavily on to the snow-covered flagstones of the battlement.

She was holding a poker like a sword. Joan of Arc came to Ben's mind. She was standing over Carter, who was rolling around on the ground, moaning and holding his head in pain. She had saved him. "Reggie," she reminded him. "Detective Constable Regina Chase."

❧

"If only we had something to tie him up with," she said, and Ben triumphantly produced the length of rope he always carried with him. And it should have ended neatly there, with them handcuffing Carter with the rope, Reggie reading him his rights and the two of them manhandling him down the spiral staircase (although the logistics of that were beyond Ben's imagination).

Unfortunately, as he was about to help Reggie tie the hands of the prone Carter (even possibly lifeless Carter), the man leapt up unexpectedly, another brick in his hand (where was he getting them all from?).

Carter was like a cornered rat. Ben might even have admired his scrappy fighting spirit if the circumstances had been different. Helmand, for instance. Without thinking, Ben used his body as a battering-ram and made a clumsy flying leap at Carter. They fell on the ground together, flailing and scrabbling in the snow. Hand-to-hand combat, Ben thought. First time for everything. And then Carter found the gun that had been knocked out of Ben's hands.

For God's sake, the man was like Rasputin. Or a cartoon villain who just bounced back after every assault.

He didn't even try to fire it, he simply lashed out and cold-cocked Ben with the butt, sending him sprawling on the hard flagstones.

Reggie ran at Carter, hefted the poker and knocked the gun out of his hands. He finally retreated, stumbling back down the spiral staircase, Reggie on his tail.

—~—

Ben felt as if he had been drained of his lifeblood. Even the smallest movement seemed beyond him, let alone trying to stop Reggie from following Carter. She was a terrier. He liked terriers, he thought woozily.

It was never a good idea to get hit on the head, and he had been hit twice now in quick succession. He was beginning to drift away. He was in the air, looking down at himself lying on the battlements. That woman in grey flitted into view again. He doubted she could help him. Was he dying? What a strange thought. Still, at the end, he'd done his best. He'd faced fear head-on. That was the thing, wasn't it? Not to be afraid. He was relieved to find that he hadn't been. He silently saluted the body he had left behind. Poor old broken Ben.

He hoped they wouldn't give him any kind of military funeral. He wanted to just pass into the air or the earth, whichever Fran chose. He hoped it would be Fran who was choosing, not his mother. She might not even come to his funeral. *Allergies,* and so on. He imagined Simon Cate would say some gentle things over his coffin, nothing preachy. He hoped that Simon would tell the bees. That he would visit Dairy Cottage and lay black ribbons on the hives.

Thinking of the bees brought comfort. He wanted to die with peaceful thoughts in his head and he settled on the quiet, industrious hum around the hive on a summer evening. The bees seemed to gather around him as he drifted away. No stinging with their little rapiers, just the occasional delicate wing fluttering on his cheek. Or perhaps it was snowing again.

Exit Stage Left

And so *that's* how Dorothy acquired the portrait," Beatrice concluded.

It seemed so long since Beatrice began her tale that a thousand and one nights might well have passed as far as Jackson was concerned. He thought he might have entered a fugue state and was only jolted out of it by the sound of another shot being fired somewhere. This time there was no room for doubt. Far too loud and authentic to be part of the Murder Mystery unless they had actually started killing each other. (For bad acting, if nothing else.) And anyway, their prop gun was sitting on the kitchen table in front of him.

Jackson leapt up and ran off, not before saying, "Stay there, don't go anywhere," to Beatrice, knowing the likelihood of her obeying this instruction was nil. Rather late in the day, he realized he had nothing to defend himself with. Even the prop gun might have been better than nothing. If there was a shooter, all Jackson had for a weapon was two fingers and a thumb. *Bang*.

He came across the Murder Mystery again. The participants, both actors and audience, were in disarray and started clamouring at him like a flock of geese. Someone was "on the rampage" they told him, and (more as an afterthought) the twin girls announced gleefully that the Reverend Smallbones was dead. "He is *not* the Reverend Smallbones," Titus North muttered. The vicar was lying on the floor, being tended to by the American couple, the woman administering vigorous compressions to the guy's chest.

"Shot?" Jackson said.

"Heart attack," the American woman said.

Where was Reggie? "On the roof," Lady Milton said, putting in a sudden reappearance. "With the man in a tracksuit who was shooting people."

"Show me," Jackson said.

Lady Milton opened a door that was pretending to be part of the wall, right down to a *trompe-l'œil* dado rail. "This way," she said to Jackson. The door opened on to a rather shabby hallway. ("For the servants," Lady Milton said.) This behind-the-scenes route would take him to a spiral staircase, apparently, and thence to the battlements, as Lady Milton called them. She meant the roof, he supposed. He pounded up the first staircase and barrelled along a long gallery and on to a landing, where he was suddenly confronted by Carter lurching along towards him. He looked like an extra in *The Walking Dead*. Wounded though he was, Carter had the advantage in the shape of an axe. A big axe, the kind that the fire brigade used to smash through doors. Not a vampire but a Berserker, the light of madness in his eyes. Jackson backed up a few steps and found himself against a wall.

Whatever frenzy Carter was in had given him superhuman energy, and he raised the axe high and prepared to split Jackson's skull in two.

The great boom of the gun deafened Jackson. The noise seemed enough to catapult him into the next world—but, no, it seemed he was still here, none the worse for wear, apart from his eardrums. Unlike Carter, who had dropped to the floor as suddenly and thoroughly as one of the game birds the Miltons probably shot on a daily basis. But it wasn't a Milton who was responsible, it was Beatrice. Not to mention Tilda and Melanie and Sophie.

Jackson stared at her, astounded. Not a prop gun after all, then.

"Never said it was," she said.

A breathless Reggie arrived on the scene. "All right?" he asked her. "Fine," she replied, a laconic exchange that disguised rivers of feeling on both sides. She glanced at Beatrice and Carl Carter equally dispassionately and then ran off again, saying, "I have to go back up to the roof and help Ben."

Jackson knelt down and took Carl Carter's pulse. There wasn't one. When he turned his attention back to Beatrice, he found that she had disappeared, possibly into thin air, although of course Burton Makepeace was in possession of all the accoutrements of a proper Gothic house, including probably a secret passage, which if you had worked here as a housekeeper you would know all about.

The sound of an engine revving made Jackson look out of the landing window. It had a view of the yard at the back, illuminated by a bright security light, made brighter by the snow that lay thickly everywhere. There was a motorcycle out there, a red Harley-Davidson, the Sportster model, the witness in him noted in case of further questioning. Not that he would ever say. His life had just been saved—that demanded a certain reciprocation.

He had expected her to be alone, but someone was waiting for her. The someone smiled at Beatrice as she handed her a helmet. Jackson couldn't hear what they said to each other, but there was no doubt who the someone was. Alice Smithson. So she had an escape plan after all, then. Two wee lassies, as Bob Gordon would have had it.

Alice put her own helmet on and climbed on to the pillion behind Melanie. Or Beatrice, or Sophie, or Tilda. The engine revved and they rode off into the night.

Dénouement

Ma'am? There's no visual evidence of the active shooter from outside the house, we've put a couple of mics on the walls but we're not getting anything helpful. No mobile signal at all around here, Ma'am, and the house's landline is dead, so we haven't been able to talk to anyone inside."

"But do we have confirmation that there *is* an active shooter in the house? Sorry, I'm still playing catch-up," Louise Monroe said. "Active shooter" weren't words you ever wanted to hear. And Carl Carter was a man whose path you were better off never crossing.

"Ma'am? Are you sending in Armed Response?" This was Cliff, she recalled. He was a traffic cop, on the portly side—his partner, Tom, was the opposite, scrawny in a way that suggested he spent more of his off-duty time smoking than eating. Neither of them looked as though they ever hit the gym. She was hoping that as the two of them were used to the high-octane pressure of car chases they could keep a lid on the drama. She didn't want anyone going all *Line of Duty* on her.

Tom had been around the back of the house and reported that it was "a fortress" and the Enforcer that the AFOs had brought along wouldn't make so much as a dent in the back door. Also, he informed her, there were motorbike tracks leading away from the back of the house. So perhaps Carter had already made his escape, Louise thought, and someone else would have to deal with the problem, and they could all crawl back into their beds and wait for spring to come. She had thrown on five layers before leaving the house and even that wasn't enough.

She wasn't supposed to be here at all, but she lived only a few miles away and when she heard it called in she couldn't justify not coming, not to herself anyway. So she'd jumped in her Range Rover and made her laborious way through the snow, because it was a case of anyone who was available.

To the bitter resentment of her teenage daughter, they had recently moved into a remote two-bedroom cottage that Louise had bought when it was nearly derelict. She had done a lot of the renovation herself, watching tutorials on YouTube. It had been therapeutic—not that she needed therapy, she was pretty mellow these days. (Really? she questioned her "mellow" self.)

Control had given her the bronze command when she arrived, so now she was overseeing Tactical on the ground. She'd set up an ad hoc command unit in what one of her officers told her was a deer park. Not a proper mobile command unit but a laptop on her knee in the passenger seat of the Range Rover. Only the most rugged vehicles were able to get through. The snow poles on the moors were almost covered.

No sign of any deer. No sign of any people. "Just keep watching and listening," she said. "The scene's too volatile. The last thing we want is to go in all guns blazing without knowing what we're getting into. Do we have an accurate assessment of how many people are being held hostage? If they are being held hostage? Any kind of assessment at all? About anything?"

"No, Ma'am."

Well, at least that made it straightforward.

~

A constable who, like Louise, lived locally, and looked as though he had thrown his uniform on over his pyjamas, had also made it here. When Cliff said Armed Response, he was referring to just the two AFOs who had managed to make it up here. That was her team—the two AFOs, two traffic cops and a PC in pyjamas.

Louise didn't like the word "siege" any more than she liked "active shooter," but she thought that was what they might have on their hands. "Let's just stay in a holding pattern," she said. There was no sign of any back-up getting through, no ambulances either. They were already carrying casualties, a couple of civilians who had been flirting with hypothermia when the two traffic cops had dug them out from a Skoda when they were on their way here. The pair were lucky to be alive and were sitting in the back of the traffic cops' Land Rover, huddled in space blankets. "Pair of pillocks," Cliff said. "Setting off in that car in this weather."

"Some people have no sense," Louise said. Most people, she thought.

She clambered out of the Range Rover and trudged through the snow until she was nearer the house. The snow was over the top of her boots. She could feel it puddling icily around her feet.

A woman in the village called Janet Teller had been shot. There'd been a silent call to the emergency services from her house, but the caller hadn't stayed on the line long enough to be put through to a police call handler. The operator thought it was a crank call, but then the woman's next-door neighbour, a man called Derek Truitt, called 999. He'd heard a commotion and went round to check on Janet and found her dead. An ARU managed to get through to the village half an hour ago. They were on their way here now to swell Louise's meagre ranks. Forensics would get to Janet later tonight. The presumption, not a hundred per cent confirmed but near enough, was that it was Carl Carter who had broken into Janet Teller's house, looking for shelter presumably. Janet Teller had put up a fight. Good for her, Louise thought. It was no consolation for being dead though.

Burton Makepeace House was open to the public, but Louise had never visited. That was a shame because she would have had a better idea of the layout inside if she had. At least the blizzard had blown itself out now.

Without warning, the front door opened. The AFOs moved fast, training their guns on the man standing on the doorstep. He already had his hands in the air. "Can't see a weapon, Ma'am," her constable in pyjamas muttered in her ear. He had his binoculars glued to the door. One of the AFOs yelled at the man to get down on his knees with his hands behind his head. He dropped obediently to the ground. The snow reached the top of his thighs. One of the AFOs kept his gun trained on the man, while the other one kept his on the front door. When it looked as if no one else was following, he yelled at the man, "Get up, keep your hands up and walk slowly towards me."

"It doesn't look like Carl Carter," the PC said. "Is it one of the hostages, do you think, Ma'am?" He glanced at Louise. The boss had gone very quiet. "Ma'am?"

"Mm," Louise murmured.

The man appeared to be unflustered by the two guns now pointing at him. In fact, he had a big grin on his face as he walked towards them. "Louise," he said. "We must stop meeting like this."

"Ma'am?"

Jackson Brodie. The great might-have-been of her life. Always turning up like the proverbial bad penny. And the sight of him still made her heart beat faster. She wouldn't forgive her heart for that. It would be getting a good talking-to later.

"You took your time," he said.

"You," she said to him.

"Yep. Me," he said.

"Unbefuckinglievable. What's going on in there? Give me a sit rep."

"Carter's dead, but you need to get ambulances through—two casualties, both serious. The major and the vicar."

"The major and the vicar?" she murmured, more to herself than anyone present. They sounded like characters in a sit-com or a farce. She worried that she might have gone through the looking glass. Or that she was still in her bed, asleep and dreaming.

"Ma'am?"

"But Reggie's okay," the man said, "in case you were worried about her."

"Reggie? Reggie's here? Reggie *Chase*?" He was trying to destroy her mind. Yes, that's what he was doing, destroying her mind. Nothing new there, then.

"Bit of a coinci—" the man began to say, but Louise cut him off abruptly. "Handcuff him," she said to one of the traffic cops. "And put him in your vehicle with the other pillocks."

~

"Fancy seeing you here, Mr. Brodie," Hazel Padgett said awkwardly when Jackson was bundled into the traffic cops' Land Rover.

"We had a hell of a time," Ian Padgett said. "Had to take the B6429 because there was an accident on the A65 and the A6035 was blocked by snow—"

"Shut up, Ian," Hazel said. "Just shut up."

Restoration

So much excitement for one evening! An escaped prisoner shooting at people (at her!) and the vicar succumbing to a heart attack. Lady Milton hadn't enjoyed herself this much in years.

They must hold more Murder Mysteries at Burton Makepeace, she thought happily. Next time, she would make sure that Derek Truitt was invited. It seemed likely that it was the kind of thing he would enjoy.

The Clean, Well-Lighted Place

I still can't believe you just watched her walk away," Reggie said, glaring at him. She was very vexed.

"Well, *ride* away, technically speaking."

It was the first time they had seen each other since the night of the shooting. Jackson had heard that she was in line for a bravery award for helping to catch Carl Carter. The snow had melted away long ago, and it was as if it had never been. For Jackson, his brief sojourn in Burton Makepeace had already taken on a dream-like quality. Or nightmare-like. Reggie had a dog with her, tucked neatly under the table. It looked exactly like the old, jumper-wearing dog he had encountered in Burton Makepeace when he was looking for Melanie Hope. "She's called Holly," Reggie said, but didn't explain further.

Jackson thought that Reggie looked exhausted. He could only imagine the kind of fallout from Carl Carter that she'd had to deal with. The debrief would go on for ever. Apparently they had no evidence for the existence of the woman who had shot Carl Carter.

"It's such an unlikely story," Reggie said. "Absurd, in fact. And I *know* that you know it was Sophie Greenway or Melanie Hope or whatever her real name is—"

"She said her name was Beatrice."

"And you *believed* her?"

But they did have the fingerprints from the Nancy Styles book from the Willows, Reggie said. "They matched them to one found at Burton Makepeace. Lifted from a jigsaw box, of all things. So she does exist. Somewhere. She's not a ghost. She's a thief. She stole the Turner."

"But she didn't make any money from it. It was a fake."

"We've only got her word for it that it was a fake. Perhaps she did sell the original and lie to Piers."

"That's a bit far-fetched."

"Maybe not. It's actually the plot of a Nancy Styles novel, *The Puzzle of the Painting*. In the novel the painting is sold on the black market to someone who doesn't care it's stolen. Then the thief claims it was a forgery when the owner of the painting wants his money. Who's to say your Sophie Greenway hasn't done that?"

"Beatrice. Her name's Beatrice."

"Whatever. We know that she read Nancy Styles novels. Maybe it's just a case of life imitating art. Dorothy's story unlocked the puzzle of the *Woman and the Weasel*, so perhaps Nancy Styles explains the Turner. I think she's more of a ruthless criminal than you want to believe. Plus, she had a gun, untraceable, and she killed someone, let's not forget that tiny detail."

"Carl Carter. No great loss."

"I don't subscribe to your theories of summary justice, Mr. B."

"Whoever she is, she saved my life. You may recall that Carter was about to chop me in two."

"Shame he didn't."

"You don't mean that," Jackson said. "How's your Major?"

"On the mend."

"Tell me about him."

"No. It's nothing to do with you."

"Humour an old man. Give me something."

"He's a beekeeper."

"That's it?"

"It's all you're getting. *Plus*, she took the *Woman with a Weasel*."

"Back with Beatrice, are we?"

"All that guff about the codicil—anyone could make that up."

"No," Jackson said, "the codicil's real, it's lodged with Dorothy's solicitor now. The house and all Dorothy's savings—quite a lot—go to Alice Smithson, the portrait to Melanie Hope. Ian and Hazel will contest it, of course. I mean, Melanie Hope's not even a real person. The probate will be tied up for years, probably."

"Jarndyce and Jarndyce."

"Who?" Jackson puzzled.

"Nobody."

"According to Beatrice—not a reliable source, I know—Dorothy thought that Ian and Hazel were quite well off enough, plus they hardly visited her, whereas Alice, on the other hand, was close to her gran and needed help to get away from her abusive husband. They say revenge is a dish best eaten cold. Dorothy feasted from her coffin."

"Talking of her coffin—what became of the hair sample you stole?"

"Nada, no trace of any dodgy substances. No crime committed there either."

"What I don't understand," Reggie puzzled, "is how did the woman formerly known as Sophie Greenway find out about Dorothy's portrait?"

"Beatrice—let's call her that for simplicity's sake—was temping at the Courtauld Institute. She claims to have an MA in Art History from St. Andrews—possible, I suppose—and was helping to clear a Covid backlog when she found Dorothy's letter and the photo of the portrait at the bottom of a pile of correspondence. She had an intuitive feeling about it and travelled up north to see Dorothy. When Beatrice appeared on her doorstep Dorothy mistook her for a new carer, then it's all tea, biscuits, a chat, and before you know it Melanie Hope has her feet beneath the kitchen table and Dorothy Padgett's heart in her hand. Metaphorically speaking."

"I suppose Beatrice will be able to get Dorothy's painting authenticated eventually," Reggie said. "Dorothy's story or confession—whatever you want to call it—is pretty irrelevant, isn't it? It's gone up in flames anyway. Hasn't it? *Hasn't it?* What does that expression on your face mean? Oh my God, you've got it. You took it out of the coffin. Because . . . ?"

"Evidence. Proof that the painting was stolen. You never know when a 'ruthless criminal' will pop up again. Trying to sell a valuable painting, for example."

"If I ask you—detective to detective—to give it to me, you'll say no, won't you?"

"Correct. Do you want another coffee? Or something sensible to eat? A girl cannot live on brownies alone."

"This one probably could."

"Enough exposition for one day. I've got to go. I've got a date."

"With a woman?"

Not with a woman. He was taking Bob Gordon out for tea in Bettys in Ilkley. Not in the Defender. He had taken the hit and traded it in for a supposedly planet-friendly hybrid. He still spent a lot of time thinking about the Defender. His lost love.

He had walked away from Ian and Hazel without being paid. He didn't tell them that he had been successful in his quest, that he had found the elusive Melanie Hope, or that he had found Dorothy's portrait. Hazel, still snarky beneath her tinfoil in the traffic cops' Land Rover, had said, "Call yourself a detective?"

Well, yes I do, he thought as he watched Reggie leave the café. She had declined a lift because "Holly needs a walk." There was a new, hopeful little bounce in her step as the old dog trotted cheerfully by her side. Sometimes things just worked out.

It wasn't the first time he'd been back to Ilkley. He'd dropped in on Bob Gordon not long after Carl Carter was killed. There had still been a lot of snow on the ground, and he had brought some groceries for the old man and cleared his driveway, which was, he concluded, definitely a job for a young man.

While he was shovelling, he unearthed a small toy fire engine, identical to the one that he had last seen with Alice Smithson's toddler, Freddie. He picked it up and brought it inside. "Look what I found," he said to Bob. "I'm sure it belongs to Freddie Smithson."

"Wee Freddie? I doubt it," Bob said smoothly. "No, one of my great-grandsons must have lost it."

When Jackson had fetched the snow shovel from Bob's garage he found there was no car inside. No *Vauxhall Corsa, ten years old, one careful driver.* In its place was a motorbike, a Harley-Davidson. Sportster. Red. He doubted Bob Gordon was about to climb on it and ride off. Bob had helped the wee lassies get away, hadn't he? It seemed that Beatrice wasn't the only one who was good at lying.

Hedge Priest

Simon had no memory of what happened immediately before his heart attack. The last thing he could recall was walking into a room and seeing a woman lying on the floor (part of the Murder Mystery, he discovered later) and then everything went blank, as though a heavy curtain had dropped suddenly on his memory. He only learnt afterwards that an American woman called Anita, a retired cardiologist, had done CPR on him, and Cosmo, of all people, remembered that there was a defibrillator in the hotel reception and had run to fetch it. Then an ambulance had made its laborious way through the snow and the paramedics had "worked" on him before carting him off to the local hospital. After a few days he had been moved to Leeds General, where he was still lingering. His heart was weak and, according to the consultant, he was "a complicated case." True on both counts, Simon thought.

He was a lucky man, the consultant said. His heart had stopped, and he was only alive now because the American woman had brought him back to life. She had returned to her native Idaho and Simon had been unable to thank her for his resurrection.

"No pearly gates, then?" Ben asked. "No angels, harps, dogs?" They had left Burton Makepeace in twin ambulances, their needs equally urgent. If there had been only one ambulance, Simon would have insisted that Ben take priority. He is young enough to have his life ahead of him, whereas mine is behind me, Simon thought.

Although they had both been unconscious and neither was able to choose anything. Ben was taken straight to Leeds General because he needed emergency neurosurgery. His heart had stopped on the operating table, and it had been touch and go for a while.

～

Ben came, attached to his drip, every afternoon to have a chat with Simon. When Simon woke up in the hospital, he found that his voice had returned. He had undergone a trial, he realized, and somehow—he didn't really know how—he had succeeded. The reward was the return of the gift of speech. He would never take it for granted again. He would never take anything for granted again.

Ben, according to his self-diagnosis, was still "not quite right." He occasionally had trouble with his speech and sometimes, in the middle of a conversation, he would seem to zone out a bit. After their daily chat, Ben would return to his own ward, where he was visited most days by his sister. Fran usually "popped along" to see Simon as well, bringing little gifts—a book, a pot of hyacinths. On one occasion, she had even smuggled in a kitten to cheer Ben up and had then brought it along to Simon as well. She said he could keep the kitten when he was better, and Simon said yes because it seemed an optimistic thing to do. "I prayed for you," Fran said, in the kind of matter-of-fact way that Simon felt he had never mastered himself. "And for Ben as well, naturally," she added. Did Fran believe in God? They had talked about many things in the past, but not God. Simon found it best to avoid the subject with most people, it made him unpopular. Fran said, "Not one bit, but that didn't stop me praying."

He would be retired from service, of course, whether he liked it or not—no longer a Man of God—and would be embarking on another, different life. He hoped he could stay in the village. Apparently Janet Teller's house was up for rent, although perhaps, on the downside, her spirit might be wandering the modest rooms, having failed the transition to a dolphin. He could take over her Thursday mornings. "At Simon's." Perhaps he could go from village to village, preaching a simple gospel. Or just laze in front of *Homes Under the Hammer* with a glass of light ale in his hand.

He would be quite happy to potter through the remainder of his life. ("You're not old!" Fran said, rather crossly.) He had no desire for foreign travel or adventure or even strong opinions. Dying had been excitement enough. Acceptance seemed to be the best philosophy to carry him forward.

Simon was surprised by how many visitors came through the door of his side ward, an endless stream of mostly elderly parishioners, some of whom he didn't think he had ever seen before. They were organized by Derek Truitt, who relished the challenging logistics of transporting the frail and infirm all the way from Burton Makepeace to Leeds. He had even brought Lady Milton on one rather unnerving occasion. It was odd to see her out of her normal habitat and he was relieved when Derek escorted her away (with great ceremony).

___

"No," Simon said to Ben. "No pearly gates." No angels, harps or dogs either. No startling revelations. He did not look on the face of God. No bright light had beckoned him. His parents were not waiting for him, which was mostly a relief, although he would have liked to apologize to them for the long adolescent years of stroppiness. "How about you?"

"Nothing really," Ben said. "Just a feeling of peace. The bees were there."

"Oh, that's nice."

"Better than the first time."

Yes, of course, Simon remembered, Ben was a man who had died twice. (Wasn't that the title of a novel?) "God must be keen to keep you here," he said, immediately regretting the G word, it sounded so vicarish. "Or the Fates," he amended. "But you're all right?"

"Me?" Ben said. "Never been better. Happy." He looked startled by the word.

___

"How are you feeling today?" Fran asked as she opened the Tupperware box she had brought with her. "Fairy cakes, George made them for you."

"Lovely."

"You haven't tasted them yet."

How *was* he feeling? It was a question Simon had asked himself a lot since the heart attack. A bit flat, he supposed, but then that was to be expected. Tired, ditto. "I think I feel all right," he said.

"That's good," Fran said. "'All right' is good."

"Yes, I suppose it is," Simon said, thoughtfully peeling the paper case off a fairy cake. "It'll do to be going on with, anyway."

"You can come and stay with us for a bit," Fran said. "We're all about waifs and strays at Dairy Cottage."

"That's very kind," he said and felt tears gathering at such generosity.

━━━⟳

He was sleeping lightly when a faint movement in the air woke him. He had an odd sensation, as if something was going to happen. For a moment he wondered if he was about to die, even though he was "out of the woods," according to his consultant. He opened his eyes, rather cautiously, in case it was visiting hour for Death, and was surprised to see Sophie sitting by the side of his bed.

"Sophie?" he croaked. Was he hallucinating? For a sudden, paranoid moment he wondered if she had taken on yet another role and had started understudying for the Grim Reaper.

Fran had told him all about Sophie, how she had stolen the Turner, how there was confusion over another painting that she might or might not have stolen. How someone said that she had shot Carl Carter. It all seemed improbable, more like fiction than life. The Sophie he knew had gasped with pleasure at the sight of a hawk in a gyre above their heads and had melted at an encounter with a tiny fallow fawn. But that was a different Sophie, a different story.

Fran knew about Sophie because Ben had told her, and Ben

knew because his new girlfriend was a detective in the police. "Reggie. She was at Burton Makepeace that night," Fran said, but Simon had no memory of her. Fran laughed. "Good old Ben, not many people acquire a girlfriend when they're lying at death's door." The door hadn't opened. Ben was lucky. So was he, of course. He must never forget that.

"Simon?"

He had drifted off, he realized. Something he did a lot of. It was pleasant. She was smiling at him. "I heard we nearly lost you. I'm so relieved we didn't."

"I'm all right now though," he said. "They say I'll be out of here in a few days." He decided he was dreaming.

"Lucky I caught you, then," the dream Sophie said. "I just wanted to say that I was sorry I never came to see you before I left Burton Makepeace. I should have said goodbye. I suppose I left in a bit of a hurry. *Mea culpa.* We were friends, weren't we? We still are, although I expect I shan't see you again. I brought you a farewell gift."

"You didn't need to do that," Simon said, even though he was pleased. Good things didn't usually happen in his dreams.

She laid something on the bedcover, on his legs. It was square and heavy and wrapped with gift paper and ribbon. "Open it after I've gone," she said. She rose from her chair and said, "I'd love to stay, but I'm afraid I can't." She kissed him lightly on the cheek and said, "Goodbye, Simon." And she was gone.

———

It wasn't a dream because the painting was still there. It was the one he had found under the altar on the day of his heart attack. Had she always intended it for him? he wondered. He presumed it was stolen. He found a card inside the parcel, taped to the frame. "It's called *Donna con Martora.* It's a thing of beauty. From me to you. Love from Sophie. x"

Curtain Call

I expect that horrid little man is going to announce who the murderer is," Major Liversedge said. "That's what usually happens, isn't it? At the end?"

"Exposition, I believe it's called," the Reverend Smallbones said.

They had been instructed by René Armand to gather in the Library and an awkward silence descended as they waited for the Swiss detective, broken eventually by Guy Burroughs saying, "How about we have a drink? Lighten the mood." The events of the day had not made for conviviality amongst those who remained.

"Good idea," Lady Hardwick said. "Will you ring the bell for Addison, Major?"

"Do you think Armand *is* coming?" the Reverend Smallbones asked. "Or do you think us all being in this room together is part of some plot?"

"Do you suppose one of *us* is the murderer?" Major Liversedge ruminated.

"It must be," Guy Burroughs said. "We've been marooned here together since this whole thing started and there is no one else. The mysterious countess is dead, as is the ne'er-do-well nephew. And poor old Dankworth, of course."

"My husband, too," Lady Hardwick reminded them.

"Unless it's Addison," the Reverend Smallbones said. "It often is. As a butler, he belongs to a profession that seems to harbour an unusually high number of murderers. Of course, I've—"

They were surprised when, instead of Addison, Hodge, the under-butler, appeared with the drinks tray. He was followed into the room by René Armand.

"Where is Addison?" Lady Hardwick enquired.

"I'm afraid Mr. Addison has disappeared, m'lady," Hodge said.

"How very irregular."

Once the drinks were served, René Armand directed them all to take a seat and took up a commanding position in front of them. "I'm afraid the news of Monsieur Addison's absence comes as no surprise, for I must tell you, he is not actually a butler, nor is his name Addison. He is called Brett Smith," he said, pronouncing the name with an expression of distaste. "Nor is he from Oswestry, as he claimed. He works on a sheep farm in Australia. And he is now the only male heir of the Hardwick family who remains alive."

The company gasped. "He is a *Hardwick?*" the Reverend Small-bones puzzled.

"A second cousin twice removed. Furthermore, the first Lady Hardwick is not dead—"

More gasping.

"She has in fact become the mistress of Brett Smith in order to wreak vengeance on the Hardwick family. The two of them colluded to murder anyone who stood in the way of them inheriting. You would have been next, I believe, Lady Hardwick, for is it not true that you are *enceinte* with a Hardwick heir, a secret known to Dr. Dankworth, which is why he had to die—"

"Oh, for God's sake, buddy," Guy Burroughs said. "Get on with it. You *know* who did it. Just say it. There are only so many times we can do this without going crazy."

"Yes," Major Liversedge said. "Do get on, there's a good chap, Armand. We all know where this is going. We've been here so many times before. We're all very tired and we want to go home."

"Such artifice," Lady Hardwick sighed. "So improbable. Really, Monsieur Armand, one becomes quite *fatigued* with it all."

René Armand bridled at their impatience. This was his moment in the spotlight and yet they never let him make the most of it. They never let him *savour* it. The reveal. The *dénouement*. The end. *Fin.*

"Very well," he said with a continental shrug. "I shall not 'beat about the bush,' as you English say." He paused for dramatic effect, puffed himself up a little and finally made the inevitable pronouncement. "The butler did it."

It was always the butler. Why couldn't they have a different ending? Perhaps one day someone else would be the murderer, but they were powerless to change anything. They were trapped in their own drama. There was no way out. The curtain fell.

CREDITS

Lyrics on pp. 122 and 179 are from "Wuthering Heights" written by Kate Bush.

Poetry extracts on p. 212 are from *The Waste Land* by T. S. Eliot, Sonnet 19 by William Shakespeare and "Going, Going" by Philip Larkin.

ABOUT THE AUTHOR

KATE ATKINSON won the Whitbread (now Costa) Book of the Year prize with her first novel, *Behind the Scenes at the Museum*. Her 2013 novel, *Life After Life*, was shortlisted for the Women's Prize for Fiction and voted Book of the Year by independent booksellers' associations on both sides of the Atlantic. It also won the Costa Novel Award, as did her subsequent novel, *A God in Ruins* (2015), and was adapted into a critically acclaimed television series in 2022. Her bestselling novels featuring former detective Jackson Brodie became the BBC television series *Case Histories*, starring Jason Isaacs. She has written twelve groundbreaking, bestselling books and lives in Edinburgh, Scotland.